The Sands o

By
John Schettler

A publication of: *The Writing Shop Press*
The Sands of Honor, Copyright©2023, John A. Schettler
All rights Reserved
Genres:
Historical Fiction, Military Fiction, Time Travel,
Alternative History

The Sands of Honor

By
John Schettler

The Sands of Honor

By
John Schettler

Sands of Honor

"Night poured over the desert. It came suddenly, in purple. In the clear air, the stars drilled down out of the sky, reminding any thoughtful watcher that it is in the deserts and high places that religions are generated. When men see nothing but bottomless infinity over their heads...."

—**Terry Pratchett**

Prologue

The *Mahdi*

Heidelberg, Germany, 17 SEP 1884

There it was, thought Max Wolf, as he peered through the lens of the great telescope. A wolf in the fold, he thought, and that was what it would be called. The name was perfect, for it was his own, and he would be the first to see and track this comet. Yes, it would be called 14P-Wolf, and its coming would be confirmed six days later by another astronomer, Ralph Copeland, who observed it from Aberdeen, Scotland on 23 September. Copeland looked like a comet himself, his balding head the nucleus, the long wild beard falling from the chin its tail. But the comet would not be named after Copeland, because the 21 year old Max Wolf had seen it first, right from the observatory built for him by his father in the garden of his family home.

It was the first astronomical discovery the young Wolf made, but it would not be the last. He would find other tailed stars in the sky, and be among the first to spot the return of the famous Haley's comet in 1910. He would find four supernovae, make pronouncements on the nature of what he called 'Dark Nebulae,' hunt dim asteroids, and find many minor planets in the outer rim of the solar system. But that night he had found his first Wolf, and he was elated.

Half a world away, there would come a time when others would find the wolf as well. It would be seen in the pristine clear night sky of the Sahara, the great desert of North Africa. To them it was a sign that had been foretold, a pronouncement from heaven itself, and an augur of the coming of one who would soon become a whirlwind of chaos and rebellion—the *Mahdi*.

1884
El Mahdi el Muntazer

"Indeed, he is the portent of the hour..." (Qur'an, 43:61)

He had come many times before, when strife and crisis lay on the land, and the Infidel was on the march. It was said He would purge the land of unbelief, cow the unfaithful, brand them, and cast them out, and this was the time of his return.

It was written that 'He is the one whose reappearance shall coincide with a sign from the sky, such that all the inhabitants of the land shall hear this cry: "Know that the *Hujjah* (Proof) of Allah has appeared near the House of Allah. So follow him, since the truth is in Him and with Him.' So it was written by Sayyid-Sadruddin Sadr, and it was said that Muhammed himself (peace be upon him) would speak of the coming of the *Mahdi*, one who would be sent from the progeny of His people.

The heavens above would announce Him, a star that leaves its place in the firmament and wanders the night with a tail of glory in its wake. So comes the *Mahdi* to the firmament of all men. It would be His to see what comes, and know what must be done in the present hour to give birth to the future. His coming heralds the time for the occurrence of every promised event, and the approach of things which no one else could know.

It is He who will wear the armor of wisdom, and bear the sword of justice; He who will free the slaves, and lead the great revolt to straighten the crooked, conquering all before Him, turning His rosy face to the heavens in thanksgiving. The whirlwind and scourge of the Dervish will lash the unfaithful and rebuke the Infidels at His behest. Not Iron nor steel will stay His burning lash, for He will brand the world with the justice of Allah. So it was said....

You will all know Him when He shows his face; hear Him when He speaks; follow Him where He leads. For He is the *Mahdi*, anointed one, and the last proof of the will and wisdom of Allah. It will be His to shake the mountains, and fling down the stars upon the Infidel. He will drive them from these lands with the lash of retribution, and their blood will stain the eternal sands, their sullied, faithless honor would flee from them on the hot desert winds.

Yet other men would stand against him as well; men of substance, will and sterling reputation. Like a magnetic force every current in history has its antipode. The magnetic charisma of the *Mahdi* would soon be opposed by that of a desert loving Englishman—major General Charles George Gordon. A great disaster saw him called to the defense of the British Empire yet again. The Army of General William "Billy" Hicks simply vanished in the Sudanese desert. What had happened to it?

Of those who fought and those who fell,
And those who bravely died,
Of those who bore our banners high,
And battled side by side
O loved ones, lying far away,
What word of love can dead lips send?
O wasted dust and senseless clay,
Is this the end? Is this the end?
—Lament, on the demise of Hicks Pasha and his entire column

Yes, the army had vanished. As for Hicks Pasha, his fate was somewhat harsher. Of the column of over 8000 Egyptian soldiers and hundreds of other porters and transport personnel, with some 5000 camels, only a few hundred survived to be taken as prisoners. Hicks was not among them. The column had been completely annihilated. A fragment of a diary entry on the day of the battle was found well after the battle and brought back to Khartum by a trader. It related a little of what is now known of this battle.

"These are bad times; we are in a forest, and everyone very depressed. The General orders the band to play, hoping the music will enliven us a little; but the bands soon stop, for the bullets are flying from all directions, and camels, mules and men keep dropping down; we are all cramped together, so the bullets cannot fail to strike. We are faint and weary, and have no idea what to do. The General gives an order to halt and make a zeriba. It is Sunday, and my dear brother's birthday. Would to God that I could sit down and talk to him for an hour! The bullets are falling thicker.' The writer would say no more, struck himself by a Dervish bullet.

That sniping would continue all that night. General Hicks had marched south into the province of Kordufan to crush the *Mahdi*, but in doing so, he allowed his line of communications to the Nile to be cut by the Dervish *Jihadis*. With the water failing, he took counsel of his guides.

"Well, Kona, we've a bit of a problem here. We need to find water. I've 5000 thirsty camels in tow at the back of the column. And they're already grumbling, or falling dead to the ground."

William Hicks had come up through the Army in India, with much experience there during the mutiny and rebellions. His skin had been tanned by the sun, contrasting with his white beard and mustache that saw him called "Old Snow Chin." Kona first advised Hicks to split his force and send half back to clear their Line of communications, while the other half advanced. This Hicks refused.

"No, I'll not divide my force in the face of the enemy now. Just get me to water!"

Kona said that a nearby dry forest held some pools or small lakes where rainwater gathered. So Hicks advanced reaching an open area between two stands of denser woodland. It was there, that the Black *Jihadis* of Abu Anga found his column, and approached it through the woods, close enough to bring fire upon it. At the same time, the *Mahdi* and his men lay hidden in the woodland on the other side of this same clearing. It was a perfect place for an ambush, the Dervish easily concealed on the woodland on either side, yet close enough to keep the column, now a squared zeriba, under constant rifle fire. Every so often a man, or an animal would be struck by a bullet and fall.

The night was terrible under that unrelenting gunfire, and morale plummeted. Hicks was not leading British regulars. His was an army of Fellahin Egyptian farmers, all conscripted. Its ranks were then filled out with convicts and the dregs of the streets of Cairo, some having to be marched this whole way still in irons and chains to prevent them from deserting. Others were Sudanese who might have otherwise been swept up in the slave trade. Few had any training in soldiery at all.

The Army was also ill-equipped, some of the farmers coming with chain mail and old iron helmets, as if it was still the Middle

Ages. It took every ounce of fortitude in the five British officers Hicks had, along with a Prussian Colonel, two Austrian Captains, and a Serbian Lieutenant struggling to hold this polyglot force together, mostly with the lash and threat of punishment than anything else.

The many followers in the baggage train brought this column to about 10,000. Hicks had marched with 50 days supply in a long train of 5000 camels behind his men. Churchill had called it "perhaps the worst army that ever marched to war." The *London Times* described the force as, "a cowardly, beggarly mob." And on more than one occasion, orders had to be backed up by a drawn pistol.

It was astounding to think that, with the British/Egyptian control in the Sudan extending little more than the range of a rifle shot from Khartum, this army represented the central core of any hope Britain had to maintain its position in Sudan. The Army had marched off into the wastes of Kordufan south of Khartum, in temperatures as high as 127 degrees Fahrenheit each day. They were now desperate to find water, with overloaded camels beginning to just drop dead from the heat and their labor. Come dawn on the 5th of November, what little hope Hicks had of ever fulfilling his mission to find and defeat the *Mahdi* would end in disaster. He no longer had to look for the *Mahdi*, for the *Mahdi* had found him, and with as many as 50,000 Dervish warriors, both Arabs and Sudanese.

The charismatic leader had offered Hicks quarter, saying any who accepted him as *Mahdi* and embraced Islam would be spared, but General Hicks sent back a message spurning this offer. It read: *"I am Hicks Pasha: my arm is an arm of iron, and my army carries an army in its belly. If the heavens fall, I will hold them up with my bayonets, and if the earth quakes I will hold it fast with my boot."* That boast would soon be put to the test.

Arrayed in three squares, Hicks' Army may have looked formidable at first sight, but it would not stand the test of real combat. Men struggling for their lives will fight, but the squares would not maintain order and they soon collapsed. Hordes of wild Dervish spearmen came at the army from both sides in a howling rage, and the battle would become a massacre. Hicks and a few other officers held forth near a withered tree where a Bugler had climbed to sound his calls. They emptied their pistols and then took to their swords, fighting until the spears of the Dervish pierced them time and again, taking them down, one by one.

As often happened, the Dervish beheaded Hicks and his officers, and brought their heads to the *Mahdi*. They were planted in a ghastly grove, the heads at the end of Dervish spears. The rest of the fallen were simply left to the vulchers and hyenas after the *Mahdi's* men stripped them of anything valuable and made off with their weapons and ammunition. The Army was gone, and there would follow a great whirlwind in the Sudan as thousands more flocked to the banners of the *Mahdi* after his great victory. That storm would not abate until Britain sent another General, one who had endured the turmoil of the bloody Taiping rebellion in China, General Charles Gordon. He had been called "Chinese Gordon" for his exploits in the Middle Kingdom after the Opium Wars, and one who would forever after be known as "Gordon of Khartum."

Part I
China Gordon

"He is superior in manner and bearing to any of the foreigners whom I have come into contact with, and does not show outwardly that conceit which makes most of them repugnant in my sight...What an elixir for a heavy heart-to see this splendid Englishman fight!"
—Li Hongzhang

Chapter 1
February, 1884

The *Abbas* was a typical paddle wheel steamer, with two coal black stacks amidships, and a tall mainmast behind them with a dark crow's nest. Knowing he would be sailing into unsettled lands, up the wild Nile into Sudan, Gordon had armed it with two cannons.

There was trouble in Sudan, all fomented by the fierce, ruthless ravaging of a man who called himself the *Mahdi*. He had the land all up in rebellion, and so when England looked for a foil against him, it was not long before the name "Chinese Gordon" was part of the conversation. And here he was.

A British officer serving with Gordon at that time described him for posterity: "a light-built, wiry, middle-sized man, of about thirty two years of age, in the uniform of the Royal Engineers. The countenance bore a pleasant frank appearance, eyes light blue with a fearless look in them, hair crisp and inclined to curl, conversation short and decided." He had aged since then, now a man of 52 years.

"So, I'm to be Governor General of Sudan again," said Gordon, "And you are likely my deputy commander and a spy for Mr. Gladstone. Yes?"

Colonel John Donald Hamill Stewart gave him a wan look and nodded his head. He was a tall man, square shouldered in his red tunic, and very proper, his hair dark and full.

"Correct," he admitted to both roles. "I'm to report on what you are doing here—directly to Mister Gladstone, and if you resolve to undertake anything too risky to life and limb, I'm to go in your place."

"It seems Mister Gladstone is overly concerned for my wellbeing," said Gordon. To look at Gordon, one would never think that here was a hero of the Crimean war, and a man who had helped lash the fierce Taiping Rebels of China into submission. Now he was Gordon of Khartum, or soon about to be.

Yet he was unremarkable in appearance, save for his eyes. Many that met him commented on those eyes, saying they were capable of looking through walls in time; looking right through men as well—that they saw things, far off, things yet to come. Even in the days of his youth, Gordon had a reckless energy about him, and a tendency to buck authority, stretch the limits of rules, and do things as he liked. The boy was the father of the man here. "If Gladstone wants me safe, then why is he so doggedly opposed to sending British troops into Sudan?" he asked the Colonel.

"Ah, the dilemmas of Empire," said Stewart. "Things start very simply in situations like this, and then they end up quite a mess. Perhaps he'll send British troops when that happens, but I rather think he's hoping we'll get in and out of Khartum without much trouble, and bring out all the necessary evacuees."

"I see," said Gordon. "Just the necessary ones—The Europeans, and British among them, of course, and the Egyptian officials and their families. I suppose that makes the 17,000 Sudanese in Khartum *un*necessary?"

"But sir, we'll barely have river transport for those you've mentioned. There's simply no way we could add in all the Sudanese."

"Because they're unnecessary." Gordon folded his arms, rubbing his disapproval in, chin up, enjoying his joust with the Colonel. "Well fancy this for your first report. I intend to stay there in Khartum and defend the place, to protect all the unnecessary rabble."

"You mean you won't be joining the evacuees?"

"Of course not. These people know me. They know I'm coming, and when you see the reception I get upon arrival, you'll understand why I must stay in Khartum."

"Then what about your orders?"

"What about them?"

You mean to say you've no intention to obey the Prime Minister?"

"None whatsoever He's misguided, a short sighted fool, and you can be sure to tell him that in your first report."

"Sir, this isn't the sort of situation to dally about in, or play games. This *Mahdi* is dangerous. Slaughter is his calling card most places he visits, and if he comes for Khartum, he'll make no exception for you. These aren't the Chinese, and wearing that gold colored jerkin they gave you will count for nothing here."

"I understand that all too well."

As a reward for his service in China, Gordon had been given a stunning garment, in the imperial color of yellow gold, a color worn only by the Imperial family by decree, or by those he gifted. Only 50 Mandarins in all of China were said to be so favored, and Gordon had been the first 'barbarian' to ever be honored this way.

"You do realize the gravity of the situation, don't you?" Colonel Stewart persisted.

"Most assuredly, which is precisely why I must stay at Khartum to organize the defense there. We're both Engineers. Surely we can fortify the place to give those people a fighting chance."

"Against the *Mahdi*? With the few Egyptian troops that still make up the garrison there?"

"That's a start," Gordon interrupted. "How many remain?"

"Sir?"

"Come on man—how many troops will be at Khartum?"

"I'm told about 7,000," said Stewart, all Egyptian *Fellahin*—farmers handed rifles and drilled an hour a day so they can pretend they're soldiers until their contract runs out. Sir, they'll have nothing else on their minds but the hour and day that happens, and the day they can go back to their families and farms. If you've a mind to make some grand sacrifice of yourself at Khartum, bear in mind that none of those men will want to join you. Why, you'll end up just like General Hicks!"

"Seven thousand... That will do nicely." Gordon seemed to have heard nothing the Colonel had said at all.

"But Sir... You *do* remember what happened to General Hicks? He had nearly ten thousand, and no more than 300 escaped alive, and that was because the *Mahdi* was generous with life that day, and took prisoners."

"Yes. Hicks hit a rough patch as I heard."

"A rough patch? If you'd call the slaughter of nearly all those troops a rough patch, then you are a master of understatement, sir. The *Mahdi* is something more than a rough patch. The man is a religious zealot, with the temperament of a dust devil, and it has been the world's woe to see more than one such individual come out of its deserts. He's not to be underestimated, and not to be trifled with. I strongly suggest you simply stick to your orders, sir."

"And I strongly suggest you mind yours, sir. Which will come from *me*, as I am indeed your commander here, if you recall. Order one—don't bother me with anything more that comes out of Gladstone's mouth. Now that I'm here, I'll do precisely what I wish, and when I wish it, and you will support me, not impede me."

"Are you proposing to flaunt the authority of the British government and become a rogue colonial administrator? This outrageous!"

"Hardly, though *you* are definitely skirting that line with all this Imperial fervor. Calm down, Colonel Stewart. I don't want to have to shoot you."

"*Shoot* me?"

"Oh yes, and I've shot men before—on more than one occasion—particularly when they became too headstrong and bothersome. Know your place, Colonel, and we'll get along nicely.

Now why don't you go and get yourself something cool to drink. It will get much hotter here before nightfall, even on the river."

The Colonel got up, in a huff, and was more than eager to go find that cool drink. In his absence, Gordon settled into a comfortable position on the couch, and considered the cards in his hand.

So, the Egyptian Government has given me authority to make use of any of its troops still in Sudan, for the purpose of facilitating the safe evacuation of its nationals, officials and family members. But I intend to use them at Khartum, for the instant they depart, it would be generally known that Britain and Egypt are washing their hands of the Sudan, and with that, any tribes here still even marginally loyal to our cause will flip and go over to the *Mahdi*. That would be most unsatisfactory. Gladstone, the doddering old fool, has it all backwards. He refuses to send a proper force here, under a proper General. Billy Hicks was a good soul, but he was a fool to let the *Mahdi* lead him off into the desert like that. A fool...

So I have to pull Great Britain back into the Sudan. If we let it go now, getting it back will be a good deal more difficult later. A stich in time saves nine. So I must get Gladstone to send me a proper General, and with a real army this time—British regulars. If we lose Sudan now, then how long before this *Mahdi* sweeps over the frontier into Egypt? How long before his Dervish fighters line both banks of the Suez Canal? And how would these poor people here ever forgive me if I hopped on a steamer and sailed away with the fat fez crowned Egyptian officials? What would they do? They would join the Mahdi to a man.

As for the *Mahdi* himself. He's to be my first order of business when I get to Khartum. I've no doubt that he'll be somewhere close, and I will find the man and speak with him. I'll talk sense into him.

Khartum~ 18 FEB 1884

The crowds began cheering the instant the steamer came into sight, thousands waving from the river quays of Khartum. The steamer reached them, was tied off, and out he came, the man everyone was waiting for, as much as hot summer rocks wait breathlessly for rain. Gordon Pasha was back, he was here again, and they loved him. With Gordon here, they would finally be safe.

Colonel Stewart would steam over Gordon's apparent impudence and the cavalier disregard of his orders, but he had to admit to the man's charismatic power when he saw him march ashore and parade through the city to the adulation of thousands.

Days later he received a letter concerning Gordon's doings at Khartum, from Lord Granville, who had been one of the officials who had first proposed Gordon's mission to Khartum, and that over the objections of Gladstone. It read, in part: *'in a matter involving such complexity and depending so much on local circumstances, it was to be expected that General Gordon might be obliged to modify or alter his views on arrival at Khartum as to... the course to be perused in order to attain the main objects in view. Her majesty's government have been anxious that, in this respect, he should have the largest discretion.'*

It seemed that forces in the government were already extending Gordon that wide discretion. Obviously Granville knows this man Gordon quite well, though he had also written that he did not expect Gordon's efforts would necessitate the dispatch of a British expedition to 'support or extricate him.' Clearly the government still did not want its white gloves sullied by the red sands of the Sudan. But how can I get Gordon to understand this, he thought? How could he get him to realize that Britain wanted nothing more to do with the Sudan and its wild heathens? Things like the massacre of William Hicks and his command had a way of jarring the nerves. London wanted no more bad headlines out of Sudan. They had enough to contend with in China, Afghanistan, and India. To Prime Minister Gladstone, Sudan was small potatoes, and with no gravy.

Yet there were those back home that would be likely to fall right into Gordon's trap, for that was what Stewart perceived it to be.

Granville was one of them, or Egerton, Hartington, and even General Wolseley had been pressing the Government to consider sending some real steel to Egypt, to assure the safety of the canal, and to have in hand should anything be needed in the Sudan. Gordon was going to make sure something *would* be needed in Sudan by refusing to leave Khartum, and accepting a siege there in lieu of obeying his orders. Gladstone would equivocate, wag his heavy jowls, and resist, slowly boiling over with frustration if I report what Gordon just told me. And of course I *must* report it. It's my duty.

Days later he would again meet with Gordon to discuss the overall situation, which was evolving from shades of grey and white to a deeper black and blood red with each passing week.

"General," he said. "The government is becoming concerned that we have not acted expeditiously to facilitate the evacuation as ordered. They have heard that the number of rebels near Khartum is increasing."

"Well, they certainly didn't expect those numbers to decrease, did they? I'm not all *that* frightful."

"More to the point, General, if our link back to Egypt is the Nile, then we ought to heed the reports that Berber is also under threat now, and might even be occupied by hostiles."

That got Gordon's attention. "Berber... why, that would cut us off, at least from anything coming up the Nile."

"Then we'd better get evacuees onto the steamers and see them off down river as soon as possible. Should we wait much longer, the Nile will start running much shallower in the winter months. Hasan, the Khalifa of Berber has already appealed for reinforcements for his garrison."

"Ah, then it *hasn't* fallen."

"This news is old, sir. Things may have happened that we won't hear about for days yet—if at all. The *Mahdi's* men are patrolling all along the banks of the Nile now—and on both sides of the river."

"Well if what you say is true, and the steamer has to run a gauntlet at Berber, then we'd better damn well arm it better."

"We've already reinforced the open areas with wood planks to make a kind of wall to provide some cover. And we can throw on a couple more guns. I've put 50 armed men aboard, but we need to Maximize room for the evacuees."

"Then let's get that underway at once. Anything more?"

Chapter 2

Colonel Stewart looked Gordon in the eyes, resisting their magnetic, jewel-like charm.

"Just this sir. The government wants me to report that, having received this news concerning Berber, if you still intend to remain here at Khartum, they ask you to state the cause and intention with which you continue to be of that mind." Stewart handed Gordon the letter, and the General scanned it briefly before tossing it aside.

"The government knows full well why I intend to remain here, irrespective of what happens down river at Berber or anywhere else. They simply do not want to make the leap of thought to the point which I am angling for—a British relief effort here. Khartum is the capital of this wild land, the seat of its government and power. Power, Stewart, *power*. I do not have it simply because I will stroll into Khartum to the cheers of thousands here. Yes, they'll accept me as their Governor General, but if I am to secure that position, and Khartum, I'll need more than the few thousand conscripted Egyptian soldiers. Furthermore, we must make preparations for what may soon be a very long siege of this city. I intent to sortie out and collect all I can of supplies and livestock, because we will have to feed 17,000 to 20,000 people after our steamers float away with the *necessary* evacuees."

Stewart thought he could move Gordon with this news of Berber, but found it had the opposite effect of seeing him dig his heels in even deeper in his determination to stay at Khartum. And now, more than ever, Gordon knew he had to find and speak with the *Mahdi*. He needed to gauge the man's mind and learn his intentions, and he wanted to look for any weakness he might exploit in the man.

The Sudanese Desert, March 1 1884

Gordon went out with a single servant, Issak, a young tanned Arab lad with coal dark eyes. They would be two men on two camels, and with barely enough food and water to reach their destination. Gordon had asked reliable locals where the *Mahdi* was camped, and that news was not long in coming. Soon he would find the place, riding for a day and a night through the sullen desert, under dark skies and brilliant stars, and then on into the sun the following morning. They stopped at mid-day, seeking some shade and relief from the cruel sun and oppressive heat.

His servant, was nervous and fidgeting, obviously sensing danger, as if he expected they might be overtaken any moment by a Dervish patrol. If so, they might be killed outright, but no one found them. They were wearing plain outer robes, and even if they were seen by patrols, they would appear no more than vagrant nomads, of which all too many inhabited that desert. When they stopped to rest in small groves of trees, Gordon would lay on the cooler shaded sand and stare up the the fluffy white clouds, wondering if they would ever hold any rain.

He had made his desire known to England, that he wanted Great Britain involved here, back in Sudan. If nothing else, they had Billy Hicks to think of, and a score to settle there. Now there *was* something else, and he explained it to Issak the best he could.

"Why do we do this, Lord Gordon?" The boy asked.

"Why? Because if I can speak to this *Mahdi* and take his measure, I will know definitively whether he intends to attack Khartum or not. Perhaps I can convince him not to make that city the object of his wrath. Then all our defensive preparations won't be necessary, though I must continue them in any wise. Men's minds change like the desert winds. Are we close to this Dervish camp?"

"Very close. Another half day's ride will take us there."

"Good, then we will rest awhile, and take some food. Later we sleep a little and ride again before dawn in the morning."

At the Dervish Camp, 2 MAR 1884

Gordon had been known for taking dangerous risks. As a boy of twelve, we might jump right into the deepest part of the pool, even though he could not yet swim. He was relying on the older boys to come to his rescue, and seemed to enjoy it. This was no swimming party.

He and Issak had huddled under a thin blanket through the desert night, watched only by the stars above. The morning came with a splendor of rose and gold, and after brewing and drinking tea and having a biscuit, they watered the camels and mounted them.

The red sands stretched out endlessly in all directions, and they were taking the Camels on the softer ground, so their feet would not be injured by sharp hard stones. These were dromedary Arabian camels, with one large central hump, not Bactrian two hump beasts. Gordon rode them as easily as he might a horse, for he had been here before when he worked to put down the slave traders.

They cleared a rise of wind scored sand and stopped. Gordon took out a small telescope and extended it to Issak. He had seen a darkness on the desert ahead. "What do you see there, boy?"

"We have found it!" said Issak, his eyes a mix of fear and excitement. "I see riders, many men around morning fires."

Gordon could also smell the Nile. Their march had described a loop out into the desert, then followed a wadi that flattened out to become a grassy *khor*, then over a field of low red dunes to find they were again approaching the river. Gordon reckoned they might be ten or 15 miles south of Khartum on the White Nile, perhaps as far as Jebel Aulia. Without a second thought, Gordon nudged his mount and they rode on. They approached the camp, looking like anyone else there, and smelling familiar Arab morning foods: toasted pita bread, Za'atar, which was a mix of sumac, sesame and salt with herbs. They saw bowls of olive oil and a dish of labneh, which made their own light breakfast seem meager.

They rode past several fires, largely ignored, until finally a man looked up, rifle in hand and ordered them to stop. "Who are you? What tribe?"

"No tribe," said Gordon, knowing just a little Arabic. "I am Gordon Pasha, here to meet the *Mahdi*"

"Gordon Pasha? Prove it!"

Gordon's hood had been tightly drawn about his face and head. Now he opened it and threw it off, also loosening his robe to reveal the formal gold braided vest beneath. The Arab guard's eyes widened when he saw this, and realized who he now held at gunpoint.

"Who has said the *Mahdi* might be found here? You are sorely mistaken."

"Not here? Then where might I find him?"

"That is not for you to know, Infidel. You are bold to come here, thus alone. Who is this?" He gestured to Issak.

"This man is my companion, and under my protection." Gordon said nothing about Issak being his servant.

"Under your protection? Then who protects you? I could easily take your head for the *Mahdi*."

"But the *Mahdi* is not here." Gordon Smiled. "Who protects me? Who else but God? It is his will that I come here, and if I cannot now meet the *Mahdi*, then I ask that you take him this letter."

Gordon produced a rolled scroll that he had prepared for this possibility. Information as to the whereabouts of a man so powerful and important as the *Mahdi* was seldom reliable. But he had to come and find this out for himself.

The Guard took it, seeming to be honored to now become a special messenger and runner, between Gordon Pasha, and the Great *Mahdi* himself. He was suddenly very proud.

"Do not open it," Gordon raised a finger. "It is for the eyes of the *Mahdi* only."

"Come then," the guard lowered his rifle. You must eat at my fire.

"We thank you for such hospitality. Should you find me in Khartum with a reply from the *Mahdi*, rest assured, you will be kept safe and well treated, and enjoy the same from me in the palace." The guard smiled, he was now so much bigger then he was when the moon shone on him the previous night, so much more.

When the meal ended, olives, pita bread, soft cheese, Gordon and Issak felt much better. Then Gordon thanked all present, and fearless, he asked them to end to their rebellion and promised them all jobs in his administration if they laid down their arms. Otherwise, he said he would have to bring many soldiers to 'disarm and break them,' and this he preferred not to do.

Two of the men at the fire laughed at that, but when Gordon fixed them with his cobalt blue eyes, they became silent, and could not meet his gaze. The guard knew they were in the presence of a very great man, a willful man, a man of natural internal power, touched by God. He had the same sense of unflagging self confidence that he had seen among the Emirs and Sheikhs who led them, only the aura about him seemed different, imbued with destiny, fateful.

"Go with the God who sent you here, Gordon Pasha," he said. "And may Allah forgive your sin of unbelief."

"Oh I am not a man of unbelief. Here, give this to your *Mahdi* as well." Gordon handed the man a small leather bound book, one of two bibles that he had brought with him, this one a pocket edition.

The letter he had handed the Guard would ask the *Mahdi* for peace, and offer him the Sultanship of all Kurdufan and Darfur provinces, which was all the land from the Nile west to the border of Chad. That land, adjoined to the Nubian Desert east of the Nile, would encompass nearly the whole of Sudan. 'And let us live in peace,' he asked of the *Mahdi*. But prophets and seers lived by their own guide marks of fate. For the *Mahdi*, nothing would be given him, but all would be taken, in the name of Allah. It was written.

And a reply to Gordon's message to the *Mahdi* was also written, and carried to him in Khartum by the very same guard he entrusted with his own correspondence. It was entirely in Arabic, but there were scholars present who could translate it and when that script was ready, Gordon retired to his chambers, sat by an oil lamp and read the document. As he did so, he felt the shifting weight of history upon his shoulders.

"In the name of God, the Merciful, the Compassionate! [1]

Praise belongs to God, the Generous Patron, and prayer with peace upon our Lord Muhammad and his family.

"From the Servant, humble in the eyes of his Lord, *Muhammad al Mahdi* ibn as *Sayyid Abdullah*, to the representative of Britain and of the Khedive, *Gordon Pasha*.

"We hereby inform you that God (Praise belongs to him the Most High) in his patience and generosity is long suffering, but he does not neglect and he does not turn aside his wrath from the guilty people, and he is the patron of the believers. The Most High said: God is the patron of those who believe; he leads them out of darkness into light; but they who do not believe, their patrons are demons who lead them from light into darkness; they are fellows of the fire, in which they shall remain forever.

It was immediately clear to Gordon that the Mahdi was attempting to seize the moral high ground, couching himself as the faithful believer, and seeing Gordon as the Infidel.

"He has pointed out [the true way of life] in the glorious Koran and others of his ancient books and by the tongue of every apostle, prophet, and faithful devotee, censuring this world and making the wise wary of it. There it is written: "Know that this present life is only a toy, a plaything, a vain amusement, a source of rivalry among you, and a striving for increase of property and children." But in the hereafter [there will be] a severe punishment [for those who seek the glory of this world]; and pardon from God, and favor [for those who renounce it]. The life of this world is only a deceitful provision.

"One who is guided aright as to the signs knows that he who acknowledges the truth of the belief in God and his Apostle is very near to God, he must attain his desire, he will get his reward and be given what souls like and eyes delight in. Verily no one can escape his punishment and penalty and every evil of this world and the next except through him [God]. Know that this world is transitory, base, deceitful, treacherous. There is no peace in it, and no pleasure in comparison with the great good which is with God in the abode of joy. But whoever loves this world and cherishes it above the next, God will cast him headlong into everlasting hell, as the word of the Most High says: "And he who has transgressed and has chosen this present life; verily hell shall be his abode."

Gordon had read similar admonishments in his bible, and thought this little more than the same, if just a little self-righteous. Then he took note of the *Mahdi*'s sense of honor. He might learn much from that.

Chapter 3

The Letter from the Mahdi... Concluded...

"So it is plain that there is no profit in the honor of this world and in its life, wealth and property, but only prolonged regret in the hereafter. The honor of this world is no more valuable than a handful of sand. Understand?"

That was a sure thing to have been said from a man of the desert, that the pursuit of honor here was as worthless as its sand, thought Gordon. He looked at the hourglass on his desk, seeing the sand falling in its steady stream. Something about it summed up the ebbing of his own life. He had come here out of a sense of honor, willing to lay down his life to save those less fortunate in Khartum, those for whom there was no place on any of his steamships heading north to Egypt. Was that all? What else did honor demand of him here? Was it his honor, or that of the British Empire he hoped to restore? The Mahdi wrote a little more...

"It was written that: 'Two hungry wolves let into a sheep-cote would not do more damage to it than the desire of man for condition and high station does to his religion.'"

With all this, Gordon could see how fruitless his offer of a Sultanship to the Mahdi had been, and he realized there was greater depth in the man than he or any others might have believed.

It is written: "There is no guide except God, as also the Most High said: "He therefore who is directed, will be directed to the advantage of his own soul, but he who errs, he will err."

Gordon could take that as a finger of accusation pointed directly at his heart, the Mahdi was, in this long diatribe, establishing himself as the only one embracing truth and truly walking the path ordained by God.

Yet here was history, the mind of the man he had sought out in the desert; the mind of a true zealot, and he could not pull his blue eyes from the scroll until he had finished it all.

"Since this is so, then it is plain that *I* am the one who invites to God, and the Khalifa of the Apostle of God (God bless him and give him peace) and that *I* am the *Mahdi*, the expected one, and this is no boast.

Now the *Mahdi* pressed Gordon to convert to Islam...

"God has authorized *me* to proclaim mercy upon whosoever obeys him and follows the direction of his prophet Muhammad (God bless him and give him peace), and vengeance 'upon whosoever rebels against him and disobeys him and follows his devil, his own inclination and desire, and cleaves to this world.' I have invited you to Islam and the faith. You should answer with submission and obedience! I tell you this only to guide you aright, and for the sake of your peace and happiness in your condition and your property, if you can know and understood the truth of what I said. *How good my intention towards you is!* And I have not ceased trying to promote your welfare and wishing you good in the hope that God might open your breast to Islam and that you might turn to the command of God, the king, the all knowing....

"Let not the success of the unbelievers in the land deceive you, it is but a slender provision and then their receptacle shall be hell, an unpleasant couch. But they who fear the Lord shall have gardens through which rivers flow, they shall dwell therein forever. This is the gift of God, for what is with God will be better for the righteous."

At this Gordon thought, what better to offer a desert people than a river flowing through a garden? Is that not the Nile Valley? Then the Mahdi finally got down to business regarding the fate of Khartum. It was conditional...

We pledge you safety upon this condition, all of you, with the pledge of God and his Apostle, and the pledge of the servant of God. So put an end to the shedding of your blood, and look to your lives and property, and let not the greatness of your number, the assistance of the army upon which you rely, deceive you. Our reliance is God, there is no other. His might cannot be measured and his army cannot be defeated. The fulfillment of the covenant is surely binding upon us as soon as you agree to the conditions in our reply, otherwise not.

Ah, thought Gordon, this is definitely a conditional offer, and he tells me the coming of the British Army here will mean nothing. We shall see, for it has also been said that "God helps those who help themselves."

"It is written: 'This world is a carcass and those who desire it are dogs.' Whether they like or not, the command of God, the Most High, is executed in spite of them. So the first demand upon them is **obedience** and a reasonable reply. If they believe in God, surely it is well for them.

Gordon had to smile, for if that were so, then why did the Mahdi wish to lay siege to Khartum? The next lines held his reason.

"**This is a warning to you**, so hearken and turn to your Lord and submit yourself to him before punishment comes upon you. Then you will not be helped. Happy is the man who is warned by another and hastens to his own good. So come to salvation before your wings are clipped!

"Peace be upon him who follows the right guidance."

Gordon took full note of the qualified wish of peace at the end. This entire letter, he thought, is the *Mahdi's* right guidance. He says he wants to spare me the suffering that he intends to bring upon Khartum, but with steep conditions. I'm to acknowledge that he is the sole authority determining who is a true believer and man of God; I'm to renounce Christianity, convert to Islam, and only then will I be worthy of his grace and spared the fate he has in mind to deliver here. This is no peace, it is merely servitude to his Islamic zeal, and to him, and this I will not do any more than I stand here in servitude to the British Government. I am warned, he says. So be it. I move now to the defense of this city.

We have a lot of work to do, he thought. First off, I'll have 20,000 people to feed here, and that will need all the livestock, grain and other food I can scour from the land here, and before the noose tightens around the city with a siege.

Then I think we will need some better defensive works. The city walls may not be enough to discourage attack.

An Idea came to him as he considered the geography of this place. Khartum sat at the confluence of the Blue and White Nile Rivers. Here they joined as one, and the city lay right between them, just south of that union. Why not dig a trench, a grand moat joining the two rivers just outside the city wall? That would make any direct assault against the walls much more difficult.

Both Gordon and his assistant Colonel Stewart had come up through the Army as Engineers, so this was a project Gordon was eager to get underway. Stewart came in and he began discussing it with him.

"What? Build a moat? Well, I suppose it could be done, but we'll have to dam up both ends while we dig the damn thing, and then introduce the water in some controlled manner. Otherwise we could flood all the ground between the two rivers."

"That would have the same effect," said Gordon.

"Yes, and it would make Khartum an island too. The only way anyone could come and go would be by boat. The Sudanese here are farmers. Many leave the city daily to go work their land, then return here at dusk for the night. So flooding all that ground would be troublesome. We'll have to carefully balance the flow of the water in any channel we dig, and make it crossable."

"For us, but not for the Dervish."

"Well, we can construct some simple draw bridges."

"Good. This will give the men something more to do than standing about on the parapets of that wall, and it might improve morale too. Doing something about their situation is the one thing every man needs to have hope. We've got to keep the men busy. Otherwise we'll start seeing desertions every night, and half of them will end up fighting for the *Mahdi*.

"We'll, I'm glad you're starting to see the realities of this situation, General Gordon. I hope you remember it was your choice to discard your orders and stay here. If there's a siege, it will be because *you've* chosen to remain. And if this city falls into chaos and bloodshed, that's on you, sir."

Part II
The Work Of The Faithful

"It is the certainty that they possess the truth that makes men cruel."
—Anatoly France, French poet

Chapter 4

Colonel Stewart had an uncomfortable feeling on that journey to Khartum. There was one place on the steamer that felt very creepy to him, and lingering there would send him into a disconsolate mood and always leave him with a chill of terrible fear and anxiety. Yes, he thought, we're headed for trouble in Khartum. That's probably what I'm feeling here. This boat is too damn slow. It's just the fight or flight reflex in me, that's all. Here on this steamer I've nothing I can see to fight, except Gordon, and nowhere to flee.

That was a good way to explain away his unsettled feelings, but no, it was something more that was bothering him, a sense of doom, of a destiny that he would never escape is he went up river to Khartum; it was a feeling that the desert would take his life and soul if he went there.

Seeing Gordon in Khartum, he put his feelings aside and approached him.

"So you've received a letter from the *Mahdi*?" Colonel Stewart was curious.

"Yes, and it was eight pages of his sanctimonious preaching."

"Well what did you expect? The man's a zealot."

"Good question. I sent a small bible along with my letter, but I don't think he regarded it as anything more than a heretical text, good for nothing more than his haughty refutation. Outrageous. Well, I've dealt with his sort before, Colonel. In China its was Hong Xiuquan, and that man actually thought he was the younger brother of Jesus! It's amazing what a man can come to believe, but there is something about a religious zealot that makes him very dangerous. He uses God to justify all his atrocities, and comes to see his butchery as the will of God, accepting no moral responsibility for it himself."

"I wholly agree sir. Anatoly France, the French Poet said it well enough: 'It is the certainty that they possess the truth that makes men cruel.'

"Well said, and there's a lunatic at the heart of most of these religious movements. Something about Islam is different, however. It has had a militant edge to it since the beginning. Its self-righteous declaration that there is no god but God and his name is Allah, is little different than the same declaration made by Christianity...I am the way, the truth, the light, and no man comes to the Father but through me. Yes, we Christians waged more than our fair share of Crusades into the Holy Land against the Muslims. We have no more claim to any moral high ground than this *Mahdi*. We all get stuck somewhere, don't we. I suppose any man stuck on one idea, like this Hong Xiuquan, becomes a dangerous man. I would lay at least 30 million skulls at his feet in China."

"Well sir, give a man a bible and you might get a priest one day. Give a man a gun and you might get a soldier. But never give him both—you get an armed zealot, and a lot of trouble."

That summed up the threat in Sudan quite well.

"Time we do something about it." said Gordon. "Look here, I've drawn on this city map. Khartum sits right in the arms of the Blue and white Nile Rivers. Here's how I want to connect them with a channel, dug right along the outer city walls." He pointed.

"Very well, I can oversee that."

"Good, then I'll lay in the stores of food and supplies we'll need."

"One thing, sir," said Stewart. "Speaking of men with one track minds. All this would be unnecessary if you followed instructions and simply withdrew as ordered."

"And how would that change the fate of all these people here? It would surely make it worse. Don't you see, Colonel? As long as I'm here, then I give Britain something to do about this situation, just like the men we'll be asking to dig our moat. And if the *Mahdi* thinks a British Army is coming up to back me here, he may think twice about trying to bring his little rebellion to Khartum."

"I suppose that's one way of looking at it. Then again, he just might think he'd better hurry his attack here, before that army arrives. What can you do here sir, really? Dig this moat? Buck up morale among the troops? Do you plan to take up a weapon yourself? Can you kill them all if they get inside these walls? There must be 50,000 Dervish out there by now."

"I have more weapons at hand than a sword or pistol. Colonel. I have a life to give, and sometimes a man willing to give his life in a cause can make a very great difference indeed."

"Then you want to die here sir? And please don't say if God wills it. You'll be no different than this *Mahdi*."

"Perhaps, but I am honor bound to stay here. Dig your moat, Colonel Stewart. I should be back in a few days with enough meat and food stocks to tide us over for a good many months if we are besieged."

Later that day, Gordon had hand picked the best of his 7,000 troops, and mounted a security detachment for his foraging expedition. Little did he know that his obstinate refusal to leave Khartum to its fate had already seen the arrival of General Wolseley at summer's end, 9 September 1884. There he began acclimating the troops that arrived as well.

Gordon's plan had worked! He was such an icon of his age, that his life weighed heavily when Britain considered the possible fall of Khartum. Increasing public pressure in England demanded a relief expedition until it became a matter of constant debate in Parliament. Gladstone had resisted sending any British troops as long as he could, until cabinet members began to threaten their resignations, whereupon he grudgingly approved a vote to pass funding for an expedition to Khartum. Then he summoned Wolseley.

"My God," he raged. "Just when I thought Gordon would go and get us out of that mess in Sudan, he pulls us right back in! Now you'll have to clean this matter up, Wolseley, and by God, don't you end up like Billy Hicks!"

"Of course not sir. I'll be leading a proper force this time—British regulars."

"Very well, then how do you propose to get there once in Egypt?"

"There are several ways it might be accomplished. We could go down the Red Sea and land at Suakin. But from there it would be a 250 mile march through the Nubian Desert to Berber, then another 200 miles or so up river to Khartum. That route is the shortest, difficult at the outset, but with the advantage of arriving at Berber without having to get around the 4th and 5th cataracts on the Nile. It might also invite attack during that initial desert leg."

"An attack you would welcome? Isn't the idea, to crush this *Mahdi* fellow and box his ears?"

"The idea is to secure Khartum and the safety of its Governor General, sir. Boxing the *Mahdi's* ears would be incidental."

"Do you have any fear of engaging the man in battle?"

"No sir, we'll handle ourselves quite well. Hicks was leading conscripted farmers. Our lads are veterans all—the Crimea, Afghanistan, India, and some have been to Egypt as well."

"Good, then do box the man's ears, General. And get that intransigent man out as well. Why did I ever agree to send him there? Wasn't it you who suggested it?"

"I was in favor, sir, but I believe it was Lord Salisbury who stirred that pot."

"Yes, and likely as a means of handing me this hornet's nest so he can step back in."

"Perhaps, sir."

"And is there any other way to get to Khartum?"

"Yes sir, the second route has some good options. We just go up river to Wadi Halfa on the Sudanese border, and then push on up the Nile to Dongola, about 245 miles. From there it's another 130 miles to Korti over desert where I would then have to decide how to proceed. This route has the advantage on moving by boat on the Nile, with adequate water that whole way, and good wells on the desert leg to Korti."

"And once there?"

"Then, should the situation need haste, I could cut right across the Bayuda Desert to Metemeh or perhaps Wadi Hamed. That would put us right on the 6th Cataract. Get past that and it's a 70 mile march to Khartum."

"Sounds appealing. I'll leave the route to you, General, but do get there if we go to all the trouble to move 9,000 troops to Egypt."

"Oh, we'll get there sir, but one cannot foresee what difficulties we might encounter. I won't be able to judge the time until I get started."

"Then off you go, Wolseley, and God go with you."

Wolseley was a good friend of Gordon, and had every good motive to see him safely rescued. Yet moving up river into Sudan was no pleasure cruise, particularly into a land that would be hostile at every turn of the river.

Khartum ~ September 1884

With the coming of the *Mahdi*, the Dervish rebellion in Sudan intensified and became a growing threat to Khartum. As the tension increased, the British press idolized Gordon as: "a solitary figure holding aloft the flag of England in the face of the dark hordes of Islam." Khartum was soon besieged, but not before Gordon organized and carried out three great tasks.

The first was a mission with the best of his soldiers, all mounted on horses or camels. They would forage for food stocks, and round up as much livestock as they could find. Of course, they would be seen doing this, and the *Mahdi* would arrange to attack them as they started back towards the city.

When Gordon saw the Dervish raiders preparing to attack, he ordered most of his riders to dismount and form up in a rocky sector, using the large strewn boulders for cover.

"Wait until they get in among us. I will give the order to fire." The rest of the column would continue driving south to Khartum.

The Dervish charged, swords waving, and with raucous shouting. As they flowed into the ravine where Gordon's troops were hidden, they flowed around the boulders, and Gordon gave the order to fire. Suddenly his 50 riflemen sprang up and fired into the backs of those who had passed through. When the survivors turned to see their ambushers, the second volley cut many more down. Then one Dervish Sheikh saw the distant column of livestock hurrying away south and pointed. Some of his riders peeled off to pursue it. That was when Gordon ordered his men back to the horse holders, hidden in a shaded glen.

They were up and riding hard on the Heels of the Dervish attacking the livestock. About 30 more men were defending that group, and they mustered in a line to try and discourage the Dervish raiders. Then coming from behind him, Gordon's cavalry arrived, carbines in hand and shooting from the saddle very effectively. Others carried long lances they plunged into the Dervish riders.

Now taking fire from both sides, the Dervish began to scatter. Gordon would lose about twelve men in this wild defense, but the Livestock and grain supplies were able to reach Khartum and pass in through the city gates before the Dervish could regroup to make another attack.

The First task was complete, and tireless, Gordon would now move to call on Colonel Stewart and see about the second task. He would find him at the trench site that was being dug to join the Blue and White Nile. A wall of thick brown tree trunks had been erected near the Blue Nile to act as a dam. Then the trench had arced along the outer edge of the city wall to the mud flats near the White Nile. When Gordon saw the wood was well underway and nearly complete, he checked off that box in his mind.

The last thing to be done was to use the few steamboats docked there at Khartum to get the "necessary" evacuees off and down river if he could. He could only spare about twenty soldiers per boat, and only one cannon each for their defense. *Abbas* would be the Flagship of the little flotilla, and he hoped that heading down river, they could get through to Berber and learn news of the relief expedition.

Gordon had been relying on messages, most channeled through a dour faced British officer, a Colonel Horatio Herbert Kitchener. Like Gordon himself, Kitchener was an officer in the Royal Engineers, trained at Woolwich where Gordon schooled in that art. Kitchener served on Cyprus in 1878 before coming to Egypt, where his stern manner made him unpopular with the other officers. When trouble broke out in the Sudan he was a liaison between Khartum and Wolseley, making telegraph contact with him and even carrying messages. Admiring Gordon, Kitchener would send him messages to the effect: "Can I do anything for you? I shall be awfully glad if you will let me know.' An entry in Gordon's diary revealed his irritation, saying it was like a drowning man being asked whether or not he might need a life preserver. Kitchener was later posted to Suakin on the Red Sea coast to become Governor of East Sudan in 1887. There he clashed with Osman Digna, the local Dervish leader in that sector.

Sir Francis Grenfell, Sirdar at that time, thought Kitchener brusque and ill-mannered, and without tact or discretion. One officer stated: "we hated the sight of him." Yet in spite of that, London believed he was a man who could get things done, and would make him Sirdar in Egypt in 1892 when Grenfell returned to England.

Gordon's fate at Khartum would affect Kitchener deeply and lead him to remarkably industrious campaigning. For now, Kitchener was eager to see Gordon relieved, and wondered why Wolseley was taking so long.

Chapter 5

Gordon would now bid farewell to Colonel Stewart. The trench moat had been built and filled with just enough water to be an obstacle without flooding. The city was plump with livestock and food. Now it was time to get the Egyptian officials and their families down river and out of harm's way. He was with Stewart at the quay, where the last of the Egyptian officials were boarding a steamship. Gordon took off his ring and gave it to the Colonel, a sign he could hand to someone else that Gordon had sent him.

"You must get through to Berber," Gordon told the Colonel, "get through and see if you can make contact with Wolseley. We'll need him here as soon as possible. Tell him we've only enough food remaining to carry us to mid November. Lord knows, he's been in Egypt since early September. What's keeping the man?"

That was a very good question.

October 1884 ~ Wadi Halfa on the Egyptian Frontier

Wolseley had it in his mind to muster at Wadi Halfa and then move up river with steamers and whaler's boats. When he reached the place, he learned that the rail line there was being extended 30 to 50 miles south to a point beyond the 2nd and 3rd cataracts. But Wolseley stopped the work.

"This expedition is not of sufficient importance to warrant the construction of a railway," said the General. Why Wolseley would have ordered this was a mystery to many historians. Particularly in stark contrast to Kitchener's approach to this same problem later. Some thought his own plan to rely on the Whaler's boats was the reason, others believed he was acting because of constraints imposed on him by Gladstone. Yes, he had been told he must go to Khartum, but not how fast he should get there. The work stoppage on that rail spur would cost him two weeks toil at the 2nd and 3rd Cataracts, where the 450 waling boats had to be fixed with long ropes and laboriously dragged up the rapids by 50 men for each boat. Some of the boats were none too sturdy, and received much damage. A few even broke up and had to be abandoned. This would delay further advance upstream beyond the Cataracts until 2 November. After that, Wolseley also would find hidden rocks, river currents, and sand bars to be unexpected obstacles.

All that laborious effort could have been avoided by simply allowing the rail line to proceed. Gordon had written a letter in July stating he could hold out no later than mid-November. Perhaps that deadline moved Wolseley to stay with his small boat plan. Once on decent open water, the boats fared better, and Wolseley began offering prizes of a hundred pounds to the first boat crews and soldiers to reach Dongola.

Gordon sent Colonel Stewart south with the steamers to repeat his call for urgent support, but the news concerning the fall of Berber had been true, and when the steam boats tried to run the gauntlet there, they faced cannon fire, and boatloads of Dervish fighters. None got through. Colonel Stewart himself was captured and killed aboard *Abass*. The same steamer he and Gordon had taken up river to Khartum. It was a sad fate, and before he died, Stewart remembered the strange feeling he had on that first journey south on *Abass*; the feelings of imminent doom. It was always at the same place on the steamer, and that was the place a Dervish spear took his life that day.

By the time Wolseley reached Dongola, he had the Black Watch and Staffordshire regiments in hand there by mid November. In effect, he was already too late, for Gordon has sent many messages saying that was the limit of his ability to hold out—mid-November. The camels of the Camel Corps were then being pressed into service, for the rail beyond the 3rd cataract had finally been completed, and supplies were being moved to its terminus, where the caravans of camels could go down from Dongola, and carry them overland.

"I can't see as if we can make any further advance from Dongola until the end of December," Wolseley pronounced one morning.

"The Light Infantry has only just departed from Wadi Halfa." That was the morning of 18 November when the Duke of Cornwall's Light Infantry moved south. That same day the 19th Hussars would also ride south under Colonel Barrow. Meanwhile, the Royal Marines, a part of the Guards Regiment, was only just reaching Wadi Halfa on the 20th and 21st of November. These men were going to be part of the Camel Corps. The Royal West Kent and Royal Irish would come up to Wadi Halfa on 1 December, so Wolseley still had regiments strung out all along his chosen line of advance, and how long it would take him to concentrate that army was any man's guess.

The Royal Irish were ordered to move by whaler boats to Korti, 130 miles beyond Dongola where Wolseley still waited.

The Colonel of the Irish protested: "What am I commanding here, the Naval Brigade? My men are soldiers, and I'd sooner march them there, right across the desert."

The colonel would get his wish, whereupon he would make that march all the way to Metemeh, a distance of 176 miles in eleven days—but not until February. That was another mystery, because Metemeh was still well below the 6th Cataract, which meant any further move up river by boat would meet that obstacle. Wolseley's plan had been haphazard, and not cognizant of the real conditions on the river, or its terrain. Once at Korti, he would still have the 4th, 5th, and 6th cataracts to navigate before he reached Khartum. He might have listened to the dour faced Kitchener, and from Korti just marched directly across the Bayuda Desert to Khartum. Instead he continued northeast up the Nile. Khartum was southeast from Korti.

Kitchener shook his head with this news and the long delays in Wolseley's advance, and he would learn a great deal on how *not* to make an advance on Khartum in the future.

The year would wear away into December. Instead of the holidays back home in England, the troops would pass their nights under the pale desert moons. What Wolseley needed, but sorely lacked, were good wagons that might have carried all his supplies and river boats across open desert, and the horses to pull them. But if wishes were horses... So goes the old saying. If this failed, it would not be the *Mahdi* or his Dervish hordes that would defeat Gordon and Wolseley, but logistics, poor planning and sluggish execution.

2 DEC 1884 ~ Sarras, near Wadi Halfa

In early December, Majors Poe and Hunter of the Royal Marines were ordered to leave Sarras and move up to join Wolseley. They would bring a battery of artillery and also be accompanied by Colonel McCalmont with a detachment of the Hussars. One night they became acquainted with the desert winds, which could rise very suddenly to a gale force and carry with them particles of yellow sand and red loess to make breathing very uncomfortable. They would also learn that the desert heat would not abate simply because it was December near the onset of winter.

They would be happy to see a tent encampment made by the rail crews under Lieutenant Vidal. The engineers were working to continue extending the line. That night, the march halted after sunset to wait for the rising full moon before proceeding. It was time for tea, oxtail soup, Bully-Beef, biscuits and tins of jam. The meal was welcome and satisfying, and the officers sat round a camp fire afterwards smoking their pipes.

The moon arrived and the groans of the camels started as they were prodded to their feet again. It would be another long night march, the men weary and sleepy until they began to hear the distant roar of the 4th Cataract. Reaching that, they saw it was a very difficult obstacle, and a close inspection of the boats revealed why they had such a hard time, many had used inferior spruce and elm planks for their siding, and some of the elm was so rotten in places that it did not hold the copper nails used to fasten it.

Days like this would stack up, one after another. Such was Wolseley's advance up the Nile, a tedious, lethargic toil, where any sense of speed or urgency was wholly lacking. Wolsey had received a note from Gordon saying not to worry, and that he could hold out forever, but that was soon proved to be a mere boast, and far from the truth. Then a second letter was more circumspect, stating that it would be difficult to hold out after December 14th, owing to lack of food. The garrison at Khartum was now surrounded by over 20,000 Dervish zealots, and the *Mahdi* was taking careful note of Wolseley's plodding advance. Even so, the General would not leave Dongola for Korti until 23 December, and all while the garrison at Khartum was starving. (The reader will compare this advance to the alacrity and ingenuity of Kitchener's campaign later.)

Soon the troops would be singing *Auld Lang Syne* and *Rule Britannia* to welcome in the new year. For some it would be the last new year they would welcome, because Dervish scouts were now marking the progress of Wolsey's advance closely, skirting its edges like wolves watching a ponderous migration of cattle.

Decision at Korti

At Korti, a base camp had been established in rows of tents at right angles to the river. There was the bivouac of all the mounted Infantry, the Light and Heavy Camel regiments, the 19th Hussars, and artillery. The Black Watch and Staffordshire regiments were present, and now they had been joined by the Sussex Regiment, with all the column's ordnance and supplies.

Here Wolseley had to make his decision on the road ahead. If Korti were one corner of a square at point A, the Nile moved along one side of that square to Abu Hamed, Point B. Then it turned southeast to Berber, Point C, and from there south west to Metemeh, Point D. That was the river route. The shorter route was to simply abandon the Nile and march overland, directly from Korti at Point A to Metemeh at Point D. That was the much shorter route.

Wolseley had thought the Nile route with his whaling boats was better, because he would have access to water the whole way, but then he learned that the route from Korti to Metemeh passed through two well sites, at Jakdul and then Abu Klea. Now he pondered what to do. Unable to decide, Wolseley would take both routes, the epitome of equivocation.

All along the bank of the Nile lay rows of the whaling boats that had brough these men here. Korti made for an excellent camp, as the Nile water here was pristine and clear, drinkable without any need to even filter it. It's flows were wide and slow. Men were still coming up river from Dongola in those boats, and others were preparing to make the trek across the desert, which would avoid the much longer river trip. The distance overland from Korti to Metemeh was a third of the river route, and in a rare moment of urgency, General Wolseley had decided to send a detachment overland immediately.

This group was composed of the Guards Camel regiment, and detachments from the Mounted Infantry, Light and Heavy Camel regiments, Royal Engineers and even 45 men from the 19th Hussars. They set off with seven days rations and with each man carrying seven gallons of water on the camels and horses, and 150 rounds of ammunition, with 40,000 more in reserve crates.

Their road ahead would take them to Jakdul, the site of a well to replenish water if need be, and then on to Abu Klea. Jakdul would also become a reserve depot, and the camel Corps troops were transporting 60,000 rations there.

It had been learned that Colonel Stewart had been murdered when his steamer was attacked near Berber by the wild tribe of the Monnasir. Wolseley's force had orders to punish the Monnasir for that should they find them, and that goal seemed to overshadow the main thrust of this entire operation—to relieve Khartum. It was pulling a good part of Wolseley's force along the longer river route to Berber.

"I've written to Gordon twice now," said Wolseley, "on the 26th of October and the 20th of September, both times asking him for information as to his position and intentions. Now here it is, new year's eve and I finally get his reply." The loss of the telegraph line, cut by the Dervish, had been a great impediment.

"Here it is, sir, Gordon's reply at long last."

"Well, what does it say man?"

The man, Colonel Swaine squinted at a tiny square paper in his hand. "It says 'Khartum all right,' sir. Gordon says he has disabled one of the Mahdi's guns."

They brought in the messenger, and Wolseley questioned him further. "Gordon is well, General, but he must spend each night on the watch, moving from one city outpost to another, and checking his sentries. So he sleeps by day. The man is in good spirits, and well supplied with good tobacco."

"Well, if he says he put an enemy gun out of action that may leave us some cause for concern. This *Mahdi* has artillery?"

"Those he took from Hicks Pasha, Lord, and many Remington Rifles."

Wolseley had a copy of Gordon's last letter and now he opened and read it again. It related how the first attack of the *Mahdi* was repulsed, then continued: *"Our troops at Khartum are suffering from lack of provisions. Food, we still have a little, some grain and biscuit. We want you to come quickly. You should Come by Metemeh or Berber, but do not leave Berber in your rear ungarrisoned. Keep the enemy in your front, and when you have taken Berber, send me word from there."*

From this Wolseley assessed that Gordon thought he could hold out until Berber was taken. Then in came a young Lieutenant with additional news.

"Sir, I'm told the local natives are saying the column sent through Jakdul has been attacked. No details, sir, and we've no confirmation. But there's been no word from them."

This sent a dark squall across Wolseley's features, and it would not be until January 4th that he did get confirmation of the state of that column. In came Lord Cochrane and a Lieutenant Hine of the mounted Infantry. Wolseley had just finished dining and got up from the table when these men appeared.

"They reached Jakdul on Friday, sir, New Year's day, and they found the wells unoccupied by the Dervish, and the water there plentiful and good. The road south was open to Metemeh and Shendi, where it was said the *Mahdi* had a small force in garrison. But it's clear that the Dervish are out there sir."

"So we go too. This desert road seems well watered, so General Stewart will command the mounted flying column and take it to Metemeh. I must continue by river to Berber to secure that base as well."

Faced with two routes of advance, Wolseley was now going to divide his force and follow both. Yet that intention aside, it would take until 14 January before the camp at Korti could complete final preparation for these movements. The place was alive with activity, and over all the awful groaning moan of the camels being pressed into service again was heard. Camels were willful beasts, and on occasion, if overburdened and in any pain, they would simply stop and kneel down. After this their burden had to be considerably lightened to get them to stand up and move again. While mules had long reputations for being stubborn, not one could match the vindictive and sullen demeanor of a camel, which might even try to bite those near him when in a mood. Some had to be muzzled to prevent this behavior, which only made the camel more surly and unmanageable.

Camels also had a good nose for nearby water, and a sixth sense for danger from the weather or other threats. By all accounts, they were none too happy to be pressed into a march again, and the men had a distinct feeling that this time, they were heading into danger.

Chapter 6
14 JAN 1885 ~ The March to Abu Klea
The Flying Column

The column formed up, delayed getting the commissariat and transport camels into line. It was a large, substantial mix of Royal Marines, British regular infantry and mounted troops. It numbered 114 officers, nearly 1700 soldiers 343 native camel drivers and 2,888 camels, so each camel driver had to manage as many as eight beasts, all strung out nose to tail in typical caravan style. Then the 19th Hussars came with 153 men on horseback.

This was obviously not the whole of Wolseley's force, but more a reinforcement of the lighter column he had sent out earlier. One officer remarked on it as "a patchwork of this unit and that, and with far too many animals. Taking a little of everything may be a good way to make a salad dressing, but not an effective or safe fighting column."[2]

There was even a herd of horned cattle being driven as part of the column, good for a food source on the hoof, but little else. Yet morale was high, and Wolseley could sense the determination of his men to get through to Khartum and save Gordon. It seemed a noble effort.

The men would find it was not as arduous a march as they first believed. The desert gave way to savas of green grass, much to the delight of the many camels, though now they wanted to stop and graze if not kept moving. They would reach the wells at Jakdul without incident, but as they approached that place, their cavalry videttes came across several tracks of other horsemen. One went to General Stewart to report.

"It's clear we're being observed by Dervish scouts, sir. They're most likely trying to assess our strength."

"Then let them beware," said Stewart, confident his column could handle itself. Indeed, scouted from any distance, the sheer number of animals in the column presented an imposing scene when all were arrayed on the open ground The riders of the Camel Corps were up front, looking grand in their light grey uniforms and white sun helmets on red saddle dressings. The wells at Abu Klea lay ahead, and it seemed that nothing would stop them.

About twenty miles from that goal, Colonel Barrow of the 19th Hussars was given orders to get well out in front and Reconnoiter Abu Klea. Major French had the point, and there were also wide flankers posted. He stopped, observing a group of Arab riders on camels off their right flank. Colonel Barrow came up and told him to take a squad and pursue them. Knowing the lay of the land well, the Arabs slipped away, and Major French came upon a wadi that was leading down to the wells. There they saw nine Dervish on camels, and several groups on foot with spears and rifles. The major rode up a low hill, whereupon he saw more footmen. He thought he might capture one or two and taking a corporal in tow, began to pursue them.

Just as they got their hands on one man, French saw many more groups of Dervish, all maneuvering to envelop him.

"Alright," he said to the Corporal. "Let the scraggy man go, we'd best get back and report this. There's more than enemy patrols here."

They would get back to Colonel Barrow who had taken the initiative of occupying a low stone outcrop overlooking the wadi. No sooner had they taken that position, when Dervish started to attack it at both ends.

"Cavalry!" came the order. "Dis-mount! Form rifle teams."

Those orders were smartly obeyed, and soon those teams of five to ten men were volley firing at the Dervish to drive them off.

"There's s good deal more out there," Major French gestured.

"That so? Well, we'll hold here until the whole column comes up." Barrow knew the value of the ground he had taken, and the fact that the Dervish had tried to take it from him underscored that in his mind. He was going to be stubborn here, and knowing the whole column wasn't far behind gave he and his men heart.

The column, however, had not formed for the march until three hours after Colonel Barrow led his men out. Still before sunrise, one segment had veered off in the wrong direction, forcing General Stewart to call a halt while riders went after them to get them back in order. That cost them another hour.

Not seeing any imminent help, Barrow left his scouts under Major French and rode back to see what the delay was. When he got back to camp he reported "The enemy is to our front! I've held him off from a piece of very good ground up ahead."

"Good," came the answer. "Then I mean to attack him at once." It was General Herbert Stewart, in overall command of the cavalry division, and already a Knight Commander of the Order of the Bath for his brilliant work in Egypt at Tel-el-Kebir and El Teb in Sudan. One of the correspondents took a photograph of him that was later developed to show an odd shadow cast over him. He shivered seeing it, for it was taken January 16th, just 30 days before Stewart would die of wounds he would receive in the days ahead.

The Bayuda Desert had largely been crossed, but now the enemy was near, and at Abu Klea there was going to be a fight.

16-18 January 1885 ~ near Abu Klea, Sudan.

It was going to be one of those battles where it would be difficult to decide who really won. General Stewart was bold and confident, but his cavalry scouts had not yet seen the whole of the Mahdist force ahead of them. While the Flying column had 1400 British troops and about 300 native men, the *Mahdi* had sent a force 13,000 strong to impeded Stewart's advance, so he was moving into real trouble ahead, and over ground that was undulating through low ravines and wadis flanked by stony hillocks. There was no commanding high point, so Stewart wisely ordered the column to form a moving square to be ready for anything.

British squares had been held inviolate throughout the Victorian era until the campaign here in the Sudan near Suakin. There Mahdist tactics were to lay low in a grassy *Khor* and then spring a raging attack on the advancing British force, which had two brigade sized squares. So it was the Madhist Dervish who laid claim as the first to ever penetrate a British square through a gap in the ranks. That was at the Battle of Tamai, and here they would soon try again.

Every man would carry a full water bottle and 1000 rounds, and they would advance in a moving square, while the transport elements and column supplies would be staged behind in a defensive zeriba. Colonel Barrow remained at the zeriba.

Two soldiers were watching the surrounding high ground closely, fearing to see the hills bristle with Dervish fighters. "This has all the makings of another disaster," said one, "Yus like wot happened in Zululand at the start."

"Corporal, you are the last I would think to be dreamin' of disaster out here."

"Oh? What do you make our odds on ever seeing the Nile again? Three to one?"

"Wors'n that. I make 'em ten to one, cause that what we might be facing in numbers out here. If Wolseley wanted to send us to Metemeh, then he should have doubled our numbers."

"Well sir, at least we gots that one slim chance, right? Look there—the bloody heathens are slipping right down our right flank!" He pointed to men in the distance, running, and clearly carrying rifles.

"Where in bloody hell did they get those rifles?" asked the Corporal.

"Off Billy Hicks and his lot," said the Private, "and if we doan buck up here, they'll be having your Martini & Henry too!"

"Not once I get me bayonet fixed." The Corporal frowned at the distant shadows, finding some backbone in his anger.

"They want that little hill, it seems. Should we tell the General?

"Tell the General? That's a damn bit above your reach, Private. I'm Corporal, so it falls to me, but I've the good sense to know that it's the Sergeant I tells, not the bloody General. Then he tells the Lieutenant, and he tells the Captain, and its the Bloody Captain that tells the General, less'n there's a Colonel about somewhere. Chain of command, boyo. Don't forget it."

The Corporal did go and point the men out to his Sergeant, whereupon he was told, "Very well, Corporal. I've seen them and reported."

In the center of the square, General Stewart and the colorful Colonel Burnaby were on horseback discussing their situation.

"I make it no more than three hours until sunset," said Burnaby. "Perhaps it would be best to wait and press our attack tomorrow."

"I'm inclined to agree," said Stewart. "Let's settle in here tonight on this little plateau. The Naval brigade has that rise on our left to watch that flank."

"Aye sir, but we've had reports that the Dervish are on that small conical hill to the right, and with riflemen, sir."

"A little too far to bother us all that much," said Stewart. "Let's get the men to sanger in with anything at hand. Use camel saddles, biscuit crates, and any of this larger stone about."

"I'll have the Sergeants put them to work, sir." Burnaby saluted. He was a big man, standing six foot four and weighing twenty stone, and by this time in his military career, he had become a notable Victorian hero, enormously popular back home. He had galivanted through Russia, through the Khanate of Khiva, and ran with the Cossacks; he had gone to Constantinople and toured Turkey and the Ottoman Empire on horseback. Back home he took to drifting about in gas balloons, and flew one across the Channel to France; and then he had come to Egypt and was with General Baker during the unsuccessful "Suakin Expedition." There he took a wound at El

Teb. Now he had thrown in with Wolseley, and was eager to join the Flying Column when he heard it was to make this desert crossing. Yet it was simple British hubris that he and Colonel Stewart were discussing an attack, when they still had no idea of the force they were facing.

The last hours of 16 January were used to build makeshift breastworks around the perimeters of the small square, and its center harbored scores of camels, which would be both an impediment and a blessing in the fight ahead. One officer remarked—"There's no place for these camels and cavalry inside an infantry square. It will mean we could never shift a company from one side to another if needed. I hope those animals are tied down. It wouldn't do well should they get a mind to stampede."

"Oh, I wouldn't worry too much on that, sir," a Sergeant replied. "They've got them lashed down good, and when the Dervish come, they'll hit us on all sides at once." That wry humor was not far from the truth.

The men who had already seen battle knew the gravity of their situation. They had three guns, positioned with the best fields of fire they could see along the outer edge of the defensive works. A kind of zeriba had been built, with small redoubts within it built from stacked crates of Bully-Beef and biscuits. The outer edge was strewn with branches cut from nearby scrub, and a single wire was run along it as a tripping hazard to any attackers.

At the same time, the Dervish were carrying rocks up the slope of the conical hill to the right, and building their own defensive position. Their work was interrupted by a round from one of the British seven pounders, which killed or injured a good many. But after sunset, they could hear the sound of beating drums from that hill, and saw it light up with flashes of light, which were soon bullets whizzing over their heads.

The camels had finally settled down and stopped their incessant spitting and moaning. But the air around them stunk of gassy farts and sweat from their day's labor, and the gentle night breeze carried this to the men on the perimeter. The sniping of the enemy lessened towards midnight, but the noise from the conical hill persisted. Bonfires were lit there and the soldiers could see dark shapes silhouetted by that light, dancing wildly in the night.

"That lot is sure getting up a head of steam, Sergeant. I hope we've sentries posted."

"That we do, lad, no worries." In spite of that assurance, there were a few false alarms after midnight, but no enemy attack was noted. It became a long, tense, uncomfortable night, the hard ground offering no comfort and the men getting little sleep. Private Gillman managed to stretch out and used a rock for his headrest. He lay gazing up at the brilliant fall of stars in the sky, the milky way prominently on display. All of that, he thought, and here am I, a rock for me pillow and death looming on every quarter. How's a man to sleep? Seven men would die that night from the sniping of the enemy, and aside from one round, the artillery had done nothing to dissuade that fire. Several camels has also been hit, and they continued to mew and groan in pain.

When the skies finally lightened, the gunfire increased and it was hazardous to stand up or move about the square. Several men were shot, some badly wounded to a point where they would not likely survive. The pickets spotted many mounted men on the left flank, and the Dervish were now thick on the conical hill.

Horsemen swelled on the right, but with the dawn the artillery opened fire on them and they seemed to melt away. The Dervish moved like the desert wind, massing with sudden swiftness, and then dissipating in a cloud of dust. They were things of the desert. But the ground here was occupied by the enemy, and they would fight to make it desperate ground indeed.

Part III
On Desperate Ground

"A hero was a person caught in the right place at the wrong time."
—**Hampton Sides,** *On Desperate Ground*

Chapter 7
17 JAN 1885 ~ Near Abu Klea

After sitting behind their defensive positions in the zeriba for several hours, all under the sniping fire of the enemy. General Stewart decided that they were not inclined to try his defenses, and so, amazingly, he resolved to press his attack instead. Had he known that his force was outnumbered fifteen to one, he might have waited behind those stones and biscuit boxes. Now he gave orders for his men to emerge and form a square for a march.

The front of the square had two dismounted companies of the Guards Camel Regiment, being the Grenadiers and Coldstreams, and two of Mounted infantry. The right side had the Scots Guards and Royal Marines, a face 128 men wide, with a couple men of the Royal Sussex thrown in.

The left wall of the square was two companies of mounted infantry, and 5th and 16th lancers from the Heavy Camel regiment. The back face had four companies, the Scots Greys, Royals, 4th and 5th Dragoons, Bays, Royal Horse Guards and 1st and 2nd Life Guards. So there were dour and experienced men in this square, mostly from the Guards. 120 camels with reserve ammo were still in the center, and they blocked any view from the front to the back side, and vice versa.

Two guns were placed in the center of the front face, and the single Gardner Machine Gun in the center of the back face. This gun was to play a dramatic role in the ensuing battle. The order to advance was given. General Stewart noted this and turned to his second in command, Colonel Burnaby.

"Get to the rear face and keep an eye on things, would you?"

"Sir!" Burnaby saluted and went back along one side as ordered. The order had sent him to a fated hour, waiting just ahead.

No one had remarked on the injudicious decision made by General Stewart that morning. He had been flanked on two sides all the previous night and under fire. He knew the enemy had what looked like good numbers of both infantry and cavalry at hand, but he had not taken their full measure with any reconnaissance; he had then split his smaller force by forming this square while leaving a portion of his men in the zeriba of the night encampment, some 200 officers and men left behind. He was now in a position to be attacked and see his forces defeated in detail.

But Stewart still had the services of the 19th Hussars, and he now put them to use, ordering them to move off to the left and confront a growing mass of Dervish horsemen at 08:30. They were told to advance, and dismount to bring fire on the Arabs, not to charge and initiate any melee. This got underway when the Hussars left the zeriba about 09:00. At 10:00, the square began a marching advance towards the wells of Abu Klea. The guardsmen on its walls presented an imposing and threatening spectacle. They were veterans all, tall, strong, and well armed, with nerve and knowhow when it came to a fight, and the will to prevail. No British square had ever been fully broken, though one had been penetrated by these Dervish here in Sudan.

The Dervish were using any cover from the *khor* grass and scrub to hide themselves while continuing to fire at the moving square. That became so hot at one point that Stewart ordered skirmishers to be sent out from all sides of the square to put covering fire on the Dervish. At intervals they would stop the square and then use the two guns to reply to the enemy fire, which sent clusters of Dervish fleeing in the clouds of dust.

A ten man skirmishing squad under Sergeant Kelly was suddenly rushed by twelve Dervish. The Color Sergeant quickly reeled his men into a line. "Alright," he growled. "Mark your targets... Fire!" That first volley took down seven of the charging Dervish at 400 yards. "Reload!" Then the second volley got three more, leaving the last two with no fervor for the fight. They turned and ran.

On the left flank of the square, Captain Campbell had a company of Mounted Infantry, each man a proven marksman. They were dismounted and watching smoke from the enemy rifle fire, to which they soon replied, all but silencing the Dervish sniping. By these aggressive defensive tactics, Stewart had boldly confronted the Dervish, all while trying to provoke their attack. But the Dervish commanders had no intention of charging that defensive square. They had prepared the ground ahead for an ambush, and saw that Stewart's small force, about 1200 men, was marching right into it.

The ground was now undulating and strewn with stone. While the soldiers avoided them deftly enough, the close packed camels in the center had difficulty, The Naval brigade at the rear was also having trouble pulling its Gardner MG gun along. Thus the slower camels began to be clustered towards the rear of the square, and they collided with the rear wall to a point where several got through and were outside the square. The ground now began to slope downwards towards a massed group of Dervish riders ahead, but the rear face of the square had lagged behind, laboring to close up with the rest.

"Come on lads. Close up your ranks there. Move it!" bawled a Sergeant. Frustrated with the rocks impeding its withdrawal, the men of the Naval Brigade started dragging the Gardner gun towards the left rear corner of the square. When the men closed up with the sides of the square, this gun was now left behind and outside the defensive walls of infantry. Colonel Burnaby saw the danger and ordered the 4th and 5th Dragoons to wheel about and cover the gun, but as they advanced, the Gardner gun was being dragged back into the square through a gap in its left side.

All the while, the Dervish horsemen were advancing on the square in a thunderous charge. The Gardner gun began to fire, a hand cranked weapon that had successfully delivered as many as 5000 consecutive rounds in trials. It hit hard, firing a .45" Cartridge, but here the desert sand and red dust was to be its undoing. It fired about 70 rounds, and then jammed.

Now Burnaby rode out to recall the men he had sent forward, for their advance had left a hole in the rear face of the square, he rode out to get after them, just as the sweeping tide of the Dervish rushed through that position, and the big man's horse reared and he fell. Red faced an angry, he found himself lying on the ground in that chaos of horses, dust and the Dervish mixed in with his covering force. Then a spear was thrown at him, its broad blade taking him in the neck at the jugular.

The rear of the square was now a jumble of mewing camels, the men of the 4th and 5th Dragoons trying to get back, and Burnaby on the ground, his hand clasping his bleeding neck as he choked on his own blood. Over all of this, came the roaring volley fire of the front and left sides of the square, which were engaging as many as five Dervish columns of infantry charging to the attack.

While hot volley fire had checked and stopped the first three columns, the fourth would reach the disorganized left rear of the square and add Dervish fighters to the chaos there, many of which penetrated inside the broken rear corner. The right rear had also hotly engaged a charge from mounted Dervish and drove them off. It was only this left rear corner that was in grave jeopardy. The men nearest the penetration were now facing foes in front and behind. Terrible hand to hand fighting ensued, the Guardsmen using bayonet, rifle butts, and even headbutts to throw back the swarming Dervish.

The enemy would now fire at any mounted officer still on horseback inside the square. The Orderly at the side of General Stewart had his horse shot out from under him and went down, and as he struggled to his feet another Dervish bullet took him right in the forehead. Now three Arabs rushed for Stewart, but his third in command, Engineer Sir Charles Wilson, used his revolver to drop the leading man, and the infantry soon got the other two.

At the position of the Gardner Gun. Lord Charles Beresford and his chief boatswain's mate were struggling to clear the jammed weapon when the mate fell from a spear thrust and was bowled over to the ground behind the gun. Not mortally wounded, he tried to crawl to safety within the square. Two Lieutenants, De Lisle and Pigott had come to the defense of the gun, but in such cases, a man's life lasted only as long as that pistol held ammunition. They would also take spear thrusts once their pistols ran dry.

The British guards were now blessing the mass of camels that had prevented the enemy inside the square from reaching any other face. Those troops now turned on the Dervish intruders, and with rifle and bayonet, they mercilessly cut down every last one of them, a ten minute brawl where the British guards and Naval Infantry could not be bested. The Dervish Emir leading that attack had actually rode into the square behind his men while reading a small verse book of the Qu'ran. Those became his last prayers, and he was shot dead.

With this, the square was again closed up, and the other Dervish columns began to withdraw. There had been 15,000 Dervish on the field, but this attack came with only a third of that force. It failed.

The square now reformed on a low hill, ready for anything. While it had been briefly penetrated on that rear left corner, it had not been broken. Major Gough and Lieutenant Wolfe in the Royals had been felled and their troops were now digging a final resting place for them. Men learning of Burnaby's death were weeping. The big man could not stem his bleeding and had died. In all, nine officers and Sergeants were killed, and 56 soldiers. Another 50 needed hospital care for wounds, with five more officers. Most of the camels had been wounded, some just nicked by a bullet, others more badly hurt. Some boxes of ammunition had to be burned for lack of transport. A count of fallen Dervish came to 1,150, with many more wounded.

The British had proved again that stout, well trained soldiers, these men among their best, could overcome the attack of many times their numbers and prevail. General Stewart would continue his advance and reach the wells of Abu Klea by 5 P.M. that evening, just 30 minutes before sunset. Even that short move had been difficult, for the wounded had to be carried on stretchers, and the men carrying the heavy ammunition boxes had to decide whether that labor or the prospect of having to use those rounds soon was the greatest evil.

When the square had advanced to the wells, there was still the matter of the zeriba. They were not spared attack, but Lieutenant Kane and his Sussex infantry would promptly rush to any threatened part of the perimeter, form line and open volley fire that was so accurate the enemy could never get within 600 yards. Meeting well aimed fire of any intensity would immediately scatter the Arabs, who preferred to find the safety of their own campfires that night.

Four prisoners presented themselves with hands up, and when one was interviewed, it was found that he, and most of the Dervish on the conical hill off the right flank of the square and zeriba had been Sudanese troops that were part of the column of General Hicks. They were among the few survivors who escaped death by joining the ranks of the *Mahdi*, but they said that in their harassing sniper fire, they had deliberately fired high, which explained the constant zipping of their rounds overhead. Much was learned about the muster of the Arabs in this region. These men also said that the *Mahdi* would never permit the British to go to Khartum without another battle, and that he was already established in the city of Omdurman.

A rider would come to Major Gem in the zeriba stating that General Stewart had the wells of Abu Klea in hand, and that night a force sent from Stewart to retrieve supplies from the zeriba would arrive about 10 P.M. That meant the zeriba had to dissolve, as its walls were partly composed of those supply boxes. They had to then be loaded on the camels there.

At dawn the next day the column would move out with laden camels, and slowly march past the scene of the attack on the square the previous day. The Arab dead still lay in ghastly piles all around the field. They would press on to reach the wells of Abu Klea safely before dusk. They also saw a good many cream colored helmets topping wood sticks thrust into the ground, the last resting place of those who fell there. Stewart's flying column had stood on desperate ground, and fought well and hard. Ahead lay the Nile River. They were now well south of Berber and not far north of the 6th cataract on the Nile.

Stewart's orders were to reach and take Metemeh, and then he would see about reestablishing communications with Wolseley, wherever he might be. This column was now the only force that might have a chance to reach Khartum, for Wolseley was far away on the winding bends of the Nile.

Chapter 8
18 JAN 1855 at Metemeh

An Arab bandit named Ali-Loda had been recruited by General Stewart as a guide, for he purportedly knew the way from Abu Klea to Metemeh. Stewart wasn't entirely convinced with what the man said.

"Captain Verner," he said. "Take cavalry and reconnoiter ahead to find the Nile."

"Sir!" Verner saluted and went to select his horsemen. He would return some hours later and report.

"General, sir, I came within sight of Metemeh, which was held by the Dervish, only they appeared to be withdrawing to the beat of their damnable drums. I saw other horsemen moving in this direction on our left."

"Colonel Barrow, take your men out there and have a look. Screen off Metemeh so we can advance to the Nile and establish a position there. Perhaps we can steal a night march on these Dervish. I'd give a five pound note to be there now with my back to the river. It would leave me only three sides to defend."

The way ahead was a series of gravel ridges with lower lying scrub and grass land flowing between them. The first ridge was broken into three segments, and Metemeh itself was screened by several outlying ridges, all being occupied by the Dervish. Captain Verner advised a move skirting the ridges and grassland by bearing right, but General Stewart saw a gap in the first ridge line, and decided to make for that. Reaching the place, they saw that passing through that gap would leave the men exposed to attack from above, and so instead, Stewart climbed a small rise to the right on one of three segments of higher ground along this first ridge line.

The General now had the same plan in mind as at Abu Klea. "This looks suitable," he proclaimed. "We'll establish a zeriba here, and the men can have some breakfast. Then I'll push forward a square as before." The General was again dividing his much smaller force, but seeing that he might be only six miles from the river, it did not seem a great risk. Bullets were coming at them from many directions once they got up. He started off to give these orders when he suddenly fell to the ground. A lurking Dervish sniper had found his mark. Stewart had been hit in the stomach, completely incapacitated. He had no choice but to turn command of the column over to Colonel Wilson, a Royal Engineer who had never once commanded men in battle.

They could now see the Dervish forming up their typical infantry formation of attack, which was a column with wedge shaped at one end, intended to try and penetrate a defensive line or a square. Five of these columns had been sent against the British at Abu Klea, and one had pushed through the confusion at one corner and gotten inside the square. It seemed the enemy was going to repeat the same offensive tactics against Stewart's same defensive moves here.

Up on the knoll, Wilson was already getting the guards behind a redoubt of biscuit boxes. It was clear the Dervish wanted a rematch, so the zeriba bulked up its perimeter for defense. As before, the camels were taking up much space in the center, and were quite an obstacle.

Colonel Barrow would be given the defense of the zeriba, with Lord Beresford. They would retain a force of 300 men, including 3 guns, some Royal Engineers under Major Dorward, the Naval troops under Lord Beresford, and half of the heavy camel regiment under Major Davidson, the men of the 16th Lancers.

A square would then be formed as at Abu Klea with the Guards, the Mounted Infantry, the Sussex Regiment and the other half of the Heavy Camel Regiment. This time they would not crowd the center with 120 camels, taking only a few with boxes of reserve ammunition and light supplies. Royal engineers would also reinforce each of the four corners, joining some of the dismounted 19th Hussars.

This all infantry square was now much more maneuverable. The men had been lying down to avoid the increasing rifle fire. Now they sprang up and off they went, the square leaving a few fallen wounded in its wake as it moved. Ahead lay the second ridge up a gravel slope. It was better ground than the thick sava grass. Knowing the ground, the enemy seemed to be pacing the square on both flanks, and the snipers moved from one covered spot of scrub and undergrowth to another, keeping up their harassing fire. Seeing this, Captain Norton of the artillery trained his three seven pounders on the Dervish and plopped down good fire on the riflemen.

The men in the square cheered with each explosion. Behind them, the zeriba was also volley firing to discourage the snipers, and to good effect. The Dervish rifle fire was broadly suppressed until the square got very near the gravel ridge. There a group of hidden Dervish with rifles opened hot fire against them by surprise. This shook the morale of several Lieutenants, who advised Colonel Wilson to withdraw to the zeriba.

In spite of his inexperience in battle, Wilson showed remarkable pluck. He later said he believed failure to advance would lead to annihilation. "We'll beat them here!" said Wilson, and with that the veteran British soldiers took on faces of grim determination. What they hoped for was an enemy attack, so they could again deliver withering volley fire against them, and when they saw the dark shapes of the Dervish infantry crest the ridge above them, some actually cheered. "Come on!" a private called. "Get on with it then!"

The Dervish rifle fire suddenly ceased, and on came that attack, with hundreds of spearmen hurtling down the slope towards the square. They were led by riders bearing colored banners.

"Ready... Fire by volley," called a burly Sergeant. "Present... Fire!" The white smoke steamed out from the Martini & Henry rifles. "Second Rank... *Fire!*" and on it went, a drill honed to utter perfection by the British Army for decades. They had fought this way all over Afghanistan and India, and all over South Africa. Now the volleys ripped into the fighting Dervish, and cut them down like a scythe in wheat. "Cease fire!" came an order. Wilson had been observing the enemy massing 600 to 800 yards out, and he didn't want the men targeting those Dervish. So he would wait until they came on, telling the Lieutenants and Sergeants to resume fire at 300 yards. He knew that was well inside the killing range of the breach loaded Martini & Henry rifles. When the Dervish charged, the square waited, and in that interval, Wilson moved a company into a third rank on that face of the square.

Soon the Sergeants bawled out their commands again: "Mark your targets...Ready... Fire! Reload! Second Rank.... Fire, Reload! Third Rank... Fire!" And on it went, a machine spewing heavy bullets that swept the Dervish flag bearing Emirs right off their horses and easily dropped 300 men, while destroying the whole front of the Arab attack. Between 800 and 1000 men had made that attack, and to lose so many as 300 right at the outset was deeply shaking to their morale. Their attack had been stopped cold, and not one British soldier had been wounded or killed. The square then pressed on, up the gravel slope to the top.

From that height they could see Metemeh on the left, no more than a cluster of mud brown huts and a few plastered buildings and low stone walls. The last ridge lay dead ahead, and just beyond it the Nile, but the ridge obscured the river. The sun was getting low now, the landscape reddening with its weary glow. So the men pressed on, seeing no dark mass of enemy on that third ridge. Dogged to the last man, they pushed on up and over the last thin ridge and there was the object of their long march, the broad gleaming flows of the Nile. A great cheer went up. There were some other small hovels on their left, first Abu Kru and then El Gubat, and both would give their names to this brief battle. Another pair of crossed swords would be drawn on the maps to mark it, but Wilson had pushed through, and now set about to build a defensive bivouac.

Without Stewart present, the elated soldiers began to requisition anything they could get their hands on, even private stores that had belonged to the General, that included several bottles of brandy. The men were allowed to go to the river for water in groups. As darkness settled over the land, they were passing tins of Bully-Beef around, and thinking of tea after.

20 JAN 1885 ~ Abu Kru on the Nile

The men slept as best they could that night, and the Dervish seemed unwilling to fight any more that day. There was no sniping at the camp on the Nile. For those still in the zeriba, they had seen the square disappear beyond that third ridge, and come daybreak, they were anxiously looking that direction again for any further sign of them. Had they survived? Was the way now clear enough for them to move? They still saw small groups of the Dervish moving along the route the square had taken. They were picking through the dead and taking anything of value.

Then thin blue-grey smoke associated with camp fires was seen, followed by white smoke later indicating those fires were being doused. Not long after, the Square again crested the third ridge. Then those with glasses studied the formation more closely and saw it was an open column of march.

"So old Charly Wilson has some fight in him, does he? Good for him!" When the column finally came marching up below the zeriba, everyone there gave them a hearty cheer. Yet when taking stock at the zeriba, Wilson would see that many of the transport camels were in very bad shape, having had no food or even water since the Wells at Abu Klea days before. The horses of the Hussars were not much better off. He realized that a march from here to Khartum would be very difficult now, particularly if further opposed.

The better animals were culled out and loaded with as much as they could carry. What was left would be guarded by Major Davidson of the 16th Lancers.

It was time to see if communications could be made with Wolseley to see what he intended for them now. In the meantime, they returned to the Nile in two squares, and then settled in for rest, food, and sleep. They had earned it.

They would all need to recover strength, because the Dervish were still in Metemeh, and Wilson's orders, inherited from Stewart, were to take that town.

Chapter 9
Dawn 21 JAN 1885 ~ Camp on the Nile at Abu Kru

The men were up and forming lines for a move on Metemeh, and Colonel Barrow had watered his horses at the Nile and was ready to move out on reconnaissance.

"They've had a drink," he said, but they're not quite fit for cavalry work yet." Barrow was all in black, even his hat, his full white beard contrasting starkly beneath the sable cap. They would make for a ridge that ran along the edge of the town, and from that height Barrow could see a large group of Dervish Horsemen across a depression to the northwest. They were obviously lying in wait should anything try that depression, so he sent one man back to the camp to report this.

Wilson was sending out the Guards, part of the Heavy Camel Regiment, dismounted, the Naval troops with their Gardner Machine gun, and Mounted Infantry, now also dismounted. Three guns went with a detachment of Royal Engineers. They moved between the double column. Only the Sussex Regiment was left behind to watch the wounded. The men would go over a hill, then down into the grassy depression. As they approached Colonel Barrow's position on the ridge, they stopped and Wilson rode out to see him. He found the Hussars dismounted on the ridge above Metemeh.

"Where are these horsemen? He asked Barrow, who pointed to the next ridge north and west.

"Right there in that notch, sir. We've discouraged them from coming this way with some rifle fire. I think they'll stay put for now, particularly after seeing your column come up."

The high ground they were on gave Wilson a splendid view of the town below, and he could see one entrenched position on its southwest corner, with a single gun. Three low hills reached down from Barrow's ridge towards the Nile, and Wilson saw the saddle between the first two would overlook that gun.

"There's the place for our guns," he said. "Good day, Colonel. Do keep those horsemen at bay."

"Right sir."

The mud hovels of El Gubat/Abu Kru were right at the edge of that saddle. Wilson was just able to get his horse to take him back to the column, having to then dismount and lead it on foot. The beast was exhausted.

He was met by Colonel Boscawen, but the column was gone!

"Where are the men, by god?" asked Wilson, annoyed. Yet he knew Boscawen to be a reliable man, and took his report.

"Sir, as we were advancing, we saw some flags below one of the villages near the river, and the column was diverted in that direction so as not to leave the camp open to attack."

"Well, we can't rush about willy-nilly, Colonel. "I've left the Sussex regiment at the camp for that very reason. Look here, I want the guns there, on that saddle, the men below El Gubat. We'll attack Metemeh from the Nile side now." Wilson's original plan had just gone out the window. "And Colonel, while I admire your initiative, do have the courtesy to send a man to inform me of any move of this nature again."

"Right sir; sorry sir."

That side of Metemeh had a low wall along its edge, loopholed for riflemen, who had fired at steamers on the river if they ever came too close. Now it lit up with bright flashes as the Dervish defenders fired on the advancing British.

"Column—lie down!" came Wilson's order, followed quickly by "Skirmishers! Suppress that fire!"

As a line of skirmishers rushed out, the men bent low as they moved. The crack of the three guns on the saddle was heard. They were dropping rounds on the loopholed wall, blowing chunks of it away. Then there came the sound of cannons from behind them. Wilson did not expect this, and turned, raising his glass. There he caught sight of four steamers, Gordon's steamers from Khartum, and they were coming to shore near the camp. There they would land a detachment of black Sudanese troops led by Khasm-el-Mus.

Seeing this, and feeling his column too exposed where it was, Wilson ordered the men back towards Abu Kru. The Sudanese also landed a pair of brass nine pounders. They had Remington rifles and swords as well, ready for a fight. This welcome reinforcement saw Wilson plan an attack with the combined force.

Khasm-el-Mus came to Wilson, proffering a polite bow. "I must inform you that the defenses of your camp must be improved, and very soon. Feki Mustafa moves with a large group of Dervish up river and coming this way." All the while the British and Sudanese guns were opening a cannonade on Metemeh.

"Well then, we can't very well move on Metemeh now. I shall take my men back to the camp."

Wilson was now flustered with all these unforeseen events. Even though reinforced, he had not seized or occupied Metemeh, but he knew his overweening goal was to get to Khartum, and it did not seem that Wolseley was anywhere near to take up that charge. It was going to fall to his column. Yet Wilson had also been told that should he be able to take possession of one or two steamers, as was now the case, he was to send a detachment to Khartum to confer with Gordon and ascertain his present situation.

Back at the camp, Abd-ul-Hamid, the Captain of the steamer *Bordein,* approached Wilson with some bad news. "I saw Gordon before we departed from Khartum. He pressed upon me to say that unless I returned within ten days with British troops, it would be too late for his city. He fears a catastrophe."

Wilson hoped that the two defeats inflicted upon the *Mahdi* might discourage his attack on Khartum, but it seemed that the close proximity of Wilson's force might now have the opposite effect. The *Mahdi* would strike and take Khartum before the British could get there.

Wilson dashed off a message to Wolseley: "In my opinion, I find it imperative that I should carry out my original mission and proceed at once to Khartum. I shall therefore hand over command at Metemeh to Lieutenant Colonel Boscawen."

Beresford had been in command of the Naval Brigade, but he had fallen ill and was quite incapacitated. All his petty officers had been casualties or were killed, so the naval troops could not serve for Wilson's mission. Stewart was down, Burnaby dead, and now the life or death of Gordon would fall to Wilson, yet with his forces depleted here, and a need to move a detachment to Jakdul to bring up more supplies, Wilson knew he could not depart before this camp was made secure. He had also learned that more Dervish were coming up from Berber to threaten his southern front.

After a brief reconnaissance by steamer down river to look for this second Dervish force, Wilson returned and began to do what he had actually been trained to do, improve defenses of his camp. He broke up one of the mud brick houses in Abu Kru and used the material to construct a triangular fortified redoubt, digging rifle pits all around it. Two of the seven-pounder guns were mounted there, though they had only 83 rounds left. The Guards and Marines would hold that post.

On the river bank he had entrenchments dug, and had wire fronting them. This work occupied all of the 22nd of January.[3]

23 JAN 1885 The camp on the Nile near Metemeh.

The steamers *Talahawiyeh* and *Bordein* were made ready to depart for Khartum at daylight. Larger than the other two, they were also better armored, and they had two guns. It had obviously been Gordon's hope that all four steamers might be used to bring British troops up to Khartum. The steamers were, in Gordon's estimation, each worth 2000 men, but he had risked them all, and their departure from Khartum had been the occasion where the *Mahdi* stormed Omdurman and took possession of that place. Any wood beams from the houses destroyed in Abu Kru had to be broken up for fuel for the steamers, and that occupied the morning.

Wilson arranged to take just twenty men of the Royal Sussex, who were all decked out with the older traditional red tunics, led by Captain Trafford. The fuel wood could not be made ready by mid-day, so Wilson resolved to leave at first light on the 24th. That was a fatal decision, yet what he thought twenty men and two British officers could do at Khartum eluded most historians. His only option would be to get hold of Gordon and come back down river to Metemeh.

Could he have moved sooner? Perhaps, but even if Wilson had moved the very day the steamers first arrived, he could have only reached Khartum late on the 26th, too late to save the city with his twenty men, and too late to save Gordon.

Friendly residents of Metemeh had come to tell the British camp there that the city held 3000 Dervish, with 500 rifles and four cannons, though they had little ammunition. That dissuaded any further plan to attack that town until more support came up river. A few nights later, the sound of beating drums and singing was heard from the town, and it was thought that was in greeting to even more Dervish arriving from Berber, but this was not the case. The singing was a celebration after news had been delivered by a rider... Khartum had been taken by the *Mahdi*. It was already too late.

When this news finally reached the camp near Metemeh, the men were crushed. All their toil and labor, and three battles had been fought and won for naught. They had left mates, good friends buried in this desert, with little more than a few stones to mark their final resting place, and surely, Gordon was dead. Indeed, he had been savvy enough to know that his stubborn refusal to leave Khartum would end as it did. So he chose his death, making it a self-sacrifice, and one that return Sudan as a province of the British Empire, a little more than a decade later.

Writer Travis Perry commented: "he fought for righteousness, against evil, never for pride as far as what history records of him, for people he had no reason to help other than he believed it was the right thing to do. He was always honest, always incorruptible, courageous, and faithful to the end, choosing to die for the sake of self-sacrifice. Not stumbling into his death foolishly..."

Gordon's body was found in the palace at Khartum—decapitated, and when news of this reached England there was a great hew and cry. They could not believe the popular administrator had perished.

It was during that time, with Gordon sending messages to the advancing relief column, that one Horatio Herbert Kitchener often carried them. Even though other wars and international crisis points beset England's Empire, there was still enough pluck in Kitchener to seek reprisal for what had happened to Gordon. He was about to write a very important letter, a formal request for the support of the British Army to support his plan to go up river and 'Avenge Gordon.'

Honor demanded it.

Part IV
The Road Less Traveled

"I took the one less traveled by,
And that has made all the difference."
— **Robert Frost**

Chapter 10
31 DEC 1897 ~ Wadi Halfa, Sudan

The hand finished its last line, and put down the pen. After reading the missive one last time it seemed a proper appeal, and a signature was appended to the end, Major-General Horatio Herbert Kitchener. That was all, he would leave off the honorifics and styles. His name and current rank would be more than enough.

The Empire Kitchener served had once controlled all of Egypt and Sudan, but the unfortunate events up river at Khartum in 1884-85 had morphed into an embarrassing defeat. Another wandering soul of the desert had come in from its vast trackless dunes and proclaimed himself the *Mahdi,* stirring up trouble like the restive desert winds moved dust and sand. In time the man had rallied all of the wild Dervish clans to his side, and rebellion was in the air. All of Sudan was in an uproar, so who better to go and restore order and impose the will of the Crown but Charles George Gordon.

Gordon was no stranger to rebellion, for he had been among other European officers in China during the terrible Taiping Rebellion. At that time, he led the Chinese Ever Victorious Army against the Taiping Rebels, earning the nickname in Britain of 'Chinese Gordon.'

Gordon had seen what rebellion could do, and he knew also the terrible fires of war and their propensity for utter destruction. He had been with the British in China when they first marched from the Taku Forts to Peking, and he had witnessed the terrible destruction of the Old Summer Palace. In fact, he had sided with Lord Elgin that hour, agreeing that a strong reprisal was necessary after the torture and murder of a British diplomatic delegation traveling under a white flag of truce. Yet the wanton destruction still bothered him, and he called it "vandal-like" saying in a letter that "it made one's heart sore" to see it burning.

When Qing China sought help from the Europeans in suppressing the Taiping rebels, it was Gordon who first caught their eye. Gordon was a name much loved throughout England and her vast empire, and so when he went up river to Khartum everyone expected a miracle, not another disaster.

Touring the Empire after China, it was not long before Gordon found himself along the Nile in Egypt, one of the crown's most important colonies, even though it was still considered part of the Ottoman Empire. Yet when the Dervish rebellion started in Sudan in the lower Nile Valley, Gordon was asked to go up river to Khartum, and evacuate Egyptian and European citizens. It was a task he accepted, but one that would morph into something quite different upon his arrival. Nothing in the desert is ever certain, and no path on its empty wastes ever sure.

His legacy would be left to those who remembered him, and those who sought to make right his time in Sudan, where he tirelessly suppressed the Arab slave trade, lifted up the poor and powerless, and ended up writing his name on the Sands of Honor.

One such man who remembered him was Kitchener, and when he was done, he vowed the world would never forget him.

General Horatio Herbert Kitchener was sharpening his axe. It was new year's eve, and the Sirdar, as he was known, the Supreme Commander of British and colonial forces in Egypt and Sudan, was restless. Thirteen long years had passed since Gordon was slain, and even the Mahdi himself was dead. The doors were open to the veranda, admitting a cool night breeze off the desert, and he could hear the gentle swells of music being played. Most anyone who was anybody among the British in Egypt was in attendance in the courtyard below, waiting for the hour to chime in the new year, 1898.

The year just finished had been a hard one, beginning with fighting on the Gold Coast of West Africa, there was trouble in

Nigeria and its capital Benin had to be put to the torch by Sir Harry Rawson. The Americans were all in a tither with their gold rush in Alaska, and oil was found for the first time in Oklahoma, Black Gold. The Greeks and Turks were fighting again, Bram Stoker published his first Vampire story, and Queen Victoria celebrated her Diamond Jubilee. A man named Thomas Edison was working on a prototype that would become the 'movie projector.' The first submarine had been built with an internal combustion engine, Britain annexed Zululand as part of their colony in Natal; and Kitchener was about to go reclaim the lost province of Sudan. His plans would write one of the first significant events into the chronology of 1898.

There was trouble in India too, but 21 Sikhs of the British Indian Army made a gallant defense against a horde of 10,000 Afghan tribals. That had caught Kitchener's eye and stiffened his resolve. So he had marched to occupy Berber, about 220 miles down river on the Nile from Khartum. Yet it was no simple march. Kitchener was a General of a different mind. He knew the harsh terrain of Egypt and Sudan had to be respected; that the desert could swallow up a column of thousands just as it might a single man. Getting from Egypt to the heart of Sudan was a journey of hundreds of miles, and Kitchener was an adherent of the principle that an Army moves on its stomach.

Campaigns were described in the history in terms of their glorious battles, the steady deployments of the brigades, the sound of the trumpets, the fife and drum, fixed bayonets gleaming in the sun and soon to run red with the blood of the enemy. The jarring shock of battalion volley fire resounded in these accounts, yet none of these things would ever happen if the Army could not first get where it needed to go. Logistics, that was the key in Kitchener's mind. To tame this wild desert land and its whirlwind Mahdist raiders, he needed to bring an army 600 miles up the Nile River, and bring it there healthy and whole. So his eye studied the map for long hours, following the circuitous curves of the Nile, noting every settlement, and then quietly marking certain locations as milestones on his planned road south into the Sudan.

Berber was now a principle focus of his interest. A few years earlier, he had tried the river from his frontier base of operations at Wadi Halfa, following it as far south as Dongola, a distance of 245 miles. From there it was 388 miles to Berber on the river, or he could cut across the desert and march 130 miles to Korti and avoid many of the cataracts, the low water rapids that so confounded river traffic. Yet from Korti it was still another 200 miles to Khartum—too far, too long. This was the route General Wolseley had taken, and the entire expedition had failed when the Mahdi stormed Khartum and his Dervish found and killed Gordon. So Kitchener was looking for another route south, and his eye fell on Berber. From that town, Khartum was just 206 miles up river, and he could make a well watered march on either side of the Nile, with gunboats on the river itself. Berber was the perfect forward base on his march south to punish the Dervish Rebels and their dissident and disruptive successor to the *Mahdi*, a man now calling himself the Khalifa. But how best to first reach Berber?

Young Winston Churchill put his finger right on the nub of that problem in his book *The River War.* He wrote: *"Fighting the Dervish was primarily a matter of transport. The Khalifa was conquered on the railway."*

The question of which route to take south was now paramount for Kitchener. Churchill put it plainly: *"The Question involved the whole strategy of the war. No more important decision was ever taken by Sir Herbert Kitchener, whether in office or in action."* All Kitchener's generalship to come in the days ahead were in Churchill's mind *"of lesser resolve than the selection of the line of advance."*

The Road Less Traveled

From Wadi Halfa to Berber, it was a little over 600 miles by following the winding course of the Nile, but if Kitchener cut right across the desert instead, he could cut that distance in half, to about 300 miles. The General had rejected Wolseley's old route up river to Dongola and Korti, followed by a desert crossing through Abu Klea to Metemeh. That route had been fought and lost, failing to reach Khartum in time to save Gordon. Kitchener would not repeat that mistake. By the same token, landing on the Red Sea coast at Suakin and then marching west across the Nubian desert was also rejected. It had been tried and also failed, with several sharp checks against competent British led forces. By process of elimination, that left Kitchener with only one last route directed at Berber. Yet to get there he would take the road less traveled—not by marching up the Nile, pasts many cataracts and following those 600 miles to Berber. No, he would cut right across the Nubian desert and see a railroad built as he advanced. The desert might not have been a good place to straggle his line of communications back to Wadi Halfa, but neither was that 600 mile river trek reliable or advisable for a supply line.

His answer was the same plan he had first tried in his move to Dongola earlier—build a rail line! It was the project Wolseley has put an end to during his failed relief effort to Khartum, but Kitchener was determined to see his rail line completed. Let two iron rails become his line of communications, and if need be, he would build it as he marched, leaving that splendid rail link in place behind him, right back to Wadi Halfa on the Egyptian frontier. Then he could traverse the 300 desert miles from the frontier to Berber in a matter of hours, not days and weeks, and his supplies would flow on that iron-railed river instead of the Nile. It was this insight and decision that was the real key to his victory, not just the battles he would fight.

A dour faced man, Kitchener's hair parted in the middle above a full mustache, and penetrating eyes. His complexion had browned with the desert sun, and he was a hard man, somewhat brusque and not much liked by other British officers. But that didn't matter, because command was not a popularity contest in his mind. He was Sirdar, by God, and like him or not, when he gave an order, men would jump to see it carried out.

Kitchener had watched control of the Sudan being slowly wrenched from the Empire's hands, saw Gordon slain and decapitated, and he wanted vengeance. Now there was a political rival center of power in Sudan, the Mahdist State, first created by a man named Muhammed Ahmad, the so called *Mahdi*, and then handed off to his successor, the Khalifa. As overall commander of the Egyptian Army, including Sudanese loyalists, Kitchener wanted an infusion of good steely British troops before he moved further south. Sudan had to be held, for otherwise the Nile might be dammed, compromising Britain's position in Egypt.

Gladstone was out as Prime Minister, for he had not survived the hew and cry in England after Gordon's death. Lord Salisbury was in, and with a mind to send Kitchener south into Sudan. Kitchener had a mind to go, but he would not see a repeat of the ill-fated relief expedition that had failed to reach Khartum in time and save Gordon. Bad logistics had been a good part of that failure, and so Kitchener would go to Berber first, to secure a good forward base.

The failed relief expedition had tried to rely on a few river boats to keep the columns supplied. Kitchener wanted something much better—a railroad. It would become somewhat of an engineering nightmare, needing more manpower, better tools and materials. Kitchener recruited local Fellahin Arabic farmers, and even pressed 200 convicts into service on the project, and they would eventually complete the line from Wadi Halfa, to Atbara, then along the east bank of the Nile as far as Khartum. As the new year dawned, it had not yet reached Atbara.

The cold iron rails were the arteries of Empire in these years, and with them in place, Kitchener was planning his campaign into Sudan to deal with the Ansar Rebels, the Dervish, as the British called them; or the Fuzzy-Wuzzies, because of their wild hair. From the outpost at Wadi Halfa, one could squint in any direction into the silent heat of the brutal desert terrain. That heat could drop the hardiest of men in a long desert march, but troops and supplies could move on that rail line very quickly, unless the Dervishes got to it first, shattering or burning the wooden ties and beating the metal rails into spear tips and swords. The General decided that must never happen.

He finished his letter.

Kitchener rang the bell on his desk and in came a servant. He had placed the letter he was writing into an envelope and addressed it. Now the General handed it to the man. "See this is posted at once."

"Yes, Sirdar." The man took the envelope, bowed and withdrew.

The local governor in Khartum had tried in vain to find and arrest the *Mahdi* while he lived, but every company or battalion of Sudanese troops he sent was attacked and destroyed by the Dervish Rebels.

Now mud brick barracks were being built at Wadi Halfa, and the place was being made into a frontier fortress, just 15 miles from the Egyptian border. Kitchener knew the Dervish were not the all conquering force many thought them to be. At Ginnis they had been stopped and forced to fall back above the third cataract. It was the previous Sirdar, Sir Francis Grenfell, that had thrown back Sudanese rebels and kept the frontiers of Egypt secure. Now the new Sirdar wanted to muster and follow his steel rails south, pushing deep into Sudan to bring the Mahdists to battle, and defeat them once and for all.

Locomotive sheds and storage buildings were being built at Wadi Halfa. Fitting shops and boiler houses were established, making the place a railway terminus. Spare rail lines and ties were stockpiled, with silos of coal and piles of wood to feed the locomotive engines. Crates of Bully-Beef would soon arrive by boats on the Nile, for the river was the first leg of the supply chain, safely inside Egypt. Everything was being laid up for the move south, into the untamed madness of Sudan, with the intent to stifle all opposition and restore the calm surety of British rule. The advance would be made along two thin iron rails spaced three feet and six inches apart.

Yet Sudan had been a graveyard for too many Englishmen in the past, with white crosses everywhere marking some fallen soldier buried beneath the hot red sands. Men at Wadi Halfa had friends out there, fellow soldiers and workers, all devoured by Sudan. This time, Kitchener was determined to make something more of their lives and deaths than a white cross in the desert. He was determined to regain the honor lost in Sudan when Gordon fell, and scoop up these Sands of Honor to fill the hourglass of Time to mark the days ahead.

Chapter 11

New Year's day, 1898, Wadi Halfa Rail Terminus

Two men were working in the hot sun, and it was a torrid afternoon at Wadi Halfa. The heat had been unremitting for the last several days, and they longed for the cooler desert nights, not knowing why their Sergeants wanted the crates off the boats by day. At least they had only another ten minutes, and then men now resting in the shade would be coming to relieve them.

"Bully-Beef," said Bill Thompson, a rat-faced Englishman from Surrey. "Oh how we're all lookin' forward to more of that. But why cart it about by day like this? It's bloody hot!"

"Aye," said Bert Campbell, a round faced, red haired Scot, Broad shouldered and with a pair of good strong arms. "That's what Kitchener says, and that's wot we damn well get to. Orders is orders Bill. Look, we've just got another six cases of this lot, then its time we head for shade."

"What shade?" Bill Thompson always had trouble finding it. There were few trees at Wadi Halfa, and most buildings offering any comfort were for the officers. "Bloody hell out here. Why all this Bully-Beef?"

"Would you rather be hauling bags of corn meal? Or what about more railroad ties? Least these crates give a man a nice hand hold, and they aren't all that heavy, Billy Boy, so don't go fainting dead away on me, or I'll have to bury you with the others."

"The others? You bringing them up again? Let them rest, Bert. You know what Johnny would say if he were still here. You either get busy living, or you get busy dying out here, but sometimes the former leads to the latter all too quick in Sudan."

"We'll be fine," said Campbell, always the optimist. "All we have to do is haul it, not eat it."

"Oh, we'll be eating it alright. Once they slap a pith helmet on us and we stand to with our rifles again. That's damn near *all* we'll be eating."

"And we'll be glad it's there too," said Bert, irrepressible.

"Wots it all for?" said Thompson. "We've only the one battalion here."

"Aye, but lots more coming from what I hear. Scuttlebutt has it the rest of the regiment is coming, and more than one or two more. First it was Hicks wiped out, then Gordon. Something has to be done."

"Why now? It's been thirteen bloody years since Khartum fell. Why now, and why us?"

"Because we're here, boyo. Simple as that. Kitchener is putting some British steel in this damn Anglo-Egyptian Army again."

"You mean he's putting some Anglo in it. A fine lot it is now—Egyptians of every stripe, Sudanese troops, and even companies of blacks. Wolseley knocked it to pieces when it was the *Turco*-Egyptian Army. Now we're trying to paste it all back together."

"Right, and we're the glue."

"Well, we've still got bloody Sudanese troops in the stew! Fancy that when we get to invading Sudan again. We won't know who's got our backside, will we. Many of this lot fought against us once. Some was with the Dervish."

"Oh, they'll stand with us now," said Campbell. "They've no love of the Dervish. Most would be quicker to slit their belly than talk with one. The Sudanese here aren't these damn religious zealots whipped up by this *Mahdi* fellow. They'll stand with us, and the Egyptians will too."

"We'll have to wait and see on that, won't we." Thompson had his doubts. "Some of them Sudanese blacks *were* Dervishes, and that after marching with Hicks. They were sniping at Stewart's Flying column all the way from Dongola to Korti. As for the Egyptians, once a man has the hell knocked out of him, like Wolseley gave it to them at Tel-el Kebir, then he hasn't much fire left for fighting after that."

"You'd be surprised what a man will do when he thinks someone else is coming at him with a sword or spear meant for his gut. They'll fight if they're well led, and our lads will back 'em too, and keep them in line."

"But what are we doing here with all this industry?" Bill frowned.

"Why, we're building a railroad from here south, that's what. And when it's finished, we'll go from here all the way to Abu Hamed in a single day instead of two or three bloody weeks in the desert heat. And the line also bypasses 2nd and 3rd cataracts on the Nile. Push it on to Berber and we bypass 4th and 5th Cataracts too. That's the way to move out here, not huggin' a camel's hump in this heat."

Private Campbell had hit the nub of all their efforts, but mentioning the heat got Bill Thompson pointing.

"Look, here comes Jess and Bob to relieve us!' Thompson stopped worrying about the Egyptians and all they were doing, and started thinking about getting down to the river and into the Nile to cool off and get a bath at the same time. Inwardly, he hoped the Egyptians would fight, because they would make up the greatest part of the army, 19 battalions of infantry (and of those six were Sudanese blacks), ten cavalry squadrons, eight companies in the Camel Corps, and five batteries of artillery. They would need them all if they went south into Sudan against the Dervish Rebels of the Khalifa—the man who had replaced the *Mahdi* some years ago.

The Egyptian battalions had six companies each with 120 men on average, and they were all decked out in the same Khaki uniforms the British troops wore, the redcoats now mostly gone. For arms, most had the older Martini & Henry, some the newer Lee-Metfords like the British. Lee-Metford rifles had a much longer range and faster rate of fire with their bolt action served by a 8 to 10 round magazine. Though the Martini & Henry had been a mainstay for the British army for decades, the Lee Metford was carried by most British regulars now. The Egyptian cavalry squadrons had 100 horsemen, with lance and saber, and the Martini carbine.

Most every battalion was led by British officers, and Noncoms. Kipling memorialized the arrangement in his poem **'Sergeant Whatsisname'** praising British non-commissioned officers who trained the Egyptian and Sudanese battalions of the Egyptian army. One stanza went like this:

"Though he drilled a black man white,
though he made a mummy fight,
He will still continue Sergeant Whatsisname."

They found the Egyptians quick learners in the artillery batteries, where they had mastered the use of nine, twelve and eighteen pounders, and the quick firing Maxim-Nordenfeldt guns.

The British army would take time to flesh out with newly arriving regulars, but its order of battle would be impressive before the campaign got underway later that year. It would be many months before the real fighting would happen, and by that time the single battalion at Wadi Halfa would be joined by many, many more, a full brigade, and then that would become two brigades in time.

British Order of Battle In Egypt, January 1898
The Cavalry & Artillery
Broadwood's Horse (8 Squadrons), 4 Maxim Batteries.

32nd Field Battery, Royal Artillery

37th Howitzer Battery, Royal Artillery

Two 40-pounders, Royal Artillery
Infantry Division: commanded by Major General Gatacre

1st Brigade; commanded by Brigadier General Wauchope

1st Battalion Royal Warwickshire Regiment

1st Battalion Lincolnshire Regiment

1st Battalion Seaforth Highlanders

1st Battalion Queen's Own Cameron Highlanders
6 Maxims
Detachment, Royal Engineers
The Rail Service troops, drawn from all battalions.
A Second British Brigade arrives later:

2nd Brigade; commanded by Brigadier General Lyttleton

1st Battalion Grenadier Guards

1st Battalion Northumberland Fusiliers

2nd Battalion Lancashire Fusiliers

2nd Battalion Rifle Brigade
4 Maxims
Detachment, Royal Engineers
Wadi Halfa, January, 1898

The barracks and shops and rolling stock at Wadi Halfa were going to try to finally tame the wild wilderness of the Sudan. If the Mahdist State was allowed to prevail, it might ally itself with the French, Britain's arch enemy. And should the French gain influence and control over Sudan, they would surely use it to cut off traffic in the Red Sea from the Suez Canal, thus breaking England's most direct sea route to her prized colony in India. To that prospect, British ministers would simply cock their heads and say something akin to: "well, we can't have that, can we."

And so when Kitchener's letter appealing for British Army support came, it would be answered. Troops enough to form two solid brigades would arrive, from Warwickshire, Lincolnshire, and the Scottish Highlands; from Northumberland, Lancashire, Sussex, and the Grenadier Guards. They would be months arriving, but once Kitchener had them in hand, he would be ready to move.

There was even cavalry, the 21st Lancers, the newest cavalry formation in the British Army. When word got out that it was going to join Kitchener and settle the matter that had led to Gordon's death, every gentleman of any standing was flocking to get into the regiment. Originally raised in India to fight the rebellion there, it still wore its navy blue uniforms, with the facings and colors of other troops fighting for the British East India Company, a pale blue grey. One such gentleman, his heart filled with the dual impulses of daring and duty, was a young Lieutenant named Winston Churchill.

The 21st had been a do-nothing regiment in India, and saddled with a scolding motto, "thou shalt not kill." It was determined to make a proper name for itself in the Sudan campaign, and that it would do, seeing its first major action and battle colors there. The Sudan lay ahead of the Army, like a man-eating tiger that none had ever tamed. This time, Kitchener was determined to set things right.

It was time for the Army to muster for the move south. The way was set, and pointed south into the red sandy terrain under a rusty haze—the Sudan Military Railroad would mark the path. It had been built with sweat, iron and blood, and why the Mahdist forces ever let it be established was in itself somewhat of a mystery. Three years further on in China, the rebellious Boxers would learn the danger of permitting these iron rails to pierce the heart of their realm, and they would attack the rail lines with vigor, burning depots, tearing up track, derailing trains and preventing their movement by any means they could find. Here the *Mahdi* and his hordes seemed to simply disdain them.

Khalifa Abdallahi was named successor to the *Mahdi*, who had suddenly died in June of 1885 of typhus after the sack of Khartoum. Now the duty and burden of *Jihad* fell to the Khalifa. A man of 51 years, the Khalifa's beard was curly grey on his chin, and he was slower than the days of his youth. He moved in a deliberate way, both in his thinking and action, but he was no less determined than the

Mahdi had been, and was dutiful to his charge. He was Khalifat-al *Mahdi*, the successor of the *Mahdi*, and one of his first acts was to purge Khartum of every occupant until it was an empty, lonesome city of clay, visited only by the desert winds.

Instead, the Khalifa made his old camp on the river north of Khartum into a new city that would stand as the Capital of the Mahdist State—Omdurman. The name derived from the Arabic (*Umm Durmān*), literally meaning "Mother of Durmān," a woman lost in the dust of history by 1897. The two cities, Omdurman and Khartum, sat at the confluence of two rivers, the Blue and White Nile, which allowed them to command that strategic region. This was one reason why the Khalifa had made Khartum a city of fallen heroes and ghosts, and refused to harbor his men there. They would build a new city instead.

Kitchener had been equally methodical in his advance south into Sudan. He first secured his base at Wadi Halfa, and it would be those shops, iron works, supply depots, and boiler rooms that would provide the steam to get his trains moving south through the desert. From there, the rail line split, with one following the east bank of the Nile as far as Kerma at the 3rd Cataract. That was the route Wolseley had taken, and Kitchener would not repeat that venture. Instead he planned to cross the desert to Abu Hamed, with the rail line extended all the way along the Nile from there to Berber and beyond.

It was 1000 miles from Cairo to Khartum, and Kitchener would take all of two and half years to march south in force. Much of that time would be spent in the building of his railroad, for Kitchener had studied Wolseley's campaign, and concluded trying to go up river on boats would never do. So in his methodical way, he built these cold iron rails instead. His advance played out like a chess game, where he would push forward to secure outposts along his route with pawns, and then defend them with his major pieces, slowly moving to corner and kill the enemy King. He knew that poor logistics had been the undoing of the Gordon Relief Expedition, and was set on securing his lines of communication back to Egypt by all means. The rail line was the key to all that, and even Private Campbell had been able to quickly see its vital importance. Kitchener intended to advance first through outposts south of Abu Hamed—Berber and Atbara. Then he would extend the rail line there before pressing on to Khartum.

He had tried the other spur in making an advance from Kerma to Dongola and was not challenged. But there were too many ghosts on that path, all those who had crossed the desert to Abu Klea and Metemeh—all who failed to reach Gordon in time to save his life. Now, advancing up the main rail spur towards Berber, the first real resistance he would meet was at Atbara, where that river met the Nile. Having only Egyptian and Sudanese battalions under command at that point, he now waited for the arrival of four British battalions, brigaded under Major-General Gatacre. They were the 1st Royal Warwickshire Battalion, 1st Seaforth Highlanders and 1st Queen's Own Cameron Highlanders; and from Malta, 1st Lincolnshire. Their arrival would set the time of his advance to Berber and Atbara beyond. He wondered what the Khalifa and Mahdists Army was doing while he advanced.

Chapter 12

Metemeh near Shendi, Camp of the Mahdist Army, March 1898

"They are coming to Berber," said the Emir Mahmoud Ahmad as he made his report. Their steel elephants can go no further unless they first take that place, and then Atbara so they may get south of the Atbara River." Like many of the Mahdist rebels, he had shaved his head, now brown from the sun, though this day he wore a traditional white turban.

"Then you must stop them there," said the Khalifa. "They must not approach Shendi and Metemeh, by any route, not on the river, or by land."

"I *will* stop them, my Khalifa. Rest assured."

The Emir had made a promise that night that he would find difficult to keep, and he would soon learn the real strength of Kitchener's columns, and the man's determination to rid Sudan of all Mahdist influences.

Shendi was an important trade center in the region of the Nubians, and the site of the ancient Pyramids of Meroe. The Khalifa wanted it to remain free of the infidels. It had also been his pleasure to take Metemeh, the place the British had come when they tried to rescue Gordon Pasha. Since the British thought it important, he would make it his own.

The Emir boasted that he would stop them, and now he considered what he might do. The enemy had advanced to Berber, but attacking them from the west was not good. Instead he wanted to maneuver around Atbara and attack it from the east so he could drive the infidels into the Nile. First he had to cross the Nile himself further up river, as his camp at Metemeh was on the west bank. That would be undertaken in Mid-March, all under the eyes of the enemy Steamboats that had managed to get up river that far. Having crossed, he would be joined by the men of Osman Digna, who had come from Eastern Sudan to join the fight. It was Kitchener's sudden advance towards Atbara that had unsettled that plan. The Khalifa told him to go and see what could be done. Osman Digna would join him near Atbara with his 4000 Ansar fighters.

So Mahmoud went east as far as Atbara, where he was thinking to swing in an arc through the desert to come at Berber from the east. Then he thought he might establish a zeriba closer to Fort Atbara near the Nile, but Osman Digna did not want this, saying it would allow the heathen gunboats to savage them on that flank. So the Emir decided to build a zeriba on the Atbara River.

"We have filled our gourds at the Nile crossing," said Digna, "Why stay near the Atbara? Its flows are weak and the riverbed is mostly dry. Let us go into the desert. If we stay here they we leave the enemy but one night march from our zeriba. In the desert, we will see them coming long before they could close to attack us. The ground here is too low." Such came the complaint from him and many other of the Emir's Lieutenants, and hearing this, but he overruled them and decided to stay where he was and build a blocking position at Atbara.

"I do not wish to play the mouse to the enemy cat, and run off into the desert. Where is the honor in that? No, we will build a zeriba right here, and dare them to attack us." he ordered. "Site it just north of the Atbara River. Its flows are weak and shallow now, so it will be no hindrance behind us."

"Of course, Emir, because we will never retreat in any case!"

"Of course... Then get started. Build rifle pits; dig trenches. Cut thistle, thorn, and scrub to build obstacles around them. We will stop them here!"

Such a defensive position was called a zeriba by the Dervishes, and they went to the work with a vigor. It would be Colonel Broadwood's horse scouts that would first find this zeriba and report to Kitchener. The General now knew where his first battle was waiting, and he was eager to get there.

March 1898

Kitchener had pushed his iron rails through the open desert, defying the doubts of everyone else to do so. As it advanced to a railhead below Abu Hamed, it carried not only supplies but also the materials and men to continue its construction along the Nile to Berber and Atbara. Before he could begin that work, he had to clear the ground ahead between Abu Hamed and Berber. He also wanted to get his new gunboats beyond the stony rapids of the fifth cataract, but to do this they would have to be disassembled, then ported by camel caravans, piece by piece, and reassembled beyond the cataract. It would be tedious, time consuming labor, but the only other way was to wait for the rail line to extend, and move the boats on the trains.

Yet Kitchener instinctively knew that it would be the picks and shovels of the conscripted rail crews that would win this campaign, as much as the rifles and bayonets of his soldiers. The Director of Railways, a French Canadian, Girouard, was as much responsible for the success of the campaign as the Sirdar himself. He had laid 500 miles of line on the two rail spurs from Wadi Halfa, a grand achievement in so little time. Now he would set his mind on the line from Abu Hamed to Berber and on south to Atbara.

To do so, he was collecting the broken, rusty bones of anything that ever served as an engine on rails, old parts, old boiler tanks for steam, anything that he could stockpile for any needed repairs along the way. The line thrust through yellow sanded desert fringed in places by purple hills, silent and still, like sentinels posted by Time itself. They frowned over the train as it passed near them, stolid, weathered, stony outcrops that seemed to have grown up from the hard ground around them. They had been carved and shaped by the incessant desert winds. Others could be seen in the distance in ragged lines, veiled by the reddish haze.

All this industry progressed south, day by day, into forsaken landscapes that had sat silent and unbothered by modernity for long ages. The coming of these iron rails, and the steel beasts that crawled along them was a dramatic and decisive change. It would mean that Armies out of Egypt could move south in a matter of a few days, where it needed a month before this line was constructed to ever reach Berber.

For the nomadic Arabs, the Mahdist rebels who appeared and vanished like the wind, these hard iron lines would become a mark of their impending doom, though at this point, not even the Khalifa was far sighted enough to see this. He believed in his Dervish *Jihadis*, had faith in Allah, and disparaged the Infidels who built such invasive and foolish things. The smoking, belching, hissing trains were wicked in his mind, but how to strike them? Even his fine Damascus steel sword would shatter and fail to harm one if he struck it.

"Its skin is too hard to suffer any harm that way, my Khalifa," one of his Lieutenants told him. "The only way to stop these beasts is to push them off the iron rails they follow, and see them tumble into the sand as wrecks. That should be easy work, for wherever we find such rails, these beasts will surely come. We have only to lie in wait for them. But for that, we must be stealthy, and very clever. The infidels are building their iron rails as they move, and they are very well guarded. Their whole army is strung out along these iron lines. Trying to get to a place where we could cut it would take us very far north. Perhaps instead, we should build our zeriba and invite their attack. It may be the wisest course after all."

The Emir believed this to be true, and now he would ride out to oversee the building of his zeriba, a great circle in the desert just north of the Atbara River. The British had fought this way when the Mahdi attacked them every step of the way south to Khartum. It was shaped like a good cut of beef steak, an in its center he would direct the building of a smaller redoubt to make his headquarters, for yes, the Emir would be right in the thick of things, daring any Infidel to try and approach his tents.

The Road to Berber

They were right on the outskirts of Berber, a town of mud huts and low muddy brown walls. But it was no longer a distant speck on a map, but the the center of the British advance. Ahead lay the Atbara River joining the Nile, the next objective, but there in the Berber camp was the Sirdar himself, Sir Horatio Herbert Kitchener.

"Look there Bill," said Private Bert Campbell with the rail crews. "There's the man himself."

"The Kitchen Man?"

"Don't ever say that within earshot of the General," Bert warned.

"Well, I'm not *daft*, man."

They saw Kitchener, standing beside a pale horse tall and straight as a wood post. Bert thought he had the look of a long distance runner, tall, lean, but strongly built. There was an air of authority about him, and a slow deliberation to every move he made. When he walked, he seemed to be stalking something. He raised a pair of binoculars to his eyes and scanned the purple veiled hills ahead, an authoritative quality to his surveillance, as if his gaze alone could take possession of those distant lands, and his will alone could dominate them.

The Private had been in line at attention once with the battalion when Kitchener strode by, finally deigning to turn his head and regard the troops. He never forgot that face, the ruddy complexion, a mix of red cheeks and tan. Two blue eyes that seemed to brand like hot coals when they fixed upon him, a straight, perfect mustache, firm chin, beardless. His was an imperious regard, domineering, bold, hard as rock and wholly determined. He was a man who led by the strength of his will and character, and not the mere rank endowed upon him by the Army. There was a quality of restrained fierceness about the General, and he had been known to snap at a man and dress him down with a tongue lashing when he was in a mood. No one ever wanted to be the object of his displeasure.

"Kitchen Man?" said Bill again. "Yes," said Private Campbell. "And he'll be one to cut the tongue right out of your mouth should he ever hear you call him that. Best mind your place, Bill. No sense hastening your way to join the others."

There had been three other friends in their tight knit group in the rail battalion, all three of them, Sam, Bob and Kelly, were already dead and buried—the others...

It had been the First Earl of Cromer, Evelyn Baring who had assumed the post of British Agent and Consul General of Egypt. He had found in Kitchener as a dutiful and competent man, and had enjoined him to protect the Sudanese frontier. After establishing the Rail terminus at Wadi Halfa, Kitchener had first probed up the shorter rail spur from the Wadi to Kerma and Dongola. Along the way, Cromer said he wanted to see if the Egyptian Army under the Sirdar's command could actually fight, and after discovering a Dervish encampment near Firket, Kitchener attacked it on 7 June 1896, two years earlier. He had a hard fight but a clear victory there, and judged that his troops were sound. Yet at the same time, he had resolved to wait for more British regulars before he pushed an invasion of Sudan to the fullest, and now he finally had them. But he would not go through Kerma and Dongola; he would not march in Wolseley's shadow.

"My," said Private Campbell. "That man has the gaze of a lion. Eyes like to see right through you, but do they sure light up when battle is at hand. Say Bill... You think we might petition to be reassigned to a fighting battalion? We've done our bit here with the rail battalion. Why come all this way without getting a rifle in hand and smelling some gunpowder in a good fight?"

"Because you might just as easily get a bloody spear in your gut, Bert, or have your neck opened by a Dervish scimitar—Damascus steel that."

"Rubbish," said Bert. "Give me a good bolt-action Lee-Metford and I'd drop any Dervish that tried to get near me."

"And what if they came in numbers too great for you to do that?" Bill Thompson would play the Devil's Advocate.

"Then they'd meet my bayonet—right in the belly."

"Sure, and all while they're hacking down on your neck and shoulder with that bloody scimitar."

"Ah, buck up, boyo. You'd be right there beside me, and you wouldn't let him get in a good hack, would you?"

"Of course not, but I could be right there beside you, only bleeding my guts out on the ground, Bert. Rail battalion is work, god only knows, but at least we get to ride the railcars when it's done."

"Not enough fighting, though," said Campbell.

"Aye, and you're just like a Scot to be looking for a fight all the time."

"Well, a man's got to have *something* to tell the folks back home, don't he? Something more than saying we hauled rail and tie to build this bloody track out in the hot desert sun."

"Sure Bert, don't you worry. Haven't you heard? There's some 50,000 heathen Dervish out here somewhere, and what are we? Half that number? Something tells me we'll have plenty to say if we ever do get back home, and more than a good chance we be stuck here with the others."

Bert frowned. "Cup is always half empty for you, ain't it Bill?"

"Well, your cup is always half full—problem is you get to thinking that half makes it truly full, and ye doan see it's half empty the whole damn time. I'm just a realist."

"Couldn't live that way," said Bert. "But I'll say this. I'm going to get my hands on a Lee-Metford, one way or another, and stand to with Kitchener and the Highlanders. Mark my words."

"Good. You can pry that rifle from the cold hands of a dead Highlander."

Private Campbell frowned at that. Thompson was trying to put the fear into him, but he wasn't having any of that. He'd stand with the Kitchen Man, hard as stone, and now he was determined not to join the others here. There would be no white cross over him here, by God. But Bill Thompson persisted.

"What about that bloody business in ninety-six? What about that disaster on the Dongola Spur? There was Hunter's cavalry, and Kitchener with a couple columns. After that carousing at Firket, he wouldn't stop with that, but had to press on to Dongola. Remember how they talked of the heat—even in a bloody storm?"

"Aye, the Death March they called it. A hard trek there."

"Damn hard. The wind came up out of the south, and the whole desert was in their faces. A man could barely breath in that, and the heat was bloody unbearable. Half a dozen Sudanese Blacks just keeled right over with heat stroke. Then the other column got caught in that hellish rain but did it cool off? Hell no! The humidity was just oppressive, wasn't it. That's when we lost the others, right? But bloody Kitchen Man just bucked up and kept us moving. Has that man no conscience?"

There were those who thought he did not, seeing Kitchener as too relentless and driven, irrespective of the cost to the men he was driving like pack animals in the desert heat. One of the correspondents would lash him severely in his account, writing:

"I have plumbed to the bottom of Kitchener now—He is inhuman, heartless; with eccentric and freakish bursts of generosity, specially when he is defeated: he is a vain egotistical and self-confident mass of pride and ambition, expecting and usurping all and giving nothing: he is a mixture of the fox, jew, and snake, and like all bullies is a dove when tackled."

"Member what the rail line looked like after those flooding rains?" Thompson stuck a finger in Bert's belly, his own bayonet.

"Member how we'd toil to fix that embankment, night and day, by God? Member Sergeant Butler with them bloody big rocks on his shoulders? Took us a week to re-lay that segment of the line, and I didn't see Kitchen Man lift as much as a single stone."

"Corse not, Billy, the man is a *General*, not a private in the 15th. He gives the orders—*we* do the lifting. Right? You want to stand around in the shade, then earn your bloody stripes, laddie."

"Well, we didn't make it to Khartum on that road, did we." Thompson folded his arms, a sullen look on his face. "That's why we're on this road, right across the bloody desert from the Wadi to Abu Hamed when there's a perfectly good river right there." He pointed west to the Nile. "Bloody hell!"

Private Campbell had heard enough. "Yah, Bill, but what happened after? We bloody well got up to Dongola, didn't we? Kitchener worked it with those wonderful gunboats. Yes?"

The British knew they could make good use of the river if they had good gunboats. Not only could they work to ferry troops and supplies or support river crossings, they could provide steady gunfire if mounted with decent cannon and the new Maxim guns[4] as well. The British had designed and built a paddle wheel steamer with a shallow draft good for rivers. They remembered the exploits of a ship build by and for the British East India Company for action in the Pearl River estuary at Canton, China. The *Nemesis* had become a Devil Ship there, and here London had sent Kitchener a wonderful gunboat, the *Zafir*, and many more. It was armored, had many quick firing guns, and six Maxim guns. Several others came with it.

Kitchener had sent men to disassemble it and port the parts beyond the third cataract between the railhead at Kerma and the village of Kafir. Once reassembled and floated on the river again, Kitchener gleefully boarded the gunboat, intending to ride it upriver into the thick of the action. Unfortunately, one of its boilers burst, and it would need repair or replacement. Kitchener was beside himself with frustration, but every time he thought of his rail line, he smiled.

It was an astounding feat, the creation of the desert spur that was now leading his men to the Dervish zeriba on the Atbara River.

Part V

Reconnaissance

"What enables the wise sovereign and the good general to strike and conquer, and achieve things beyond the reach of ordinary men, is Foreknowledge."
– Sun Tzu

Chapter 13

The night of 7 APR 1898 ~ The Dervish zeriba on the Atbara

That night the Emir Mahmoud was in his tent when two British prisoners were brought in. the recalcitrant and unreliable Osman Digna's eyes were bright as he pointed at them sharply and spoke in a harsh voice.

"These we took near Suakin, and I regret that I did not skin them alive. Now they are here, but after their kinsmen have killed so many of my people, they still live! It is an insult. Make them speak!"

One of the prisoners, a British officer, raised his chin and spoke. "So this is Osman Digna," he said. "I have never seen your face before, though I must say, I have often seen your back!" At this many of the other Emirs laughed, for Osman had a bad reputation for avoiding battle, often fleeing when things got difficult. Of course, that enraged him, and he reached for one of his pistols, intending to shoot the Infidel there and then.

"No!" Mahmoud shouted. "His life is mine. If you dare harm him I will have to shoot *you* as well."

Steaming, Osman glowered at the officer. "Then you would permit these two to live—Infidels, in the very heart of our zeriba?"

Mahmoud considered, his eyes narrowing. "I will do this... They will be placed in the very front line of battle. There the bullets of their own countrymen will slay them. Yet if by some miracle they survive, then I deem it the will of Allah, and no one will touch them. Should that happen, it will be up to the Khalifa to decide their fate."

"That is a fair judgement," said one of the Emirs, Abdala Hamed, and Wad Bishara spoke in agreement. "As Allah wills it!"[5]

"Why do they come again?" said Emir Mahmoud Ahmad as he surveyed the zeriba defenses by the dry riverbed of Atbara.

"Because we killed their *Mahdi*—Gordon, that is why, Effendi."

"Their *Mahdi*? Now they come for our Khalifa? They could never lay claim to the title of *Mahdi*. Never."

"Except in their own minds, Effendi. They revered Gordon, and many even worshipped him. That he was treated so poorly at Khartum was a great sin."

"He was an Infidel!" the Emir took offense. "He was treated as the Qu'ran proclaims."

"Was he, sire?"

"Of course. Does it not say in 5:33: *They shall be slain or crucified, or have their hands and feet cut off.* Then Sura 9:5 says, *'Slay the infidels wherever you find them ... and lie in wait for them ... establish every stratagem (of war against them).'*"

"But Gordon was beheaded."

"Surely, because Sura 47:4-9 promises paradise to whoever cuts off the head!"

"That may be so, sire, but how would we react against those who cut off the head of the *Mahdi*?"

"That never happened. Allah summoned him to his side. The infidels had nothing to do with his demise. It was the will of Allah!"

"But they still blame the *Mahdi*, do they not—for Gordon's fate."

"And wrongly so! Where is it written that the British Infidels should have sway over Sudan? Why them? This Gordon was no *Mahdi*. Haven't the British an island of their own? Why do they war on the Dervish Ansar, disciples of Muhammed Ahmad. This is *our* native land, and they come not for glory and vengeance I think—no not for Gordon's death, but to conquer this place, and keep it from other greedy hands like the French. They came once before, and we stopped them. The *Mahdi* dealt with Gordon as well. What was the man's name again? The one the *Mahdi* led into the desert?"

"Hicks Pasha, sire."

"Yes, and we crushed him!" The Emir clenched his fist. "So we must do the same to this new Pasha. And what does *he* call himself?"

"Kitchener, sire. He has been diligent. The steel elephants lead his advance, and all the way to Berber, right across the desert! So we must stop them, sire. Right here. The zeriba is strong."

"We shall see." The Emir, Mahmoud Ahmad, got up, left the tent in the center of the zeriba, and resolved to walk the perimeter.

30 MAR 1898, The Camp at Berber

It was a land where 'men hold life cheap and regarded suffering with callous indifference.'[6] Kitchener was also such a man, stony in his indifference to both setback or suffering—at least the suffering of his soldiers. He had secured Berber, and now he wanted a reconnaissance in force to locate the main Dervish position. Of course that task would go to Lieutenant Colonel Broadwood's Horse, eight squadrons with two Maxim Guns on two-wheel carriages.

Lieutenant Colonel Robert George Broadwood was a slight man, tall and slender, with just the dusting of a mustache below a thin nose, and short hair, which he wore flat on his head. His was the life of the soldier, and it would not end until he joined the "Bloody Red Tabs" during WWI in France when he died of wounds after being struck by a shell while crossing a railway bridge over the River Lys. But that hour was a long 19 years in the future, and he would soldier on from this day to that. He was sharp-minded, adept in the saddle, and would one day rise to the rank of commanding General of the British 1st Mounted Division.

This day he had the honor of screening Kitchener's infantry force, and conducting a general reconnaissance to locate the enemy strength. It was difficult work in the heat, let alone the fact that the Dervish had a large mounted force, which his scouting squadrons ran into all too often.

Berber was now secure, and the Army had gone forward to the confluence of the Atbara River with the Nile, occupying Fort Atbara there. They then advanced to Hudi Ford, and pushed further up the

Atbara through its scrub strewn river banks to Ras al Hudi. There the river bent south and the columns pushed on to another ford at the small village of Abadar.

Kitchener had made this move to widen the front between his columns and the Nile. The General knew it was the habit of the Dervish to make wide envelopments of an enemy force so as to take them in the flank and rear. Occupying this eastern outpost at Abadar, the Dervish would have to go much farther east to get round his flank. To prevent that, or at least hamper any such attempt, Kitchener had Broadwood's eight squadrons of cavalry.

5 APR 1898 ~ Broadwood's Reconnaissance

The riders were Egyptian, but well trained and all led by British officers. It was Broadwood's task to scout aggressively each day as Kitchener's army came up, and that led to more than one skirmish with the Dervish horsemen with his isolated squadrons. This time he would lead all eight forward in a tighter group, a reconnaissance in force.

Earlier news had revealed that the Dervish had come along the Nile to the west near the village of Aliab between Shendi and Berber, then cut straight across the desert some 40 miles to reach the winding watercourse of the Atbara near Nakheila and Fahada. In this they demonstrated their ability to move swiftly and boldly through the desert terrain, and over great distances. In their train, followed wives, children, slaves, and hangers on, for the Dervish army was of the people, and where the soldiers went, friends, relatives, and many others always followed. The Dervish were a nomadic people in any wise.

The morning dawned clear and cool, but with the promise of the usual mid-day heat, which often reached 115 degrees Fahrenheit. Broadwood took his eight squadrons, a horse battery, and four Maxim gun batteries on the quick march, cutting across the open desert where the river made a sharp dogleg rather than moving through the thick scrub near the water. Thorn and scrub grew in any depression in the land where water might gather after a rain, and the riverbed was, of course, the low point in all this ground.

Nothing was seen of the enemy during this march, which would soon reveal the position of the Dervish zeriba near the river. Broadwood was at the head of his cavalry, and he stopped, peering through a short telescope to surveil the land. All seemed empty and quiet, and it left him with an uneasy feeling. He and his men had scouted this far days earlier to first find the zeriba, but only by squadrons, which had always met superior forces of Dervish horsemen. Now he could feel there presence, though he could not see them. He knew they were out there somewhere, swarming in the reddish rose-colored haze.

Broadwood looked over his shoulder and waved his squadrons into two lines of four. Then he raised his arm and pointed forward, but advanced cautiously at the walk until he spied the Dervish zeriba on the right near the river. Then, seeming to manifest from swirls of desert dust and sand, a large force of enemy horsemen was seen ahead. Broadwood peered at them through his glass, but could not get an accurate estimate of their strength.

"But they match us at the very least, and probably exceed our numbers," he said to Captain Gallais at his side. Philip Walter Jules Le Gallais, was from Guernsey, commissioned as a cornet into the 8th Hussars on 23rd April 1881. Tall and straight, his red hair and mustache distinguished him from the other cavalry officers.

Seeing the Egyptian cavalry, the Dervish began to retire southeast.

Gallais smiled. "Well, they certainly don't like the look of us sir, do they."

"Look again, Captain, they move to stand on our far left flank, and should we make any move towards that zeriba, they would then be right on our backside. We haven't the numbers to cover our rear and do much of anything else. No, we must either disperse them or get them to retire up river. Otherwise we must retire ourselves and call it a day. I can't have them haunting our left like that. Then we'll have another good look at that zeriba." They had scouted this position four days earlier, and found it a warren of Dervish strength.

At this, the British rode high in the saddle, eager for a good cavalry action here. Broadwood had his bugler sound the advance, but he moved deliberately, at a slow pace coming parallel to the zeriba until his squadrons were opposite its southern end, no more than 1000 yards off. Broadwood spied along the line of tall palms and scrub near the river below, as the land descended in a gentle depression. Now another large body of mounted Dervish fighters issued from one end of the zeriba, and that entire encampment now came alive as men rushed to take up positions on the perimeter of the zeriba behind a thorny fence or abattis. There they fell into trenches and maned some rudimentary cannon emplacements. Through the green foliage of the palms and scrub, he saw many banners attended by swarms of white robed troops carrying spears and rifles. The morning sun gleamed off those spear tips, more like broad bladed cleaving knives that narrowed to sharp ends. The coming of Broadwood's cavalry had raised the alarm.

It was not long before the Dervish started firing their cannon, giving obvious warning to Broadwood that they were ready for a fight. The rounds were badly aimed and high, soaring overhead to fall harmlessly into the scrub.

"Note the positions of those guns," Broadwood pointed, wanting that filed away for his report to Kitchener.

"It seems we're being enveloped sir," said Captain Gallais.

Broadwood watched this new group closely, seeing a thin stream of skirmishers ride out ahead along the river in the scrub, where some dismounted and hid themselves in the undergrowth. The main body stayed very near the zeriba.

"Captain, find Captain Persse, and then the two of you stand there on our right rear quarter."

Broadwood looked behind him. "Captain Baring!" he shouted, and the Captain rode forward to his side. "Go find Captain Firise and then your squadrons are to move well out on our left. Site the horse artillery between your position and mine. See if they can discourage that mob."

Broadwood had discarded all thought of dispersing the enveloping Dervish force on his left and rear with a cavalry charge, and though it was dangerous, he was now extending his front to prevent being flanked. Perhaps the guns could discourage the Dervish force on his left, or so he reasoned.

The Dervish force on the left was milling about, like a swirling storm of horsemen, but it did not advance or attack. The horse artillery hastened into positions, and soon there came the crack of the guns as they began firing. That fire was accurate, the rounds exploding in and near the Dervish to compel them to fall back. In reprisal, they waved their swords overhead and cursed their enemy, a threatening storm, though it came no closer.

Broadwood wanted some fire on the other Dervish horsemen that had emerged from the zeriba. He sent his runner, Lord Tullibardine out with that order, waiting until he saw two guns being turned smartly to the right and opening fire. These rounds fell closer to Broadwood's men and the loud explosions set their mounts to chaffing. The accurate fire, across some 1800 yards, sent exploding rounds into the thick of that northern group, and caused great confusion, Broadwood saw riders and horses felled and a wild swell in those ranks. But under continued fire, the group fragmented and dissipated. The Colonel saw wounded horses on the ground, some still, another still kicking with pain. Then men rushed to the fallen men and dragged them off, carrying their bodies back into the zeriba.

Broadwood then heard the chatter of some of his Maxim guns. The quick firing MGs had sprayed a group of dismounted skirmishers, the sand around then nipped by rounds that sent all of them running for deeper cover in the scrub. The Colonel smiled. He had been well outnumbered in men and horses, but his guns were wreaking havoc.

The Dervish had not attacked, but now Broadwood saw that the northern group had formed into a thick line in the scrub, and they began to fire rifles at his four squadrons. That fire hit no one, but the bullets nipped at the sand around them, with obvious threat. At the same time, the Dervish on the left had moved into a farther enveloping position, and now they were advancing.

Broadwood looked at his watch, seeing it was just 09:00. The Dervish movement now looked much more threatening, and he decided he would not do well to remain where he was. He had the bugler sound withdrawal. So, instead of dispersing the Dervish, he himself would be forced to retire. The Maxim guns continued spitting out their chattering fire, covering the retreat of the horse artillery. Then, some 200 yards on, the artillery would stop and give cover fire to the Maxim batteries so they could fall back.

The northern Dervish group now regained order and began to advance with a threat to the artillery. Broadwood had already sent one of his squadrons to reinforce Baring on the left, now he needed to reinforce Gallais and Persse on his right.

"Come on then!" he drew his sword, and pointed it towards the river. His officers would now get the charge they had been longing for. Broadwood was right out in front, waving his sword. He saw what looked like a force of 400 Dervish riders ahead, and his squadrons slammed into them, bursting right through their lines, dropping many Dervish with their lances. A melee ensued, wherein Broadwood spied a man who was obviously an emir or Sheik. He spurred his mount in that direction, but the man edged away, declining Broadwood's challenge only to come face to face with a bugler and his pistol, who fired and shot him right off his horse.

Then Broadwood saw another man, his headdress that of a Sheik, make a sweeping cut of an Egyptian rider, scoring him from shoulder to hip with his Damascus steel. There was sublime vengeance in that stroke, and Broadwood heard the lilting call of the Sheik, his voice rising in triumph. He had done something honorable, spilling his enemy's blood on the desert sands. But he could see his men had been badly disordered by the Egyptian cavalry charge, and now Captain Baring arrived with two squadrons from the left.

The Sheik screamed an order, and the Dervish began to disengage and withdraw. Broadwood heard the word 'zeriba' in that order, and now he saw the two squadrons of Gallais and Persse dismount and take to their carbines, peppering the retreating Dervish and dropping many more.

The Dervish were brave today, thought Broadwood, but my men were braver. Now the dismounted Dervish skirmishers coalesced in the scrub near the river and began firing rifles at Broadwood's force. It was answered by vigorous carbine fire, but in that action, Captain Persse was hit and fell from his mount, badly wounded. The withdrawal continued by degrees, through the one gap behind them that the Dervish riders had not yet reached. It was two hours before the cavalry got clear of the enemy, whereupon they took stock of their casualties, which had only been one officer, Persse, six Egyptian riders killed, with ten others wounded. Yet as many as thirty horses had been hit by the Dervish fire and put out of action.

Broadwood would now retire, a thirteen mile march back to Kitchener and the infantry, which he reached at 13:00. He found that the two brigades of Sudanese troops had been ordered to stand to arms, and the British brigade had been making ready to advance and assist the cavalry. Kitchener had heard the artillery and Maxim gun fire, and believed that Broadwood's cavalry had stung the

Dervish enough to see them issue from their zeriba and make a general attack south. He thought the whole of the Dervish Army was raging at Broadwood's heels.

Chapter 14

6 APR 1898 ~ Preparations

As Broadwood's cavalry slipped away, the Dervish dragged the six Egyptian dead away, taking them back to their zeriba. There they were beheaded, and those heads were nailed to the trunks of Palm trees, like trophies recovered to spur the morale of those in the zeriba. A great racket rose up, the hooting and trilling of the Arabs, the bawling of the Sudanese. They were singing their war cries in readiness for the battle that would soon return. They were ignoring the fact that some 200 of their own lay dead on the the ground, and that Broadwood had extricated his cavalry with little trouble, and slipped away.

Winston Churchill would hold this gallant reconnaissance and withdrawal under attack as second only to the remarkable achievement of the railway crews who forged that line across the desert to Berber over a hundred miles from Wadi Halfa. Broadwood would praise both his stout hearted British officers and Egyptian troopers alike for their dogged efforts. His assessment of the Egyptian troopers was both critical and generous:

"Initiative they did not possess, high resolve they did not know, but they would ride out boldly into the desert on patrol, would fire steadily when dismounted, would charge—if not with dash, at least with discipline."[7]

With Broadwood's report, Kitchener was now determined to advance and destroy the Dervish.

"They're in the zeriba? All of them?"

"Except those we engaged attempting to enfilade and envelop us, sir. The horsemen."

"And with how many guns?"

"Not more than I had at hand sir. Our artillery will surely overmatch them and have good effect. And the Maxim guns were very useful."

"Your estimate of their strength?"

"About 15,000 sir, give or take a few hundred, and we certainly removed 200 of those from their ranks this morning."

15,000, thought Kitchener. It was fewer than he feared. His own force was around 10,000 strong, and Broadwood had his 500 cavalry. He had thought the enemy could be as many as 50,000, and at least twice his numbers, but if Broadwood was to be relied upon, that was not so. Were there other Dervish hosts near at hand? That would take time to ascertain, and attacking this known enemy position would likely answer that question. He thought he might be advancing into a hornet's nest, attacking an entrenched zeriba, the enemy behind an abattis of thorn and thistle, and in numbers greater than his Army. What if another host were to swell up out of the desert in the thick of my attack? He struck that fear from his mind like the hard swipe of that Sheik with his sword that Broadwood had seen.

"Very well..." Kitchener would now look to his Brigadiers. "We assemble the brigades for action—but tomorrow, you and your men can rest tonight and we'll press on soon enough. A few units are still straggling into the forward camp at Abadar. "

"Is there anything more for us sir? What of the communications back to Fort Atbara on the Nile?"

Broadwood knew that a supply depot had been established at Fort Atbara near the Nile, and goods were moved from the trains at Berber to the fort, which then caravanned up the winding Atbara River to reach Kitchener's camp at Abadar. The General had been surprised the Dervish had made no attempt to strike at his line of communications back to Berber, but the Sheiks and Emirs had no mind for such raids, all waiting to prove their honor in the bigger battles.

"Camel Corps is minding that LOC," said Kitchener. "I'll probably want you back on that same flank when I bring up the infantry, so get your men rested, and find any more horses you may need with the trains. That's all, and well done, Colonel."

"Sir!" Broadwood saluted crisply and withdrew. Yes, he would be out on that flank again soon enough, and his 500 Egyptian cavalrymen would be facing off against 5,000 Baggara, the nomadic Arab horsemen of the Sahel in Chad. Many had migrated to the new capital in Sudan, Omdurman, and further east to join the Mahdists. They were good horsemen, bold, and fierce in combat. The successor to the *Mahdi* himself, the Khalifa Abdallah, was a Baggara.

Kitchener knew the minds of his subordinates. Gatacre, commanding the brigade of British regulars was of a mind to attack, but Hunter, overall commander of the Egyptian and Sudanese brigades was still cautious that night in conference. He voiced the same fears Kitchener harbored.

"We know the Khalifa's main army was at Omdurman. What if it's strung out before us even now. We haven't looked southwest at all along the Nile." Later Hunter suddenly reversed himself.

"Well sir, the Khalifa bloody well knows where we are, and he's known it since we took Berber. If he hasn't made an appearance in all this time, then maybe he's no stomach for it. He's obviously sent this force here, but they're not of any mind to attack us. I say we get after them."

That decided the matter for Kitchener, who was determined to attack anyway. While the British battalions squared themselves away, mending up their kits and boots, the Sudanese troops prepared with wild drumming and full throated song. Kitchener sent orders back to contain the correspondents and allow no telegraph traffic back to Wadi Halfa or Egypt, at least until he knew the outcome of his battle. Would he have the victory, or would this be another embarrassing Isandlwana if the rest of the Khalifa's army should suddenly appear on the scene. That, he thought, was up to fate. Ahead of him lay the Sands of Honor, and he would tread upon them, undaunted. His written orders that morning all ended with the phrase: "Remember Gordon. The men before you are murderers."

Night, 7 APR 1898 ~ The Advance

As if still harboring an inner fear, Kitchener ordered his brigadiers to form their troops in elongated squares, and they would advance in that formation, not a column of march. It was as if he thought he might be ambushed right before he could close on the enemy zeriba. Even so, he increased that prospect by ordering a night march on the evening of April 7th. There was no need setting the men to march in the morning heat, but there would be no avoiding it on the 8th when that sun got well up. The squares would move along the outer fringe of the scrubland edging the riverbed. They trundled past a small settlement at Mutrus, advancing on Nakheila. The British Brigade led that march, and behind it came the Egyptian and Sudanese Brigades under Maxwell, MacDonald and Lewis.

The sun set, painting the landscape in hues of rose and amber that slowly deepen to azure and vermillion in the twilight. The land itself was quiet and still, for the Dervish were all in their zeriba, many feasting on skewers of lamb and rice. The troops marched in silence, hearing only the crump of their own boots on the sand, and the sound of an occasional canteen. Kitchener knew he was making a risky move if the Dervish were watchful and had videttes out screening their encampment. The men were keenly alert, listening for any sign of the enemy, their eyes straining against the darkness, trying to make out any movement ahead. All they saw were occasional gazelles that had been coming down to the river for water. They fled like grey ghosts before the lumbering squares of Kitchener's army.

The squares plodded on, over the wide desert of mostly bare sand with occasional outcroppings of weathered stone, and small stands of scrub. At intervals they would traverse a *khor*, which was a narrow depression in the land where sweet grasses flourished. Few would forget that night march, and how keen their senses were as they probed ahead into the darkness of that desert. Two hours on, light winds rose and stirred up the reddish dust, making the scene even more obscured.

At Mutrus, they had covered half the distance to the zeriba, and Kitchener stopped. He did not wish to arrive in the dark, and as they were very close to his objective, he had the men lie down and light food was distributed. Bert and Bill with the headquarters got some too, the very same Bully-Beef tins they had been hauling off the river boats at Wadi Halfa, and as Campbell had predicted, they were glad to have it, and a few biscuits.

Kitchener ordered his brigadiers to post sentries and then told the men they could catch some sleep from 9PM to about 1AM. There they were, just four miles from the zeriba, the men wound up and most unable to get any real deep sleep the remainder of that night. They all knew they were dozing on the edge of history, and that all they would do the following day would be inscribed and read for generations to come. So it was a restless sleep for sure, with false alarms when a Highlander cried out when he was kicked by a nearby mule. His sudden outburst startled the rest of the battalion, and the Camerons nearest the front all stood to arms, ready for trouble, but there was nothing but the night and wind.

Some 12,000 men under arms had crept right to the doorstep of the enemy camp, and the Dervish seemed completely unaware of their presence. Such was their lassitude that had enabled Kitchener to get so close undiscovered.

As dawn approached, Kitchener sent orders for his desired deployment. At the top of the ground sloping down to the river, Kitchener established a laager of wagons in a square. He posted the companies of the 15th Rail battalion on watch in that laager, and Lewis sent one of his Egyptian battalions as well. That is where Privates Bert Campbell and Bill Thompson held forth, and

Campbell finally had his Lee-Metford, with fixed bayonet. Within that laager, Kitchener established his headquarters, with stores of food, water, and additional horses and ammunition. A little down the slope he arrayed his four brigades right to left—Maxwell's Sudanese troops, MacDonald with three Sudanese and one Egyptian battalion, Gatacre with the British, and Lewis with Egyptian infantry on the far left. Guarding that flank, was Broadwood again. The artillery, all of 24 guns, was in the center, behind and above Macdonald and Gatacre, and he posted the six companies of the Warwickshire battalion, 960 men, between his other battalions and Lewis.

As was often the case, the Sudanese troops would be pressed into battle first, while the Egyptians were held back with Lewis. Perhaps it was a kind inherent disdain the British held for Sudanese troops, or perhaps a feeling that the Egyptian Fellahin, being conscripted farmers, would not be as inclined to attack. In any case, if any part of the force could be considered "Cannon Fodder," it was the Sudanese, yet their performance was admirable.

The zeriba, night, 7 APR 1898

For their part, the Arabs in the zeriba had tortured and mutilated a few stray Sudanese captives taken from the earlier reconnaissance, chopped off heads and nailed them to trees, and then sat around numerous campfires to cook and eat their evening meal. The two British officers were taken to the south edge of the perimeter, and tied to tall wood posts. The Emir Mahmoud was in his tent behind a square redoubt in the very center of the zeriba. He had promised the Khalifa that he would stop these invaders, but his method had been quite passive. Rather than aggressively scouting as the British had, or even striking at the supply caravans shuttling along the Atbara River, he elected to simply build this redoubt and sit in it. Even his vaunted Baggara horsemen had been easily repulsed by the fast firing Maxim guns, and they talked among themselves on how devilish the weapons were, and how unseemly.

"The British fight without honor," many said. "They will not stand face to face with us and fight us like real men. No, instead they bring these abominations: steel elephants belching smoke and screaming as they move, cannons that send exploding rounds that shower the ground below them with lead, and those devilish fast firing guns. Where is the honor in that?"

"We must leave the zeriba when the fighting starts, and ride them all down!" another said. "What are we? 5000? How could we allow so few enemy horsemen to escape us some days ago? We should have many more heads to nail to the trees here."

"That is finished. Now let us go and eat." And not one among them thought it wise to picket the encampment or send out mounted videttes. These failings would allow Kitchener to come creeping right up on that encampment come dawn.

06:15 ~ Guns Herald the Dawn ~ The Artillery Preparation.

The Arabs had not yet grasped the significance of the so called abominations that the invaders brought to this war. They were just the leading edge of new weapons of war, all meant to kill the enemy before he could ever contemplate doing the same to you. The Maxim guns would evolve into a host of deadly machine guns, the artillery grow to enormous sizes capable of trembling the earth itself with their thunderous barrages, the rail lines would multiply and carry soldiers to every quarter, but the way of the Dervish fighting would diminish and die. These were also among the last hours where British cavalry would charge gallantly into battle as it had done all through the earlier part of the century against Napoleon. The day of the horseman was slowly waning, and in their place there would soon come even more abominations, massive treaded metal beasts that looked like water tanks, and were called by that name.

And before the next great war would end, the well honored names of the old Guards cavalry regiments would be given to armored divisions and regiments of tanks, and the skies would be aflutter with moth like machines, sweeping and battling one another with abominable machine guns, and then dropping small bombs on ground positions. This says nothing of the heinous shells that would not simply shower the ground with lead, but deliver noxious poison gas. The ways of War would get darker, more relentless, more merciless and horrible with each passing decade. Yet here, this day, both sides still clung to some hope that they would be the ones to prevail, the Sands of Honor still firmly beneath their feet.

The Chinese master Sun Tsu had remarked that he who waits in a fixed position on ground of his choosing would be well rested, and the enemy seeking him tired by his march. That may have been true, but it had been a very short march, and the British would be quite fresh. One thing Sun Tsu overlooked were the abominations... He who has weapons that range farther than that of his enemy shall have a very great advantage. That edge lay in the hands of the British regulars that morning—the Lee-Martin Rifle.

It was going to be a grand attack, and Brigadier Gatacre was very eager to lead it. Lance Sergeant Wyeth unfurled and raised up a Union flag, there was a a rousing wave of fife and drums, and of course, the pipes of the Highlanders. The men were formed, and Volley fire was directed at the edge of the Zeriba. Gatacre drew his sword, ready to lead the British brigade to the attack,

Part VI
Atbara

"Rouse him, and learn the principle of his activity or inactivity. Force him to reveal himself, so as to find out his vulnerable spots."
— **Sun Tzu, The Art of War"**

Chapter 16
06:15, Morning, 8 APR 1898 ~ The Battle of Atbara

The Advancing squares opened their northern sides and reformed in a more elongated formation, like a letter U that had been flattened and stretched out. They were on higher ground, which sloped down to the zeriba on the river, about 900 yards off. The men had been moving as silently as possible, preserving the element of surprise. Kitchener did not want a horde of Baggara Horsemen to muck up his battle deployments.

The first thing to be done was to site the guns in the center, and then the Brigades would go forward to make their attack after the preliminary bombardment. The Dervish defenses were seen easily as the morning brightened with dawn. Behind the outer rim of thorn and bramble, there was a trench, with many rifle pits and four gun pits studding it, all around the perimeter. Within the circle were many thatched huts, and a second redoubt protecting Mahmoud's tents. Kitchener noted a total of ten enemy gun emplacements, but only four facing his direction of attack. He had 24 guns, and he planned to use them for a good long while before he attacked.

Thin trails of bluish smoke rose from the interior, the fires for the morning meal that would soon be rudely interrupted. All was quiet, as if both sides were just glaring at one another, holding their breath. Then Kitchener gave the word and a single sharp report opened the battle. It was followed by a string of loud bangs as one gun after another went off. They were firing explosive shells, one of the abominations the Arabs had been complaining about, and yes, when they exploded, they sent a hail of lead shrapnel and grapeshot straight down at anything below. Other shells would strike the ground before exploding and sending up a welter of dust and sand, all laced with shrapnel. Shells began bursting over the thatched huts and shaking the distant palm trees. As they swayed back and forth the disembodied heads nailed to the trunks leered at the defenders with what looked like an evil grin. Their comrades had come to avenge them.

Soon all 24 guns were laying it on thick, and working all the ground in the interior of the zeriba, with much attention given to its hard outer crust. With the artillery there were two rocket sections, and they sent hissing, twisting rockets up and then down into the zeriba. One plummeted into a thatched hut and set it on fire. All the Dervish foot soldiers had leapt into the pits and trenches, crouching low.

There was a great stir at the back of the encampment near the river, and a shroud of dust rose up. Kitchener studied it with his telescope and saw a large body of horsemen exiting the zeriba and pushing out onto the sloping ground on his left flank. Those were the 5,000 Baggara riders, fully a third of Emir Mahmoud's force. They would be no good inside the zeriba, but they had rested the long night there. Off on the left there was a swell in the ground where the four batteries of Maxim guns were deployed. As soon as they saw these fierce horsemen forming up, the gunners leapt to their weapons and started raking them with machine gun fire, which would mow down men and horses alike in scores.

That was enough to discourage the Baggara from making one of their wild charges. Instead they moved farther out on that flank, stopping only when they spied the lines of the Egyptian Infantry under Brigadier Lewis.

As the artillery continued to lash the ground of the zeriba, the infantry began to move into their planned assault formations. The front of each brigade would form in a double line, and behind, a column of companies would stand like human battering rams to be thrust against the outside of the defenses, all while that double line in front blasted away with well aimed volley fire from their Lee-Metfords. At the point of attack, they encountered a thicket of thorns and branches, some four feet in depth. Breaching parties of Royal Engineers were issued thick leather gloves and long metal hooks. It was their task to use those hooks to pull the thorny abattis open and allow the infantry to enter. Other men carried heavy wool blankets to throw over the lower brambles so the infantry could enter to reach the trenches unscored by the thorns.

The British troops led the attack, showing the other brigades how it was done. Soon the wail of the pipes was heard from the Seaforth and Cameron Highlanders, the burly soldiers kilted to the knees. They pushed through the outer crust of the zeriba and were in the trenches, guns leveled, bayonets thrusting, officers hacking with their swords in one hand and a pistol in the other. "Now you're into them!" shouted an officer. "Give them the bayonets, lads!" No quarter was given. The British wanted no prisoners or new recruits for their Sudanese battalions.

Emboldened by this attack, the Sudanese battalions of Maxwell and MacDonald began pounding their drums and charging to make their attack. The Dervish, assailed by abominations everywhere, offered scattered defensive fire with the few muskets and Remington rifles they possessed. It was even odds now, with 10,000 Dervish within the zeriba against an equal number under Kitchener. Now the sound of rifle volleys predominated over the shock of continued artillery fire.

As it hit the edge of the zeriba, the assault slowed and piled up, then the perimeter was breached and the fighting moved into the trenches, hand to hand. If the Arabs wanted their opponents to fight honorably, man to man, that was what they would get. The blood stained sands would uphold the honor of both sides, but the British assault, particularly the Highlanders, was irresistible, without remorse or mercy. They tore the defenses apart, silent, resolute, unstoppable.

Major Urquhart of the Cameron Highlanders was shouting encouragement as he led his men forward, until a thrown spear took him full in the chest and cut his voice short. He would die there on the field, and major Napier, and Captains Findlay and Baillie in the Seaforths all received mortal wounds. All these officers led from the front, none shirking behind their men. The attack came into the zeriba like a flood, swamping the trenches and carrying deep into the interior, where 20,000 men on both sides were crowded into an area no more then 1000 yards wide and 800 yards deep.

The British troops made for any gun emplacement they saw, finding nothing more than brass seven-pounders. They overturned them all. In those pits, shelled by the British guns, the dead lay atop a few living survivors, terrified that they would be buried alive there with their fallen comrades. It was a ghastly scene all through the zeriba. Every trench was filled with the Dervish dead, their limp bloodied bodies lying among slaughtered sheep in a ghoulish tangle.

The living Dervish swarmed and screamed, but were always driven back towards the river. The Arab fighters were the most stubborn, refusing to break and run. They had to be faced down and defeated, man to man, but there was not one among them to match any of those strapping Scottish Highlanders.

In among them, was Bert Campbell, having pleaded for permission to join the attack, which was granted. He fixed his chin strap, checked the fit of his bayonet, and ran gleefully down the slope, a one man company. He would fall in with the trailing company of the Cameron Highlanders, and fight his way into the zeriba, there to do his part. Up ahead he saw two Arabs standing tall, side by side, and he sighted on one with his Lee-Martin. A sudden wind blew the man's hood aside, and there was light blonde hair. The more he looked the more he realized that these were a pair of British soldiers, so with fixed bayonet he drove towards them with two other highlanders at his side. Five Dervish had the misfortune of facing him, and three he gunned down, the last two dying by his bayonet thrusts.

He reached the two men, a highlander on each side to guard as he cut them free from the wood post with his service knife. They had survived all through the intense artillery preparation, though one was nicked by shrapnel and was bleeding. They had survived the opening volley fire against the edge of the zeriba as well. It was a miracle. It was the will of Allah. Bert could see nicks in the wood posts and rounds embedded there, just above their heads. Now it was Bert Campbell's sharp eye and the nerve and brawn to get to them that saved their lives.

"Gods grace!" said one of the men. "Thank heaven for the Scots."

On the right, the 11th Sudanese battalion was through the thorns and saw the second redoubt where the Emir Mahmoud held forth. They sent a company forward in line, which met terrible fire from Mahmoud's elite guardsmen firing their Remingtons. That dropped the company to a man, but other companies behind it pressed forward, join by the Sudanese 10th Battalion, and they reached the defenders before they could reload. Their attack carried the center redoubt, where they found the Emir Mahmoud hiding in a revetment and reading from a book of prayer verses. They seized his ankles and dragged him out, hooting and hollering the whole time. They had paid dearly for the prize, but they had the Emir, standing amid the tall black soldiers who had so gallantly brought him to heel. His turban was lost, and standing bare headed before them, a British officer took charge of him and led him away with two highlanders.

The scene dissolved into chaos and carnage, the bodies of women and children in the thatched huts were soon mixed in with the fallen Dervish soldiers. The attack swept all before it, driving relentlessly towards the river, with blood dripping from the British bayonets. The Dervish were desperately trying to retreat across the riverbed, many gunned down there by independent rifle fire.

At 08:25 the cease fire order was finally given, and the carnage ended. Kitchener came forward, and when the men saw him they took off their pith helmets and raised them high on the bloodied ends of their bayonets, cheering him wildly. It was the only time many had ever seen his stony reserve melt into a broad smile, his blue eyes glittering in the sun. It was not just a victory, but a massacre. Mahmoud's force had been annihilated, destroyed, and scattered.

Several hundred prisoners were taken, mostly black Sudanese, who all begged to be allowed to join the ranks of the Sudanese Battalions. So the 11th Sudanese Black infantry, one company short in this slaughter, would take these to restore its ranks. The Sudanese would fight for either side, and by joining the conquering enemy they might get food, fair treatment, and even a much prized rifle. Otherwise their fate as prisoners could be much worse.

As for the 5000 Baggara Horsemen, those were the men of Osman Digna, a wayward and acerbic leader on the Dervish side. His failure to do anything at all but look threatening with his cavalry had contributed nothing to the Emir's fortunes, and now he turned and led his men off into the desert, sullen and angry. He had once again showed the enemy his back.

Retreating up the Atbara River, no more than 4,000 Dervish from the zeriba would survive, and they would eventually be collected by Ahmed Fedil. Osman Digna would make for the Sudanese capital at Omdurman, along with another emir, Wad Bishara.

Counting their own losses, Kitchener found he was short 525 men and 18 officers. They left the zeriba, the bloody sand clumped and clinging to their boots, and reformed on the higher ground above. Thankfully, the day was not yet hot, and a cool morning breeze was blowing. Some flinched from the stench of the battlefield inside the zeriba, but the British battalions just lay down on the red sands and started doing the one thing any self respecting denizen of the British isles would do—they were brewing up tea.

By early afternoon it was scalding hot again, and there was no shade in the thin scrub. Some of the highlanders removed their kilts and lay them on the branches to huddle beneath and screen off that burning sun, but for most, it was a misery unbecoming to the valor they had showed in combat.

At three in the afternoon the order was given to take up the spades and dig a shallow trench for the fallen. It was hard work in the sun, but when they had it a foot deep the officers relented and the men then started laying the bodies of friends, officers and fellow soldiers of every stripe who had fallen. The pipes would wail out a dirge for five to ten minutes, and then the men buried them in the Sands of Honor. Every man there knew that this could have easily been their own fate, and some whispered gracious thanks to whatever god they worshipped. Others thought the dead had acquitted themselves with valor and nobility, if the slaughter they had inflicted could ever be thought of as noble. It would be nothing compared to the ravages of wars yet to come, but here, in this hot red desert, in that burning hour, the living were still glad, in spite of their misery in the sun.

Their only regret was that this victory would now be followed by a withdrawal, back to the camps closer to Fort Atbara, and not a further advance. For most, that regret soon fled on the wind. They knew this little war was not over, and that their rock hard General still had a mind to bring the Khalifa to heel, and march to his capital at Omdurman, and then on to Khartum. For now, they all just waited for the blessed cool of the coming night, cursing the sun and bidding it begone.

Kitchener's army had flung 1100 artillery shells, 18 rockets, 4800 Maxim rounds and 225,000 rifle rounds at their enemy, but not one had hit the two men rescued by Bert Campbell. Now the Khalifa would have nothing to do with their fate, nor would the Emir Mahmoud, who was himself a prisoner. Ironically, when Kitchener spoke to the men and asked them "What's to be done with this Mahmoud?" the two men spoke in the Emir's favor.

"We owe him our lives. They were going to kill us, but he forbad it. Instead we were taken to the front ranks of the zeriba, and thank god your highlanders spotted us and recognized a good British soldier when they saw one."

Such was the cost for regaining the honor sullied when Gordon fell, but the Campaign was far from over, and the price would get ever higher. The main Dervish Army remained unfought. Questioned later, the captured Mahmoud remained proud and defiant. "You will pay for this at Omdurman," he said. "Compared to the Army of the Khalifa, I am but a leaf."

Chapter 17

Kitchener would take his army back to encampments along the Nile, north of the Atbara. He left four Egyptian battalions in Fort Atbara, and the rest of the army was strung out between that fort and Berber. There they would wait out the summer, as Kitchener was wanting cooler weather for the days remaining to his campaign, and the arrival of a second brigade of British Regulars.

There was disease in the camps, particularly among the Sudanese at Berber, and the heat was unremitting, as high as 120 degrees Fahrenheit, and nearly 110 in the shade. Even the wind denied the men any comfort, for it too often just stirred up the cinnamon red dust of the land. Kitchener would send out welcome rations of bacon and biscuits with jam twice a week, with tots of Rum in the evening, There were even a few cases of Typhoid Fever, but these were rare and it was not widespread.

The troops only had to parade on drill for about an hour each morning, having all the rest of the day and night to themselves. They enlarged their skills at fishing the Nile, hunting Gazelle, or shooting at birds. Any felled or caught would be on some squad's menu that night, the best food the men had to cut the monotony of the Bully-Beef tins. A race course was soon made for sport in the evenings near sunset, and a ground set aside for polo. Some of the officers secured leave and returned to Cairo for better digs, but most just stayed with their men.

The correspondents that had come on the train to Berber went about interviewing men and officers to write up their stories. Bert Campbell's exploits were read into the record. Then they gleefully disappeared on the next train south. For the men, the best of it was the long, cool desert nights, with a bunk roll beneath their heads, staring up at the star sewn skies in awe. The darkness in the desert night was complete, and the men could even count the streaks of meteors in the sky.

The battle recently won was talked over endlessly. Questions were asked among Kitchener's staff as to why General Gatacre deployed the Cameron Highlanders as he did. Some thought the Seaforths and Lincolnshire battalions would get all mixed up with them as they passed through. To this Gatacre answered that he had expected the Camerons would be badly hurt in their task of tearing open the zeriba abattis. He would rather have but one battalion so harmed than all of them taking losses in that effort. As it turned out, the outer edge of the zeriba had been much easier to penetrate than he feared.

Others thought the artillery preparation of about 90 minutes too short. "We might have just pounded them for three or four hours," said a Lieutenant.

"Aye," said a Captain in the Cameron Highlanders, " and then they might have skedaddled out the back side of that zeriba, and still be out there somewhere right now as a functioning army."

As for the captured Emir Mahmoud, Kitchener had him paraded through Berber, hands tied behind his back, and beneath a sign that read in Arabic: *"This is Mahmoud, who said he would take Berber."*[8]

Kitchener would then wait for three new gunboats, christened *Sheik, Melik* and *Sudan* to arrive from England to join the *Zafir* and others, fresh out of the shipyards. They could be brought to Berber by rail, reassembled there and then launched onto the Nile, which ran all the way to his distant objective—Omdurman. Only one cataract, the 6th remained, but it was the most navigable of all six, as long as the Nile was not too low. Everything in his mind as Kitchener planned the next phase of the campaign had relied entirely on that splendid rail line.

One thing was heavy on his mind. He expected the Khalifa at Omdurman to have as many as 50,000 troops, and even with newly arrived British regulars promised, he would just make half that number. It argued that he should now be the one to establish a strong zeriba, and let the Khalifa bleed his forces against it. Another thing he knew—he would need more than Broadwood's eight cavalry squadrons, and he was glad that the relatively new 21st Lancers were coming to him. He most certainly wanted more guns, twice the number he had on hand at Atbara, and many more Maxim guns. These abominations in the Arab mind would break them, first instilling fear, then carnage and slaughter when they were employed.

A whole new British brigade was coming, organized as follows:

2nd Brigade; commanded by Brigadier General Lyttelton

1st Battalion Grenadier Guards

1st Battalion Northumberland Fusiliers

2nd Battalion Lancashire Fusiliers

2nd Battalion Rifle Brigade

4 Maxims

Detachment, Royal Engineers

This would put eight British battalions in the field, and to mitigate the effects of that awful desert heat, Kitchener would wait until early autumn, and plan his battle for September. In the meantime, it was his to muster supplies, reorganize his brigades, bring up those river gunboats and additional forces, including 9 squadrons of Egyptian Cavalry under Broadwood and an expanded Camel Corps to eight companies. He would field two full divisions now, the 1st with the eight British Battalions and 21st Lancers; the 2nd had 16 Egyptian and Sudanese battalions. It looked like this:

Second Division; commanded by Major General Hunter

1st Brigade; commanded by Colonel Macdonald

2nd Egyptian Battalion

9th, 10th, and 11th Sudanese Battalions (IX, X and XI)

2nd Brigade: commanded by Colonel Maxwell

8th Egyptian Battalion

12th, 13th, and 14th Sudanese Battalions (XII, XIII and XIV)

3rd Brigade; commanded by Colonel Lewis

3rd, 4th, 7th, and 15th Egyptian Battalions

4th Brigade: commanded by Colonel Collinson

1st, 5th, 17th, and 18th Egyptian Battalions.

Camel Transport

Kitchener planned to make his advance from the vicinity of Berber, up the Nile to Wadi Hamed, which was just below the 6th Cataract. All the other cataract rapids were bypassed by the rail line to Berber, so his gunboats would only have the 6th to deal with on the way to Omdurman. It was the smallest and most easily navigated cataract region. Wadi Hamed would become his new forward base, 155 miles up river from Berber and about 60 miles below Omdurman. The Army was concentrating, with the new battalions of the British 2nd Brigade arriving. When Kitchener saw the Grenadier Guards leaping off the train, he knew England was now fully behind his enterprising campaign, and he would not disappoint.

He had already sent the Egyptian Division to the march. Now the river boats would take horses, artillery, transport animals, cattle and officers. A flock of new unwelcome war correspondents had arrived, and they would go under escort from two Squadrons of the 21st Lancers. Among them was young Winston Churchill, both an officer in the 21st and a correspondent for *The Morning Post* back home. Kitchener wanted nothing to do with him, for he disliked Churchill, seeing him as a meddling glory hunter out on a medal hunt, which was not far from the truth.

Many units would be taking the right bank of the Nile, others the left, and the boats also served to ferry men across. Most piled onto barges that the already laden boats could then tow across the river. There were a good number of steamers for the work: *Bordein*,

El Teb, El Tahra, Fathe, Nasr, Firket, all transport steamers, then the gunboats, *Zafir, Tamai, Sultan, Hafir, Abu Klea, Metemma, Sheikh, Melik* and *Sudan.* Some were armored screw driven boats instead of paddle wheel steamers. They came up by rail in sections, and were then reassembled at the Army concentration point near Fort Atbara, all under supervision of Lieutenant Gorringe and major 'Monkey' Gordon, the nephew of the late famous General Gordon of Khartum. Once tethered to heavily laden barges, they could make little more than two knots against the flows of the Nile. Painted slate grey, they were soon given the nickname "Monkey Gordon's Greyhounds." Four were painted black, but the moniker stuck to them just the same.

The Greyhounds were mounted with quick firing guns, two 6-pounders fore and aft, and one or two bigger 12-pounders, along with field howitzers. Some had 3.5 inch Krupp guns, and .45 Caliber Nordenfeldt Machine Guns or up to six Maxim MGs. Added to Kitchener's 44 gun artillery contingent, this brought a great deal of additional firepower to the battle ahead. The gunboats also had wireless telegraph systems, searchlights, circular saws to cut wood for fuel, and they were shallow drafted boats, drawing only two feet of water fully laden.

One of the gunboat commanders, on the *Fateh*, was the famous David Richard Beatty, and in this battle, England came within half an inch of losing their commander at Jutland, and future First Sea Lord of the Royal Navy. Attacking Dervish positions near Hafir, Beatty took a bullet right through his helmet, but it missed his head by that narrow margin. That incident, and that fact that Winston Churchill was also galivanting with the 21st Lancers, left a good amount of coin in the pot for England. The loss of either man would have caused dramatic repercussions through the history ahead.

The Boats were assembled at Fort Atbara, now being called England's Portsmouth in the Sudan. The Dervish hated the gunboats, calling them "The Devils," just as the Chinese had when they first saw the paddlewheel steamer *Nemesis*. The Khalifa would promise a wife to any gunner who could hit one with a shell. This they largely failed to do, and the gunboats would smash and sink any small boats they found on the river, at great cost to the movement of Dervish supplies. The Dervish actually drilled holes in the bottom of their smaller boats to sink them by the shore in order to hide them from the British gunboats. Then, they would drag them ashore and stop up those holes to use them.

If the first stake in the heart of Sudan had been Kitchener's rail line, these gunboats on the Nile were the second stake.

The Khalifa's Dream

As Kitchener's Army moved ponderously up river by march and by river boat, the Khalifa at Omdurman took careful note of any news marking its progress. As August wore away and the heat began to abate, he lay in a feverish dream in his quarters, wherein the *Mahdi* himself appeared to him and promised him a great victory over the Infidels.

He had been shaken by the defeat of the Emir Mahmoud at Atbara, but this dream restored his confidence. He awoke refreshed and confident, summoning his generals.

"We will not sit idle in a zeriba as Mahmoud did at Atbara! No, we outnumber the infidels by more than two to one. Instead, when they draw near, we will attack and simply crush them with the rage of all our 60,000 warriors, and a great victory will be had, just as it was when Hicks Pasha came for us. This Kitchener will be no different."

"But what of their devil ships! What of the many other abominations the heathens bring, those chattering guns that kill our *Jihadis* in such great numbers? And their cannons are much better than any we have."

"So it was with Hicks Pasha, and that did not stay our victory."

"Then will we withdraw into the desert and lead them into a desolate place as we did with Hicks Pasha? What if they do not follow, and instead sully the streets of Omdurman?"

"No, we will meet them long before they can make any close approach to the capital. It is written! The *Mahdi* himself appeared to me in a dream this very morning!"

"So it is written!" The Emirs all took heart, now eager to lead their men against the Infidels. Yet such things may have been written in the mind of the Khalifa, but they would first have to be proved on the field of battle. That was a proving ground that Great Britain had used time and again to rewrite the history of nations as it pleased, and this time, Kitchener was going to do the writing.

Chapter 18
The March to Wadi Hamed and beyond, August, 1898

Bert Campbell was elated when he returned to the rail battalion and found Bill Thompson. "Got me at least five of the buggers," he bragged, "and they never laid a hand on me. If one so much as looked my way with fire in his eyes, I put a bullet in his belly, and when I ran out, the bayonet served quite well against those heathen wild dogs. What did you do back here? Hit on the Bully Beef?"

"No, I contemplated on Rosie back home, glad that I might be likely to see her again, along with me Bairn. You ain't be married off, Bert, so you can afford to be bold like that. I've me family to think of, mate."

"Hell Billy, half the men or more have wives and Bairn back home, and they never shirked from the fight."

"Nor did I, damn your mouth. I never went to beggin' the Lieutenant to let me get on down into the thick of it, that's all. We had our orders up here, just like all the rest in the battalion. There was 5,000 Dervish riders on the loose, and we all stood to around the HQ tents. You're the only sheep that was out of the pen."

"Filthy lot they were," said Bert, speaking of the Baggara horsemen. "They thought if they screamed at us loud enough, we might break and run, but I stood with the Queen's Own down there, and I was proud of it. That said, it was even odds at Atbara. When we go south to Khartum, the buggers will outnumber us by a good measure. No matter. If they have us two-to one or better, and the other lads take down five like I did, then we'll have the victory, by God." Bert Campbell's math could not be argued with.

Now they marched, for the Rail battalion was coming with the rest of the army, there being porters and transport crews enough to manage the trains to Berber and Fort Atbara. They fell in behind Lewis and his Egyptian Infantry, trudging over the red sand. A listless, wind was in their faces, hot, weary, and harrowing as they marched. It carried no promise of a cooler night, devoid of moisture. The only consolation they had would be the close proximity of the great river Nile, ageless, its waters coming all the way from the great lake named after Queen Victoria. Both its great flows, the Blue and White, would meet where they were now headed, at Khartum and Omdurman.

"That's where we're bound for, Bill. Omdurman."

"I thought we was jus' headed for Khartum?"

"Oh Aye, the two cities sit like two eggs in the same nest, close on one another, right where the Blue Nile meets the White."

Before they would ever see them, there would be miles and miles of pale red sand, the river offering their only relief from the long hot march, for the dark scraggly trees were nearly leafless this late in the year. Sleeping at night near a grassy depression of a *khor*, they would find hordes of angry ants on the march, driving them from their bedrolls in a way the Dervish never could.

The march had been as hard on the animals as the men. Horses went lame, camels hurt their feet on the rough ground, being led over terrain they would never traverse on their own. Some had to be put down, such was the agony of every step they took, all heavily burdened in the heat. In one spot, they came to a pleasant grove of tall palms, close by the wide flows of the Nile, which was nearly a mile wide there. They saw steamers tugging barges laden with British Infantry, and Bert was glad he at least had the use of his legs to walk about. Out on the river, the sun gleamed on the water, and beat down on those barges like a hammer on an anvil.

The Army came with no intention of seeking any terms with the Khalifa. The men knew they were in for a fight, and one that would dwarf the previous engagement at Atbara.

"You think those Arab scum will billet themselves in a huge zeriba?" asked Bill.

"Not when they have the numbers on us. It will be more likely that we get up there and have to dig in when they come. Can you imagine what would happen if 60,000 Dervish were to take us on the march?"

"Why, we'd form squares, right Bert?"

"Better to be well set somewhere, and sitting in a freshly dug trench."

"'Wot? Dig in with this heat? The men would be falling left and right with the work."

"Nah, I was in with some strapping big Scots when we fought. They'll get any job done, and right quick, heat or no heat."

"Well, you can forget no heat, Bert, it'll be heat, ruddy hot, all the day long. That's fer sure. May not be up at 115, but it'll sure be 90 or more. Say, wot ye think of Kitchen Man paradin' the bloody Emir about with that big sign over his head?"

"Not a thing I'd advise," said Bert. "These Arabs are proud men. In the zeriba, they fought us to the death, and we happily gave them that, but nah a one would ask any quarter. Proud men, that lot. Say Bill, who's that proper English gentleman that came up on the last train before we marched? You know, the tall fellow, all in a nice tweed jacket, which I have no doubt he's shed by now."

"Probably a correspondent," said Bill. "Why else would any proper English gentlemen want to be out here touring with this army, lessun' they had some job to do."

"Right, it does seem odd. This one actually had his footman with him. Can you believe it? Does he think this is a stroll in Hyde Park?"

Camp on the Nile, the 4th Day of the march ~ 22 AUG 1898

Sir Roger was late to the party, but he had finally arrived. He and his Footman Ian Thomas had been able to catch a clipper to Calicut, and there in India, Sir Roger wandered off to find a lonesome temple. Deep in the earth beneath that place, he found and entered a maze of catacombs, which eventually led him to a great metal door. Ian recognized it at once.

"Another Time gate?" he asked the Duke.

"Right you are. More of them about than any might know, but I know them all. This one will do nicely, and with the Key I found at the Summer Palace, I can tune things to nudge us just a few years ahead to 1898."

"Tune things?"

"This is a very special key, my good man. Its shaft can be rotated, and the damn thing is finely calibrated. I can set the direction of desired movement in time by which direction I rotate the shaft, and there are fine marks that set the duration. Then, any rift we enter will deliver us to that new Temporal location, and not merely the one native to the rift."

"A handy thing to have."

"Indeed, which is why I labored so diligently to obtain it. It's a shame I didn't do away with Mister Parkes. I might have known that his temperament would lead him to do what he did at the Palace."

"1898," said Ian. "Forgive me if my history is rusty. What are we doing, heading back to China? Wouldn't that be the years of the Boxer Rebellion?"

"No, the real game there gets underway in 1900. We'd do best to stay out of China now, particularly after what happened to Mister Fortier."

"Sad that, sir."

"He got what he wanted—mindless oblivion. Did the man think he could lounge about and smoke opium all night and have it wreak no havoc on his body? Fortier was not a hardy man, and I've seen Bully Boys twice his size brought down by opium—stopped their bloody hearts, just as it did with Fortier, and that was a very grave loss."

"Sorry for it, sir."

"Oh, don't misunderstand me, it was no sentimental thing for me, Mister Thomas. To be honest, Fortier was a bit of a rogue, quite undisciplined. That bit he pulled with Zheng He was a typical example. The gall of the man! I'd say good riddance to him, but he had the temerity to kill himself before we had the opportunity to reset our game in China. God only knows, that was going to set off alarms back home. So no, we'd best get well away from China, because the Directorate will have Agents out after me now, which is why I came here to make our next little jump. And then, since the Directorate would certainly pick up our use of this rift, we skedaddled onto the first ship to Alexandria I could find, and here we are—the scene of our next little adventure. I've even found a new opponent—Sheikh Ali. I've known the man a good while, and he's very much interested in my Churchill diamond, which you made possible, my good man, when you foraged his remains for me at Bladon. Do you know he's here as well—yes, the living, breathing man himself. Strange that I have what was left of him right here in my pocket, while he's still kicking about the desert here with dreams of daring do."

Ian did not quite follow all of this. "Sir, what's the Directorate?"

"Well, someone has to oversee the comings and goings through all these Time Rifts, yes? That's what the Directorate does back home. Every time someone uses a gateway, particularly with a key, that signal goes forward to the directorate. They may think I'm in India now, which should give us time for a good game here with Sheikh Ali."

"Back in 2021 sir? When we took that tunnel under Lindisfarne? The Directorate is there in that year?"

"Oh, no, Mister Thomas. That was your native time, but I hail from much farther on, a time well into the future. You see, I'm an Agent too, a Time Walker, we call them. But now after that failed reset at the end of the last game, I'll likely be branded a rogue, and a wanted man. I have no doubt that Agents in place have already investigated our walk through those catacombs back in Calicut. That's why we slipped out of port on a fast ship here. Oh, if I make any adjustments or interventions here, they'll get wind of me too, but this is a very delicate situation. Churchill is here, and my opponent is likely going to be gunning for the man. Beatty too. Well, England can't afford to lose either one, which is why we're here to look after them."

"I see."

"Yes, be ready with that rifle of yours, my friend. We'll certainly need it for this little adventure." Sir Roger smiled.

They had been on the Gunboat *Fateh*, where Sir Roger met its commander, the stern faced Lieutenant David Richard Beatty, who was just a 27 year old man at this time. Sir Roger was thrilled to see him.

"He's every bit the maverick he turned out to be," he told Ian. "Do you know they had to beat the man three times for infractions during his tenure as a cadet in training? He's like a horse you could never quite break to the saddle, always skirting the line between order and chaos, and quite headstrong. Stanly Coleville commands the Gunboat flotilla here, but he was Beatty's old commander on HMS *Trafalgar* and HMS *Alexandra*, so he brought Beatty in on this business, and made him his deputy commander. When Colville was wounded in the action against Dongola, Beatty was quick to take the reins here, and he'll still think he has them in hand, even though Colville has mended."

"Interesting how these men climb so high," said Ian.

"Oh, he's a climber alright, and well connected. He one day takes command of a cruiser, HMS *Arrogant*, and I thought that quite ironic. Fits the man. Well, he sticks his neck out in adventures like this, and much too far. I'll want you to help me impart some caution in the man."

"Me sir? What can I do?"

"I'll let you know. First off, we'll jump ship to the *Nasr* today. I've made arrangements with Lieutenant Hood."

They changed gunboats, and the next day the flotilla proceeded up river to the sepia toned mud hut town of Metemeh. It was the place where the ill-fated relief expedition to rescue Gordon had finally reached its end, only to learn they had come too late, and that the great man was dead. It was also the place where the Emir Mahmoud had camped before he marched on Atbara, and the smelly remains of fallen or butchered animals, and some local farmers, were strewn around the town. Ahead lay Wadi Hamed, where the rest of the Grand Army of the Nile was intent on establishing its forward base.

There would be one more day's march, past the sullen brown hills of Shabluka, looking like burned out cinder cones, their flanks scorched black. Beyond them, they would make for the Kerreri Hills, the infantry marching in khaki columns, preceded by troops of the 21st Lancers and Broadwood's Egyptian Cavalry.

The Army had been moving along and astride a thin track that found its way back to Metemeh, and approaching the Kerreri Hills. Kitchener surveilled the ground near the river. It seemed suitable ground for his encampment that night, and he stopped. Events would soon convey the dangerous proximity of the Dervish Army, and he started issuing orders for the placement of his troops in a line of battle. He would form a guarded camp that night.

The day was old, the hot sun low, and he did not think there would be fighting that evening. But the darkness was never a friend, for the Dervish would think nothing of launching a surprise night attack. So he arrayed his troops in a crescent, its open end backed to the Nile, and he told told them to dig in along the camp perimeter. They would sleep at their battle stations that night, but the Dervish never came.

Part VII
Omdurman

"Every man should lose a battle in his youth,
so he does not lose a war when he is old."

— **George R.R. Martin,** *A Feast for Crows*

Chapter 19
Night 31 AUG 1898 ~ The camp on the Nile

General Kitchener had seen a battle lost trying to reach Khartum some years ago when he was younger, and in organizing this campaign, he was methodical; determined to see a battle won. The night of August 31st would be the first of two tense periods of waiting for the enemy, for thus far, only light Dervish patrols had been seen.

Kitchener was of a mind to think of them like smoke, and for him, where there was smoke, there was fire. That night, he sent word of the situation down the long telegraph cable that had trailed behind the army, a thin connection to the world outside, and everyone back in England. Then a stiff wind came up, and with it the skies began to vein with white lightening.

The men had been sleeping on the perimeter of the vast encampment, which had been improved in some areas by the digging of a trench. In the British sector a typical zeriba wall of thorn and bramble had been trussed up, four feet thick. Sentries had been posted, men taking turns at the watch to extend all night, for the fear of a night attack was on everyone's mind. No enemy came that night, but the rare desert rainstorm brought its own brand of misery to those trenches.

Where there had once been oppressive heat and seemingly eternal dryness, now the skies opened and hard rain began falling all along the camp. Waking at two AM, Bill Thompson and Bert Campbell looked out over the camp, illuminated by lightning. They could dimly see the makeshift lean-to shelters the men had staged with bedroll blankets, sleeping instead directly on the sand. Now that sand was wet with rain, and sodden on the ground, the telegraph wire lost conductivity, thus cutting off the expedition from Alexandria, Cairo, and the world beyond. When the Prime Minister was informed that there was no response to their last telegraph query, he became concerned.

The disaster of Hick's Pasha and the demise of Gordon were still both raw memories. It was again in September of 1883 that the Hicks expedition had ventured out to find and destroy the Mahdist Army. His column had vanished into the barren wasteland of Kordofan, south of Khartum.

His soldiers had never been paid, and they were raw, with little to no training and an undisciplined temperament one might expect of such men. Led astray by their Guides, they were soon surrounded by the Dervish forces of the *Mahdi*. By great exertion, the British officers managed to form them in a square. Some accounts claim it held for two days before collapsing, others said it just disintegrated under attack. None of the British officers returned, including General Billy Hicks. Of the 8000, perhaps 500 Egyptians and Sudanese would survive, who had deserted to join the *Mahdi*, and the *Mahdi* had 5000 camels and a lot to loot in that supply train, including many rifles and ammunition—even cannons.

Was the ominous lack of communication from Kitchener a sign of yet another disaster? Was that bleak, empty city of Khartum cursed? Must any foreigners who dared its approach suffer some sad fate or calamity? No news was bad news, or so they believed, but in fact, it had only been the rare desert rain that enforced this silence. Yet that did not mean that the shadow of calamity was not still a very grave possibility.

No attack came that night, and the 1st of September dawned with the men drying out near their morning fires, growling, spitting, rubbing their sore backs and lamenting their sodden uniforms. Kitchener did not want to spend another night like that, not knowing where his enemy was. It was time for an aggressive reconnaissance by the cavalry.

The 21st Lancers formed up on the left closer to the river, with Broadwood's squadrons covering their right flank. Kitchener's orders were to reconnoiter towards Omdurman, and the cavalry got underway. The Lancers saw a number of gunboats heading south on the river, intent on bombarding the Dervish capital.

As the cavalry advanced there seemed a deep silence on the land, but the men could feel that eyes were on them, a sense of unseen menace that became more palpable when a large flock of hundreds of vultures appeared, fluttering above the horsemen, then passing on ahead of them and perching on the thin branches of trees and scrub, their necks craned to stare back at the cavalry. It was as if they saw the horsemen as their next meal. A sense of deep unease settled on the men of the 21st.

When Broadwood's Egyptians saw this they began to whisper nervously with one another. The coming of vultures over any man found in the desert was always considered a sign of bad fortune, and a harbinger of death.

Coming to the Kerreri Hills. The Egyptian cavalry found them empty and deserted, with no sign of the Dervish. Yet from the heights the signal detachments of 21st Lancers waved down at the others, and the message was simple—Khartum in sight. It had been a long time since any Englishman had laid eyes on the city. Not long after, as the advance continued, the 21st could see the high white stone dome of the *Mahdi's* tomb in Omdurman.

"There it is lads, the resting place of the fabled bugger himself, the *Mahdi*. Guess he was just a mortal bloke like the rest of us." They would later hear the sound of distant gunfire, and as it happened, the gunboats had also spied that high dome, and after shelling the walls of the city, they turned their 12-pounders on it, and took a number of bites out of the stony white structure. To the Dervish this was a great shock and sacrilege, and further evidence that the Infidels were ravenous devils. Yet for the British, it was evidence only that the

Mahdi, who had sewn such discord and chaos in Sudan, had finally gotten his due—the silence of death.

From the high ground they could see the two flows of the Nile joining, like two steel wires coiling together.

"There it is—I can see the ruins of Khartum!"

"Well don't think we'll see any sign of Gordon there. He's long dead and buried, unless the heathens left his body to the bloody vultures."

Moving on from the Kerreri Hills, they would see just one more imposing height ahead, known as Jebel Surgham, sitting with its highest point at its westernmost end, and a lower plateau saddle reaching east for the Nile. The water was slate grey this morning, and they could make out a few mud huts near the river. It was the tiny village of Egeiga, which would be the place Kitchener would select later that day for his next encampment. As he had done at Atbara, he was making a slow, cautious advance on Omdurman, using his cavalry well to give advance warning of any significant body of enemy troops ahead. That is exactly what they would find.

The cavalry had seen nothing to report, and now they hastened to the lower ridge of Jebel Surgham. Once there they would be able to see if there was any enemy force at hand. When the scouts rode up to the top, they stopped, one man pointing at something to the northwest.

"Something there, sir," said the corporal, handing off his telescope.

Lieutenant-Colonel Rowland Hill Martin, took a look and frowned. All he could discern was a long brown line on the lighter sands of the desert.

"Looks like the edge of a zeriba. Could that be where they're hiding out? Better that than nothing at all, I suppose."

"That edge appears to be at the top of a slope, sir. The camp must surely be below."

"Let go an have a closer look, shall we?" Martin waved his squadrons forward, no more than 320 men. He was riding at a slow trot, directly towards a force outnumbering him at least twenty to one, but he could not yet see that. When the 21st had advanced to within three miles, a few riders came out from the distant zeriba, slowly approaching the British horsemen.

"Permission to say hello with my Carbine, sir? A trooper asked.

"Kindly announce ourselves," said Martin.

The trooper fired, dropping two Dervish horsemen at some 800 yards. "I guess they are not acquainted with the range of our guns, sir."

"It seems not."

Those were the first shots of the Battle of Omdurman, unless Beatty would claim his gunboats opened hostilities, and they might have hit someone important, or so Martin thought. The 50 year old Lieutenant Colonel then saw the edge of the zeriba thicken considerably—and move!

"Bloody hell!" he breathed. "That's no zeriba! It's a line of Dervish soldiers."

Out on that vast plain came the Khalifa Abdullah beneath his great black banner, waving unfurled in the morning wind. There came the Khalifa's son Sheikh Ed Din. There came Khalil, and the fiery Osman Azrak, Emir Unis, Ali Wad Hulu, and Abdel Baki surrounded by 500 dark spearmen in black robes. There came the notorious Yacoub, scourge of the desert. These were the men who had stirred the restless sands of Sudan in wild rebellion; the men who had thrown down Gordon of Khartum, one of England's dearest heroes. They were fierce, proud, relentless as they came, and endowed with a fanaticism that would drive them into the teeth of all the firepower Kitchener's army could bring to bear on them, the quick firing artillery, Maxim Machine guns; the incessant volley fire by lines of steady infantry with their magazine fed Lee-Metfords.

This vast army, approaching 60,000 in number, could have come the previous night, like wolves in the dark, but instead they waited for the dawn, choosing to attack beneath the eyes of Allah. Why should they creep and snipe in the dark against these, who they would now surely destroy? Now, there was nothing between this vast host and Kitchener's Army of 22,000 but the 320 men of the 21st Lancers, watching from that lonesome desert promontory. With them, was a young Lieutenant, out to make a name for himself, a medal seeking, glory hunting 23 year old named Winston Churchill....

On came the venomous Dervish fighters in their fearless fury, and they were raging out towards the cavalry. The mass thickened as more men surged up from beyond the edge of the rise. It was a mass of Dervish soldiers, easily four miles wide and thickening by the minute. They could soon see hundreds of white banners waving from the hordes, and Colonel Martin reckoned that he had just found the entire Dervish army of the Khalifa. The sunlight winked and glinted on their spear tips, by the thousands. It was very much akin to the discovery of the Great Zulu Impis before the battle of Isandlwana nineteen years earlier, and every bit as chilling.

"That's done it," said Martin.

Winston Churchill said that it was the impression of a lifetime, and that he did not ever expect to see anything of the kind again. But that life might soon be cut short if the British troopers didn't stop gawking and get moving.

The Khalifa himself was there, somewhere in that wide brown mass of swarming men and horses, looking like a horde of army ants on the barren plain. He had given much thought to the demise of the Emir Mahmoud at Atbara, seeing that victory only came to the Dervish when they attacked. This is how they defeated Hicks Pasha, and by sitting on defense, Emir Mahmoud had been crushed. So he declined to build a zeriba this time, or to fight a defensive or delaying action against Kitchener's forces as they advanced. Instead he would strike and crush him, as the *Mahdi* had defeated Hicks Pasha.

It was written.

The Khalifa's legions were all marked by colored flags. Ali-Wad Hulu was on the left, under a broad green banner. Then came Osman Sheikh-ed-Din, and Osman Azrak, the former under a darker green flag. Other tribes in the host bore red flags, but the Khalifa rode with his guardsmen under a broad black banner. Most carried swords or spears, but there were at least 12,000 with Remington rifles or older muskets. Each broad colored banner may have led about 15,000 men.

"Soldiers," said the Khalifa, pointing. "See how the Infidel has desecrated the tomb of the *Mahdi!* Who among you would live and still permit that? There they are, on Jebel Surgham. Go and kill them all! Become a raging desert wind, and blow their heathen souls to hell!"

Chapter 20

The Road to Hell

Kitchener had paved it well, and with no good intentions. Now he was reaching its end. Fewer than 800 cavalry under Colonels Broadwood and Martin were all that lay between his columns and that massive army of the Dervish. Riders came in, breathless, their horses blown, and gave the news. One was young Winston Churchill, sent back to report by Colonel Martin. He had been loathe to have to report to Kitchener himself, for he knew he was disliked, but he nonetheless found the General dressed all in white, and riding his white Arab charger. By this time some units of the army had formed on the plain and was marching towards Jebel Surgham. Mainly it was to guard Kitchener, who was thinking to reach Jebel Surgham and have a look for himself.

Then Churchill rode to his side, saluting and hoping Kitchener would not even recognize him. He reported the huge mass of Dervish now approaching the hills. Kitchener did recognize Churchill, but only asked him a single question: "How long do you think I've got?"

"About an hour, Sir. Perhaps an hour and a half." Then Churchill saluted and pulled away to make for the zeriba for a little food before the long ride back to the 21st Lancers. He was invited to join a set table by a Major L. B. Friend of the Royal Engineers, and he sat and ate with Colonels Wingate and Rhodes, and a German officer attached to the column as an observer. Other men also found the General with similar news, but less composed than Churchill's report.

"They're coming sir—thousands and thousands of them. We must get laagered at once!"

"Calm yourself, Lieutenant," said the Sirdar. "Here, see those men? That's the Guard. Go and give them to order to stand to where they are." Kitchener was pointing at his encampment.

After eating, Churchill would ride back to the 21st Lancers, and join as that unit conducted a halting retreat, stopping to dismount and fire at intervals to try and delay the Dervish advance. This wore on through the afternoon, but it seemed the danger had passed. The entire Dervish Army suddenly halted, fired their rifles into the air as a jubilant warning, and then began to make camp for their evening meal.

Kitchener's army was now within five miles of this huge force. They had come to the small village of El Egeiga on the west bank of the Nile. Sir Roger knew the big battle was close now, for that was where it had been fought, but he was not in the camp, being out on the gunboat *Nasr* up river.

Whether the camp could get ready now depended on the cavalry, and how much time they could buy the infantry. Yet Kitchener's position was not yet in any danger. The Dervish were not coming that day. Flags started waving, trumpets calling, and the whole column began moving to locations marked by their commanding officers. They would fall in exactly as the previous night, in a great arc, a letter "C" with its open end backed right against the Nile.

Kitchener was not immune to the rising sense of alarm among his men. He had seen he had sufficient force to defeat the Emir Mahmoud, but here he would be facing three times the number of Dervish fighters, among the Khalifa's best troops, and all fighting under his eye. At least he had that second brigade of British Regulars up, but there had been too many disasters here within reach of Khartum, and he did not want another one. In this next battle he had to decisively defeat the Khalifa to break his power over this land, and restore the honor of the British Empire.

Thus far I've done everything right, thought Kitchener. Atbara is secure, and with 90 days supply for the army. I've fifteen gunboats up with a good river link back to Atbara. I've sturdy troops in hand, plenty of artillery, even two 40 pounders, and I found the enemy just in time to set for defense. Give me two hours and I'll make him regret he ever dared to challenge the British Empire, by god.

One thing is certain, this will either end with the Khalifa dead or captured, or with the same to me. That I strongly doubt. No, this will not be another Isandlwana. We'll hold!

It was as if Kitchener was commanding the field with the power of his will alone. He noted the arrival of the second British Brigade. Compared to his veterans from Atbara, the newcomers looked pale, and struggled with the heat. They had not had enough time to acclimate themselves to this land, but if they could snap to in their lines, take aim and pull the triggers of their rifles, they would do nicely enough. Gatacre had the British division of two brigades, Hunter the Egyptian division. They were good men, steady and competent in the field.

All around the field, the perimeter was soon in place. Behind it, groups of men and officers, clustered around crates of biscuits and Bully-Beef, brewing tea. Kitchener allowed himself a smile at that. There seemed no impending crisis that was ever capable of keeping an Englishman from his tea.

1 SEP 1898 ~ On the River with the gunboats

Lieutenant Beatty had been eager to get into action. He was leading a flotilla of gunboats up river aboard the *Fateh*, and off his starboard rear was the *Nasr*, commanded by Lieutenant Hood. Several others were present in train, and they were all armed with quick firing 12-pounders, howitzers and Maxim machine guns. This represented a great deal of extra firepower, as well as a force able to reconnoiter up river towards Omdurman. Up ahead they had seen groups of Dervish on the shore, and some light boats that Beatty took to be enemy supply boats. The gunboats had been routinely sinking any they could find, but now he had bigger fish to fry.

Beatty led his flotilla south just able to make out the dark rise of Jebel Surgham where the British 21st Lancers were about to write their name in this history. But headstrong and thinking himself invulnerable on his gunboat, Beatty was out on the foredeck, in plain view as the Dervish on the shore fired back at his boats with their rifles.

"There," said Sir Roger, pointing at Beatty as bullets whizzed by the Nasr. "See that man there, Mister Thomas? He's like to get himself killed there. Let's put some caution into him. Do you think you could put a round on the edge of his helmet without any harm to the fellow?"

Ian Thomas was an ex-Marine commando, and a highly trained sharpshooter. "I reckon I could sir."

"Then do so, but be very, very careful here. This man must *not* be injured."

The gunboats were now firing their cannon, and Maxim guns at the shore, scattering the Dervish. "Take a shot at the Dervish first, will you?" Sir Roger looked around to see if anyone was watching them, but the other officers and crew were busy at their tasks.

After firing a round shoreward that dropped a Dervish dragging a small boat inland, Ian adjusted his sights and scope, peering though as he took aim. It would be a difficult shot, for the boat was moving with the swell of the river and he was moving with it. But he had taken shots from moving vehicles before, and had been dead accurate with them. He sighted, took a breath and then slowly pulled the trigger. There was a sharp crack, and then Sir Roger, looking through his field glasses, saw Lieutenant Beatty's white helmet spun to one side and set ajar. Beatty took it off, peered at it, and then two other officers were at his side. He saw Beatty run his hand through his hair and look at it. Then all three men hustled into the enclosed cabin of the gunboat.

"Well done," said Sir Roger. "I just hope to god the only thing Beatty saw on his hand was hair cream."

So the bullet that had come through Beatty's helmet in this history had not been an act of fate, but one delivered by Sir Roger. It was a kind of warning shot for Beatty, and if it drove him to a covered location, that well aimed bullet might spare him another, or so Sir Roger believed.

"Yes..." Sir Roger could still see Beatty in the cabin, now pointing and shouting orders. He seemed unhurt, which was a great relief. "Now," he said to Ian Thomas. "There's just one more prima donna I'll have to look after, and I think he will soon be right out there near that dark rise."

"Who would that be, sir?"

"Why, Mister Churchill, of course. He's with the 21st Lancers on this flank. Drat, if Kitchener weren't so acerbic, he should be attached to the headquarters staff, but Kitchener never liked Churchill, so he schlumped him off and he fell in with the 21st."

"Can't see a thing out that way sir, so I don't think my rifle will help."

"No, Mister Thomas, in this case, Fate will have to run its course. I must only hope that Sheikh Ali isn't working this flank."

1 SEP 1898 ~ With the Cavalry

Kitchener had intended to fight a defensive battle all along. To provoke the Khalifa, he had sent his gunboats out to shell Omdurman, and his cavalry to locate the Dervish army. Yet the work of one would frustrate the work of the other. The gunboats had collapsed the side of the dome of the *Mahdi*'s tomb, and put several holes in it. This had the desired effect, but it had been like a man poking a hornet's nest with a stick. Kitchener now wondered how bad the enemy's sting would be.

Its first result was a rush by groups of angry Dervish horsemen, all after the videttes and scouts put out by 21st Lancers. Those men had to make a hasty retreat back to the ridge line where the main body of the regiment had formed. There, Colonel Martin had dismounted several squadrons, and formed a line. Now they looked and saw movement by masses of infantry, flowing out onto the plain below and obviously moving to flank the cavalry on both sides.

'"Fire on those men!" came the order, and the dismounted line began to volley fire at the advancing infantry.

Kitchener did not really need to provoke the Khalifa. He had already been persuaded by his Emirs that taking a defensive position and waiting for the Infidels to attack had always ended in defeat. "We must smite them!" the Emirs argued, and this is what the Khalifa now intended to do. He was on holy ground, close to Sands of Honor where he had two good victories. Here he had destroyed the column of Hicks Pasha not far to the south, and then stormed Khartum to deal with Gordon. So he would strike, but not this day.

Beatty's attack on the *Mahdi's* tomb had lit the fuse. Now Osman Digna took his horsemen on a wide envelopment, all racing towards the Nile. But the greatest mass, both mounted and infantry, was now coming rapidly towards Jebel Surgham. Several rounds of volley fire were made to try and discourage them, but on they came, heedless of any casualties.

Colonel Martin looked and saw he must have been outnumbered by as many as twenty to one. The real number was closer to 50 to one, and so he wisely told the buglers to sound the withdrawal. The 21st flowed down off the saddle of that high ground, following the line of a wadi towards the Nile. They could see Dervish riders pacing them several hundred yards off, and marveled at the great mobility of the horsemen. They were natural light cavalry; superb in the saddle.

At the same time, Broadwood's Egyptian cavalry was on the other flank, up on the Kerreri Hills. There, the advance of Osman Sheikh Ed-Din, the son of the Khalifa, and Ali Wad Hulu, was a dark stain on the plain, flowing up to envelop those hills. As with Martin, it was soon clear to Broadwood on that flank that he could not hold his position screening those hills given the numbers advancing on him. He waited just long enough, then mounted up and withdrew north towards an extension of the Kerreri Hills. It was Osman Sheikh Ed-Din's men that pursued Broadwood, forcing him to circle above those last hills and then turn east towards the river. Soon both Cavalry forces were maneuvering to reach the two flanks of Kitchener's position, right where they touched the Nile.

Then, unaccountably, the dark hosts stopped. They waited in suspended animation, their ranks still clamoring with war cries. The the last of the Cavalry saw they appeared to be settling in behind the hills to make camp. They would not fight that day, but wait until the following morning, a reprieve that was only too welcome by Kitchener. It would give him ample time to position his brigades and see them well dug in overnight—just in case the enemy planned a night attack.

In doing this, the Khalifa was ignoring the advice of Sheikh Ali, given the previous evening in his conference of the Emirs. Ali had come with about 3000 men, good Arab riders, and so he earned a voice in that council.

"Why do you fight here?" asked Ali. "To protect the Capital? Have we not seen the folly of that? The *Mahdi's* tomb has already been defiled!"

"I would not have the Infidel set foot in Omdurman, for then it would be spoiled even more," said the Khalifa. "They would shell it night and day with their river cannons."

"Yet Omdurman presents us with a bastion of defense. Do you think the Infidel could move us, house by house, and ever take that city with the numbers we have?"

Most Emirs present nodded at this, agreeing that Omdurman could easily be held. Then the Khalifa spoke again, revealing his mind.

"I do not wish to sit in a place and wait upon the enemy's pleasure to attack me."

"Yet they are not great enough in numbers to besiege us in Omdurman," said Ali. "We could hold it with a third of our forces, and still outnumber them in the field two to one."

"Was it not you, Sheikh Ali, who advised that we should strike, and with every *jihadi* we command?"

"This I did, but now we stop—why? Do we fear the sun this afternoon?"

"Of course not! Today we have fixed the enemy's attention," said the Khalifa. "I do not think they will be so bold as to come to attack us. We are between their position and Omdurman, and so the capital is protected. Let the men rest tonight, and in the morning, we will crush them. Here is how it shall be done..."

The Khalifa began to draw a map in the sand on the floor of his tent. "Here is the Nile... Here the enemy camp. We have chased off the few horsemen they command. In the morning, Osman Azrak will drive back any outliers from their camp, as they often deploy them. Then my son, my brother, and I will lead the main attack, and we will squeeze the last breath from their lungs, and drive them into the Nile. This was the great victory I saw in my dream when the *Mahdi* visited me. It is written!"

This got the reaction the Khalifa expected, and there was broad agreement among the Emirs. Then Sheikh Ali spoke one last time, a lone dissenting voice.

"Beware, my Khalifa," he said. "The strength of the Infidel does not lie in their numbers, but in the terrible weapons they carry. Their rifles are much better than ours, and every man among them has one. And then there are the abominations—the river boats, the chattering guns, and they have many times our number in cannons. This, they call firepower, for they do not wield the sword, except among their commanders. Yet this firepower can have terrible effect.

It is how they have won all their victories, and remember, they are both impudent and stubborn. I would not attack them in a prepared zeriba, and by waiting today, we give them much time to improve their defenses."

"No prepared position is insurmountable," said the Khalifa. "They themselves did exactly what I have ordered now, and against the Emir Mahmoud, who was also in a well prepared zeriba. You all know he was brave and strong. They crept near by night, and then attacked at dawn, and they crushed him. We have just crept near behind these hills, and in the morning we will crush them as well."

"But Mahmoud's numbers were none so great as we have now," said Ali. "And a third of his men rode off with Osman Digna."

The Osman's[9] eyes flared at this. "What should I have done in that zeriba? There was no room to fight as my horsemen do, I went to envelop their flank, and by so doing, I lessened the numbers they had to attack the zeriba.

"True, and it is with the sheer mass of our forces that we must prevail tomorrow morning. As Allah wills it."

"And if he does not will it? What if their firepower, as they call it, is simply too great?"

"We will storm right through it, burst into their zeriba, and then destroy them, just as they did with Mahmoud."

"This I ardently hope for," said Sheikh Ali. "Yet if we fail in this, then the stratagem to be used can be one of two things. We can withdraw to Omdurman and dare the Infidel to try and take that from us. Or, we can withdraw into the desert, force them to follow us, and then slay them, as we did with Hicks Pasha."

"As Allah wills it," said the Khalifa. "But I expect neither option will be necessary. We will crush them."

"One thought more," Sheikh Ali raised a finger. "What of a night attack? Would this not limit the range of their gunfire? We might get much closer to them before we felt the hard rain of their bullets—close enough to overwhelm the edge of their defense, and break inside. Then, in that darkness, confusion and chaos would reign. Their transport animals would stampede in all directions. How few might survive, thinking only to reach their boats on the river, to sail away and report the shameful defeat."

At this the Khalifa's brother, Osman Sheikh ed-Din, spoke his mind. "Such a victory, stolen at night in the dark, would hold no glory for Allah. Yet if we strike by day, under the eyes and beneficent gaze of Allah, peace be upon him, surely then we would win the day."

Sheikh Ali frowned, but could only say. "Allah sees all—be it day or night. Who dares say otherwise?"

"Yes," said the Khalifa, "and you see much, Sheikh, but I have seen their river boats at night, and they have long white eyes that will search the ground on both sides of their encampment. Besides that, the moon is full, and they might even be expecting such an attack. I will not oblige them. No it is not by surprise in the darkness that we shall prevail, but boldly, as my brother says, in the clear light of day. Let them sleep in fear all night. We attack with the coming of the sun!"

Chapter 21
2 SEP 1898~ The Battle of Omdurman

It was half past four when the first bugles sounded in the encampment. The men had spent a long and restless night under the moon and stars. All the while it was as the Khalifa described it. Beatty had the gunboats in two groups covering each flank on the river, and all night their long white searchlights scoured the desert on the flanks, extending a thousand yards inland. At one point the Khalifa thought they were searching for him, and moved his tent well inland, behind the imposing heights of Jebel Surgham.

"They are looking for me," he said. "I would not have their eyes upon me as I sleep or conduct my evening prayers!"

Sentries stood like shadows at the edge of Kitchener's zeriba, their eyes following the slow sweep of the search lights, and peering into the desert where the white moon illuminated the ground out some 400 yards.

Kitchener's dispositions revealed that he was going to rely on firepower to win this battle. He arrayed his men in a two rank line, all around the edge of the zeriba. Behind each brigade, he held but two companies in reserve to reinforce any hard hit spots. Behind them, he had men with stretchers to go and remove the wounded and fallen, and to also act as runners to replenish ammunition when called. Between each brigade, he placed batteries of artillery, and at intervals along the line, he set his Maxim Guns, 20 along that line, and another 34 on the gunboats protecting the flanks

The cavalry had patrols out at night, to give early warning of any attack. Nothing was seen. They would be up early to again move out towards the Kerreri Hills and serve to delay any attack aimed at enveloping Kitchener's right. Most of the British troops were on the left. Broadwood would again take his force out, with the Camel Corps attached, and try to distract and delay the enemy advance on the right. In doing so, he was placing himself in grave danger, because the Dervish infantry was fleet footed, and the camels would be slow to descend the reverse side of the ridge, which was quite rocky.

When Broadwood saw the Dervish coming for his troopers, he shouted an order: "Camel Corps, withdraw to the zeriba!"

The camels lumbered back towards the zeriba, and the cavalry skirmishers gave them good covering fire as they withdrew.

"Cavalry! Mount up!" Broadwood now took his Egyptian cavalry into the hills, where he planned to conduct a classic delaying action, much like Dunford had attempted at Isandlwana. The men would dismount, fire at the approaching Dervish, then remount and ride off to do this several more times. This led Osman Sheikh-ed-Din off into the Kerreri Hills trying to close with Broadwood, and it was a significant diversion. Yet among the Emirs that were in that group, was Sheikh Ali. The Egyptian horsemen were an elusive quarry, and they would eventually make it back to the Nile and move to the right flank of the zeriba.

"Do you not see what they are doing?" said Ali to the Khalifa's brother. "They lead your entire force off into these hills, and away from the place Osman Azrak will soon strike! These Egyptian horsemen are of no concern. Their numbers are too small to do us any harm. They come here merely to provoke you to chase them! Let us regroup and be ready to join the attack on the zeriba. Find Ali Wad Hulu and let us join him."

This was very good advice, but communications across the field were not fast or accurate, and recalling the disparate arms of his force of over 15,000 troops would take Osman Sheikh-ed-Din a good while.

In the meantime, Osman Azrak had over 13,000 men ready to strike the center of Kitchener's zeriba at a little before 06:00. The Osman was a fanatical adherent and believer in the *Mahdi*, and now a most loyal servant of the Khalifa. He was known for his lightning swift raids, his cruelty, a real fire breather in the field of battle. He had wheeled out two guns, an old French 75mm gun and a smaller mountain gun. They were two of only five possessed by the Dervish army, all manned by captured Egyptian soldiers who were literally chained to the guns to prevent them from fleeing. Their desultory fire was all short of the enemy perimeter, and harmed no one.

Behind them, Azrak had 4100 spearmen, 7650 men with swords and some with rifles, and 1450 cavalry with swords and spears ready to attack. Their rising war cries could be heard in the Allied camp. These formations extended across a front about 1,500 yards wide, and advanced toward the left flank of Maxwell's brigade and much of Wauchope's British Brigade with the Lincolnshire Regiment, Seaforth and Cameron Highlanders, and Warwickshire Regiment.

The British battalions had about eight companies each, and deployed six forward in a two rank line, with two companies in reserve. It was a formation designed to Maximize firepower. As the clamor of the Dervish increased to a fervent welter, the British guns from land batteries and the gunboats began to open fire. These guns had a 3,000 meter range, and some had the Lyddite shells using a new highly explosive chemical.

As the Dervish charged they kicked up a large brown dust cloud that was soon blooming with the deadly black roses of these exploding shells. Their effect was immediately noted, but in spite of the casualties the enemy still came on, waving spears and shouting at the top of their voices. Winston Churchill described the carnage this way: *"Out on the plain, bullets were shearing through flesh, smashing and splintering bone; blood spouted from terrible wounds; valiant men were struggling on through a hell of whistling metal, exploding shells, and spurting dust—suffering, despairing, dying. Such was the first phase of the Battle of Omdurman."*[10]

Had Osman Sheikh-ed-din been in his original starting position on the field, his 13,600 men might have joined this attack, but his men were still scattered through the Kerreri Hills in spite of Sheikh Ali's attempt to reverse that.

Kitchener and his staff were all up on their horses, and Kitchener was riding from one position to another to check the deployments, a very hands on General who preferred to be in the thick of things. He saw the dense Dervish formation coming at the center of his position, with colored flags wafting over the heads of those men. They gave the gunners good targets, and the crack of British artillery reassured him. He knew Wauchope's brigade would stand, but was a little concerned over Maxwell's position, which had three Sudanese battalions and and one Egyptian. They had dug into a shallow trench the previous night and they were well prepared.

The Dervish were charging into the rising sun, the light of that dawn glinting off their spear tips. As they came on, flag holders were hit and went down, the banner then picked up by another until he was hit. The Sudanese troops were remarkably cool, their officers calling out the volley fire, and the troops responding smartly. The Maxim guns were wreaking havoc and carnage on the attackers, who began entering a killing zone about 800 yards from the British Brigade. There the edge of the attacking swarm just seemed to dissolve as it came on, leaving mounds of dead and wounded men on the ground. The slaughter was terrible, the defensive fire so intense that the attack was halted, men given to crawling forward instead of running, but still being cut down by one volley or artillery shell after another.

Kitchener was watching, and set his jaw. *Firepower*, he thought. *They won't even reach our lines. We'll break them, by god, and then I'll march right out and take Omdurman.* He was seeing the first half of that thought playing out before his very eyes, the Sudanese every bit as cool and steady as his British troops. They had the shorter ranged Martini & Henry rifle, so the Dervish were able to get as close as about 400 yards to their position. The British, with the

Lee-Metford rifles, had stopped the edge of Osman Azrak's charge about 800 yards out, and few if any got beyond that mark. Those that did were gunned down and died that hour, along with thousands of their Dervish comrades behind them. The dense ranks of the *Jihadi* infantry were just shattered, the 1400 riders simply swept off their horses or tumbled to the ground when rounds killed their mounts. They would struggle to their feet, wave their swords with futile rage overhead, and then be gunned down by the next volley of well aimed rifle fire from the Guards, some of the steadiest and most experienced infantry in all of Europe, if not the world.

If Sheikh-ed-Din had not run off after Broadstreet's cavalry, his 13,600 men would have also been aimed right at Maxwell's Brigade, charging towards the 8th Egyptian and 13th Sudanese battalions. But that did not happen. It was an ill-timed attack, and it failed miserably, but behind the rise of Jebel Surgham, the Khalifa still held an enormous force in hand. There stood the 14,000 men of Yaqub, a gathering of many tribes and clans, the Ta'aisha, Habbiniya, Humr, Rizauqat, the Bani Halba, Zaiyadiya, Kababish, and Danquala. With them stood the Khalifa's personal bodyguard of 1486 men, and the Khalifa al-sharif with another 1,700. Osman Digna was also present with about 2000 men. This force of nearly 18,000 men was the Khalifa's trump card, which he now prepared to play.

On the other side, Kitchener was about to make a most unwise assessment of his situation. "That's done it," he said, seeing the slaughter of Osman Azrak's attack. Azrak himself rode forward, one of the last to fall, hit by several bullets at once. If his men died, then he would die with them.

"We've broken them," said Kitchener. "Now I'll drive the whole lot off the field and march to Omdurman." Kitchener was of the mistaken mind that his battle was won, and he was now about to order an organized pursuit of the defeated enemy. If he had see the strength of the reserve the Khalifa still had behind Jebel Surgham, he might have stayed right where he was, but he mistakenly thought his battle was over.

He was wrong.

2 SEP 1898, 06:00 ~ With the 21st lancers

The 21st Lancers were already trotting out of the zeriba and fanning out by sections to send out patrols on the left flank. Some went out as far as Jebel Surgham as they had the previous day, and there they saw much the same as they had encountered earlier. Winston Churchill was among them, reporting the sight of a great mass of Dervish warriors, at least five miles wide in his estimation.

He saw the Emirs on their proud steeds, riding back and forth and shouting out in loud voices, rallying their men. Then the whole mass was in motion, advancing swiftly towards those hills, the sound of their war cries resounding from the heights of Jebel Surgham. Churchill said it was *'like the tumult of the rising wind and sea before a storm.'* The Dervish advance was so intimidating that Churchill moved to look back at Kitchener's forces, reassured by their calm lines. He saw the main body of his 21st lancers below keeping watch on them.

The banner of Ali-Wad Hulu was seen, which had joined the Khalifa's bodyguards with his additional 5,400 men. This meant the force Churchill and the other scouts were observing was now about 23,000 strong, nearly twice as strong as the attack made by Osman Azrak. It was an enormously impressive force, the pride and might of the Dervish State; all the disparate tribes that had rallied to the banners of the *Mahdi* years ago. Now this little empire would stand or fall on the outcome of this one great battle.

Near the single black banner of the Khalifa, there were some 500 riders, all carrying white flags inscribed with verses from the Qur'an. Their order was perfect. The Dervish came on to the heights of Jebel Surgham like a rapidly rising tide. For Churchill's little patrol, it was time to be somewhere else. The Dervish had seen them and some of their riflemen were sending bullets at them, badly aimed, which either nicked the sands underfoot or whizzed overhead. The patrol galloped off, hearing the crack of fire behind them, but none were hit.

Somehow coming under fire like that had stirred up the ardor for battle in the Lancers. They saw the Dervish host starting to climb the lower slopes of the ridge they were on. This prompted the patrol to move some 300 yards to their right, to get in behind the cover of a scattering of rocks and boulders. There Churchill saw another body of men moving east towards the Nile, not knowing that he was seeing the men of Osman Digna, who was always on the outer flanks of any attack, but seldom in its throng.

Churchill saw the British gun batteries beginning to fire, for the range to that ridge line was known and the guns calibrated to strike it accurately. He knew that as soon as the Dervish crested that ridge, they would be under that terrible artillery fire joined by Beatty's gunboats and the British 32nd Field Battery. The Dervish on the ridge would be hit by as many as twenty rounds in the first minute, some bursting above them and sending lead shrapnel down into their ranks, some erupting with terrific fire and anger as the Lyddite exploded. Other rounds plunged into the flinty shoulders of the ridge, sending up torrents of red smoke and fire. Churchill saw the sea of white banners toppling in all directions as their bearers were struck and killed. But that forest of banners reanimated as other men took them and forged on. It was range and firepower that was now weighing in on the outcome of this campaign. Kitchener's forces could strike and kill the Dervish warriors long before they could close to use their obsolete medieval swords and spears.

Now the patrols all withdrew, returning to the main body of the 21st Lancers. Churchill's patrol reached the Nile and watered their horses, listening to the thunderous roar of volley fire from the British brigades. The Dervish were trying to send up their riflemen to contest the enemy fire, but Churchill saw them falling under the merciless volleys of the British soldiers, who stood in their stern and resolute lines. An order came for his troop to rejoin the regiment.

They watched the volley fire as one regiment after another engaged in what Churchill called *'a mechanical scattering of death which the polite nations of the earth have brought to such monstrous perfection.'* When they opened volley fire on the Dervish, it was indeed machine like. The drilling and ordering of lines and columns all meant to move the soldiers into positions where they could inflict this terrible carnage and send hails of metal at their enemy, piercing flesh and shattering bone. It was but a pale prelude to what would transpire in WWI in the next decades, where all of Western Europe would become entrenched zeribas, and soldiers would make futile, suicidal charges like this into the intense killing firepower of these defensive positions.

No trenches had even been necessary here at Omdurman, for the Dervish would never get within 300 yards of the British lines. The rifles began to heat up with the intense and steady fire, so much so that some men ran back to the reserve companies to get more ammunition and exchange their hot rifle for a cool one. On the receiving end of this withering gunfire, skulls were broken, bones shattered, and blood poured from mortal chest wounds. Limbs were torn and hundreds upon hundreds were maimed and killed.

Even so, the Khalifa held some 15,000 of his host behind Jebel Surgham, and that portion now under this terrible fire was about 8,000 men. Ali Wad-Hulu had another 15,000 hidden behind the Kerreri Hills. That represented half the Khalifa's army, still holding 30,000 men in reserve.

On the left, amid the low Kerreri Hills, Osman Sheikh-ed-Din had been off chasing Broadwood's cavalry, which removed his considerable force from the attack on the center by Osman Azrak. His men had forced Broadwood to retire, and the Camel Corps was in some distress, encumbered by wounded and moving slowly on the stony ground. Broadwood saw that a sudden turn by the Dervish infantry was now threatening to overtake and destroy the Camels, who were moving slower than those charging men on foot.

The camels neared the Nile as Broadwood ordered his Egyptians to be ready to charge. It was the only way he thought he could take pressure off the Camel Corps and save them. While they formed up for this, The Colonel could see they were none too eager to execute such an order. The mass of the enemy alone would make a charge now suicidal. Perhaps, he thought, we should just dismount and fire.

Part VIII

Consequences

"In Nature there are neither rewards nor punishments—
there are consequences."
Robert G. Ingersoll: *Some Reasons Why*
"The hardest strokes of heaven fall in history upon those who imagine
that they can control things in a sovereign manner, playing providence
not only for themselves but for the far future—reaching out into the
future with the wrong kind of farsightedness, and gambling on a lot of
risky calculations in which there must never be a single mistake."
English Historian Sir Herbert Butterfield

Chapter 22

Broadwood hesitated. What was this massive Dervish formation here to do? Were they set on his cavalry as their objective, intending to drive him off, or were they merely maneuvering to join with the other Dervish marshalled behind the Kerreri Hills? What should I do, he wondered? I'll be throwing this cavalry to the wolves if I charge, all to save the Camel Corps. Then, at this critical juncture, he heard the boom of artillery and saw the gunboats on the Nile beginning to open heavy fire to cover the withdrawal of the Camel Corps. Their guns were accurate and deadly, slowing the advancing Dervish horde, and that settled the decision for Broadwood. It was time now to save his horsemen.

Much to the relief of his troopers, he ordered the bugler to sound the withdrawal and led his squadrons east in a wide circuitous maneuver. The hour had been saved by the appearance of the Devil ships on the Nile. The Camel Corps slipped out of danger and reached the zeriba, and frustrated to see this, the men of Sheikh-ed-Din then turned to go for the cavalry. But the horsemen were much faster, and all that did was lead those Dervish away from the main attack on the zeriba. In this, the inability of the Emirs to execute more control over their men once they were launched in any given direction was clearly seen. By the time the Osman had recovered control and reformed his men, it would be too late for them to support the main attack. Sheikh Ali had tried to prevent this wild goose chase from repeating itself, but his pleas had gone unheeded.

In doing what he did, Broadwood exercised admirable initiative, for he had been ordered back to the zeriba much earlier, but lingered to do all he possibly could to interfere with the advance on that left flank. Now, on the right flank, the 21st Lancers were about to write their name into this history. They were going to make the regiment's first major cavalry charge, and the last for the British Army at the same time.

Now, more than ever, the Sirdar, Kitchener, was convinced his battle was won, and he began issuing orders for his brigades to advance out onto the plain. He would have done this earlier save for this second big attack, and in spite of his confidence, such a move was still very unwise. Yet Kitchener now thought he had the inside track to Omdurman, and he was going to go for the city at once.

As the terrible volley fire slackened and stopped, the men of the 21st Lancers mounted for action. They had withdrawn from the rocky heights back towards the left flank of the zeriba. General Gatacre came riding to the edge of the zeriba with orders for Colonel Martin, and he was pointing to the ridge where Churchill's small scouting section had first seen the second attack coming.

All the men of the 21st, little more than 300 in number, were now up in the saddle and ready. A few patrols led the way with the bulk of the regiment following at the trot. The first patrol gained the ridge and took in the sweep of all about it. They could see the white high tide line of the latest attack, where the Dervish had been stopped and lay in heaps on the ground as if they had encountered some impenetrable barrier in the desert heat. They ran right into the thick of all that volley fire, and no man among them could advance further and remain alive. Looking through binoculars, the troopers saw the occasional horse standing amid scores of dead, and a few men here and there limping back towards the hills, some helping wounded comrades on the ground as they went.

A report was flashed back to the encampment via heliograph, and an order returned—*Advance! Clear Left Flank.* Ahead lay a shallow *khor*, and there could be seen a thin line of Dervish along it in what looked like a deliberate blocking position. Colonel Martin studied it for a time, and then decided he needed to act promptly to clear it from the flank as ordered. He gathered in the squadrons and as Churchill described it: *"he ordered 'Right wheel into line' to be sounded. The trumpet jerked out a shrill note, heard faintly above the trampling of the horses and the noise of the rifles... All the sixteen troops swung round and locked up into a long line, and the 21st Lancers were committed to their first charge in war."*

The Dervish line looked to be no more than 700 men strong, yet that was still over twice the number of Martin's troopers. Yet that did not deter him in the least. He intended to use the shock and speed of a full cavalry charge to sweep them off the field. But earlier, the Khalifa had been informed of the movement of the 21st Lancers, and Sheikh Ali was with him when news came of the British cavalry advance on the river flank.

"My Khalifa," said Ali, "That is Osman Digna, and not the most reliable of your fighters. It would be wise to quickly reinforce that flank!" That was well given advice, and the Khalifa was of a mind to heed it. So while reports and orders were being flashed back and forth via heliograph by the British, the Khalifa sent four groups of 500 men each to reinforce the flank, where Osman Digna held that line in the *khor*. Instead of only 700 to 1000 men, there were now 3000 Dervish hidden in there, and the 21st Lancers were thundering forward at the gallop towards a force more than seven times their numbers.

Yet none of the troopers would know this until they would reach the outer edge of that *khor*. Only then could they look down and see how many more enemy Dervish were there before them. It was simply too late to rein in at that point, the charge could not be stopped.

An eye witness, Churchill described it: *'The collision was prodigious. Nearly thirty Lancers, men and horses, and at least two hundred Arabs were overthrown. The shock was stunning to both sides, and for perhaps ten wonderful seconds no man heeded his enemy. Terrified horses wedged in the crowd; bruised and shaken men, sprawling in heaps, struggled, dazed and stupid, to their feet, panted, and looked about them. Several fallen Lancers had even time to remount. Meanwhile the impetus of the cavalry carried them on. ... the officers forced their way through the press; and as an iron rake might be drawn through a heap of shingle, so the regiment followed. They shattered the Dervish array, and, their pace reduced to a walk, scrambled out of the khor on the further side, leaving a score of troopers behind them, and dragging on with the charge more than a thousand Arabs. Then, and not till then, the killing began...*[11]

The charge came into the *khor* with so much force and momentum that the Lancers plunged right through the greater mass of the enemy, and up the far side of that shallow depression. When the killing began, they started jabbing with lances, hacking with swords and firing their carbines and pistols, while the Dervish stabbed at the haunches and breasts of their horses to bring them down and then leapt upon the fallen riders to slay them. In the midst of all this chaos and carnage, was a young man Great Britain could simply not afford to lose—Winston Churchill.

The lancers had plunged right through a mass of Dervish, twelve ranks deep. It had been a rare event, even in the time of the Napoleonic wars for cavalry to collide headlong in a charge with infantry. More often than not the infantry would have formed square and the horsemen would flow around these tight formations, but not here. Nothing could be done to evade or maneuver away from that densely packed line of Dervish infantry. This titanic collision was inevitable.

Men were thrown head over heels, bowled over. Terrified horses fell on them, their weight crushing them to the bottom of the depression. Frenzied, flailing combat soon ensued, with both sides trying to kill any enemy within reach, and most simply trying to get out of that seething trench of death. The cavalry plunged into the Dervish mob, and right through it to the far side of the *khor*.

Reaching the far side Sergeant Major Veysey's face was bleeding badly from a sword cut. He was ordered to 'fall out to the rear," but remained adamant.

"Fall out be buggered!" he replied, and raised his carbine to fire. For that he was recommend for a Victoria Cross, and at the same time for a court Martial for disobeying a direct order and swearing at his superior officer. Nothing was done with either recommendation. +1 and -1 equaled zero.

Now, as if some great unseen clock had just struck a fateful hour of doom, the history of these events was about to change.

Churchill was not among those who made it through the Khor! There, with a sweeping blow from a broad bladed spearhead, Young Winston was knocked off his horse and fell into the raging mass around him. That had not happened in the history Sir Roger knew, but this time this event played out differently. Unhorsed troopers struggled, dazed and bruised, to reach their feet, and Churchill had drawn his pistol. He fired, killing the two nearest Dervish, then realized he was bleeding from a chest wound, and his head was light. Blood stained his khaki tunic coat in a dull smear where the spear tip had scored him, but the cut was not deep.

The Dervish who had rifles pushed the barrels right into the sides of the British horses and men and pulled the trigger. They hacked at the reins of the cavalry troopers, and at the legs of their horses. They brandished their cruel swords and slashed until the crush of the collision prevented their use. Then many simply threw themselves at the troopers with daggers, or pulled them from the saddle to choke the life out of them. Most attempting this received a bullet from a pistol, and Churchill, fired, killing at least five Dervish before he felt the cold hard steel of a killing knife in his back, and the strength of his legs gave out. He fell into the throng of writhing men and horses, weak and in pain.

A stillness settled over him, and he lay upon three of the four men he had gunned down in the struggle. There, in that nightmare of pain and agony, he stared into the open eyes of one he had fired at. The man looked at him, fear in his eyes there at the edge of death. Then Churchill saw the light and energy in those eyes flare up briefly... *rage, rage against the dying of the light,* he thought, and then they dimmed and closed. He now felt his own awareness fading, his vision dimming, heart slowing, and his consciousness waning into a cold darkness. While the greater part of the 21st pushed on through, he was one of those that failed to reach the other side, and now three other Dervish started hacking at his back with their swords. They were the comrades of those he had gunned down, and they sought retribution, but he felt none of those cruel blows. His soul had already left his body. It hovered over the scene briefly, faded away, like a dying trumpet call, and was gone. History took a deep breath, and sighed in its wake.

Time shivered and shook with each blow on Churchill's back, for this was in no way supposed to happen here. Churchill was to have been one of the lucky riders to break through unscathed, just as Colonel Martin had, riding through without even holding a weapon, but something had changed, something was different. Osman Digna was to have held that *khor* with only a thousand men. It was Sheikh Ali who tripled that force with his appeal to the Khalifa. Because of that, this Prime Mover on all the history yet to unfold during his life was struck down.

Aboard the Gunboat *Nasr*, Sir Roger Ames thought he felt a palpable shock wave emanate out from the collision of that cavalry charge with the Dervish. He felt an impending disaster, a sense that some fundamental supporting beam in the history had been sheared away and now lay broken in that shallow *khor*, though he could not know that Churchill had fallen at that hour.

Yet he felt it, doom, calamity, the twisting and breaking of taut cords of fate and destiny; the shattering of all Churchill would do in the days ahead. No one knew it just yet, but everything would be different now—*everything*. Sir Roger had labored to save Beatty, and then to bring the gunboat *Nasr* to that flank, because he had known what Colonel Martin would do here. Even now the gunners started firing at the Dervish in the *khor*, the Maxim guns chattering out their death knell. But it was too late, too late, too late, just as the last expedition to push this far up the Nile into Sudan had been too late to save Gordon. England lost a much loved hero with Gordon, but here a man of even greater stature lay prostrate and cleaved by swords and spears, each killing blow a deep stab at the history yet to come.

Riderless horses stood among the surviving troopers, some with blood streaming from as many as ten or twelve wounds. Troopers saw their own horses' legs and sides bleeding from gashes, many limping. 65 troopers and five officers, Churchill among them, had been swept off their horses in that crush and killed. More than a hundred of their horses had already fallen and died.

The troopers looked back at the Dervish, who still glared at them, with both sides showing grudging respect for the valor and bravery of their foes. The Dervish line had already started to close the great gap that had been forced in it by that charge. As Martin's cavalry began to reform, the Dervish began leveling their broad tipped spears, ready to receive another charge should it come.

By some miracle, Colonel Martin had survived the fray, but seeing the cost of that charge, he was loathe to launch another. Instead he would take his men away to maneuver towards the river and find the extreme flank of the Dervish in that depression. There he chose ground, dismounted his men, and let them pour carbine fire into the *khor*. The *Nasr* was just off that flank, and its six Maxim guns raked the *khor* mercilessly, joined by a six pounder and then a twelve pounder cannon. That was how Sir Roger had hoped to save Churchill, for he was to have survived that first plunging collision. The gunboat was to have kept him from any further possibility of harm where Colonel Martin stood now. But it was too late. Churchill already lay dead, and though Sir Roger did not yet know this, he could feel in his gut that something was terribly wrong.

This fire was too much for the brave Dervish to bear, and they withdrew towards the ridge of Jebel Surgham. Among them was their leader, Osman Digna, who had not shirked from the fight this time. As the Dervish fled, Colonel Martin was left with his dead.

In his own account of this engagement, Churchill once wrote that he had come through horse and all, completely unscathed, as if Time and Fate had conspired to save him, surrounding him with a nexus of peace and preservation. He had no stain of blood on his uniform or helmet, and not the slightest wound, nor even a bruise. Here it was all a different throw of the dice, and young Winston lay dead in the Dervish throng, four of his assailants dead around him in a ghastly embrace, his blood now flowing into the Sands of Honor in that shallow *khor*. The consequences of this single death were terrifying to contemplate.

Sir Roger would not know the fullness of this disaster for some time, though he labored now to get off the gunboat and reach the shore. His intent was to get to Martin's cavalry and see for himself if Churchill was unharmed. Churchill had written that his mind seemed to shut out all sound as the charge carried him through the Dervish line unscathed. *"The yells of the enemy, the shouts of the soldiers, the firing of many shots, the clashing of sword and spear, were unnoticed by the senses; unregistered by the brain."* Yet a great shockwave was rippling far into the distant future, with seismic effect that could not be fully known for decades—a Heisenberg Wave...

One man, slated to have died, was Lieutenant Grenfell. He had every promise for a sterling military career ahead, and now he would have that time, while Churchill died in his place, and surrendered the next 57 years he was to have lived in this world to the void.

"What's wrong sir?" said Ian Thomas as the two men finally made shore, sloshing out of the Nile.

"I can't say as I know, Mister Thomas, but I've got a feeling in the pit of my stomach that something terrible has happened here—utterly terrible. And knowing what was at risk, I can only guess at what it may be.

"What sir? Kitchener looks to have won his battle. Look, his regiments are coming out of the zeriba and advancing in open columns on the plain."

Sir Roger's eyes narrowed at this. "The fool!" he breathed. "Come, let us get to that group of men there, the remnant of the 21st Lancers. I must find Mister Churchill, god save him, or all has been lost here."

He started off towards the dismounted cavalry, but with each step he and Ian took, it seemed he was walking into deepening shadow and fear.

Sir Roger would soon learn why, for Great Britain had just lost its Roaring Lion, and his death was a finality that would now be on Sir Roger to try and reverse.

"Oh, dear God," he said, weeping to hear the news of Churchill's death. "What in the world have we done?"

Chapter 23
Lawrence Berkeley Labs, May 12, 2023
The Meridian Project

Kelly Ramer came rushing into the main control room, a warning in his eyes. He was the computer savant of the project team, and he had just been monitoring his Golem module in the other room.

"Trouble," he said flatly, his tone accentuating the gravity of his discovery.

Chief project physicist Paul Dorland looked up and cocked his head. "Golem 7 again?"

"Right," said Kelly, "but six more chimed in as well." He was speaking of his so called Golem Modules, programs that were kept running 24/7 to ceaselessly monitor recorded history, and compare it to that which was stored in a vast database, the Touchstone database they kept inviolate. Any difference was flagged and a colored display would change the line of causality for this Meridian to indicate the gravity of the discrepancy. In this case, Kelly had seen the line suddenly go from a sedate calm green to blood red. It was a sure fire sign that someone had tampered with the past.

"Big variation," he breathed. "Where's Nordhausen?" He spied the history professor through the glass wall in an adjacent room talking with Maeve. "Robert!" he shouted. "I need you—now!"

Kelly was not one to ever much lose his cool, and his manner now alarmed Paul, who sat up, and then looked over his shoulder to see Nordhausen coming through the sliding glass door.

"Yes, yes, hold your horses, Kelly. Can't a man enjoy a simple cup of tea? What is it? What's the matter with you?"

"1898!" said Kelly quickly. "The golems just flagged a big variation, late in the year 1898. What was happening? Where should I look?"

"Late in the year? What month?"

"September, that's all I got before running in here to look for you and sound off."

"Let's see," said Nordhausen, lowering his glasses from his forehead to the bridge of his nose. "No use trying to pull things out of memory. Here, let me log in to one of the research terminals." He settled into a chair before a computer screen and started typing. He scrolled down to September and read the first data he saw:

1898: Sep 1, *Lord Kitchener's army bombarded Omdurman, Sudan. Lt. Winston Churchill approached Omdurman, the rebel capital, as a scout in the cavalry along with the rest of Gen. Kitchener's army of 25,000 men. [see Sep 2]*

1898: Sep 2, *Anglo-Egyptian lines under General Kitchener were charged by 50,000 fanatical Dervishes, which were mowed down by howitzers, machine guns and rifles. Lt. Winston Churchill led one of the last (and most useless) cavalry charges in history. Sir Herbert Kitchener led the British to victory over the Mahdists at Omdurman and took Khartoum. The Dervishes left 11,000 dead and 16,000 wounded. In 1899 Winston Churchill published The River War, An Account of the Reconquest of the Sudan. This was the 1st use of the machine gun in battle.'*

"A few inaccuracies there," said Dorland. "Churchill didn't lead that charge, but he was part of it. Colonel Martin was the commander of 21st Lancers there. And also—this wasn't the first use of Machine Guns. Kitchener had them weeks earlier at Atbara. But I'll concede they had a great impact on the outcome of that battle."

"Could this be it? The continuum line just turned blood red, right at September of 1898. Anything else of any significance happen that month Robert?"

"Kitchener destroyed *Mahdi's* tomb in Omdurman, they pulled General Electric out of the DOW, 20,000 Paris construction workers went on strike, Howard W. Florey purified penicillin, George Gershwin was born... not much else."

"Then it had to be Omdurman," said Paul. "It's a little known battle these days, but it was actually very significant. The line went red, you say? How bad is that."

"It's only got one more color shift after that—black, and you know what that means."

"Death of a Prime Mover," came a voice. Maeve Lindford, head of Outcomes & Consequences had drifted in, joining the others, a concerned look on her face. Who was there, Robert?"

"Well, I just read out that Churchill was present."

"And David Beatty," said Paul, "not to mention Kitchener himself."

"Who was Beatty?" asked Maeve.

"The Admiral commanding the British fleet at Jutland, for one thing," Paul had long studied history in terms of its decisive battles.

"Was he ever in danger?" Maeve was fishing.

"Well, a bullet practically knocked his pith helmet off, but he wasn't injured."

"What about Churchill?"

"He was in the charge made by the 21st Lancers, but came through without injury."

"That's what's in our Touchstone database," said Kelly, "but the Golems are screaming mad. There's been a big variation. Something's wrong and it starts right there, September 1898."

"Anything else, Robert?"

"Not much, the Spanish American war was already over by September, and in Asia, the Boxer Rebellion was brewing but it would not get real traction for another two years in 1900."

"Well, can't we fine tune the variation on the Golem Modules, Kelly?"

"It needs time. I just got the preliminary alert that something had changed."

"How soon before we can look at source data?"

"Probably an hour. The Golems are collating now; sampling resonance, and running things into your station at Outcomes & Consequences, Maeve."

"Alright, we're all here," said Maeve, "so let's get on this gentlemen. Robert, you get with Kelly on the Golems and see about Churchill and Beatty—or anyone else who might have been involved. I'll see what sifts through to Outcomes. Paul?"

"I'll start prepping the system and open a Nexus Point here. With our combined intent, and capability with the Arch, we can probably stop Heisenberg wave propagation here and spare the future a bad time-quake if this is as serious as it looks at first blush."

"Good." Maeve was all business as she headed to her station.

Within 40 minutes they were starting to get altered source data, and the mystery did not take long to solve. It was Churchill, just as Maeve had feared all along, and now she was looking hard at the events in the man's life in the years preceding 1898, trying to find some place where they might easily lever him out of his trip to Egypt and the Sudan.

Kelly was watching the red line as it progressed forward from 1898. It stayed red, a dire warning, all through the First World War, and then, as the line reached 1939, the color deepened to dark burgundy, and then went black in 1941. It stayed that way, obscuring all the history of WWII. That was trouble indeed.

They were getting detailed information now, and yes, Churchill was reported to have been killed at Omdurman in the charge of the 21st Lancers. So he would never become the Foreign Secretary and then First Lord of the Admiralty presiding over the naval race against Germany. Nor would he be there in 1939 to counter the appeasement of Neville Chamberlain. Landmark photos that existed in the Touchstone Database were gone in this new data, never taken.

There was no photo of Churchill walking stoically through the ruins of Coventry Cathedral in 1941, or sitting on the quarterdeck of HMS *Prince of Wales* with the US President Roosevelt later that same year. The famous Tehran conference photo of the big three, Stalin, Roosevelt and Churchill, was never taken with Churchill, in that third chair sat another man, unknown to Maeve at first glance.

Churchill never walked with his riding crop through the amphitheater at Carthage in North Africa of 1943. Nor would he ever meet with an enterprising Russian Captain in the deep desert, and learn much of what was to come in the terrible second World War. And Churchill was never there in the boat next to General Montgomery, crossing the Rhine in 1945. It was all gone, expunged, lost, eradicated, every footstep in his life after Omdurman, every thought that ever passed through his mind, every word he would write, every speech he would give had never happened; and Great Britain was so very much impoverished with his absence, particularly in those crucial war years where Churchill became the symbol of stubborn British resistance.

It was all gone. All his books had vanished from the annals of the world: *The History of the English Speaking Peoples, The River War, My African Journey, The Gathering Storm, Never Give in, Triumph and Tragedy, The Grand Alliance, the Hinge of Fate, The great Republic, the Power of Words.* All were words never even written; gone.

Maeve could not bring herself to see what his removal from the Meridian had actually done to the rest of the history, but she knew it could only make Britain's fortunes darker and more perilous. She lowered her head with fatigue. How to fix this? How do you replace Britain's Irrepressible Roaring Lion? She knew they had to *prevent* this death, no matter what the cost, and that work had to be done *before* September of 1898. In her mind the object of all their efforts must be to prevent Churchill from ever getting into the 21st Lancers in the first place. But how? She would have to get with Robert Nordhausen and scour the history of those years.

Far away, in another space and time, another man was sitting with the misery of this same problem, even as General Kitchener completed the route of the Khalifa's Mahdist Army and marched on Omdurman and Khartum—Sir Roger Ames.

West bank of the Nile, noon, 2 SEP, 1898

When Sir Roger and Ian Thomas finally found the mutilated body of Churchill, the full weight of what had happened settled on Sir Roger's shoulders. They joined two other troopers to give him a burial in that *khor*.

"This is terrible," Sir Roger lamented. "A catastrophe! I knew he was here, but gambled that he would ride on through the Dervish as I knew he had in this history—unscathed. I just did not take heed of the principle of Inherent Variation."

"What is that sir?" asked Ian, hoping the time theory would not be too thorny.

"Well, history is not fixed, as we have both seen well enough in these adventures. It might be scraped into the grooves like a vinyl recording, but it's subject to change. Imagine a song that might vary slightly every time it is played, in a note or two, its beat or tempo, or in some accompanying harmony. Very odd, yes? That's the principle of Inherent Variation. It doesn't work that way with music, but it does with causality and time progression. Every time an event plays out, it is liable to change somewhat. Most changes are small, but as I have come to know, small things can often have big consequences. This is a perfect example."

"But sir, what could we have possibly done to change this outcome and see Churchill dead like this?"

"Oh, it was no direct action on our parts, save one—I allowed this history to replay by coming here and interfering. You see, it's nothing we did. In fact, I should not have had to do anything at all to see Churchill come through that cavalry charge alive. That was the outcome as I knew it. Yet in allowing it to replay, I permitted the whole matter to be ceded over to Mother Time and her lovers, Fate and Destiny. They are the real culprits here, not you or I. Every time events replay, they are subject to change—an inherent tendency to see variations, like mutation in cellular replication, I suppose. Even the replication of our own DNA is subject to this variation and mutation. The replication process makes mistakes, which is why we see all this great variation of life about us here, men, horses, birds, trees, scrub, grass, insects—the whole lot. It's this sublime error made by DNA that gives rise to all of this. And in temporal matters, the principle of Inherent Variation on replay also has a life saving role. It is what spins off alternate threads in the history after a major deliberate intervention is badly resolved and creates a Gordian Knot."

"But you said yourself, sir, we made *no* deliberate intervention to see Churchill to death's door here."

"Correct, of course not. I was here to look after him but I was remiss. I just assumed he would come through that charge unharmed as before, but Inherent Variation changed that outcome. I thought we'd help by getting the *Nasr* here to provide heavy cover fire for Colonel Martin's troopers after their charge. After all, there were still about 2000 Dervish in this depression, and the cavalry remained in grave danger. Many of their horses had fallen and those they still had came to near madness with that charge. There was a real chance their rifle fire would not hold Osman Digna's men at bay. So I persuaded Lieutenant Hood to bring his gunboat here and lend a hand. That seems to have worked, but alas, with Inherent Variation, the damage to the continuum was already done. Churchill's death is a hard blow."

"Can't we just reset things again sir, like you explained before?"

"Oh Yes, we can and we must go through the motions at least. Yet whether or not that will save Churchill is in no way certain."

"Why sir? I thought it would reset, just as it was."

"Oh, it will, but as I said—you and I did nothing to cause Churchill's death, save one thing—we permitted this battle to replay here. Inherent Variation then saw Churchill killed in that charge, and that set a Precedent."

"A Precedent, sir?"

"Yes, it created an outcome that Time can now see as plausible. As in legal matters, Mister Thomas, once a precedent is establish in Law, it has the ability to influence the outcome of other cases. Before we came here, there was no such instance where Churchill died here. Yet in all things, and this is the great mystery, Ian, in all things, every possible variation in the progression of events is like a number on a roulette wheel, and every number has an equal chance to come up. This death might not have happened at all; it might not have happened in each of ten more replays of this battle, but this time, it did. Churchill's number came up."

"And if we reset now, sir?"

"Then we spin the wheel again, but now a Precedent stands where this death occurs, which puts just a little more spin on that roulette ball, and makes it ever so much more likely that Churchill might die here again—even in a reset. That may not be so, which is why we must definitely reset the table, but then again, the Precedent might cause a repeat of this death—or it might even kill David Beatty as well, for all I know, or the two of us, even with absolutely no interference from us at all. This is the great risk we take in tampering with time, and I should have been more mindful of this possibility.

"Well, I suppose we'd best get to the meeting point with Sheikh Ali and own up. Then we reset and just hope for the best. Come we'd must get to Omdurman before Kitchener desecrates the place."

Chapter 24

There was chaos for a time in Omdurman, until the infusion of Khaki clad British troops restored order. It had been agreed that Sheikh Ali would meet Sir Roger at the *Mahdi's* tomb to settle their game, and this before Kitchener came to the place. In making this arrangement, each man pledged to be the guarantor of the other's well being. Sir Roger would see no harm come to the Sheikh if they arrived with the British in charge, and vice versa if the Dervish still held Omdurman when the meeting was convened. The former was the case, and British regulars were already in the city. The Khalifa was escaping out into the desert with about 30,000 survivors, and with 20,000 left dead or wounded behind him. His vision had been shattered, and not even the *Mahdi's* assertion that this would be his great victory held true.

The Sheikh found Sir Roger outside the city, and they entered by the north gate. Sir Roger told the nearest British Officer that the Sheikh was a personal acquaintance, and had provided much information on the Khalifa's movements, so they were let inside the shrine of the *Mahdi's* tomb without any problems. It had already been pounded by Beatty's gunboats, half the dome collapsed, which distressed the Sheikh a good deal when they entered and saw the rubble and broken stone scattered all over the interior.

"Regrettable," said Sir Roger, "And I must tell you, it will get much worse when Kitchener arrives. The man is out for vengeance, and he'll go so far as to disinter the *Mahdi* and decapitate his corpse, in reprisal for what happened to Gordon. The body will then be thrown in the Nile, but the *Mahdi's* skull, that will be taken by Kitchener for use as an ink well on his desk. Then he'll completely demolish this tomb."

"Barbaric," said Ali. "Is it any wonder why our people gather in such numbers to attack you British? This is *our* land! Why are you even here?"

"To keep out the French, to restore lost honor, to avenge Gordon, to prop the British Empire back up in Africa—take any reason you prefer. History isn't pretty, in fact it is indeed barbaric, and all to often. If it is any consolation, Lord Kitchener will later have to write a formal letter of apology to his Queen for what he did, and what he permitted his men to do here."

"So how do you judge our game?"

"As a terrible loss—on my part."

"On your part? But you and your soldiers have the victory. We are chased from Omdurman to see its streets sullied by the tread of Infidels, and this precious tomb will be desecrated. It is unbearable. I strove mightily to bring the men of Sheikh ed-Din and Ali Wad Hulu to the center to join our last attack against your general's foolish deployments. But their men were too headstrong, and I failed. So I must judge your side the victor here."

"No, my good man, that is honorable, but we have suffered a loss greater than all you describe. There was a man, and you wagered to secure the diamond that was made from his remains, so great was he. He was to have lived here, and so I did nothing to disturb that, yet as it happened, he fell..."

"Who was he? Where did he fall?" asked Ali.

"On the river flank, where the British cavalry charged the Dervish hidden in a low depression. This man was named Churchill, and you know of whom I speak."

"Churchill? I see... I had no idea he was there." The Sheikh was being duplicitous, for he knew that very well. It had been his urging the Khalifa to reinforce that flank that thickened the Dervish ranks in that *khor*. Was he now responsible for this great man's death?

"Here then," Sir Roger said solemnly. "I give all that remains of him to you willingly, and honor my debt. For in failing to prevent his death, I judge I have lost everything. What was Omdurman? A city in the desert. What was Khartum? An abandoned city, desolate of life and haunted by Gordon's ghost. But see in this the obstinate fervor for vengeance, and how it can lead both single men and armies to such carnage? The Dervish saw 20,000 casualties in this battle. I weep for so many dead left on this field that will not have the decency of a burial. And more, I weep for the loss of one bright star in the skies of British history—Winston Churchill."

Sir Roger reached into his pocket and handed the Sheikh a bundled cloth where he had kept both the Churchill Diamond and that of Wellington, wrapped round with a simple white silk handkerchief.

The Sheikh took it, his eyes glittering like the gemstone, but there was only one diamond there now. Sir Roger saw that and was struck by the realization.

"You are magnanimous, even in victory." Ali said nothing of how he had convinced the Khalifa to reinforce the river flank, but inwardly, he felt ashamed. "This is the Churchill Diamond?"

Sir Roger squinted at the Diamond, seeing the faint blue tint to it that told him it was the Wellington stone. Of course, he thought. If Churchill died here, then he was never buried at Bladon, so Mr. Thomas never could have found his remains there, and my Churchill diamond could have never been created. He confessed this to the Sheikh. "I'm sorry, but that one is Wellington. I hope you will accept it."

"Of course," said Ali.

"I ask only one thing of you, Sheikh. You must agree to reset these events, erase all our interventions, and allow them to play out one more time, with neither of us on the field of battle to interfere in any way. The outcome may not differ, but if by chance this one man—Churchill—should live, then the darkness that has fallen upon my soul would lift and I could breathe again. Will you do this? If so then you will have the Churchill diamond as well."

"Of course, my friend." Ali knew he had to agree, thinking now that he was responsible for this death, and that it was no failing on his opponent's part. "I will abide by the most important rule of any temporal game—*reset the board*; leave all as it was before you came."

"Then *you* are magnanimous, Sheikh, a worthy man. Very well, you have your prize, so let us both return to the moment when we first met here." That was well down river, below Berber, before the battle of Atbara. As it was some great distance, Sir Roger said he could gain passage there on a steamship, if the Sheikh would come.

"Me? Go on the river aboard one of those abominations?"

"There is much you might learn about them, and the world that made them."

"Oh, I know all about that world. You forget I hail from Saudi Arabia, Sir Roger. I know it all too well, which is why I came here, to a time when the fervor of the faithful was great, where men still believed in honor, and where they were willing to risk all for their unshakable faith in Allah. But I will come with you, if your British friends will permit me." Ali fingered the hardness of the Wellington Diamond, amazed at its size and perfection. He felt like a thief in taking it from Sir Roger, and his shame forced him to acquiesce and agree to completely reset this game.

"I can arrange it," said Sir Roger. They would need to reach a time one day prior to the day they first met. That would prevent that meeting, and erase all their interventions in this history.

"Come, let us leave here and ride to the river."

And they did.

Sir Roger's only play at the end was to retreat to the beginning and reset. Then he would just hope fervently that Churchill would survive that charge. But back in Berkely California, the Meridian Team was already making other plans.

Lawrence Berkely labs, Meridian Project, 2023

"There's no use trying to alter the outcome of the battle," said Maeve. "Besides, it would be too dangerous. We had our desert romp with Lawrence of Arabia. What we need to do is find a good place to intervene in the years prior to the battle."

"And do what?" asked Paul.

"That should be obvious. We must see that Churchill never joins the 21st Lancers, or goes to Egypt to partake in that madness. Removing him from the scene of the battle is the only way to be sure about saving him. Otherwise we'll have to face things like Inherent Variation and Precedent now that he was found dead on that field. That violated the standing order of things, so it had to be a case of Inherent Variation."

"Agreed," said Paul. He had devised this time theory, and all these terms were listed in a nice lexicon now. "But where to remove Churchill from this campaign?"

"I was thinking about trying to prevent his posting to the 21st Lancers. Why did he join them as opposed to some other unit?"

"Because Churchill's program at Sandhurst made him a Cavalry cadet. So when he went to the War Office looking for a new assignment after leaving India, they naturally posted him to a Cavalry unit. He had no training with the infantry."

"I see... How can we stop this? That has to be the job for us now. You know how determined that man was when he set his mind on something."

That was certainly true. Churchill had been military minded from an early age as a boy, and he was somewhat of a visionary. He had an inherent belief in himself, and at one point in his schooling, he actually said this to a schoolmate: "I have a wonderful idea of where I shall be eventually.... London will be in danger, and in the high position I shall occupy, it will fall to me to save the Capital and save the Empire."

That prognostication was somewhat eerie, as if Churchill could actually peer into his distant future and see the fate that awaited him. It shook Maeve when she read that in her research on the man. Even the boy knew he would one day be great. He was a Prime Mover, through and through, and how could they hope to derail the sure course of his life, even if it was to save it so that future could actually be lived?

"The man was a bloodhound for danger," said Maeve. "He got himself into the 4th Hussars, and when they went to India, what does he do? He rides off with the Malakand Field Force on the North-West frontier of India, intending, as he put it, 'to establish a reputation for personal courage.' Probably aimed at greasing the path for his career in politics. One had to be *somebody* in England to get into Parliament or a post like Foreign Secretary, and certainly Prime Minister."

"A Bloodhound for danger?" said Paul, "Yes, the Malakand Field Force. It was commanded by a General Bindon Blood."

"After that Churchill set his eye on Africa, and began getting all his connections to lobby for his posting to Egypt, including his mother. Ah, here's something... Kitchener didn't like Churchill, and he was against his being posted to Egypt. He thought Churchill was just a climber, out to use the post to serve his own interests, and not to really serve the Army."

"Well, he was right about that," said Paul. "Could we use that? After all, Kitchener will be Commander in Chief there."

"It wouldn't be easy." Maeve was trying to imagine a scenario where they could use the arch to get to Egypt of 1898, and then so poison Kitchener's mind against Churchill that he never gets to ride with the 21st Lancers.

"Churchill was posing as a war correspondent," she said.

"Yes," said Paul, "and Kitchener hated them."

"Could we use that?"

"How? The problem is where do we fit in to get on the scene in any capacity where Kitchener would even listen to us? How would we even get close enough to his headquarters to do something like that? Tourists would not be welcome on a venture into the Sudan."

As they tussled with this problem, in came Kelly Ramer with a new report.

"Something is happening," he said. "The root of the alert line is changing color. It's moved from Red to orange in the last five minutes, and I think it will progress from Amber to yellow soon."

"What does that mean?" asked Maeve.

"That the situation is not as grave as we first thought. I'm trying to fish out more source material from the Golems. Who knows, we may find Churchill alive and well after all. I think there's a replay in progress."

He shrugged. "Then again, we might not."

The real news would come minutes later, when the Arch itself signaled that there was a breach underway within its domain. That was rare, something that shouldn't be happening at all. Paul checked the power track and saw it had been idling at 40% for the last hour, just enough to create a Nexus Point here, but now it was rising. The Arch was programmed to provide power required to manage and maintain a breach of the continuum, but they had not ordered or programmed any such activity. The only way this could be happening was if someone was inbound, trying to use the Arch as an anchor for a temporal shift initiated somewhere else, at some other time.

He had been reaching, reflexively, for the power control lever, intending to pull it back, but realizing what must be happening, he pushed it forward instead.

"I'm taking the Arch to 80%," he told Maeve and Kelly. "Would one of you go down and have a look—but don't enter the Arch shift zone."

"What's going on?" asked Maeve, confused.

"We've got unexpected company. Someone is coming through the Arch."

Maeve looked at Kelly, quite surprised. Then she took him by the arm and off they went. She was now very curious as to who this was, but she did not want to go down there, creeping up to the edge of infinity with the Arch up at near full power. So Kelly was going too.

Part IX

The Uninvited Guest

"If history starts as a guest list, it has a tendency to end like the memory of a drunken party: misheard, blurred, fragmentary."
— **Sarah Churchwell**

Chapter 25
Lawrence Berkely Labs ~ Meridian Project
May 12, 2023

Maeve and Kelly had taken the elevator down to the Arch, then opened the enormous metal door, thick as that of a bank vault—thicker. Down the hall they could see a kaleidoscope of color wavering and dancing on the walls. There in the chamber opening on the left, there was a great metal arch, and the approach to it was clearly marked with thick lines on the concrete floor that delineated the Arch Domain, the area that would be affected by any opening of the continuum. The Arch opened a rift in time, and anyone within that domain could travel in time to the destination in Spacetime that had been programmed into the system's controlling computers.

The power required was enormous, and 95% of the operating cost of the project was paid to Pacific Gas & Electric. It was a love hate relationship. The power company loved receiving that payment, but hated the drain and stress it put on its systems. Because it was crucial to keep the power at certain levels during a shift, backup generators running on diesel were always operating when the Arch cycled up to anything more then 40% power. Even if all outside power was suddenly lost, the generators could hold the power level steady enough, long enough, for the system operators to slowly power down or abort a planned shift.

Shifting was dangerous! The stresses it put on the human body were legion. They had all shifted in the Arch numerous times, but Paul, Kelly, and Maeve could never open their eyes during a shift or they would suffer intense dizziness and nausea. Only Nordhausen could bear it, and he routinely commented on the incredible beauty of the light show as the continuum opened. The Arch was playing with fundamental physical forces, right down to the Quantum level. Yes, it was dangerous, the only known place on earth in 2023 that was capable of doing what it did, and still a closely guarded secret.

To the world outside the complex, the project was just conducting physics experiments. No one knew they involved the possibility of traveling in time.

This situation was now much different than a programmed shift. There were no coordinates governing it, for it was incoming, a shift originating from somewhere else, something that had happened only one time before. Then it had been a visit from the future, perhaps the only place where anyone would have the technology and knowhow to do this. Paul was certain that was the case again—someone in the future was using their Arch as an anchoring point to help them shift.

As he monitored the incoming shift, he was wondering who it was this time. Was Mister Graves returning for some reason? Why the need to use the Arch here? That told him that something was wrong in the years ahead to require this assistance; or that there was some king of temporal anomaly between this moment and the one the incoming Walkers were coming from, whoever they were. He would know soon enough.

Maeve had gone to the medic station and picked up a first aid kit, which included an air syringe with mild stimulants in case anyone arrived unconscious or injured in any way. Heaven forbid that anyone would arrive here dead. She knew the danger.

She put on a set of goggles and handed one to Kelly. The lenses were designed to filter out certain wavelengths of light, making the dizzy whirl of light and color palatable. Wearing them, she was able to focus and see the actual manifestation of a Time Traveler, there, just beyond the thick yellow line on the floor that marked the outermost boundary of the Arch Domain, the edge of infinity, as she thought of it. They also wore a set of wireless headphones to muffle the terrible sound, and allow them to hear anything Paul was saying as he monitored the shift from the control room above.

A figure appeared, first a slowly forming shadow that gained substance with each passing second until it bore the shape of a human being, a man, wearing a full trench coat and felt hat, and dangling from his right hand, he carried a briefcase. His other hand held a pipe, and as the sound diminished in a sickening descent, as if it was being sucked into a drain, she could actually see a thin trail of smoke rising from the bowl of the pipe.

The man moved, swayed just a bit, but recovered his balance easily. He turned towards Kelly and Maeve and spoke. "Ah," he said. "Do I have the pleasure of meeting Miss Lindford... and Mister Ramer, I think?"

"Indeed, said Maeve." The sound of the arch was winding down and down, the lights gone now, the power moderating as the level reduced to 40% again. Paul gave them the all clear, and Maeve noted how the man waited patiently, not moving further until they started approaching him. *This one has moved in time before,* she knew immediately.

"Maeve Linford," she said removing the headset with one hand and extending the other to take the visitor's hand. Kelly introduced himself and also shook the man's hand.

"Please forgive this unscheduled intrusion," said the visitor. "I'll explain why it was necessary in a moment. My name is Director Pavel Kamenski."

"Director?" said Maeve, a question in her eyes.

"Yes, Director of Temporal Intelligence and Outcomes & Consequences in my Milieu. It's a pleasure to meet the Founding Fathers, and the mother of all consequences, Maeve Lindford."

There was no question now that this man was from the future. None. Maeve smiled and pointed the way, and now the three of them would make their way back up to the Arch Control room. While in the elevator, Maeve punched the intercom panel and notified Paul.

"All's well," she informed. "We're coming up, and with a Director Pavel Kamenski."

Paul scratched his head. He knew that name... He quickly googled him—Pavel Kamenski, Deputy Director of the old Russian KGB at one time. He vanished mysteriously some years ago while in retirement at Vladivostok. How in the world could he be here? What did Russian intelligence want from them? How did they even know the Arch complex existed here, and how could they have possibly targeted it like this with an incoming shift—and from where? One question piled on top of another in his mind.

The three arrived from below, and Kamenski smiled, shaking Paul's hand. "A great pleasure, Professor Dorland, the man who first opened Time. This is such an honor." Nordhausen came in, very curious, and introductions were made. Then they all went to the nearest conference room, where Robert had been flipping through a pile of books involving Churchill and Kitchener's campaign in the Sudan.

"I beg your pardon," said Kamenski. "We are not ones to make unscheduled visits like this, but it was necessary. We needed an anchor here, or I could not be here at all."

"Why so?"

"Surely you must be aware of an aberration in the continuum. We know your Golem system looks for such things."

"Yes," said Maeve, glad to have a kindred soul here with them now. "We've been looking at the year 1898, during Kitchener's campaign in the Sudan."

"Precisely," said Kamenski. "Then you know what happened—to Winston Churchill."

"As things stand now," said Maeve. "We were hoping that might change. Kelly had just reported some retrogression of the color shift of this event."

"Just a temporal flux around it. If you look again, you'll see that things remain very bad. Here, may I show you?" Kamenski opened his brief and took out a pad device, on it was a colored display much like their own monitor. It was zoomed in to the first half of the 20th Century. They leaned forward as the Director pointed out the problem. "This is what it resolves to in the future—my point of origin, though you will please excuse me if I cannot say exactly when that is. It's a security protocol. A remnant from the Time War."

"Well I hope to God that's settled down."

"Oh yes, we have an understanding now with the Assassins, and a Peace has held since you first forced it on them. That said, things happen, and I'm afraid we are as much to blame as anyone else, and by we, I mean the Russians."

Maeve's eyes narrowed. "You mean the ship—*Kirov*, not Putin and his ilk."

"Exactly. We have found *Kirov* to be most useful, and I've come to Captain Fedorov with one or two missions that helped us a great deal. That man is very clever, yes, very intelligent and with an excellent sense for temporal mechanics. Well," Kamenski slid the pad device closer to the others. "You'll see how the line deepens to black in 1939, and how it remains so all through the Second World War. That's a Gordian Knot, and it casts a rather significant Penumbra forward, so profound that we had to have the assistance of your Arch here for me to get even this far back."

To illustrate this, Kamenski tapped a spot on his screen and they saw a larch arcing overlay of charcoal grey extending well beyond WWII on the continuum.

"This Arch has a lot of power," Kamenski continued. "From here you are well forward of the crack and snap of the Heisenberg Wave. From here, you can still get back to the point of divergence in question, which would be the death of Sir Winston Churchill, on the second day of September, 1898, in the Sudan."

"We were just discussing that, and trying to reach a solution. Then Kelly reported the color shift from the original variance was lightening, so we were hopeful this might self correct."

"It doesn't," said Kamenski flatly. "What you were seeing was the probability of correction due to a reset operation performed by the Agent responsible for this anomaly—a certain Duke, Sir Roger Ames, and his associate."

"Jean Michel Fortier?" said Maeve.

"Not any longer. He died on their last misadventure. You may have picked it up a few years earlier, say in 1842?"

"Ah," said Maeve, "The Opium Wars. Yes, we saw that, but it did not seem to cause much of a stir."

"Thankfully so," said Kamenski, "because those are now permanent variations woven into this Meridian. We got very lucky, because those outcomes closely paralleled the actual history. The Duke was not able to reset his intervention there, because this other man, Fortier, died before they could do that. Well, this sort of meddling gets our attention rather quickly, and we tracked this man, Sir Roger, as far as Calicut in India. Then his trail went dark, until this happened." Kamenski gestured to the pad device. "Quite a mess, wouldn't you agree? And it originates in a very bad spot—1898, because we had to run an operation ourselves in 1900. That has become a very sensitive region on the Meridian. "

"Another operation? Whatever for?" asked Maeve.

"You won't know for a while yet, but a Chinese destroyer goes missing in the Tsushima Strait soon, and it causes quite a problem. So I had to call on the Russians, and I mean the officers and crew of *Kirov*, to lend a hand. Now I think we may need them again for this trouble in 1898."

"What could they do?" asked Maeve. "How would a battlecruiser help with this?"

"Well now," said Kamenski. "You good people ran a mission once when you discovered the *Bismarck* had not been sunk on its maiden voyage. Yes?"

"Correct," said Paul. "I was point man on that mission. It's how we reversed the second Palma Event, when Professor Nordhausen dug up the genealogy and identity for the man responsible for it."

"And refresh me on that, if you would."

Robert sighed, and spoke up now, for he was the one who had nailed down the suspect responsible for the eruption of the Cumbre Vieja volcano, which had one flank that collapsed into the sea to send a massive tsunami all the way across the Atlantic that smashed the Eastern seaboard of the United States. He explained it to Kamenski: "The eruption wasn't a natural event, but a willful one, because the man I ferreted out of the history managed to set off a nuclear warhead on the flank of that mountain—Cumbre Vieja. So our team worked to find out who he was, and how to eliminate him from the Meridian, and this we did. Yet it involved that wild naval chase mounted by the Royal Navy to sink the *Bismarck*. When we discovered that had not happened, the mission involved sending Paul back and see if he could bring more assets to bear on the German raider to insure her sinking."

"Otherwise," Paul chimed in, "the *Bismarck* reaches Brest safely, remains undamaged by British air raids, and weeks later it sinks a ship in a British convoy bound for the middle east, and a most important man goes down. The man was supposed to lead a commando raid that ended up killing the father of the operative who engineered this attack on Cumbre Vieja."

"Complicated," said Kamenski, "as these things often are. Well, here's another bit of spice for that stew. This convoy you mention was the back half of the so called "Tiger Convoy," a Winston Special, which is why it had the designation WS."

"Yes," said Paul. "WS-8B."

"Precisely." Kamenski looked from one to the other. "Now then, given what happened in the Sudan in 1898, there *were* no convoys designated 'Winston Specials' in the war. So the *Bismarck* would have had nothing to shoot at."

"Unless the British simply named it something else. Look, we know the ship that was sunk, the *Orduna*, so it should not be difficult to track it down."

"You may find a lot of cards have been shuffled in that deck," said Kamenski. And the British had a lot more on their hands than just the *Bismarck*. The whole progression of the war was skewed without Churchill, and this bit here is a perfect example of why. That man had his thumb in a good many pies. His absence changes everything. The cords of that war are all tangled up now. It's very bad."

Chapter 26

"**I** don't think I could stomach just how bad things got," said Paul. "The question now is this. What can we do about it? We've been trying to find a way to reverse Churchill's death."

"That won't be easy. What were you thinking?"

"Trying to make sure he never gets posted to the 21st Lancers, for a start," said Maeve.

"Ah, but you underestimate the fervor and will of that young man. Even in his youth, Churchill had all the drive and fortitude that made him so formidable when he became the Prime Minister. Let me lead you off that trail. He'll get posted to the 21st. We've tried a number of times to prevent that, but every mission failed. Our last shifts could not get through the Penumbra caused by Churchill's death. so we had to use Agents in place—we have them all over the Meridian, you know, and we could at least send information back, if not our people. The Agents still failed us."

"Is that why you're here?" asked Maeve. "To send someone back from here?"

"Not exactly. We did have one success with Agents in place, but there was a problem. This man, Sir Roger Ames and his accomplice, or rather his opponent. He took up here with a Sheikh Ali, and we have now determined that Ali was affiliated with the Assassin cult."

"The Assassins?" Maeve's eyes flared. "Then they were behind this? *They* killed Churchill?"

"Not directly, but yes, they were trying to encourage that as well, and the two efforts collided and dissipated. We worked it, and managed to get Churchill posted to Kitchener's staff instead of the 21st Lancers, but then found out that he was instructed to carry the order to Colonel Martin to advance on that flank."

"Oh?" said Paul. "I thought it went via heliograph signal."

"Yes, but those signals were always backed up by riders carrying written orders. Churchill was sent, and instead of simply handing off his orders, he saddled up and just joined the Lancers. We've looked at it from a number of angles, and we've come to conclude that the initial replay that resulted in Churchill's death was just a case of Inherent Variation, not a deliberate act. The error was meddling in the first place, which allowed Inherent Variation to become a possibility. Then, once Churchill died, a Precedent was set, and all subsequent interventions aimed at replaying that history now seem to produce the same thing—Churchill's death. It was history that should have been left completely alone, but this Ames fellow has been up to a good deal of mischief. We were going to try something else, but we can't get through the penumbra now being caused by his demise. Hence, I've come here, to get a better vector for a shift."

"What can we do for you?" asked Paul.

"Well, this man Ames has really done it this time. He was mindful enough to reset after he discovered Churchill's death, but that seems to have just made things worse. The reset also saw poor Winston die, and now there is a double Precedent, a groove getting dug just a little deeper in that history. Now we're looking at Ames himself. We know he's a Keyholder. That's what his tampering in the Opium Wars was all about. He was after the master key hidden in the Summer Palace near Peking, and we are certain he found it. That key gives him enormous latitude, almost as if he was in possession of a Time Controller."

"But we thought *you* had the Master Key, and that it was left for the Russian Captain to find aboard *Kirov*."

"I may have boasted about that key, as it was number one in that set of seven, but no, it wasn't a true master key. Yet Ames got his hands on one, and now he can move with very great precision, Tracking the man will be very difficult. We can pick up an opening in the continuum, but we can't get a fix on where it leads until he gets there and does something to cause a variation. Then our systems pick that up, just like your Golem modules, Mister Kelly. So we were able to track him to the Sudan in 1898, then we detected this major change—catastrophic, really."

"Just as we did. We've been in mission ready mode ever since."

"Good for you. Now then, this will get thorny. You ran a mission to reverse the *Bismarck* incident, and to see the ship got sunk on its maiden voyage. Now a good deal is different. If you call up that history, you'll see that *Bismarck* isn't alone. You brought *Rodney* into action on your mission. Yes?"

"I did," said Paul, still proud of that mission. "And I also made a very interesting discovery. You see, *Rodney* had been enroute to the United States, with her hold filled with tons of Gold bullion, and other valuables—like Lord Elgin's marbles. Stashing them away in the tubes under London just wouldn't do. The British wanted them safely out of the war theater. Well, I had occasion to get down below decks on the *Rodney*, and I saw those marbles, one in particular being the Selene Horse. Its case had been jarred, fell, and one side broke open, chipping the statue on one lower corner. There I found a key—a very special key, with microscopic etchings on the shaft indicating geographic coordinates. They were for Gibraltar."

"Yes, the rifts beneath St. Michaels Cave," said Kamenski. "This Mister Ames already had the Lindesfarne key, which took him to 1815 for Waterloo, but he dearly wanted that key hidden in the Selene Horse, as it activated all the many rifts under the Rock of Gibraltar. Every last one led to a place in the 19th century—the Age of Imperialism. So it's no surprise this man Ames turns up at the Battle of Waterloo, then in Zululand, and after that in the Opium wars. Then he makes an appearance in the Sudan of 1898. Now, he's got a real master key—not just a Set Master, and we've put out an all points alert to apprehend the man, to every Agent in place on the Prime Meridian."

"Strange," said Paul. I took that key while I was aboard *Rodney* in the guise of an American, one Lieutenant Commander Joseph H.

Wellings, USN. Then later the key just vanished, and I have no idea what caused that."

" It was stolen from you, that's all," said Kamenski.

"Solen? By who? I was very careful with it."

"By a very adept thief, Professor Dorland—Mother Time herself. I can tell you why. Mister Ames was searching ardently for that key, because the man simply loves the Age of Imperialism, and we think he had a mind to live out the rest of his life there. He and Fortier were touring, and meddling with the history, and they were very careful to reset things each time—until 1842 when Fortier died before that could be done. In any case, there was a ship sent back by the Watch—a secret group within the Royal Navy that was first established by Admiral Tovey in the 1940s. It was meant to keep watch for the comings and goings of the Russian battlecruiser, which was jumping about in alarming ways after the accident that first displaced it in time. My goodness, *Kirov* caused more havoc than a stampede of buffalo through a tulip garden in the 1940s." Kamenski shook his head.

"But I straightened them out. I worked long and hard with the key Prime Movers aboard—Volsky, Fedorov, Karpov. In the end, they performed admirably, and I still call on them for special assistance on missions. That is, in fact, one reason why I am here. But to finish with your vanishing key... The ship the Watch sent back was the *Argos Fire*, a corporate security ship owned by Fairchild Enterprises. They were asked to find and secure the key you found aboard *Rodney*, Mister Dorland.

"But it seems the Germans got to *Rodney* before that battleship ever made it to Boston safely. So everyone thought that key would never be recovered—until Miss Fairchild accidentally discovered one time rift beneath Gibraltar that we had not been able to secure. The resourceful woman had a plan. She knew that Lord Elgin had loaded the Marbles he pilfered in Greece aboard a ship, the *Mentor*, for shipment to England, and she also knew where that ship ran aground and was wrecked enroute. So she decided to use that rift under Gibraltar to go back to the site of that shipwreck, and managed to get to the key *before* the Elgin Marbles ever reached England. Quite remarkable, really.

"Then, on that very same mission, who does she encounter? Sir Roger Ames, and he is most interested in getting his hands on that key. He couldn't just take it, because Miss Fairchild was accompanied by her Argonaut Marine Commandos. But Ames proposed a trade. He gave Fairchild his Lindisfarne key, number two in a set of seven, for the one recovered from the Selene Horse, number three in that set. This meant that the key was already recovered from the Selene Horse by the time you first discovered it on the *Rodney*, so of course, there was nothing there for you to find, and when Mother Time found out you possessed that key, she stole it away from you the instant Miss Fairchild recovered it in the wreck of the *Mentor*. I hope I haven't confused you."

"No Director, that is most enlightening," Paul said politely. "Of course, that makes perfect sense. Yet you mentioned you were here because of some need to employ that ship—*Kirov?*"

"Ah, yes. You are a very good listener, Professor Dorland. Have I said what an honor it is to be here to speak with you—all of you, the Four Founders. Your Time Lexicon is required content for memorization by every cadet in our academies."

"Thank you... but as for your present interest in the Russian battlecruiser?"

"Of course... why, it's to look after *you*, Professor Dorland. Yes, we knew of your mission in the guise of Lieutenant Commander Wellings, and we knew you were aboard the *Rodney*, but things have changed because of Churchill's demise, as I said earlier, and now *Bismarck* won't be out there alone. In fact, Lütjens isn't even aboard that ship for its maiden voyage. He's on the *Hindenburg*, an even more powerful ship. So when you appeared on the *Rodney*, the *Keiegsmarine* had a good deal more at sea to try and save the *Bismarck*. In fact, they have the *Hindenburg*, the *Tirpitz* and their aircraft carriers, *Graf Zeppelin* and the *Goeben*, with a good number of cruisers and destroyers. So your mission to *Rodney* is much more hazardous now. I wanted to see if I could use your Arch to get to *Kirov*, and employ my friends there to look after the *Rodney*—to save *you*, Professor Dorland, because otherwise, we assess a high probability that you will not return safely from that mission."

"Well, we ran that some time ago," said Maeve. "And there he stands—he *did* return safely."

"Yes, and he's supposed to have a key around his neck that he finds on the *Rodney*. Where is it? I've explained what happened to that. Yes? In much the same way, he could up and vanish just like that key. That is a very real possibility now, but I cannot explain it further aside from saying that those events are now in replay—all because of this sad situation involving Churchill. The whole war is twisting in the torment of a replay now, and a good many things are changing. Take that marvelous modern armored brigade that intervened at Bir El Khamsa in the history you might have recorded. Well, that doesn't happen now, because the British never did establish an oil concern at Sultan Apache in Egypt, and Kinland's Brigade was therefore never sent to Egypt to guard it. I'm sure you haven't had time to read up on all the many changes Churchill's death set in motion, but we have. I'm just here to see if I can close up a few stiches in the loom of Time. That's all. After all, if *Rodney* goes down, then you go with it, Professor Dorland. We don't want that. Yes?"

Kamenski smiled.

Chapter 27

"Then what about Churchill?" Said Maeve. If his death is the root cause, then shouldn't we keep our focus there?"

"I have an idea on that as well, but it's something I'll discuss with the Russians." Kamenski looked at his watch. "Now then, if I might prevail upon you to allow me to use your Arch, I'll be on my way."

"Use the Arch? You mean to shift forward again?" said Paul.

"Not just yet. I'll need to get back to speak with the officers aboard *Kirov* first, and enlist their support for a dual mission—to save you, Professor Dorland, and then to try and save Churchill." Kamenski fished about in his brief and produced a small memory key, handing it to Dorland.

"All the location data is there. Both physical and temporal—all the calculations." He looked at his watch again. "Yet we must time the shift to go at precisely on the hour. Can you do this?"

"Yes, we can bring the system up and have it open a rift at any time we program."

"It's all on that key," Kamenski reassured. "Just feed that data to your shift control module, and then I just need to be in the Arch domain when it happens."

"Very well. Is there anything we can get you before you shift?"

"Oh, I'm fine, thank you. Is there a lounge below on the Arch level?"

"Yes, there's a ready room adjacent to the Arch on the left."

"Good, I'll just sit there and have a smoke while I wait. Thank you."

"But Director...What is your target?"

"*Kirov*, of course."

"But won't they be at sea? A moving ship will be a very difficult target to hit, and I'd hate to see you manifest over empty ocean and plop down into the water."

"My good man, this was all worked out by an array of quantum computers so powerful that you would blush to think you ever shifted anywhere with those you operate here. Believe me, they will hit the target with absolute precision. The physical locus and exact time is there. It will even compensate for the swell of the sea."

Paul shook his head in amazement. Yet he was thinking of everything that could go wrong. The slightest miscalculation could see Kamenski materialize partly within a bulkhead or deck of the ship. In their own shifts they had always looked for an easy open area, devoid of any such complications, but he realized the computers generating the shift data would be enormously powerful compared to their own, as Kamenski said.

"Unfortunately," said Paul, "we have not yet moved to quantum computers here, though that is on the horizon. That means it will be our computers actually running the shift and storing your pattern profiles in memory here."

"They'll do. Hopefully there will be no need for duplicate pattern profiles. Tell you what, Professor Dorland. When I get home, I'll see that we send a little thank you gift to you for your Arch here. I'm sure it will help you a great deal."

"You're too kind, Director. We're happy to do anything we can for you."

"I am indebted to you, sir."

Maeve escorted the Director back down to the arch, explaining how and when he should cross the thick yellow line on the floor, and what he might feel. He told here her had made a good many shifts, and that he would be fine. Then, before she left, he extended his hand to shake farewell, and she felt him press another memory key into her palm.

"A little something for Outcomes and Consequences," he said. "Don't worry, the tech transfer has all been analyzed and approved. Enjoy your work, Miss Lindford. It's been an honor to meet you."

BCG Kirov ~ Atlantic ~ 25 May, 1941, 04:00

It was still dark when the shift resolved, right on the long empty foredeck of *Kirov*. It was one of two places on the ship where there would be little in the way of superstructure or equipment to complicate a shift. The other was the helo deck, but that was busy this morning, a KA-27/40 being prepped for takeoff.

Fedorov was on the bridge and just happened to be near the forward view panes when he saw a swirl and flash of light on the forward missile deck. His eye was drawn to the spot, first thinking they had been hit by something. But what? Then he squinted into the predawn darkness.

"Nikolin, please illuminate the missile deck."

"Aye sir. " he switched on spots and running lights there and the deck lit up. Now Fedorov saw a single man in a dark overcoat standing there amid the missile cell hatches. He went to the intercom and ordered the watch on that deck to go out and see what was going on. No one should be on that deck, and unless there was some unscheduled operation there, it should be completely empty.

Fedorov watched as a crewman came out to meet the interloper, and he saw them shake hands. The unexpected visitor then pointed to the bridge and even waved a hand in greeting. Fedorov wondered what was going on here. This was most unusual. Who could it be? How could someone just appear there out of thin air? One part of his mind was already solving the problem, but he did not yet want to listen to it.

"Secure from forward deck illumination," he said to Nikolin again. "The ship will resume running dark."

"Aye sir, all deck and running lights off."

It was not long until they heard footsteps on the ladder up to the main bridge hatch. Fedorov went over to open it, seeing Rodenko watching him closely. There, at the top of the ladder well, stood Director Kamenski, a smoking pipe in one hand, a briefcase in the other. It had been a perfect shift, accurate to less than a centimeter. The physical locus and temporal numbers had been spot on target.

"Director!" said Fedorov, quite surprised.

"Always good to see you, Mister Fedorov. I have some urgent business with you. May we speak?"

"Certainly sir, we'll use the Ready Room. I was wondering what happened to you. I visited your quarters and you were not there. We searched the entire ship."

"Yes, I had a short leash when I first came aboard, but now I have a little more time. But I'll have to be leaving again soon."

"Sir, how in the world did you—"

"I know you will have many questions, Mister Fedorov, but time is short. This is about the *Rodney*. Are you presently in command?"

"I have the bridge at the moment. Admiral Volsky is still in his quarters, and he should be here after breakfast."

"And Mister Karpov is not present. Yes?"

"No Sir."

"Very well, concerning the British battleship *Rodney*, do you have its position?"

"Yes sir. the ship is enroute to Boston, presently about 575 nautical mile to our northwest."

"And the Germans are out looking for it. They know about the Gold Bullion, and they would like nothing more than to sink that ship. But there is something else aboard of even greater value."

"You mean the key, sir? Yes, we're aware of that. In fact, Miss Fairchild is here with us aboard the *Argos Fire*."

"Ah, that is excellent, but it is not the key I worry about now, Fedorov, but a person—a very important person. He is presently aboard *Rodney*, under an assumed identity—one Lieutenant Commander Wellings. Nothing must happen to him. He must not be injured or killed should the Germans ever find *Rodney* and engage her. Unfortunately, he is presently thinking to steer *Rodney* into the hunt for the *Bismarck*, unaware that *Bismarck* had quite a few friends at sea this time."

"A man under an assumed identity... May I ask who this person really is?"

"An American Physics Professor, Paul Dorland, and he is what we would call a Prime Mover, someone who must be kept from harm at all costs. He is one of two men I seek your help with here. Well, I knew you were involved in this little affair, and so I came back to see if I could persuade you to intervene; keep *Rodney* safe, and by extension keep this Professor Dorland safe as well." Kamenski looked at his watch. "Am I correct in seeing the time here is now 04:55?"

"Yes sir, that is correct."

"Then the German recon planes off the *Graf Zeppelin* will have just sighted the *Rodney* heading west."

"I wish there was something I could do here. I can inform *Rodney* they have been sighted; warn them of the German carrier, but we have no weapons with the range to intervene just yet. However, two British battlecruisers are close by, *Renown* and *Repulse*. But we do not yet have the location of *Graf Zeppelin*." Fedorov activated the tactical display in the Ready room and zoomed in on *Rodney*.

"I can help with that," said Kamenski. Group Böhmer, presently composed of Carrier *Graf Zeppelin*, battleship *Tirpitz*, battlecruisers *Scharnhorst* and *Gneisenau*, heavy cruiser *Prinz Eugen*, and destroyers *Thor* and *Loki* will presently be here." He pointed to a position a little north of the *Rodney*. "The Germans have just spotted *Rodney*, and they have a good many Stuka strike planes."

"I see... That's also a little bit more than the two British battlecruisers could handle." Fedorov had a grave look on his face.

There came a knock on the ready Room door, and Rodenko peeked in. "Captain, sir. Nikolin just received a sighting update. Five ships, bearing 373 degrees northwest, range 340 miles. Report indicates capital ships and one small carrier, sir."

"That will be Lütjens," said Kamenski. "The five ships are the battleships *Hindenburg*, *Bismarck*, light carrier *Goeben*, light cruiser *Rommel*, and destroyer *Wolf*. The battlecruiser *Kaiser Wilhelm* was also present earlier, but it was detached at 02:00 and is presently heading back to Brest."

Fedorov started keying that information into the tactical display, which would also update the bridge display. "Then *Rodney* should come under air attack soon. Rodenko, have Nikolin warn them-in code please. I'll be there shortly, and please inform the Admiral we need to go to battle stations."

"Aye Sir. Will do."

"Lütjens is just 40 nautical miles outside our firing range at the moment," said Fedorov. "But we might be able to fire just after sunrise. That won't help *Rodney*, but we might get that light carrier and improve the odds a bit."

"Well, it's *Graf Zeppelin* in the Böhmer Group that worries me now." Kamenski was re-lighting his pipe, which always calmed his mind in such situations. The battle he had feared would soon be joined, but this version of *Kirov* had no Zircons. He could not have gone to Fedorov in the future to bring a better loaded *Kirov* here, because this one was already here, and would prevent that due to the prohibition against co-location. That reminded him of something.

"Mister Fedorov... You have been worried about what you call the second coming. Yes?"

"Well, we have some time yet. That is slated to happen late next month. I'm not sure what to expect, but yes, I'm worried."

"Don't be. Kamenski smiled. Your ship has also been just a little unstable of late, hasn't it. Well, I have something here for you to help with that." Kamenski reached into his briefcase and pulled out a small spherical device. There was a single on-off switch and he toggled it on. It emitted a quiet hum, and a green light lit up on the top. "There, that should help."

"What is that, sir?"

"A temporal stabilizer. It will hold you steady here, with a good stable Nexus Point around the ship and crew. I know you've had some trouble lately. This should correct it."

Trouble was just half a word for it. *Kirov* had been pulsing, very unstable, and it had led to the death of crewman Lenkov, his torso imbedded in the galley deck, his legs somewhere else. Beyond that, people had been disappearing. Dobrynin, Orlov, and then Kamenski, though Fedorov was very glad for his return here. Tasarov had been bothered by a confounding deep sound as well, and he wondered if that would abate.

"Everything should be fine," said Kamenski. The ship will be stable, even at high speed. You will lose no more crewmen, and your people should perceive no ill effects. And as for your worry about the second coming, forget that. It will not happen."

"What?" Fedorov looked confused. "But sir, how is that possible. It *must* arrive, otherwise how could we even be here now?"

"Yes, I'll admit that you've exposed yourself to Paradox by ending up in a time prior to your first arrival here. You have forced Mother Time to make a choice—does the ship arrive here as before, or does it fail to arrive while you remain here. You see, it already did shift back, which is why you are here now. You are inching closer to that time, what you call Paradox Hour, and of course Mother Time hates a Paradox above all else. She must decide, and I already know her choice. Your ship will remain here, stable now in this milieu, and no other ship will arrive that hour as you fear. This is how she resolves the Paradox, my friend. She just chooses, and in this case, the prohibition against co-location prevails. So do not fear. Just focus on your sea battle and do all you can to save the *Rodney*."

Fedorov did not quite understand it all, but he was very relieved to hear this from Kamenski. At the same time he realized that this was a major change. A very big change in the fate like of *Kirov* and crew. It would mean that he never appeared there on that ship to convince *Kirov* to return to Severomorsk, that another version of Karpov would not be able to take over on *Kirov* there, and on and on it went.

"Sir," he said. "May I ask where you have been? I thought you were among the men going missing on this ship."

"I was, but it was only because my visa here expired and I was automatically pulled out. I left you a little something on the nightstand in my quarters. Careless of me. I should have given it to you directly, and also said goodbye. Please forgive me. Did you find it?"

"Yes sir, if you are speaking of the key."

"Exactly. Keep it safe, Mister Fedorov. Keep it very safe."

"I will sir, I'm wearing it along with my missile key for the special warheads."

"Well, hopefully there will be no need to use either one. Keep it safe. You'll learn more about it later."

"Is this like the key on the *Rodney*, sir?" Fedorov had to ask.

"Yes indeed, but you need not worry about the key on *Rodney*. It's not there." he explained how Fairchild had preempted that. "Just keep this one safe. I'm sorry to say I cannot stay long—another short visa."

"I don't understand, sir. A visa? What do you mean?"

"I cannot say just now, my friend. Trust your instincts in the days ahead, and your judgement. You were correct to get rid of that thing you threw into Peake's Deep."

"The Devil's Teardrop?"

"Yes, that was a good choice. Well, Karpov is not here, and Volsky has been somewhat cautious in naval combat. This may all be on you, Mister Fedorov. You have to become a fighter now. Save the *Rodney*! Then I have one more mission for you, to save another very important man. It's too complicated to discuss now, but here is a memory key with all the details. Study it well, and I wish you good luck."

"I'll do my best sir." Fedorov put the memory key in his pocket, wondering what it was all about. Then he heard Rodenko announcing 'Admiral on the bridge.'

Kamenski looked at his watch. His time was very short. so he excused himself, wanting to go out and greet Admiral Volsky.

"Hello, my old friend!" Volsky was elated to see him, and the two men came back into the Ready room.

"I've very little time left. Admiral, I've asked for the support of your ship and crew on two very important missions. I hope you will permit that. Captain Fedorov will explain everything."

"Never fear," said Volsky, "We will do everything we can. It will be good to have you at my table this evening."

"Oh, I wish I could stay for that—truly—but my time is very short. Farewell, my friends. Please excuse me. The retraction is starting."

Fedorov saw a strange arura begin to surround Kamenski, undulating like a heat sheen in a desert, only with shades of green and blue. Then the Director vanished, right before their eyes.

Lawrence Berkeley Labs, 2023

"Fish on the line!" said Kelly looking at Dorland. The Professor pushed up the power lever to sustain the retraction, which had been pre-programmed by the data fed into their system on that memory key. Kamenski's stay on *Kirov* was just a brief two hours, enough time to brief Fedorov and stabilize the ship. He had every faith in the young Russian Captain, and was glad he had the time to reassure him about his worry over Paradox Hour.

Kamenski could not get all the way back to his native time in the future because of the Churchill Penumbra, but he could get back to the Arch at the Meridian Complex, where that shadow was not very deep. From there he would be able to use the Meridian Team Arch to power through the Shadow, with a strong assist from the future making that possible. His mission was over....

Part X
The Last Battle

"I was going to say I wished we'd never come. But I don't, I don't, I don't. Even if we are killed. I'd rather be killed fighting than grow old and stupid at home and perhaps go about in a bath-chair and then die in the end just the same."
—C. S. Lewis

Chapter 28

Professor Paul Dorland, now in the guise of an American Naval officer, Lieutenant Wellings, was going below. He had been aboard this ship once before, on the mission teed up from the warning provided by the Number Seven Golem Module. They had called it the Golem 7 Mission[12], an effort to prevent the *Bismarck* from surviving its maiden voyage. He had made a discovery. But here, now, things were very different.

He was a tall, thin man, dark eyed, clean, and dressed out in proper US Navy whites. The stripes on his cuff and shoulder insignia made him to be a Lieutenant Commander.

But Wellings was more than he seemed.

He had first come on the scene in Bristol, England, near the Clyde anchorage where HMS *Rodney* had been waiting to escort Convoy WS-8B on her initial outward leg, before breaking off with *Britannic* and heading west to Halifax and then Boston. WS-8B was the second half of a convoy bound to reinforce the British position in Egypt, or so Paul believed, but it was not called that now. It was simply called CO-8B. The first half had been designated CO-8A, once dubbed the Tiger Convoy by Sir Winston himself but not this time. Sir Winston had died in the desert of Sudan, long ago.

So Tiger Convoy had become a domestic cat instead, with CO-8A passing safely round the cape, and making a much needed delivery of precious Matilda and Crusader tanks, and Hurricane fighters, to General Wavell. Those tanks would soon help Wavell and O'Connor hold off Rommel's new offensive aimed at Tobruk.

Rodney was still at sea, bound for Boston. She had rendezvoused with Convoy CO-8B for a time, then veered off to the west with the big ex-liner and new troop ship *Britannic* in her charge. Wellings was out on the main deck that morning, when he heard the distant drone of aircraft. He could see nothing above, but the pilots of those planes would surely have a much better view of *Rodney* and *Britannic* down here. He was worried, were they British planes off a nearby carrier, or German? He decided he had better get below and check on that key.

Yet as Wellings descended into the lower levels of the ship, every question in his mind led him on to another, a long corridor of unopened doors that perhaps would be breached with this very key if he learned how to use it. First off, how was it that the object itself could have moved forward with him in time when he returned from his last wild ride aboard HMS *Rodney* in the Atlantic ocean? Never mind that, he thought. It did come forward, and he once had it well in hand.

He remembered how he had placed the key on a chain and wore it around his neck, under his shirt at all times, from that moment on. He also made an entry in Kelly's protected RAM Bank, describing the key, how and where he found it, and including a set of images. It was well encrypted, so he had no fear of that data ever being discovered. If something did slip, he wanted to know it immediately—at least insofar as this key was concerned. He had the RAM Bank programmed to notify him once a week about the hidden file, and ask him a question only he would ever know the answer to before allowing him to view the contents. If the key ever vanished, he wanted to know it immediately—know that it had existed, where he had found it, and what he had discovered about it since.

Yet how would any of them ever know again what was real, or what was the contorted product of another Time intervention by unseen agents like Sir Roger Ames or others? They were the first, or so they thought, to ever open Time. They had created the device, the Arch, their gateway to a thousand yesterdays, or a thousand tomorrows. Yet now they would have to keep the Arch spinning on low standby mode at all times to keep a stable Nexus Point open, an enormously expensive proposition, and one that also presented challenges involving maintenance and engineering. Thankfully the cost was no longer a concern. He had all the money they would ever need, just by selling stocks he had bought on a personal mission to the dawn of the Computer era.

He had spent every nickel he had to but shares of Apple, Microsoft, Google, Facebook, and other companies he knew would have rabid success. The Meridian team was now fabulously wealthy, so money as never an issue. It's just that it was getting more an more difficult to get their hands on required resources. You could not buy what was not there.

He worried that one day, by some means, his machine would falter and fail when it was most needed. Yes, there were others operating on the Meridians of Time now. The team was not alone. They had discovered that two sides in a distant future were at war with one another, one known as the Order, the other labeled Assassins, each side attempting to bend the lines of fate and time to their liking—Time War.

They had met some of these nefarious agents in time, and eventually forced the two sides to agree to a truce and end their Time War. How the Assassin cult had managed to restore the Palma Event again and send half of the Cumbre Vieja Volcano into the sea still eluded them. They had been working up a mission to try and reverse that, then got distracted by the latest dark Golem report and the coming of Pavel Kamenski.

Now he wondered if the Golem alert system would be efficient enough to pick up any potential violation of the truce they had negotiated. Clearly something had to permit the Palma Event to happen again and wipe out the Eastern Seaboard. What if the warring parties used some unknown technology, or even a principle of physics unknown to his day, to spoof their system and conduct another stealthy operation? Was this key evidence of exactly that?

He said nothing of his discovery of the key during those negotiations, but kept that thought in the back of his mind. What were these future agents really up to, he wondered? Was it *Rodney* they had been gunning for all along? Old lumbering *Rodney*, with a secret cargo, in more than one way—the King's business, the gold bullion, the Elgin Marbles, the hidden key... and me!

We had to threaten them, both sides at war in the future, before they would listen, for they knew we had power. We were the first, the Founders, Prime Movers all, and from our unique position on the continuum, we had the ability to frustrate any move they made. What if the Assassins took our threats to heart, and decided that their next and only mission must be to eliminate the meddling Founders from the continuum in a way that still permitted Time travel to occur in the future? They must have discovered how we had used the *Bismarck* mission to reverse their second attempt to trigger the Palma Event.

Physicists were still taking pokes at Einstein. The CERN research institute near Geneva recently announced they had measured particles that had to be exceeding the speed of light, presumed to be the elusive Tachyons. It was only a matter of getting somewhere 60 nanoseconds sooner than expected, but it was enough to raise a lot of eyebrows in the physics community. It meant, in one possible application, that it would be possible to send information back through Time, something Wellings could clearly confirm now if ever asked around the water cooler conversations at the Berkeley Lab facilities, though he could never speak a word of this to anyone outside the four core members of the project. Even the interns and lower level staff had been banned from the main facilities after that first mission. The team could take no chance that the true purpose and utility of the Arch would ever become generally known. If the government ever discovered what they were doing here, it would be confiscated and shut down in a heartbeat. In that event he had little doubt that a new Time War would soon begin.

It was a very slippery slope, he knew. Others would reason that if information could be sent back in Time, matter and people would come into the discussion shortly thereafter. He smiled inwardly when he learned that Steven Hawking had remarked: "It is premature to comment on this. Further experiments and clarifications are needed."

He could write them all a book, he thought, but the more he considered things, the more questions piled up, one on top of another. Be careful what you wish for, went the old Maxim... *You may get it.* And what did he have hanging round his neck that day when he first revealed the existence of the key to his good friend Kelly Ramer. The key... a strange relic that should never have been found, or left, where it was discovered—the very same key he was laboring to find again now as he reached the lower decks of *Rodney*, and began to make his way forward towards the main cargo hold.

A curious man, he had immediately applied a little forensic investigation to the key, regretting that he had twiddled with it in his pocket and largely extinguished any finger prints he might have found on it. Yet a little non-invasive scan revealed something very interesting, for this key was not what it seemed at all. There was something machined on the side, a series of numbers that could only be read under intense magnification. Beyond that, it was hollow! There was something inside it, and he would spend a good bit of time thinking about that before he went any further, or even whispered the fact to his closest associates.

There was something inside it! The metal end, machined to engage lock tumblers, had clearly been designed for some other purpose as well, and this turned the cylinders of his mind, opening a universe of possibilities. What was it, he wondered? Surely the contents would tell him where it had come from, and what its purpose was, he thought.

Now all he had to do was find out how to open the damn thing. Yet, being inventive and resourceful, he soon answered that challenge. He found that the head of the key could be turned with sufficient torque, and slowly unscrewed. He still remembered that moment of breathless opening, when everything he ever knew and believed turned at the head of that key, and its slow untwisting became the great unraveling of all that ever was. When he finally had it open, and tilted the shaft ever so gently to urge the hidden contents out onto a lab dish, he stared with amazement and perplexity at what he had found.

Days later, he knew the answer to many of his questions, and he also knew why there had been no answer from the distant future when others had called out to their successive generations. From that day forward his life, and his entire understanding of the world he lived in, was never the same. But who to tell?

He spent a long time thinking about that before he ever spoke a word of this key again. Yet it was something too big for him to carry alone. Like Frodo's ring, it began to weigh upon him, seeming heavier and heavier with each day that passed. But unlike Frodo, there was no place he could take it and cast it away, and there was no way he could simply forget about it either... not this... not this...

Then one sunny afternoon at his cottage in Carmel, he was sitting with his good friend Kelly, down on a getaway visit while the other team members stood watch back in their Berkeley Lab facility, the Arch complex as they called it now. They had been walking on the coastline of Asilomar that day, and later dined at a favorite restaurant, the *Sardine Factory* in Monterey. Afterwards, they were drinking wine in the cottage, looking at some of Kelly's photo albums, and listening to the music they loved and shared together, talking over things in a way only two very old friends could. The music played on in the background and Kelly came in with a good bottle of Pinot Noir from the wine rack.

The man who would be Wellings knew that he had to finally unburden himself concerning his discovery of that key. Yet he knew the moment he opened his mouth, he would pass this hidden knowledge on to his friend, germ like, and Kelly's life, and his awareness of life itself, would change forever. He, too, would never be the same. He hesitated briefly, thinking to leave his friend in the relative innocence and simplicity of his life, to leave him unbothered, unburdened, unaware. But if this would eventually lead them all to renewed Time missions, the whole project team would have to be informed. He could bear it no longer. The sheer loneliness of carrying the key, and all he knew about it now, was like a great weight crushing down on his soul.

He reached into his shirt and slowly drew out the key on its chain, feeling like Gandalf visiting Frodo in the Shire, there to tell him what the quaint little magic ring was really all about.

For one last moment he waited. Then he spoke. "It's about this key," he said...

* * *

Now here he was on *Rodney* again, out to go right down to the cargo hold and find that bloody key again. He knew just where to look this time. There would be a marine guarding access to that hold, but his rank as a Lieutenant Commander could back him down. He got in by simply saying he was the American liaison sent to look after this cargo, and he had a duty to inspect it. The guard had hesitated briefly,

"Well, don't think I'll try to make off with a bar of gold man. You can search me as I exit." Yes, he got in. Now all he had to do was find the correct case, get the damn thing open and get to the base of the Selene Horse. There would be tools in the hold to let him chip away at just the right spot, and he labored the next hour to do this, but all for naught. He was certain he had the right location on the horse's base. One last chip and off came that corner. He was thrilled to see the imprint of the key in the stone piece that came off—but he found nothing else. The key had been there once, but now it was gone. He fished about the case, running his long fingers through the straw packing material but nothing was found.

He looked at his watch, seeing he had a good bit of time left before the retraction program kicked in. Time on the *Rodney*, a grand little adventure. So he closed up that case, went out and satisfied the guard that he had taken nothing, and then headed aloft to the main deck. The ship's Captain, Dalrymple-Hamilton, had taken a liking to him, so he was welcome on the bridge. The sound of those planes overhead was worrisome.

Chapter 29

Group Böhmer, Carrier Graf Zeppelin, Atlantic
64 nautical miles North of HMS Rodney

The flight deck of the carrier *Graf Zeppelin* was still and calm, with the first of the morning fighter contingent was already aloft, two BF-109s. Six more fighters were scheduled for launch at 07:00, to be followed soon after by the first squadrons of *Stukas*. The carrier had sortied *streikschwere*, with a strike-heavy compliment primarily composed of modified *Stuka* dive bombers. There were two *Stuka* squadrons aboard, a baker's dozen in each, for a total of 26 strike aircraft, and a dozen BF-109Ts, with four *Arado* seaplanes to make 42 planes in all. But Böhmer never liked the Arado search planes. They were just too damn slow. He much preferred just sending out BF-109s on a recon sweep, and now he had found his quarry, and within easy striking distance.

A signal came from his first two fighters indicating the position of a large merchant ship and a battleship. Now he was watching the first of the strike Stukas coming up on the elevators. It was a pity that Marco Ritter and Hans Rudel were still on the *Goeben* with Lütjens. Then again, he had faith in his own pilots. This had to be the fat British battleship *Rodney*, and it was very slow. It should make an easy target for his Stukas, and if they didn't finish it off, *Tirpitz* and his two battlecruisers would certainly do the job in time.

The former first officer of the *Admiral Scheer*, Kapitan zur See Kurt Böhmer, was now in command of the *Graf Zeppelin*, arriving on the bridge early that day to oversee the morning launch.

Brinkmann is in Prinz Eugen *out in front, and I have the new destroyers* Loki *and* Thor *to either side. We must have a destroyer abreast of us at all times, and that failing, one of the heavier ships must stand in for that duty. We can take no chances that those demonic rockets will find us again, and we seldom ever know where the devil that fired them is lurking. Yet for now, the sea is empty,* and we will pluck out the eyes of any aircraft that come looking for us. The British carriers are well to the south and west in any case, so we should rule the day here. Now to get our boys up and after the British. If I can sink that old battleship we're looking for, I can save Lütjens, Topp and Lindemann the trouble. Then they can turn and slug it out with the enemy battleships.

The *Schweregruppe* of the task force was out ahead of *Prinz Eugen*. He could not see the tall main masts and superstructure of *Tirpitz* in the darkness, but he could feel the ship's presence, the cold hard Wotan Hart steel plying through the waters like a great shark. *Scharnhorst* and *Gneisenau* were cruising to either side, guarding the battleship as the destroyers stood watch over his carrier. Once bitten, twice shy. Now that the Germans had faced the British rocket weapons, they sailed in shieldwall formation, with one ship protecting another from the deadly sea skimming missiles.

Kurt Böhmer looked at his watch, seeing the elevator bringing up another two fighters, wings still folded as they rose to the main flight deck. The big bent wings of the Stukas were already in place, the planes lined up in a long line for takeoff. He would send squadron Number-1 out this morning for the first attack. Perhaps the second Squadron would not be needed.

Now he heard the engines revving up, and saw the deck master waving the first plane off. The others would follow until all twelve planes were circling like a flock of angry crows over the task force. That was their nickname, the crows. Then they started south to get after their quarry, dark birds of prey in the grey dawn.

Soon the Type 281 Radar set on the *Rodney* would begin picking the Stukas up, and battle stations were sounded. LTC Wellings headed for the bridge. Dorland did not want to be down on the main deck during an air strike. The conning tower had 12 to 14 inches armor.

The Stukas peeled off into flights of three to four planes, the first diving on a defender, the destroyer *Mashona*. Another flight made for the big troop liner, *Britannic*, and the last four planes maneuvered to attack the *Rodney*. The sky was already blooming with smoky explosions from all the many flak guns on the ships. *Rodney* was putting out most of this, with her six barreled 45mm Bofors guns and ten twin 114mm dual purpose secondaries. The other three destroyers, *Eskimo, Somali* and *Tartar* all joined the flak defense. It was a very rough ride in for the Stukas, and the first flight of four took a loss as it dove on the *Mashona*. Three targeting *Britannic* all dropped their bombs just shy of the ship, and the four overflying those ships to get at *Rodney* ran into a hellstorm from her flak and were cut to pieces.

As they screamed down, parts of wings, tail rudders and the wheeled undercarriages were blown away, and all four Stukas spun down into the sea. None of their bombs had even been released before they were fatally hit. That left two planes, and they both circled around to get at *Britannic*. They got into a good position above the ship, tipped over and dove with a wail of their Jericho trumpets. These were the only 500 pound bombs to find their intended targets in this strike, one coming in at an angle to blow through the steamer's side and damage her propulsion. Three boilers were down, and her speed began to fall off.

The surviving Stukas radioed ahead and requested permission to land before another squadron went up. Some of them had damage, and one pilot had taken some shrapnel through the cockpit for a minor wound. Böhmer gave orders to hold the second squadron below until Squadron-1 was recovered. That accomplished by 10:15, the second squadron roared off the deck for the short flight to the target. This time, the entire squadron was ordered to go for the *Rodney*, and they first maneuvered to the south side of the Task force before they made their diving run.

One plane would be hit and explode on the way down, but the other eleven all released their bombs. Three of the 114mm twin mounts would be hit, with two destroyed. Another bomb destroyed a Type 268 Radar gun director system. There were no serious fires or flooding, as the ship's armor had absorbed most of the shock of these 500 pound bombs. Back on Graf Zeppelin, the survivors of Squadron-1 were now strapping on heavier 1000 pound bombs.

Aboard *Rodney*, a signal was sent out requesting fighter cover, but the British carriers were not close. *Arc Royal* and *Illustrious* were still 500 miles to the northwest. Captain Wells was on *Glorious*, about 300 miles to the south of *Rodney*. She had plenty of fighters, a dozen Seafires, but they only had a 230 mile mission radius. Her second squadron had six fireflies armed, but with 1000 pound bombs. The other six hastened to arm for fighter missions, and they would have the necessary range, with a 380 mile radius, but not for about three hours.

Down in the Azores, about 520 miles from *Rodney*, a single Seafire had been rigged for long range ferry, and it was being sent up to replace the Sunderlands that had Spotted Group Lütjens earlier that morning. Fedorov had gone all ahead flank to try and close on the Germans, but the Sunderlands had turned for home and they had lost the target sighting track. This Seafire had been rigged out with a good surface search radar set, and it would soon re-acquire the targets for *Kirov*.

At 11:00, the destroyer *Thor* was let off the leash and ordered to go out after the *Britannic*. Twenty minutes later it had come over the horizon and was closing to gun range. *Britannic* had fallen well behind as *Rodney* altered course to the southwest, but destroyer *Somali* was sent back to watch her, and it began to rush to attack *Thor* as the big cruise liner was being pummeled by 127mm rounds. The gun crews on *Somali* could see fires breaking out all over Britannic, and wanted revenge.

Signals to the *Rodney* from *Britannic* advised Captain Hamilton to carry on. The troop ship was too badly damaged and could not run or keep up. Her Captain said he did not think they could keep the ship afloat very much longer, as they had both fires and severe flooding.

While Captain Hamilton hated to leave his charge, they had detected a line of German ships coming south, and his situation did not look good.

"Ah, Commander Wellings," said the Captain as Paul reached the bridge. "We're in a bit of a pickle here. Our destroyer, *Somali*, has done a bang up job. We detached her to look after *Britannic*, and she ran into a wolf—a German destroyer. She engaged and got the better of that ship. But now she reports a large capital ship, and more warships behind it. *Britannic* says she can't run or follow us, and I'm in a quandary. If we turn back to render assistance, we'll have to tangle with whatever the Germans have back there."

"What do they have there sir. Any ideas?"

"Large capital ship has to be a German battleship. Could be the *Tirpitz*, the *Oldenburg*, anything. It might even be one of the Twins."[13]

"As I see it, this is just a question of *when* you go to battle, not *if* you go. Any German battleship out here will run up towards 30 knots, and what, we can work up to 21 knots if I'm not mistaken. So if they want a fight, they'll catch us. Have we any help at hand?"

"We'll have *Renown* and *Repulse* over our left shoulder, about 138 miles off now from their last signal. The rest of the fleet is 300 to 400 miles to the north, Tovey and Holland, each with two battleships."

"Well sir, seeing that you can't *avoid* battle with the Germans, and seeing that you've all your guns forward, running isn't the answer here. I'd come about and work back towards your two battlecruisers.

This is a battleship, and built for a fight at sea. They'll need your 16-inch guns if they come up into this."

The Captain raised an eyebrow. He had a belly full of gold bullion, the King's business, and that weighed as heavily on him as it did on the ship. Then he decided. "Yes," he said, "Of course." It was always better to choose a fight than to have one forced upon him. Look at brave *Somalia* out there. He gave the order to come about, and signals were sent to his last three destroyers to follow. If the Germans wanted a fight, *Rodney* and her 16-inch guns would oblige.

Battleship Tirpitz, 12:30, 25 MAY 1941

It was a fine morning, with no clouds, a fine sea and good visibility. Captain Zur See Friedrich Karl Topp was out on the weather deck with his binoculars, peering south at the distant edge of the sea. He could barely make out the squat shadow of the destroyer *Loki*, well out in front, and now a Watch officer came out to say they had just received a signal from that ship.

"Ship sighted by *Loki*, sir. Just over the horizon—but no details."

"Signal *Graf Zeppelin*. Have them take a look and report. Tell Loki to make for that burning troop ship."

Topp returned to the bridge, and by 13:00 that sighting had firmed up—a battleship, obviously the *Rodney*, and three smaller ships, most likely destroyers. *Rodney*, but on a heading of 46 degrees. They're working back towards that damn troop ship. The fools. Well, I suppose they can't run from us. So someone out there has found some backbone. The crew was already at action stations, but he told the forward turrets to be ready for action at any minute. They were already loading the massive 15-inch shells as *Tirpitz* pushed south through calm seas at 24 knots.

Tirpitz was about to see its first major engagement of the war. Now we see what this ship is made of, thought Topp. I hope they built it well.

Chapter 30

13:00, 25 MAY 1941, Battleship Rodney

Destroyer *Eskimo* was about seven nautical miles in front of *Rodney* when they sighted *Loki*. The German destroyer was turning away and increasing speed, as per Topp's order to go to the troop ship. The *Eskimo* immediately engaged and the enemy replied. Soon both destroyers were taking hits as the *Eskimo* slowly closed, with a slight two knot speed advantage. The British destroyer took several superstructure hits, the radio smashed, the antennae down, and the magazine for one of her ASW Mortars blown up in a hit that might have looked much worse than it actually was.

The last signal from *Eskimo* was reporting a large capital ship to the north, just breaking over the horizon. *Rodney* soon had it on its surface search radars, but the ship was still out of range. Captain Hamilton was glad it was a single ship, and not a whole German flotilla. He knew that *Graf Zeppelin* was up north, and that the Stukas were probably rearming to get after him again. But this German ship coming at him now was his main concern. What was it? If this was a *Bismarck* class ship it would have only two twin turrets up front—four 15-inch guns. He had the advantage now as the ships closed on one another.

Rodney's three big turrets were all forward of the conning tower, nine 16-inch guns against the four German guns. He gave the order to fire, and the concussion and roar shook the ship when his guns started blasting away at a shadow on the far horizon. In these opening salvos, both ships would be hit, but both shrugged off the hits with their heavy armor.

On *Rodney*, the conning tower shuddered with a hit low on its base, but the heavy 14-inch armor was not fully penetrated. Shrapnel damaged sensors above, but no one was hurt. Feeling that hard hit made Paul wonder at the wisdom of getting back into this fight. If *Rodney* went down, Britain would lose all that Gold Bullion, the

Elgin marbles, priceless artwork, and he would go into the sea, assuming he could even get off the ship alive. He looked at his watch, still almost three hours to retraction time at 16:00.

Come on, old girl, he thought, pulling for *Rodney*. He could hear the drone of planes above, but they did not sound like Stukas, and none came at them... yet they would in time.

Captain Hamilton saw the distant shadow elongate on the horizon. He knew the German ship had turned to get his rear turrets into action and even things up a bit. He ordered his guns to continue firing at will. *Tirpitz* replied as the range closed, and both sides were getting heavier hits. *Tirpitz* had 13 inches of armor at the belt, 14 inches on her turrets, and deck armor at a little over 4 inches.

Rodney had equivalent armor, except her turrets were a little better protected with armor as thick as 16 inches. But the German ship was very well built, her bulkheads were sturdy, and interiors had good protection, particularly the magazines. She was nearly 20,000 tons heavier in displacement than *Rodney*. It was a slugfest, like two heavyweights going toe to toe in the ring, and both landing heavy handed punches. *Tirpitz* had a higher rate of fire, so the Germans were landing more of those punches than *Rodney* returned, but *Rodney* was hitting harder. It's 16-inch guns were fully capable of achieving a full penetration of 14 inch armor.

Rodney rocked with the heavy 15-inch hits, and in time, nearly all her secondaries and most of her AA guns were ravaged by that fire. But she penetrated *Tirpitz* to put heavy damage on her steam plant, and the German ship's speed fell off to 7 knots, the ship just moving on its earlier momentum.

In the German's favor, they scored a direct hit on *Rodney*'s B-turret, disabling it and taking a third of her firepower out of the fight. Both sides had serious trouble, but *Rodney* had controlled her fires and had only minor flooding. Her next problem would be the Stukas that were already coming up on the elevators on *Graf*

Zeppelin, and lining up on the main flight deck for takeoff. They would not be needed.

At 13:30, a major fire broke out and the flooding on *Rodney* worsened with three solid hits on her forward hull that penetrated. The battleship was shipping water fast, and it was soon clear to Captain and crew that *Rodney* was going down at the bow. Captain Hamilton had learned that *Renown* and *Repulse* were just 88 miles away, but they would be too late to this fight. If they did come on the scene, it would be to face down the Twins, which were still back with *Graf Zeppelin*. In that fight, the German carrier and her Stukas could be the deciding difference. That and the better armor protection on the German battlecruisers, even though their 11-inch guns were outclassed by the British battlecruisers 15-inchers.

Closer yet was Group Lütjens, with the *Hindenburg, Bismarck* and another light carrier. Things did not look good for the British. They were losing *Rodney*, but now another ally was thinking to get involved.

13:50, 25 MAY 1941, BCG Kirov

"Sir," said Samsonov. "We have the range with our Onyx and Sizzlers."

"How many Onyx?" asked Fedorov.

"Only ten, sir."

"Fire four. Choose your target, but see if we can get the bigger ships. Then make your next salvo a set of four sizzlers."

Samsonov could not tell what was what, so he selected the lead ship and fired. The four missiles would streak out at 1450 knots, and soon find the light cruiser *Rommel*, a new German design. It would not survive those hits.

"I think we killed that target," Rodenko confirmed. "I'm losing radar returns on it."

"Good, said Fedorov. Admiral, with your permission I would like to proceed with this attack."

"You are doing well, Fedorov. Fire at will."

"Four Sizzlers, Samsonov. Let's keep them looking over their shoulder."

"Just to let you know, Captain," said Rodenko. "We now have a firing arc on the whole battlespace to the northwest, but I am sorry to report that we have lost returns on the *Rodney*."

Fedorov shrugged. "There goes the King's business," he said sullenly. In effect, the Mission Kamenski brought them had just failed. They could not save *Rodney*, and both the gold and the Elgin Marbles would be lost. But Fedorov was not aware that Professor Dorland was still out there, alive in the sea, and with his retraction clock still ticking.

Paul had gone over the side, and being an officer, he got space on a small life boat, which was a better outcome than his first encounter with the *Bismarck*.

15:00, 25 MAY 1941 ~ The Hindenburg, Lütjens Group
205 Nautical miles NE of Kirov

Admiral Lütjens saw the hot tails of three naval rockets racing past the *Hindenburg* and continuing to the northwest. He saw *Rommel* erupt with fire, its side torn open, and watched as it keeled over and capsized within minutes."

"Good Lord, that devil ship is back!" he breathed.

"Those rockets came from the southeast, sir," said the OOD. "Look, you can still see the contrails."

"So they are behind us, and they have just crept into range."

Kirov's Sizzlers were soon spotted inbound, and this time Samsonov had guessed right. *Hindenburg* took a hit aft, the missile popping up to strike Dora turret, which took heavy shock from the explosion and was enveloped in fire. That turret was out of action. The next missile struck the battleship amidships, blasting a secondary gun and its fire director. The last missile slammed into the battleship's heavy side armor. There was a fierce explosion, but the glancing blow saw the armor hold and the damaged did not penetrate into the ship's interior. The ship's steam plan was untouched and the chastened battleship continued on course.

Captain Lindeman on the *Bismarck* saw those hits, but then saw the *Hindenburg* emerge from the smoke, still running at good speed. He saw no major fires on the superstructure. What *are* these weapons? We have nothing that can track them and shoot them down. If it were not for our armor, he realized, *Hindenburg* would have been sunk by those rockets. This changes everything…

Kirov was perhaps 20-30 years ahead in naval technology. Lindemann could not understand how this enemy ship could find them, let alone have a weapon that could reach out hundreds of miles and hurt them. He hoped *Hindenburg* would still be in shape for a gunfight up ahead, because *Tirpitz* had already gone toe to toe with a British *Nelson* Class Battleship. She had prevailed, but had significant damage, and Germany could not afford to trade battleships with the Royal Navy.

He looked warily over his shoulder, hoping those rockets would not find the *Bismarck*. A message was received from Admiral Lütjens: *We are slowing to look at damage. Proceed ahead to find Tirpitz and Böhmer's group. I will look after the Goeben.*

The Captain gave the order to take point and increase speed. Radar returns were now showing many ships in the area. DD *Wolf* reported two large capital ships to the north, and suggested they were the British battlecruisers. Then came the alarm from the watch. "Ships ahead! British destroyers!"

These were *Mashona* and *Tartar*, sent east to look for Group Lütjens. They found it, when *Bismarck* suddenly loomed ahead and started firing on them. Neither destroyer would survive that encounter, with *Bismarck*'s secondary batteries more than enough to take them down. But before they sunk, they were able to identify their assailant. In reprisal, the British battlecruisers would see and sink destroyer *Wolf*, in short order.

16:30 hours, 25 MAY 1941
BCG Kirov, 205 miles behind Bismarck

Rodenko reported that the target, presumed to be *Hindenburg* or *Bismarck*, had fallen off in speed. "We hurt them," he advised.

"And we're going to hurt them again." In Fedorov's mind, any harm he could put on the *Keiegsmarine* would be helpful here. It could only improve the chances of the Royal Navy in the war, even if they were too late to save the *Rodney*.

He looked at the tactical screen. There he saw that *Renown* and Repulse were moving south into the gap between *Hindenburg* and *Bismarck*, which was now 28 miles ahead of the bigger German battleship. They had seen the light carrier *Goeben*. And *Renown* was opening fire as the carrier turned in front of *Hindenburg* trying to run south.

Goeben had just launched Hans Rudel and five other Stukas before *Renown* started getting hits on the carrier. 15-inch shells were doing a good amount of damage, shutting down all flight operations. Marco Ritter was trapped below decks, wishing Rudel well, but he knew he would not get up in a fighter again any time soon.

Now Fedorov saw that *Hindenburg* was replying to the fire of the *Renown*. He watched the battle on the screen, six planes diving on the *Renown*, but only one scoring a hit. Now he saw the battlecruiser turning into the wake of *Bismarck*, which was 26 miles due west. *Renown* had no business trying to exchange fire with *Hindenburg*, and accelerated west.

"Samsonov, four more missiles on that leading target." He was going after *Bismarck* now, then he would look for the *Graf Zeppelin* if it could be found. Fedorov would watch that missile train, Moskit-IIs with extended range, until he saw all four plow into the target. But none had the popup reprogramming, and *Bismarck* had turned broadside to the attack. So all four missiles smashed into the battleships heavy side armor, and it mostly absorbed that heavy impact.

"What's left?" he looked at Samsonov.

"Sir, I have six more Sizzlers, two Moskit-II's, and six Onyx received from *Kazan*. Then three missiles mounted in cells for special warheads, the P-1000s."

The Cupboard was running bare, and after those last strike missiles were expended, *Kirov* would be toothless. With its temporal stabilizer active, the ship would not vanish this time, for it was nearing the hour when they had lost contact with Admiral Tovey and disappeared into that thick mind-numbing fog. That wasn't going to happen here, and their presence was also going to stop the Second Coming. The arrival of *Kirov* from the future, with full magazines, had allowed *Kirov* to remain a dangerous adversary in the years ahead, mostly in the Pacific when Karpov was in command. And when Fedorov vanished, he found his consciousness right there on the ship that arrived with *Kirov*'s Second Coming. That wasn't going to happen now, though Fedorov was as yet unaware of all those events. He had a battle here, and that was all that mattered.

I'll do what I can, save the special warheads, and then see what we might do later. There's no sense getting stingy now, even if we will soon be toothless, save for those three nukes.

Then he remembered the other mission Kamenski had talked about—Churchill. For that they would have to break off here and get to the Red Sea. But not before get *Graf Zeppelin*, he thought. Without that ship Lütjens will think twice about his battle here.

Part XI
While the Iron is Hot

"Do not wait to strike till the iron is hot; but make it hot by striking."
— **William Butler Yeats**

Chapter 31

A dark hour lay waiting for England in the years and days after Omdurman. She would stand alone, with all Europe prostrate at the feet of a raving madman. There were only three things that might save her. One of them was engaged in that struggle now, the Royal Navy. If it could put such harm on the *Keiegsmarine* here that it dare not sail again, then England's shores might stand inviolate, her vulnerable sea lines of communication might be preserved. That was now the plan in Fedorov's mind, and he had fourteen missiles to accomplish it.

The second thing that might save England was a powerful friend, the United States, across the Atlantic waiting like a brooding storm. The Royal Navy had to survive and prevail for the power of the United States to flow east over the Atlantic to Great Britain.

The third thing that could save England was a man, a single man with indomitable will and strength of character, and a gift for oratory unlike any modern era leader before or since. That man was Winston Churchill, the one man who could make sure that England would never lose her faith and steely will to live, or its capacity to guide and govern, but on the 2nd day of September 1898 that man had died. Fedorov had no idea at this point how he could do anything at all to change that, or how he might move his ship to a place where he could even try. It was a long way, across the whole of the Mediterranean to the Red Sea. Once there, shifting with Rod-25 was a haphazard affair, and he would have no control over the outcome of such an event.

Fortunately, there was another man working the problem, Director Pavel Kamenski, and he left Fedorov detailed instructions on the memory key explaining what he wanted him to do. So now, in this brief hour, in May of 1941, Fedorov was the man who might save England, both on the tempestuous seas around them, and in the strength of his will to prevail on this mission to save Churchill.

They had been sailing from one crisis point to another, with Admiral Tovey and HMS *Invincible* by his side. Yet this was the hour when Tovey had been shocked to see *Kirov* vanish, as it had so many times before. That would not happen now. Everything was changing...

The battlecruiser *Renown* had come up on the brooding hulk of the *Hindenburg* and briefly engaged the German battleship. She now had a secondary battery destroyed, several sensors flayed by shrapnel, and a half dozen flak guns smashed, but otherwise, she was still fit and in action, all her main guns intact, and with no flooding or serious fires. *Repulse* had turned to come up smartly off her starboard side, but for both ships, it was now a case of 'out of the frying pan and into the fire."

Four Germans ships loomed ahead, out on the grey edge of the sea: *Bismarck*, *Tirpitz*, *Scharnhorst* and *Gneisenau*. There were 34 big guns between them, and the two British battlecruisers combined for only twelve. The battlecruisers had been built during the First World war, once the fastest capital ships afloat, but that was no longer true. Not only were they outgunned by the force that lay ahead, but they had belt armor of no more than six inches compared to more than twice that on the bigger German ships.

If *Rodney* had already been slain by *Tirpitz*, the Captains of the British battlecruisers knew they had no business at all trying to engage what lay ahead, so they turned north at their best speed to try and escape. They would only rejoin this fight with the arrival of Holland and Wells, with *Hood* and three more *KGV* class battleships.

Repulse came about and started north and *Renown* turned into its wake. Then *Hindenburg's* guns came to life again, behind both ships, and tall geysers from heavy rounds began to bracket *Renown* again.

It was at this point when a Seafire off one of the British carriers confirmed the sighting of a large German carrier that had to be the *Graf Zeppelin*. Fedorov had already sunk the *Goeben*. Now he wanted to get this one, and sent two more Moskit-II missiles out after it.

Admiral Volsky was on the bridge now, his heart heavy as he saw the tactical display, seeing *Renown* being hit by heavy shells from the *Hindenburg* as it fled north. How many more will die before this is over, if it will ever be over?

"Now then," Volsky adjusted his officer's coat. "Mister Rodenko has a good read on thing here Fedorov." He looked over his shoulder for Rodenko.

"The KA-40 was up just after sunset," said Fedorov. "We could fly any time, but why waste the air defense missiles if those German fighters are about. In any case, we've had a good look forward, and can now report the locations of both German battlegroups.

"A lot of power there," said Volsky.

"Perhaps," said Fedorov, "this single German group near the British battlecruisers could match anything the British have in range. I hope they have the good sense to find safe water until their battleships arrive. My enigma decrypts show the *Tirpitz,* with two battlecruisers, another heavy cruiser, two destroyers and the wild card, *Graf Zeppelin*. The two British battlecruisers will not be able to stop them, and now *Bismarck* and *Hindenburg* are there as well, wounded by our missiles, but still dangerous. The remainder of the British heavy ships will arrive piecemeal, behind the action from the northwest. Admiral Tovey tells me that they are also bringing *Duke of York* and *Hood* down from the Denmark Strait, and they would be the last to arrive."

"Then we must give the Germans something to think about." Volsky tapped the enemy contacts on the Plexiglas screen. "We are in missile range now with the weapons we received from *Kazan*. They range out over 600 kilometers—the Onyx. Unfortunately, they are not our heaviest warheads, only 200 kilograms, and firing at this range will also expend most of their fuel, so the fires will not be as much of a factor. You know these enemy ships, Fedorov. How do you suggest we proceed?"

Fedorov took a deep breath, realizing he was now about to plan their battle action, and sign the death warrants of many men with each word he spoke. Yet it could not be helped. They had committed themselves to this course, to this battle, and now it had to be fought. It was either that or they would surely see the British take heavy losses. The *Rodney* was already gone, and the two battlecruisers could not stand against the German fleet. They had to act.

"Given the situation," he began, "I think we need to get after the German aircraft carrier first, *Graf Zeppelin*. I believe they will be launching *Stukas* any time now, and so we must strike them quickly, and attempt to either sink that ship or take it out of the action. The *Stukas* will be a grave threat."

"And the battleships?"

"We've hit several, particularly the *Hindenburg*, but we may have to leave those to the British. Let's get that carrier."

"Agreed," said Volsky. "Always get the carrier first. That is a rule that will stand even to our time in 2023. Let us give them a rude awakening with the Onyx missiles we stole from *Kazan*. They will do the job, yes Fedorov?"

"*Graf Zeppelin* has armor, but not anywhere near the protection of the battleships. Yes sir, they should do the job if the two Moskit-IIs I just sent fail to sink that ship." Fedorov rubbed his forehead, a worried look on his face.

"I know what you are feeling, Fedorov," said the Admiral. "Legendary ships out there, commanded by men you have read about, and perhaps idolized in your mind these many years. But you must kill them."

"Correct, sir. Once, after *Yamato*, Karpov told me it would get easier in time, but I have not found this to be the case."

"That is because your conscience is still intact. Killing is never an easy thing to do for a man of conscience. Karpov sees things otherwise, because his soul is darkened. He is an efficient and deadly man at the helm of any ship he commands, but he kills wantonly, and without regret. So be thankful that you feel some of the pain our missiles may inflict on these men and ships out there. Yes, I say ships as well, for we live with them, bond with them, whenever we take to the sea. They are the raft of life itself for us here. Without them we are like Lenkov, sinking into the depths of oblivion. So when we sink one, we know what it is to put men into the cold sea, and know we cannot save them. Never forget that, but also never let it prevent you from doing what is necessary to win the day."

"I understand sir, but this does not make it any easier."

Volsky nodded. "Once I relied on you to do what we should do in these situations, and on Karpov to do what we must. Now I'm afraid that you must wear both hats, Fedorov. You are Captain of this ship, and I may not always be standing at your side here."

"I will do my best, Admiral."

Carrier Graf Zeppelin ~ Norwegian Sea ~ 7 May, 1941, 04:00

We are missing Marco Ritter these days, thought Kurt Böhmer. I was thinking to see him down on the flight deck with that red scarf flapping in the wind. But he'll be out there. Word is that the *Goeben* did very well in the Med as a scout ship, and Ritter cherry picked the best *Stuka* pilots from my flight crews here to look after *Hindenburg*. That said, they could not stop those rocket attacks. Nothing we have can stop them. So the only thing we can do when the sky lights up with those missile trails is put up a good shieldwall.

Brinkmann is in *Prinz Eugen* out in front, and I have the new destroyers *Loki* and *Thor* to either side. After what happened to *Sigfrid*, we must have a destroyer abreast of us at all times, and that failing, one of the heavier ships must stand in for that duty. We can take no chances that those rockets will find us again. Yet for now, the sea is empty, and we will pluck out the eyes of any aircraft that come looking for us. The British carriers are well to the south and west in any case, so we should rule the day here. Now to get our boys up and after the British. If I can sink that old battleship we're looking for, I can save Lütjens and Topp the trouble. Then they can turn and slug it out with the battleships.

The *Schweregruppe* of the task force was out ahead of *Prinz Eugen*. He could not see the tall main masts and superstructure of *Tirpitz* in the darkness, but he could feel the ship's presence, the cold hard Wotan Hart steel plying through the waters like a great shark. *Scharnhorst* and *Gneisenau* were cruising to either side, guarding the battleship as the destroyers stood watch over his carrier. Once bitten, twice shy. Now that the Germans had faced the British rocket weapons, they sailed in shieldwall formation, with one ship protecting another from the deadly sea skimming missiles.

Kurt Böhmer looked at his watch, seeing the elevator bringing up another two fighters, wings still folded as they rose to the main flight deck. It was then that he saw what he had feared since that first astounding attack near Iceland. There were lights in the sky, high up, rising like shooting stars fleeing the earth and seeking the darkness of the night again. But they would not stay high for long. The watchmen had seen them as well, and alarms were ringing all over the ship. He looked to see men running to battle stations, and reached for his field glasses, his heart beating faster.

One... three... four rockets were in the sky now, climbing, then appearing to hang in the darkness like a line of cold steel stars. Then they fell, one by one, as if they were a formation of precision fighters peeling off to attack a target at lower altitude. Down they came, as the men shouted and footsteps rattled the decks. Guns were turning and training, barrels elevating, and then he heard a gunnery officer shouting at his men.

"Not there!" he pointed with a baton. "Lower your guns. They will come in right over the wave tops!"

It was something his men had been oblivious of in that first attack, but forewarned was now fore armed. The Germans knew what to expect. According to plan, they tightened up their sailing order, like a school of fish seeking safety in a group of closely packed ships. *Graf Zeppelin* held *Loki* on the right arm, *Thor* on the left. Now the guns began firing, for the director had been correct, and the missiles were diving for the sea.

Böhmer knew what to expect, that dizzying dance over the wave tops, as if the rockets were deliberately taunting the gunners to try to hit them. The roar of the AA guns now became deafening, the bright fire of the exploding rounds lighting of the sable sky and glowing on the dark waters below. He watched, spellbound again, thinking they must surely miss. How could the British even know where his ships were to target them? Did they have a U-boat nearby to give away his position? They could never find him with a random shot like this. He was thinking of them as a spread of torpedoes, dangerous, but something that might be avoided by maneuver. Yet nothing would stay these lethal weapons from their appointed round...

On they came, low on the sea, the bright fire from their tails now suddenly visible. They were so fast that it was impossible for the gunners to adjust for the range. Böhmer would see them come right at his ships again, unerringly, as if they had eyes, bat-like things, creatures of the night that flew with senses unknown to man, vampires. To his utter amazement, the first of five came boring in right towards his formation.

"Hard to port! All ahead full! All ships to match speed and turn!"

He scarcely had time to shout out the order when the first lance struck his shield on the starboard side. *Loki* was hit just forward of the bridge, smashing right into a 4.7-inch dual purpose gun turret as it fired in futile reprisal. The turret exploded, completely obliterated by the 200kg warhead, and bright orange fire lit up the scene with its angry light.

Then the second missile pummeled *Loki* amidships, the small 6800 ton destroyer rolling with the heavy punch. It was just the size and type of ship the missile had been designed to kill, and it would do exactly that.

Then, to Böhmer's amazement, he watched the next two missiles alter their course. They were not simply well aimed lances thrown from beyond the horizon, a feat that was astounding enough. They *maneuvered*, making lightning quick turns that not even the most agile fighter could have achieved. They *maneuvered*—right into the gap between *Prinz Eugen* and his own ship, but it was not the veteran Prince they were after that morning.

Graf Zeppelin was struck on her port side, about 200 meters forward of the main elevators. There were two 15cm guns there in twin-gun *Dopp MPL C/36* casemate mountings, with 1.2 inches of armor. It was not enough to stop those 200kg warheads, and the turrets fared little better than the smaller guns on *Loki*. The fury of the fireball glowed orange and red on the grey hull of the ship, and then the second missile smashed right behind the heavy anchors suspended on the bow, piercing the thin armor and blowing clean through the ship and out the Starboard side.

The last thing to strike the bow of the ship had been a bottle of champagne during the launch, but now it was a blackened wreck, with heavy fire and smoke coiling up from the wound.

Böhmer soon learned that neither rocket had penetrated to the arming deck, where the *Stukas* were sitting like a flock of densely packed black crows, with heavy bombs mounted beneath the stubby, folded wings. How in god's name could they move like that, he thought? These are precision guided weapons! Nothing on earth could fly so fast, and turn so smartly to find his ship in the middle of the formation like this. It was almost like magic!

Chapter 32

Aboard *Kirov*, Volsky was standing by the Captain's chair, where he had insisted Fedorov take his seat to lead the opening action against the German fleet. He was watching his young Captain closely, as if he thought Fedorov might wince when Rodenko reported that all missiles launched had found the target. That was no surprise. Karpov had said it many times before—*what we target, we hit, and what we hit we can destroy.*

Yet Fedorov did not feel like Karpov that day. Yes, he was bothered by the thought that each order he gave here was sending men to their death, and burning their ships, still unseen over the far horizon. At least it was not as bad as that day when they had faced off against the great battleship *Yamato*, its mighty guns flinging massive shells at *Kirov*, coming within a hair's breadth of striking the ship at one point, and sweeping away the top radar mast as it passed overhead like a merciless hammer of doom, striking the sea with a thunderous roar.

Thankfully, they had replaced that system when they returned to Vladivostok, and now it spun rapidly on that same mast overhead, its electronic fingers seeking out the German task force in the early pre-dawn hours.

Fedorov looked at Volsky. "Two hit's sir."

"What is your assessment, Fedorov?" said the Admiral. "Will they be enough to put that ship out of action?"

"We will not know that unless we get the KA-40 back up for battle damage assessment, or unless they begin launching planes. In that instance, I believe we must fire again."

"Agreed," said Volsky. "This is an armored ship?"

"No more than 100mm on the belt," said Fedorov. "45 to 60mm on the flight deck."

"Then it is vulnerable to plunging fire as well." The Admiral folded his arms. "We might do more damage that way if it becomes necessary."

They had decided to strike in the early pre-dawn hours, thinking to pre-empt any air strike that may be launched by the German carrier. Now they sat like a dark spider at the center of an electronic web spun out by the ship's powerful radar systems. All about them, their adversaries were creeping into that web, unaware of the danger that lurked over their horizon... until those first missiles broke the stillness of the dawn, and the battle began.

Fedorov knew it was to be a one sided affair. Their enemy could not even see them, let alone strike at them in reprisal. With their speed, they could stay well beyond the range of the massive guns on the German battleships, so it would be a simple and merciless equation as he saw things. It would be a contest of fire and shock against German steel. How much of a pounding could their ships take before the steel broke in the wills of the Admirals and Captains who commanded them?

Before the action he had discussed the situation with Admiral Volsky, and came down to a grim conclusion. Fedorov had pointed out that they had only 28 anti-ship missiles, still more than a normal combat load, due to the fact that they had pirated missiles from the submarine *Kazan*.

"This is the heart of the German fleet, is it not, Fedorov?"

"It appears so," said Fedorov. "We've identified all three battleships, the two battlecruisers, the carrier *Graf Zeppelin* and the light escort carrier that was with *Hindenburg*."

"Then if we use the power we now have, we can literally take the German fleet out of the war. Yes? I am not speaking of a nuclear option here. Yet my question to you is this—can we cripple the German navy for good here by using the conventional warheads we still have?"

"Very likely," said Fedorov. "That will depend on how we hit them."

"Hard, Fedorov. We must hit them very hard. A carrier must be saturated to achieve a certain kill. I know this is our tactic in modern times, but will it apply here?"

"The *Graf Zeppelin* has only a third the displacement of a typical *Nimitz* Class carrier, sir. And the *Nimitz* could sustain three times the damage of even the best built carrier in WWII. We may be able to mission kill this German carrier with two or three hits."

"Yet that would allow it to survive, would it not? Now I begin to sound like Karpov, but would that mean we must fight this same battle all over again, and without the missiles we fire here today? No. I think we must take a hard line here. If we engage, then we must do so with the intent of killing these ships, not just putting damage on them to discourage them. Do you agree, Fedorov?"

After a deep breath, Fedorov nodded his assent.

"But you still have reservations," said Volsky. "I can see it in your eyes."

"It's not that, sir," said Fedorov.

"Then what? Tell me why you hesitate?"

"It isn't the tactics, Admiral. I agree. If we fight here now, and with a limited missile inventory, then we should seek a decisive engagement. Yes, I know I also sound like Karpov now, but we both admit that in many ways he was correct when it came to battle. I was thinking about something else—how the Germans could have learned about *Rodney*."

"Volkov? Might he have tipped them off?"

"I've wondered about that, but cannot see how he would be privy to that information Miss Fairchild disclosed. Yes, he might be able to look up the service record and see that *Rodney* did have that gold bullion aboard, and the Elgin Marbles, but that would be of little consequence. It would not be anything that would compel the

Germans to maneuver as they have here, and seek out that single ship."

"Could we be reading more into their maneuvers than they really know, Fedorov? After all, both task groups now appear on a course to rendezvous by mid-day, and they are merely heading away from the British battleships behind them."

"Yes, and directly towards us. I think they must know we have followed them through the straits of Gibraltar, sir. Yet that northern group is not bearing on our position. It is on a course to intercept *Rodney*. So is the *Hindenburg* group."

"Mere coincidence," Volsky suggested.

"No sir, they knew the position of *Rodney* well enough."

"And don't forget that we have that previous message intercept. It appeared Lütjens was ordered to take this course—ordered to seek out *Rodney*."

The Captain nodded, again with some sense of misgiving obvious on his face. Minutes later they began their attack, and now the next move was plotted in this uneven chess game, where the Russian ship could move to develop all its pieces before the enemy could lay a finger on a single pawn.

"Fourteen missiles remaining," said Volsky. "Two must have struck a smaller escort ship."

"They are learning, Admiral," said Fedorov. "They are trying to steam in tight formations around the carrier to protect it."

"Correct," said Rodenko. "I can now read two ships in close proximity to the primary. They must have redeployed the cruiser escort to replace the ship we hit with those first two missiles."

"All the more reason to change our angle of attack," said Volsky. "I was told we still have several *Moskit-IIs* programmed for vertical strike profiles—is this so, Mister Samsonov?"

"Correct Admiral. I have three of six missiles in that system programmed for vertical strike."

"Then I think this is the next move, Fedorov," said Volsky. "A knight leaping from above, and not the slashing, sea-skimming attack of the Bishop."

"I'm seeing air activity over the primary," said Rodenko. "I think they're launching."

"So our first strike was not enough," said Volsky.

Fedorov hesitated, just long enough for Volsky to turn his head from Nikolin to regard him more closely. Then the young Captain swallowed, nodded, and turned to Samsonov.

"How many *Moskit-II* missiles remain?"

"Six missiles loaded and ready—one in the number ten bay." Samsonov was reminding Fedorov that one of the six was mounted in the special weapons bay, where a nuclear warhead could be loaded onto the missile if so ordered. The other two were on P-1000s. The reserved Moskit was not armed today, but Fedorov took note of that. They still had three special warheads, and if they ever had to use them, they would need missiles. So instead of 14 missiles available as reported earlier, he actually had no more than 11 if he wished to retain three for those special warheads, and he had already fired two Onyx. It was time to do some heavier hitting.

"Ready one *Moskit-II* for immediate launch," he said. "Vertical attack profile. Target the primary, carrier *Graf Zeppelin*."

With over twice the warhead weight of the missiles they had received from *Kazan*, this was the ship's premier ship killer. It was normally programmed to be a fast supersonic sea-skimmer, but they had found that the heavy side armor of the battleships of this era had been able to survive hits at the water line. So it was decided to reprogram missiles to pop up and hit the superstructure, or simply strike from high above, where the thinner deck armor could easily be penetrated by the big 450kg warhead moving at the blistering speed of Mach three.

"Very well," said Fedorov. "Mark your target and fire."

18:00, 25 MAY 1941 ~ Carrier Graf Zeppelin

Two of three fighters on deck had been damaged by shrapnel hits from the earlier missile strike that struck *Graf Zeppelin* near the bow. This had prompted Kapitan Böhmer to urge his flight engineers to get as many *Stukas* up on the deck as possible. He was determined to launch, even if it meant his planes would have to storm right through the smoke forward, blinded by the dark smoke now rolling right down the flight deck when he turned into the wind, and licked by flames as they took off over the bow. The British had done the very same thing with those fluttering moths of theirs. So he urged his crews and pilots on.

While Fedorov and Volsky had discussed how to proceed, sorting through what the Germans knew about *Rodney*, they got up a flight of six *Stukas* and had them all airborne.

And then it came...

It was the same as before when Böhmer saw it, a bright light ascending from the purple edge of the coming dawn, climbing, climbing. Then it arced over and began to fall, a fiery comet that seemed to grow larger and brighter with each passing second. Down it came, swift and silent, as it was moving three times faster than the roar of its own engines. The eerie silence of its coming was deceptive, and then it thundered down on his ship, plunging right through the armored deck amidships with a shattering explosion.

Graf Zeppelin rocked with the blow, the orange fire erupting from the guts of the ship in a broiling mass. It was as if the carrier had been struck by a swift kamikaze, but one weighing over 4500 kilograms, and with a 450kg explosive penetrating warhead. The rest was the great fuel laden mass of the rocket itself, which penetrated the deck, exploded with torrential fire and shock below, and plunged right through the maintenance deck where another twenty *Stukas* were still being armed. The explosion erupted from the machinery spaces below, and set off 500 pound bombs, one after another, in a terrible sequence of death and destruction. Planes and flight crews were immolated, bulkheads blown apart, fuel set fire in a raging inferno. The damage extended all the way down to one of the two propulsion shafts, severing it, and then the shock of the attack blew completely through the hull.

Graf Zeppelin keeled over to one side as the hull was breached below the water line. But it was the raging inferno within that would consume the ship, the fires reaching one plane after another, the ordnance and aviation fuel feeding the conflagration. The ship was doomed. Germany's first aircraft carrier, famous even though it never steamed on the high seas or saw combat in the war Fedorov knew, would not survive the hour.

High above, the six lucky *Stuka* pilots who bravely took off through the deck smoke, now saw the volcanic eruption below, and gasped at the fireball that now consumed the ship. Yet the Goeben was already gone, and they were over 900 miles from a friendly coast. They knew they were doomed, but they would not ditch until they had first found an enemy ship and dropped their bombs. The destroyer *Thor*, steaming off the port side, had to make an emergency turn away from the carrier to avoid the holocaust. Even so, the sides and superstructure of the smaller ship were lacerated with shrapnel. *Prinz Eugen* had fallen off to take up a position to the starboard side of the carrier when it turned after the initial missile strike. Now the men aboard the heavy cruiser gaped in awe at the scene unfolding.

The carrier was soon in a heavy list, still burning fiercely when it began to keel over, the hot fires hissing into the sea. All the remaining fighters and *Stukas*, and the elite pilots that had trained to fly them off the carrier, would die in those desperate, violent minutes, along with nearly 1,700 officers and crew of every rank.

There would be twenty two survivors.

Chapter 33

"That's done it!' said Rodenko. "I'm losing radar returns of the carrier. It's sinking."

"Good job Fedorov, Samsonov," Volsky commended both men. "I see the British battlecruisers have escaped north too."

"That was wise," said Fedorov. "They will wait for their battleships now, but I wonder what Lütjens will do."

Numbers clawed at Fedorov now.... Facts that he could call up from the library of his mind, or look up if he ever forgot them. Carrier *Graf Zeppelin*, 33,550 tons displacement, 262 meters in length, four geared turbines producing 200,000 shaft horsepower. Aircraft carried: 42. Ship's Compliment: 1,720.

It had taken just one missile, angled at the right attack, and falling into what amounted to a readymade explosive mass of 500 pound bombs and volatile aviation fuel. The damage was violent, catastrophic, and final, and this was a ship they would never have to face or fight again. *The legend was gone—killed by me*, thought Fedorov. *All those lives... I'm responsible...*

Admiral Volsky was watching him closely again, understanding what he was feeling. He knew that he could never reason away the emotion, and the heavy burden of having to kill. It was not even as if the ship itself were in any danger. They struck down their enemy before they even knew they were in harm's way.

"It had to be done, Mister Fedorov," said the Admiral.

"I understand, sir." Fedorov tried to clear his mind of his dark thoughts and feelings of guilt. Volsky was trying to help him.

"Yes," said Volsky. "I know it was a hard blow to those men out there. Yet we must be prepared to do more here. This was a ship that was never even supposed to be at sea in this war."

"Another interloper," said Fedorov, "as we are, sir."

"Very well," Volsky nodded. "Now we must consider the battleships. There will be time enough later to think about what we have done here. At the moment, the enemy is approaching our horizon, but they present many targets. We may have only one missile or two to put on each ship." Volsky shook his head.

"I'm afraid that the battleships may not die so easily," said Fedorov. "When Tovey caught the *Bismarck* in our history with three British battleships, *Rodney* included, they put 2,878 rounds of all calibers into that ship, and *Bismarck* was still afloat. It took three more torpedoes, and some say deliberate scuttling, before the great ship went down."

"Nothing is unsinkable," said Volsky.

"Yes sir, that we know all too well. Oh, we'll hurt what we fire at, but it will take a good deal to sink these ships."

"Then our intention will be to disable them, mission kill them, and leave the rest to the Royal Navy."

"In that case, we may wish to program more of these high angle attack profiles. And I would also suggest we use the Vodopads"

"Torpedoes?" said Volsky. "I see. That was how we bested that big Japanese battleship."

"Yes sir. Our missiles hurt the enemy, but have not really killed any battleship we engaged. Yet a torpedo hit, particularly one designed to break a ship's back, or follow its wake to the rudder, is a very dangerous weapon, for any ship."

"Agreed. We are in range of this same task group now. The Vodopads rocket assisted approach can take it out 120 kilometers. How many rounds do we have remaining on that system?" Admiral Volsky looked to Tasarov, who seemed lost beneath his headset, his eyes closed, listening very intently to something.

"Mister Tasarov?"

"I'm sorry sir..."

"An undersea contact?" Volsky moved to the young Lieutenant's station now.

"No sir... I do not think so..."

Fedorov was still musing. "I see *Hindenburg* is gaining a little speed. They must be getting back underway. I wonder what he will do now that they have no air cover?"

"We need you now Tasarov. Ready your torpedoes, Vodopad and Veter."

"Yes sir, standing by."

"Let us see if the Germans still want a fight here." Volsky folded his arms.

That was the question on the mind of Admiral Lütjens that hour.

He was sitting on the *Hindenburg*, looking at the damage control reports, and receiving the same from *Tirpitz* and *Bismarck*. Only *Scharnhorst* and *Gneisenau* remained undamaged. Both his carriers were gone, and he now had no air cover. The few planes still aloft could do nothing but ditch near his ships so the pilots could be saved, and that was the order he sent them.

Wilhelmshaven had intelligence for him that the British were coming with *Hood, Duke of York, King George V*, and *Prince of Wales* to join the two battlecruisers that were lingering nearby. Those battleships would bring 38 big guns to join the 12 on the battlecruisers. And the British would have carriers too.

His own ships would have 24 big guns, and 18 more 11-inchers on the battlecruisers. Now he was thinking he would do better to turn and head for French ports. Except for *Hood* and the battlecruisers, the British battleships made only about 28 knots. If he could get his ships moving east now, he might just slip away.

That was what he decided to do, sending an 'all ships change heading and follow me' order. He turned northeast for Brest at 19:30.

Seeing this, Fedorov concluded the Germans were retiring to Brest or St. Nazaire. He asked Admiral to meet with him in the Ready room.

"Sir," he said. "Before you came on the bridge, Director Kamenski briefed me on an important mission. He says it is vital to Britain's prospects in the war here now."

Then Fedorov briefed the Admiral with all Kamenski had told him. "He says that we are to coordinate with *Argos Fire* on this mission and enlist their support, for they possess a device that can receive instructions he gave me on a digital memory key with code to coordinate a shift."

"A shift? Where?"

"My assumption is the year and time of these events involving Churchill, 1898, in the Sudan."

"The Sudan?" We cannot sail the Nubian deserts, Fedorov."

"No sir, but we can get close enough for the KA-40 by entering the Red Sea. As the Germans appear to be retiring, I suggest we disengage here and conserve our missiles for the trip through the Med to the Suez Canal. From there, we can get well down the Red Sea, and very close to this action in Sudan."

"And do what? Are we to throw our remaining missiles at these Dervish you speak of?"

"No sir. But we have other means, along with *Argos Fire*. This will be a mission for Troyak and our Marines, and hopefully with support from the Argonauts on *Argos Fire*."

"You are proposing we mount a rescue operation for Churchill?"

"Something like that. It will be aimed at the Dervish position the 21st Lancers charged late in that battle I was describing a moment ago—Omdurman."

"And if we do not do this?"

"Then Churchill dies and England is bereft of his considerable services in this war. I haven't been able to look at any of the history, but it will certainly change the course of the war, and that affects everything we fought for, and any future that arises from these years—all our many interventions."

"So you are telling me that all our chips are on the table for this mission?"

"Yes sir, that about sums it up."

"Then of course we must do whatever we can. Sinking another German ship here will not matter. Let me inform Admiral Tovey. You go and ask *Argos Fire* to come along side and then go brief them and gain their support."

"Thank you, Admiral. I knew you would understand."

20:00 25 MAY 1941 ~ Aboard Argos Fire

Fedorov went over to the *Argos Fire* by boat, hoping Elena Fairchild and the others would be as supportive as Volsky was. He would meet with Captain Gordon MacRae, and Mack Morgin, his Intelligence Officer in Miss Fairchild's stateroom.

"Greeting's Captain Fedorov. What's this about? Something too hot for radio traffic?"

Fedorov nodded. "I received some rather ominous intelligence, which I think you might easily verify. Churchill is dead." Fedorov just came right to the point.

"What? Dead?" said Morgin. "I've heard nothing at all on that, not a whisper on the wire."

"How did it happen?" asked Elena, a shocked expression on her face. "Was it the bombing in London?"

"No," said Fedorov. "In fact he was not harmed here in the war at all, because he wasn't involved."

"What?"

Then Fedorov came out with it. "He died in the year 1898, in the Charge of the 21st Lancers at the Battle of Omdurman. So he never became Prime Minister, and everything he did to help steer Britain through these rough waters never happened."

"Are you serious?"

"Deadly serious. I'll give you the whole briefing I received, and the plan I've come up with to try and reverse this catastrophe, because that's what it is without Churchill in this war."

Elena wanted to cooperate, but now she first looked at Mack Morgan and asked him to check on it.

"Mack, find out who the bloody Prime Minister is, but don't mention Churchill directly on the call."

"Right Mum," said Morgan, and he excused himself. It was all too much to believe, but he would get to his Dark Intelligence web and ferret out the answer easily enough. In the meantime, Fedorov briefed Elena and MacRae.

When he had finished, Elena spoke. "Assuming this is all true. What do you propose we do about it?"

"Well," said Fedorov, "I haven't had much time with this to work out a finished plan, but I was thinking we could give this to our Marines, and perhaps with the support of your Argonauts. We can get in range of the site from the Red Sea."

"Yes, but we're here in 1941, Captain," said MacRae. "How do you propose we get to 1898?"

"I was given this by Director Kamenski." Fedorov produced the memory key Kamenski had given him. "He said it could interface with a device you have here on your ship."

"You mean that bloody Box?" MacRae's eyes widened. Then in came Mack Morgan, a grim look on his face.

"It's all correct," he said "Lord Halifax is Prime Minister now, and there's not a whisper of anything to do with Churchill—nothing."

"God in his heaven," said Elena. "Captain Fedorov—we're in. May I assume that Memory key has instructions?"

"That's what I'm thinking, but I haven't had a chance to look it over. I think our first task is going to be getting safely to the Suez Canal, which means we have to run the Strait of Gibraltar."

"Then I suggest we lay in that course and get moving. Tovey can handle the Germans from here on out."

"Yes, my Admiral Volsky is briefing him, perhaps just that we need to break off and attend to something. I don't think he'll mention Churchill."

"Wise of him," said Elena. "Though I'm sure he knows the man is dead. Then again, he'd know nothing of his time at the helm as we know it. Alright, we'll take point, let's get headed for the Straits of Gibraltar, and that will give you time to digest what's on that key. Let me know what you find, because I may have a plan B for us if we hit any roadblocks."

"Thank you. I knew we could rely on you. I'll look the content of this key over and then we'll meet again for a mission briefing before Gibraltar."

Part XII

Men of Valour

"Arm yourselves, and be ye men of valour..."
—**Winston Churchill**

Chapter 34
30 NM west of Tangiers, 20:00, 26 MAY 1941

They left the chase in the Atlantic at 19:00 on 25 May, and ran at 28 knots for Gibraltar. By 20:00 the following evening, they were west of Tangiers, ready to run the Straits. The Germans had seen them coming, but Fedorov did not fear any strike by aircraft or surface ships. *Argos Fire* and *Kirov* could defeat either threat easily, but it was the undersea threat that gave Fedorov worries.

Kirov's forward Bullnose sonar dome had been damaged earlier, but Tasarov was listening on the side hull sonar sensors, and a towed array.

There were only a few Axis submarines in Gibraltar at that time, and Captain Guissepi Caito of the Italian Submarine *Narvalo* was one of them. He would be joined by Kapitan Walter Kell in *U-204*. Another boat was in the harbor, but undergoing repairs. Kell's boat was just commissioned in March of 1941, but it was out from Kiel early in this turn of events. After running the Denmark Strait, Kell had lean pickings on his first patrol. He had been scheduled to return to Brest, but was instead diverted to Gibraltar where his boat was refueled and ready to take on this duty in attempting to block the Strait.

Fedorov planned to run south, closer to Tangiers and Morocco, and so he would run afoul of Kell on that course. Captain Caito was to the north, covering routes closer to Gibraltar. Both boats had just dipped into the ceiling on the thermal layer, and were creeping at 5 knots through the Strait heading west.

It was to be a battle of sensors and ears, and the best side would win this confrontation. At his post for the planned night run of the Strait, Tasarov was settled in under his headset. He had the day shift off and was well rested. The deep humming sound he had heard earlier, both on and off duty, had finally abated after Kamenski activated the Temporal Stabilizer he gave Fedorov. Tasarov's head was now clear, and his ears were fine for the work ahead.

Aboard *Argos Fire*, Captain MacRae and Commander Dean were on the bridge, with *Kirov* following them into the strait. They saw German search planes rising from the airfield at Gibraltar on radar, but as soon as they gained any elevation MacRae put Aster missiles on them, and shot two down before the Germans got the message. The squadron of Stukas stationed at Gibraltar was armed and ready, but they would get no orders after those two search planes were destroyed within minutes after takeoff.

In a well choreographed plan, *Kirov* was following the wake of MacRae's ship, about 2.5 miles behind. As the two ships passed north of Tangiers on a very dark night, they reduced speed to 20 knots. Captain Caito on the Italian sub was now angling southwest to get a little better coverage over the center of the channel. Both boats were beyond the sub nets, and out of the minefield defensive area. The night was tense after they had received a signal that the enemy ships were entering the Strait.

Not surprisingly, Tasarov was the first to hear something. "Undersea contact," he said, "bearing due east at just under five miles."

"Kill it, Tasarov. Use the Starfish."

That was the SS-N-15 Starfish rocket torpedo, also called the RPK-6 Vodopad. Tasarov fired that weapon, and a minute later he picked up a second undersea contact, the Italian boat, bearing 45 degrees northeast and five miles out. Captain Caito's boat had not yet detected the two intruders, even though he was creeping at just two knots. Then his sonar operator heard a splash followed by an underwater explosion. U-204 had been found and killed by *Kirov's* Starfish. The *Argos Fire* was an air defense destroyer, and not well equipped for undersea contacts, but Tasarov fired a second Starfish, which found and killed Caito's boat with little trouble. The air threat and now the undersea threat was cleared. They saw no sign of anything else, not even local fishing trawlers or patrol craft.

They would run just outside shore battery range from Gibraltar, and no one on the southern coast in Morocco seemed ready to challenge them, so it was up to the minefield. When Tasarov detected it, they would have to slow to 10 knots and he would call out contacts left and right, as Fedorov eased the ship through that field, making minor course corrections. Men stood ready on deck with machineguns to target floating mines, but most were moored at various depths and not visible. The field had mainly been laid to keep out allied submarines, as it was thought the Stukas and surface ships would hold against an allied surface threat. Captain MacRae was also steering a careful path through the field by 23:00.

It was easier than we feared, thought Fedorov. It's good that there wasn't a battleship out there to try its luck with us.

That wasn't entirely true. The Nazi-French battleship *Jean Bart* was in Gibraltar, but it was not ordered to sea or ordered to fire; not against these targets. The Germans preferred to retain that ship unscathed, an made no further effort to stop the little flotilla. The Axis powers had put their money on those two submarines, but they had not counted on someone like Tasarov.

Now it would be a thousand miles to the Sicilian Narrows, the next possible choke point, with plenty of German air power in Sicily and Tunisia. Fedorov wondered whether the Germans wanted to lose more planes with a challenge there. They had plenty of SAM's left, as did *Argos Fire*.

That night, Fedorov went to his quarters and looked for his copy of Churchill's *The River War*, the account of the entire campaign mounted by Kitchener to defeat the Mahdist rebels. He could not find it, and was chilled to see an empty space in his bookcase, right where that book should have been.

Of course, he thought, it was never written. So instead he took to reading everything else he could find about that campaign: Battle Story: *Omdurman 1898* by William Wright, *Onwards to Omdurman* by Keith Surridge, *Omdurman* by Peter Ziegler, *Sudan: The Reconquest Reappraised* by Edward M. Spiers. He wanted to learn everything he could about the charge of the 21st Lancers. How was he to prevent it, and that failing how might he aid it.

He had discussed their options with Captain MacRae and they decided that using valuable missiles against the Dervish position would probably not be effective.

"I'll tell you what," said MacRae. "They get one look at our X-3 helicopters spitting hellfire missiles at them and rolling in with mini-guns, and they'll most likely run like Satan and all his demons were after them. Just the sight and sound of a helicopter will likely terrify them."

Fedorov thought about that. It would indeed be a shock, but one the historians would have great trouble explaining. Would eye witness reports of that survive? Wouldn't the British Lancers see it too? Might a keen reader in the future correctly interpret what these witnesses were describing? How could it possibly be explained as anything other than the wild imaginings of terrified men at the edge of death's door?

A second option was to get the Marines and Argonauts in under cover of darkness, landing them behind the Dervish line that was attacked by the Lancers. Then they could dismount the choppers and come up behind the Dervish. With every man carrying a weapon more deadly than a Maxim Machine gun. They could quickly thin the herd. But that would also put them all at risk. Would there be casualties? How would they find Churchill? Should they try that, and attempt to bring him back to the ship? What would that experience do to him—a ride on a helicopter flanked by dour faced Marines? It was a lot to think about.

Hitting the Dervish defenders with as much shock and awe as they could might just disperse them. They might truly believe they were being assailed by demons and flee. That would allow the 21st Lancers to charge and mop up the stragglers, but what if one spear or rifle bullet were to still find Churchill? Picking him out of a crush of riders all in khaki uniforms would not be easy. What if Mother Time stubbornly claimed his life, if only just to spite their attempt at interfering here? There were too many questions.

Now he considered other assets that might be at hand, and his mind fell to Beatty's Gunboats. He knew that several gunboats were cruising off each flank of Kitchener's position where it met the Nile. Could their firepower be used?

He read and reread accounts of the charge, one of the last charges made by cavalry in history, along with the charge of the 20th Hussars against Turkish infantry during the Chanak Crisis of 1920. Yet Omdurman was indeed the last charge of a full British cavalry regiment.

Now Fedorov got to thinking about the orders the commander of the 21st Lancers was operating under, Colonel Rowland Hill Martin. He had been told by Kitchener to reconnoiter from the southern end of the *zeriba* to the outskirts of Omdurman. When the Dervish line in the depression of the *khor* was first sighted, Martin signaled back to the Zeriba with a heliograph to make a report. Some minutes later he received a reply, again flashed by heliograph: "advance and use every effort to prevent the enemy re-entering Omdurman."

This gave him an idea, but it would be complicated to try and interfere with that heliograph signal, at either end of the communication.

Reading further he determined that Colonel Martin did not immediately order a charge. He first sent out patrols to see what lay on their immediate front. That was when Lieutenant Grenfell spotted the *khor*, a place called Abu Sunt, and incorrectly estimated the enemy Dervish there to be between 700 and 1000 men. Might that moment provide a lever on these events? Then he remembered another event, on the previous day, and his eyes sparkled. Now he finally had a good idea.

He had been worrying about the more direct options he might take. Just using the shock of the helicopters appearing, or landing the men to creep up behind the Dervish and decimate them would dramatically shuffle the deck in terms of who died here and who lived. His Marines could kill hundreds, but an attack from behind would give the Dervish no route of retreat.

Now he looked at the ground south of that *khor* called Abu Sunt. If any attack was made, it should come from that side, driving the Dervish from that depression. Then he thought of something else.

The next day he would invite Captain MacRae to *Kirov*, and asked Major Troyak to attend (who still considered himself a Sergeant Major in spite of his promotion).

"Alright," Fedorov began. He had drawn a good map the previous night on the back of a navigation chart. "So here's the position for the action involving 21st Lancers, this wadi here. There is the Nile, these are the saddle and rise of Jebel Surgham. The Charge that killed Churchill was fought here, in this wadi I've drawn, called a *khor*—Abu Surt. Now I've thought of every possible way we might attack that *khor* before the charge, and I don't like any of those options. Yet it's the ground between the *khor* and the Kitchener's encampment on the Nile that most interests me. And I'm looking at operating the day *before* the Cavalry charge, Sept 1st, not on the day of the battle."

Fedorov explained Kitchener's advance that day, and how he received the first reports of the massed Dervish Army north of Jebel Surgham. "Churchill delivered one of those reports, which means he had to ride from the vicinity of those hills, or this saddle to find

Kitchener somewhere here. That's where we bag the man—on his way to make that report."

"Bag him?" said MacRae.

"Yes, I want a night infiltration to this islet on the Nile here, directly opposite this ground. We will wait through Sept 1, and observe the far bank of the Nile, particularly the gunboats on that flank. Both he boats and cavalry will move out early on 2nd September. After that the men will move by inflatable rubber rafts, cross this arm of the Nile and gain a position on this open ground. There you hunker down and wait for Churchill. Your mission is to spot, contact, and apprehend Churchill as he rides back to make his report to Kitchener the morning od 2nd September. So you'll want to have teams strung out all along this area, because who knows what route Churchill took. You bag him, hustle him back to the inflatables and get him across the river to that islet again. That's the plan, and we can discuss details if anyone has questions."

"Damn clever," said MacRae. "I like it. But how do we get out there night of September 1st? Won't we be seen from this encampment? Particularly with the helicopters."

"It wasn't there yet," said Fedorov. "Kitchener's Army was camped farther north on the river that night. He broke camp the morning of 2 September and resumed his advance and then set his final camp by 10:00 that morning. So we'll need to get the helicopters in on the night and early morning of September 1st. We'll have the cover of a storm. Yes, it may be a slog for the Marines, but they can handle it. Then we cross the river on the morning of the 2nd. That was when the Lancers spotted the Dervish Army and Churchill was sent back to report."

"Just one question. How do we get from 1941 to the night of 1 September 1898?"

"There's the rub," said Fedorov. "It's all up to Kamenski and how they programmed that memory key. I can only hope his people thought this through."

"Was this his plan?"

"No, his plan was only to deliver our ships to 1898. I put this together after reading the history."

Chapter 35
The Red Sea, BCG Kirov, 28 May 1941

It was, as MacRae had put it, "damn clever." Instead of trying to engage and maul thousands of Dervish fighters, or spook them so badly that they would flee, they would use a smaller force and employ stealth. Fedorov could think of no way they could nab Churchill or have any chance of completely assuring his safety once the cavalry charge began. They simply had to get to him *before* that charge, but MacRae's question was the problem now—how to get to September 1st of 1898? They would just have to see where they ended up after the shift to 1898. It was a roll of the dice.

They ran the Sicilian narrows without much difficulty, only having to discourage a flight of Italian planes and then take down one U-boat. Even though the Axis powers had marked their progress through the Med, it seemed they had little ardor for battle with these strange and powerful mystery ships. *Regia Marina,* the Italian Navy, made no effort to send a surface action group against these ships any more than they wanted to face off with the Royal Navy. So they made it safely to Suez, and on through the Canal to the Red Sea. Now they were hovering off the coast of Sudan south of Suakin and the port that was named after Osman Digna in their own time. Fedorov finally knew why.

The closest point in the Red Sea to Khartum was about 30 miles south of Suakin, and that's where they were now the two ships close by each other for the planned shift to 1898. From that point, it was 385 air miles to the islet on the Nile that Fedorov wanted to target as their Landing Zone.

Fedorov read the instructions on the memory key Kamenski had given him. They said that by merely inserting the key in a side port in the box on *Argos Fire,* all the necessary programming would be in place for that device to take them to the battle of Omdurman, but when? Kamenski's notes were not specific, though he stated that they would appear in the Red Sea, at any position their ships occupied when the shift was initiated. What if that shift delivered them to the second day of September? That would make the helicopter entry more difficult, easily seen from the encampment. "I'll leave you time on both ends of the cavalry charge," Kamenski had written, but he wasn't clear as to what that meant.

Fedorov asked MacRae about this device on *Argos Fire*, but the Captain could only describe it in broad terms. Fedorov asked if he might see it, and he arranged to visit MacRae's ship. All Fedorov knew was that Elena Fairchild had found the device at the oracle of Delphi in the Greek isles, and that it had something to do with the keys they had been looking for. At this point, he knew nothing of the device Kamenski would later give them, and its ability to precisely control a temporal shift. So while Fedorov thought he had come up with a great plan, the risk and uncertainty around it was still troubling him. Aboard *Argos Fire*, he met with Elena and explained the mission plan with MacRae.

"Then that memory key has all the coordinates to get us there from 1941?" asked Elena.

"So I was led to believe," said Fedorov, "but have you used this device to shift before?"

"Only with our first arrival here, and at that point, I knew virtually nothing about it. I believe it was pre-programmed to move us to 1941, and I have no idea how it might be coaxed into taking us to any other time. It's as much of a mystery to me as these damn keys are. As you can see, there are seven apertures on the top, all in the shape of a key. But I don't know whether they must be mounted there for this thing to work or not."

"Does it have any ports that could receive this memory key?"

"Yes, I've looked it over many times, there are three ports on the right side, and my man Mack Morgan says one is a USB 4.0 port, with a 40 Gigabyte data transfer rate per second. He didn't know what the other two were."

"They might be even faster ports from future tech evolutions," Fedorov suggested. "I was able to read files on it from a desktop computer on *Kirov*. But I'm not sure what will happen if I were to plug it into that device, which is what Kamenski's instructions tell me to do."

Then I guess we'll just have to take a leap of faith here," said Elena.

"For that matter, I'm not even sure how we'll know what the date and time is after we shift. This is maddening." Fedorov shrugged.

"I think we'll just have to trust this Director Kamenski. We've already failed to save *Rodney*, so let's just hope this mission plays out as we need it to."

"Kamenski's notes say we'll have a 48 hour window in 1898, or a visa of 48 hours, as he calls it. That gives me some hope that window will open some time prior to the climactic cavalry charge that would include our target date of 1 September."

"Sounds reasonable," said MacRae.

"Alright, who goes on this mission?" Elena folded her arms.

"I'm sending in our Marines, a single eleven man squad under Troyak, and he'll hand pick our men. I've decided to come along too. I was hoping you might lend us at least one English speaker. My plan is to form smaller teams for a picket like—a king of human trip wire to catch Churchill. I can manage a little English, but a native speaker would be best."

"No problem, we'll put all our men at your disposal. Assign them as you see fit."

"Thank you. We'll be on our KA-40, which can take 16 men. We'll have the range to get out and back too, and with only 12 men aboard, we'll have room for the inflatable boats. Can you make the 385 mile range to the Nile on your choppers?"

"No problem," said MacRae. "We can even carry reserve fuel in external fuel tanks."

"Same with us," said Fedorov. We'll take in a dozen Marines, counting myself, and your English speaker. You'll be bringing ten Argonauts."

"Armed to the teeth," said MacRae, "And I'll go too. We'll make a pair of Captains courageous."

"Hopefully, we can get in to the Nile before dawn on Sept 1st, but we'll have to run without lights. It will be dark in a good storm, but the moon will be up and full, so if it breaks through the cloud cover, we'll have some light on the ground."

"We'll have FLIR," said MacRae, which was forward looking Infrared. The Russian Helicopter could also mount such a sensor. And they would all have night vision goggles as well. The only variable out of their control was the target date Kamenski had programmed into the device. For that, unless there was some way to alter the shift program once the device activated, they would just hope to go with whatever Kamenski's people programmed.

The Shift 30 miles south of Suakin, Sudan, in the Red Sea

Troyak had hand picked his very best men, which of course included Zykov. Fedorov briefed everyone, and it was decided that the men would break into three man teams, and dot them in positions across that desert once they crossed the Nile. Each team would deploy with the men about 20 to 50 yards apart, using any cover they could find. They had camo rain parkas, plenty of water, and plenty of energy bars and ammo too. It was decided to mix the Argonauts, all English speakers, in with the Marines after they crossed the Nile. Each team would be composed of two Marines and one Argonaut. That would make six teams in the desert. Then two Argonauts would would remain with the inflatable boats, with Fedorov and MacRae; and the last two would remain with the helicopters and pilots.

"This is a snatch and grab," Fedorov briefed the men, "with a Russian speaking Argonaut acting as a translator for each team. We aren't going to kill hundreds of Dervish, though you'll defend yourself if attacked. The target will be a single rider on horseback, wearing Khaki British kit and a pith style helmet. He'll probably be coming at a fast trot, but we should be able to spot him well before he reaches our picket line. It will be the responsibility of the team closest to this rider to stop an secure him, and that without harming a hair on the man's head. If necessary, you can kill his horse, but without him on it please. Get Churchill to ground and keep him safe. Use the Comms to immediately notify me when you have him, and be aware, there may be more then one rider coming back to report, so you'll have to stop anyone who crosses our deployment line. Unless you encounter Churchill, let them pass, but you'll first have to ascertain who they are. If questioned, your English speaker will tell them you are a picket line deployed from the camp. Our uniforms will be odd looking to them, but I don't think that will matter much."

Fedorov wished they could have gotten hold of British kit for this mission, but he could not think how they could pull that off.

"Now, when we get Churchill, the whole line folds in and back to the inflatables. We want this to be a quick extraction. You're all professionals. I'm sure you'll know what to do. Get Churchill to the boats, and off we go to that river islet. From there the helos get to the ships and then we just wait out our visa and there will be an automatic retraction to 1941. Questions?"

"We're taking Churchill to the ships?" asked MacRae.

"No, we're taking him across the Nile, and then leaving him on that island. I'll brief him there, and tamp down the shock factor. The man has some living to do between 1898 and 1941. We can't take those 43 years from him. In that time he'll enter politics in England, and rise to become Prime Minister. I'll want an interpreter with me to explain things to Churchill before we board the helicopters to leave. The last thing I want is for him to try and get back to 21st Lancers before that cavalry charge."

"What if he's hell bent for leather and tries to get off that islet?"

"That's why I'll need to talk with him, and get him to understand the gravity of the situation. He already believes he has a grand destiny, so I'll play on that."

"You're just going to tell him we've come from the future? He'll laugh in your face," said MacRae.

"I think I can get through to him," said Fedorov. "Leave it to me."

Fedorov looked at his watch. "Alright men, deploy to the helo decks on your ships. I'll accompany the Argonauts back to *Argos Fire*. I'll want every man on the ready line or on board their assigned helicopter in twenty minutes. We'll be shifting in thirty minutes, so you may feel something. Any man have any trouble, contact me immediately, then the squad leaders will summon a replacement."

"We'll all be fine, sir," said Zykov, and he gave Fedorov the thumbs up.

After reaching *Argos Fire*, Fedorov, MacRae, and Elena Fairchild met in her Stateroom. An interpreter stood by to translate what Fedorov said. They opened a channel to *Kirov* so they could give notice of the impending shift.

Fedorov watched as Elena removed the clear covering dome over the device. Then Fedorov solemnly handed her the memory key. There had been no instruction to use or mount any of the keys, so Elena would just insert the memory key into the any port where it seemed to fit. That worked.

A few seconds after she did that, they heard a sound from the box, and its panel lights winked. Fedorov saw two arrows light up, one green flashing on and off, the other red, steady on. Kamenski's instructions were to wait for the green arrow to go steady on, and then press the red Arrow.

Elena watched with great interest, and when the green arrow stopped winking, Fedorov sent a message to *Kirov* to stand by for Temporal shift. That done, Elena took a deep breath and pressed the red arrow. There was no audible sound, but the room suddenly filled with auroras of whirling light, then Fedorov heard a tearing sound, high pitched at first, but deepening to a lower and lower pitch, as if it was being sucked into oblivion. They all were.

The device had all its instructions from the memory key, and Elena saw a date light up in digital numbers. The message read: 02:00 hours, *09/01/1898 ~ Visa Duration: 48 hours.*

When Fedorov saw that he sighed with relief. Kamenski's 48 hour window had been from 02:00 on 1 SEP 1898 through 02:00 on 3 SEP 1898. After that, a retraction scheme would kick in automatically and return the ships to 1941, their point of origin.

"Kamenski gave us the time we need," said Fedorov, greatly relieved. He could barely feel the shift in progress, and physically, he was fine, as this was a younger Fedorov, with fewer time shifts on his clock. Once the shift concluded, the Date readout displayed 02:00, 1 SEP 1898 and flashed three times. Then the digital numbers started counting down those 48 hours"

"Well," said Elena. "Looks like I'll hang out here and watch that countdown. You can synchronize watches if you want. It was as easy as taking an elevator ride. They just had to make sure everyone was back aboard the ships before that 48 hour clock ran out. To make that a certainty, Fedorov got on the radio and told Troyak that everyone was to set a watch timer of 47 hours. That reserved a one hour safety interval before the retraction.

"Everyone needs to be on the ship before your watch timer runs to zero," he explained to the Marines on the radio. Alright, Mount up Marines. I'll be on one of the X3 helos and see you on the river island. You are cleared for takeoff. Fedorov out."

Chapter 36

The KA-40 on *Kirov* was the first to take off, laden with extra fuel, and 11 well armed Marines. The big bird rose ponderously from the aft helo-deck, slowly gained altitude and then seemed to disappear into the darkness of 1898. They had turned off their running lights, and would now fly with sensors, like a great night bats out over the desert.

The weather was close, clouds thickening rapidly, and Troyak could feel the tension in the air. It was not in his men, for they were loose and ready, but in the atmosphere around them, the energy of a rare desert storm about to become thunder, lightning, and driving rain. The first spray of a squall lashed the forward view pane, so he told his men to don their rain parkas before they landed. It would be 385 miles to the Nile, and at a Maximum speed of 170MPH, the KA-40 would get them there in two and a half hours.

Ten minutes after they departed, a pair of X3 helicopters rose from the *Argos Fire*. Each had five Argonauts and one section leader. MacRae in one bird, Fedorov in the other. The X3 was a hybrid, with a prop driven engine on either side in addition to its five bladed rotor. It was a much faster machine at just under 300MPH, so they would sweep past the KA-40 in the night and reach the planned LZ in just 90 minutes.

Those two birds raced through the gathering storm with ease, and Fedorov soon saw the gleam of moonlight on the Nile as the X3 descended. The moonlight came and went with the movement of rain heavy clouds but in the cabin the dull green glow on infrared and night vision allowed the pilots to easily pick out the warmer mass of the river islet from the cooler water of the Nile. They descended and hovered briefly before settling down in an open field near an orchard. As soon as they landed the Argonauts slid open the doors and leapt out, quickly fanning out in all directions to secure a perimeter around the two helicopters.

To any farmer or sheep herder on that small islet, seeing the coming of these two craft they would have been like seeing the Gods appearing out of the stormfront to walk among men. The sight of the helicopters would have been terrifying for there were no aircraft anyone in Sudan would know in 1898. The Wright Brothers would not make their daring first flight for another five years. Airships had been invented in 1852, but no one in the Sudan had ever seen one, another abomination of modernity.

That night, the Argonauts seemed to be alone, so Fedorov radioed the KA-40 telling Troyak that the LZ was secure and that they would flash running lights on their approach.

By the time the KA-40 arrived, its heavy rotors beating the night, the rain was thickening. The pilots saw the lights winking at them through the wet haze, and made for that spot. They would use Infrared as well, to pick out a safe spot away from the other two helos, and the KA-40 set down. Doors opened and Marines leapt out at the ready, some were already opening the cargo hatches and dragging out the long boxes containing five inflatable boats in tightly packed cases. They would open them and then the men formed up. The six three man sub-teams were formed, with one argonaut joining two Marines, Fedorov had decided to go into the Desert with the last group, Team-6 instead of waiting on the islet.

That same early morning Winston Churchill was in the Zeriba encampment to the north on the Nile, awakening at 02:00. As he described the storm: "Great blue flashes of lightning lit up the wide expanse of sleeping figures, of crowded animals, and of shelters fluttering in the wind." Kitchener's camp lay sleeping.

The mission teams pressed on west across the small river island and reached the edge of Nile, which was about 243 meters or just under 800 feet wide at this point. The boats were self inflating, and so they were taken out of the cases and hissing into their shape in a matter of minutes. Each came with a small outboard in the back as well as several paddles. They were special forces commando boats, weighing only about 275 pounds when fully inflated with the fast inflation kit. The men got the five boats deployed, but Fedorov had them conceal them with scrub and branches. They would not cross the Nile until well after dark that evening, and the dawn for 1 September had not yet come. This day was to achieve an unseen helicopter insertion to the river islet under cover of darkness and that rare desert storm. Now they would wait until the pre-dawn hours of September 2nd.

At this hour, 04:30 on the 1st of September. Kitchener's army was well south, the men up and moving to get warm in the rain. Everyone from the lowest Private to the Sirdar himself was sodden and wet. They were too far north to have seen the coming of the helicopters, which moved like dark shadows in the inky night, their engines and rotor thump lost in the roar of thunderstorms. Kitchener's troops had already broken that wet camp, with Reveille sounded at 03:45 to begin forming the army for another march south to the little village of Egeiga on the Nile. There Kitchener would make his final zeriba before the fighting started the following morning on Sept 2nd. But they would not be forming that zeriba until 10:00 that morning on the 1st. In this way Kitchener had made slow, short but steady advances towards Omdurman, knowing his enemy was near. Fedorov's men set out scouts to observe Kitchener's encampment, and particularly the ground on the opposite back of the Nile they would use later. They watched as a small flotilla of gunboats started up river, and saw the British cavalry once again forming up for their reconnaissance on that same flank.

That morning a dark flock of vultures circled over the cavalry of the 21st Lancers, a bad omen indeed. Now Fedorov had to rely on his exhaustive reading of the history, hoping it was all correct. The 21st Lancers had scouted Jebel Surgham this day to discover the Dervish army. Reading Churchill's own account of the battle, Fedorov knew he would be sent back to report to Kitchener at about 13:00 on 1 September. He was out there now on Jebel Surgham.

Fedorov looked at his watch, seeing it was approaching noon. Now was the time. The gunboats were all up river. Kitchener's men were busy preparing their zeriba, all the cavalry was up beyond those dark grey slopes. "Alright men!" he shouted. "Let's get to the boats and cross. All teams then move out by number and deploy your picket line. We've little more than an hour to be in position!"

The men seized the boats and ran then quickly down the covered slope to the water. They leapt in, for this was a drill they had completed many times, particularly the Marines. The five boats would reach the west bank of the Nile in a just a few minutes, turning off their outboard motors and paddling in the last few hundred yards so the sound would not draw any attention. It was their moment of greatest jeopardy, but no one saw them make that swift crossing. The zeriba was still being formed and no sentry lines or pickets had yet been posted.

Then the boats were gathered into one spot and concealed with overlaid scrub and tree branches. Fedorov gathered the men low and out of sight in a shallow *khor* depression that met the Nile.

Troyak had a small military drone with a camera, and Fedorov asked him to send it up so they could scout the ground they would soon be entering. To any observer, this might seem like just another vulture or bird at a distance, and it enabled them to see that the ground they needed was now empty, and to watch the movement of 21st Lancers out beyond Jebel Surgham. Troyak reported the cavalry had gone up on the saddle of the hill, and that they were starting to signal with the flash of a heliograph. The ground between the hills and the encampment was now empty. It was now or never, and it had to be now.

"Alright men, let's move. This will need stealth. Three man teams will go in order, and when team one reaches its position they will radio back. Then we move team two. That way no more than three men might be seen moving at any one time. Stay low, use any cover you find, and then do your best to conceal yourself and watch for lone riders. Churchill will be getting his orders to report to Kitchener soon, so we need our picket line in place. Move like the wind!"

Stealthy infiltration was a specialty of both the Marines and the Argonauts, and team one moved out. A few minutes later they radioed they were in position. Then Team two followed, reporting all clear and in position minutes later. Each successive team had less ground to cover, as they were picketing the line from its outermost point in the desert with Team-1 with each team deploying closer and closer to the river. Fedorov hoped the ground covered was a wide enough net to catch their fish. He used his binoculars. Once in position, he could seen nothing. It was as if his men had just vanished.

At one point they saw riders coming back towards the camp. Fedorov maneuvered the drone to look them over, and saw they were two British troopers bringing back a group of four prisoners, native Jaalin who had been caught by the Lancers. He radioed his teams to disregard that group and stay hidden as best they could. There came the boom of cannon, and Fedorov realized these were the gunboats firing on riverside positions that had been built closer to Omdurman. He was glad the boats had moved south, because Beatty was among them, and he had been looking for Dervish boats to shell in the proceedings days. If they were seen by a gunboat while on the river, they would be assumed to be Dervish scouts or men moving supplies, and most likely engaged.

It was a situation where the threat could come from either side in this battle. They were intrusive shadows in Time, men that were never meant to be where they were, and with great power to change the course of this Meridian. Now they lay low, waiting and watching, until Fedorov's drone finally spied a lone rider picking his way down the slope of Jebel Surgham. He maneuvered the drone closer, his heart thumping. Might this be Churchill riding back to make his report. He marked the rider's progress, and then gave warning on the comms. "Be ready to stop that rider—this could be our man."

Out in the desert, Zykov was lying prone in Team-3, his field glasses peering over the rise of a small sand dune looking for their quarry. He saw the rider, and signaled Fedorov.

"Team-3 reporting. A lone rider coming right at us, now about 300 yards out."

Fedorov had briefed the Argonauts well back on *Argos Fire*. "You men are the English speakers, and should you contact this rider, he'll likely be startled. So you have to immediately let him know you are friendly. Say you're a British picket line. The key thing is not to spook him so he tries to evade you at a gallop."

"Looks like he'll be hitting Team-Four," said Zykov. The number one team was the farthest out in the desert, so number four was right near the center of the picket line.

"Stand Ready Team-4," Fedorov signaled. "All other teams, be ready to move to the boats."

The rider came on at a brisk trot, and rode right into the center of Team-4. The man there was Argonaut PFC James Litton. When the rider was about ten yards off, he suddenly stood up, and raised a hand.

"Halt! British Picket line!" he shouted. "Stop and identify yourself."

The rider was startled, and reined in coming to a stop. He saw two other men getting to their feet on either side of him, in odd looking uniforms, but clearly soldiers, and certainly not Dervish scouts.

"Lieutenant Churchill," he called, "21st Lancers. I carry a report for General Kitchener."

"Right sir," said Private Litton. "We've orders to look for all messengers. The General won't be found with the Brigades. We've orders to take you to him directly."

Churchill cocked his head, not knowing what to make of this. Colonel Martin might have sent a heliograph saying he had been dispatched with details on their sightings. It wouldn't be unusual for Kitchener to be in an odd location, and as he might be difficult to find, help from these men would be welcome.

"This way," said Litton, coming up to Churchill. "if you please, sir." The Private reached up and took hold of the reins, leading Churchill on his horse towards the river. This was the great point of departure, where these events flowed off in a tangent from the main Meridian, and began to rewrite the history in a way that might save Churchill's most valuable life.

Churchill was going to order Private Litton off, but he could see these men were no threat, just very odd looking. He had been in and out of Kitchener's headquarters many times, furtively, and he was dreading any encounter with the man, knowing he was roundly disliked. At this point the whole of the picket line was up and moving at the crouch back towards the river, still making use of any cover they found. Churchill was astounded by their stealth—moving, going to ground, using any cover the barren desert offered. These were obviously well trained, experienced men. It looked like ten or twenty men posted here, and all to look for messengers? It didn't make sense, but if these men could get him to Kitchener quickly, that would be good. His intelligence was urgent. So Churchill allowed himself to be led, but his hand fingered the automatic pistol he had on his hip, just in case these men turned out to be hostiles.

"Who are you?" Churchill asked the private, "I don't recognize your uniforms. Why aren't you wearing proper kit?"

The Private had to be a quick thinker. "Special detail sir. We're attached to Kitchener's Headquarters guard. The General knew he'd be getting reports and he wanted them right quick. We were told to picket this ground and get any messengers to him safely, and on the double. Be glad you came upon us here sir, otherwise you might be an hour or more trying to find the old man, and if you've information he needs, the quicker he gets it, the better. So we were told, sir."

"Oh I've got information alright. See those hills there on the right? The Bloody Dervish are swarming like locusts south of those hills. Saw them with my own eyes. 21st Lancers will try to buy the Army some time, but they're coming, and by the thousands."

"Then we'll just have to see them off by the thousands sir, or drop the bloody buggers if they come at us. Right this way sir, down by the river there. The General is very close." The Private pointed.

They reached the cultivation and thicker scrub near the river and picked their way through. Moving swiftly, teams three, two and one were now right on their heels. Teams five and six had already reached the boats. They pushed through a line of thick scrub and there stood Fedorov, with Captain MacRae and another man dressed just like Private Litton. Churchill looked about, seeing many soldiers, but no sign of General Kitchener. What was going on here?

"Easy Mister Churchill," said MacRae. "Would you please dismount. My name is Captain Gordon MacRae, the Guards. We've been posted here to collect message riders and see they get where they're needed."

"Is Kitchener here? I've urgent information."

"He's close, but not on this side of the river."

"What? Well where the hell is the man?"

"Just across the River Lieutenant. We've small boats at hand, and we'll take you over. You can tie off your horse right here and we'll ferry you back here smartly once you've made your report."

"Strange," said Churchill, "I thought Kitchener would be with the Army." And why would a single messenger need an escort of twenty men like this?

"Oh, he'll be back on this bank soon. Had to go meet with Beatty and the Gunboats this morning, and tell them what he wanted. They met right over there on that river islet, and the General took breakfast there. Shall we get moving Lieutenant, it's just a short crossing." Now MacRae looked at his commandos. "Alright men, lets get to the boats and be done with it. You men there, see the Lieutenant gets safely across." He pointed to the east bank of the Nile.

Churchill still found all this very odd, but he was already down off his horse and two men, both Argonauts, came up and took him by each arm. "Right this way, Lieutenant, one said in a fine cockney accent. There was no question in his mind that these men were British, but one of them had been watching him very closely, and now that man was speaking in another language. The soldiers jumped to obey, and it was clear he was their officer. So here was a Captain, a Scot from the sound of him, and then another group speaking what Churchill thought was Polish, or perhaps Russian.

Then he saw the boats, they were sleek, jet black water rafts, with bulbous sides and a rounded front, and two sharp tails. Something was mounted between the two tails, and the whole craft looked like an inflated innertube from a bicycle, bent in a U shape, but with a hard rubber floor. He was helped aboard one of several of these boats, and watched all the other soldiers. MacRae, Fedorov, and a bilingual Marine translator who spoke English and Russian was there, Private Garin. When the rear outboard was started, Churchill looked over his shoulder, amazed. There was some kind of engine mounted there, and it was moving the craft swiftly out onto the river. He looked to see the other boats racing over the water, and the speed of these craft amazed him. Looking up river towards Omdurman, he saw what could only be one of Beatty's gunboats. It was the *Nasr*, with Sir Roger Ames and Ian Thomas aboard, there to put some fear into Beatty and give him a little caution.

The boats reached the river islet very quickly and they started to disembark. Standing on the shore the Russian officer came to his side and smiled. "Mister Churchill," said Fedorov. "It's an honor to meet you. Can you come this way?" He gestured inland.

All the others were now apparently puncturing these water craft and packing them up like tents! Churchill gaped at their work, hoping they wouldn't forget to leave one boat to get him back across the river. But the Russian Officer, who introduced himself as Captain Fedorov, was leading him quickly to the center of the islet, and there he was amazed to see three squat shapes, two identical, the other larger, looking like three great metal insects. They had long props on top, with blades that extended so far that they curved and bent towards the ground.

Churchill saw the soldiers opening hatches on these things and climbing inside. Now the Russian officer spoke, in halting English.

Epilogue

Fedorov & Churchill

"Please don't be alarmed. We came to save you." Then the man switched to Russian, looking at one of his soldiers, Private Garin.

"Mister Churchill," Garin translated, "My Captain wants me to tell you that he is very sorry to have diverted you from your duty to report, but he says General Kitchener will be informed well enough. You, however, are a man of great importance. We have come a very long way to find you here, and at this particular moment. I know you are young, eager to make a name for yourself, and very courageous. But it is imperative that you do *not* return to the 21st lancers."

"Not return? Why?"

"Because they are now in a most dangerous position. They will soon withdraw safely towards the encampment, but then after the battle here, Kitchener will order that regiment to sweep this river flank and try to do all possible to prevent the Dervish from entering Omdurman. A line of Dervish fighters will be seen by your regiment, and incorrectly estimated to be a force of about 700 men. Colonel Martin will order a charge, but it will turn out that the force attacked is much larger, more than 2000 strong. Your Regiment will sustain very heavy casualties, 70 men, and nearly 120 horses. Now listen carefully. You must *not* partake in that charge. Yes, it is a grand moment on any field of battle, and you have longed to put yourself at the center of such events, but not this one. No, never. You must not be with 21st Lancers when they make that charge."

"But sir, it is my duty to return to my unit, just as it was my duty to make this report to General Kitchener. Why do you say this? Of course I must rejoin my Regiment." The light of battle was in Churchill's eyes, and Fedorov perceived his steely resolve. There was nothing else to do but come out with it.

"No sir," he said himself. "If you make that charge, you will not survive it." Now he spoke through Private Garin again. "You will *die* here on this river flank today, and forfeit all the years that were yours to live. But the tragedy is more than the loss of one life. Your death delivers a great blow to England, for you have a grand destiny, Mister Churchill. A dark hour will come one day, when England stands alone, but your leadership, in a position of great authority, will steer your country through those rapids to find safe and calm water beyond. Die here, however, make that charge and you will not be there when England most needs you. Go to try and win your medal here and you will forsake so many other laurels yet to come. Your body will be buried here, just across that river and a little to the south, and for lack of your future leadership, England falters and fails."

"What? Why, this is nonsense! How could you possibly know what would happen to me, or to England years hence. You make no sense man. I Must go back. They'll say I deserted, shirked my duty, that I'm a coward. I can't have that."

Now Fedorov pinched off his collar microphone and gave an order. "KH-40, cleared for takeoff now."

He pointed across the way, pulling Churchill's attention to the larger fat metal insect in the nearby field. "Watch there closely, sir."

Churchill heard a swelling mechanical sound and he could see those great metal blades were turning about and working up to a frenzy. Then, to his utter amazement, the entire contraption lifted right off the ground in a haze of blowing dust. Alarmed, he instinctively reached for the pistol on his side holster, but felt an iron hand grip his arm, and secure his weapon. It was Troyak. Then Churchill saw the helicopter in a hover above them, and its lights winked three times before it growled louder and banked away, flying off to the east. He gaped at it in utter astonishment.

"Mister Churchill," said Fedorov. "We call that machine a helicopter, and the first practical flight of such a craft will happen in September of the year 1939—41 years from now. The first time you will fly on one will happen 20 years later, in 1959, and you will be with a Mister Eisenhower, the President of the United States. You are a clever man, Mister Churchill. For you to see such a craft now, in 1898, must surely tell you how and why we know the truth of what we are saying to you here."

"Why, you say this as though you lived in those future years, and beyond. You say it as if all this is just dusty old history to you!"

"Yes," Fedorov said flatly. "That is all true. So mark my words. Your death is very near, and if you leave this island and rejoin your regiment before sunset tomorrow, your corpse will lie buried here in this desert before dusk that day. Do that, and England dies in 1941; then a long night of barbarism will descend on all of Europe. Understand? Live and become the man we know in our future, and you will *save* your nation, and with it the British Empire. You will lead your people out of darkness, to a great victory. "

Churchill had often dreamed that he had a great future destiny, and so Fedorov's words were playing to that, kindling that sense he had of achieving greatness in the service of his nation. But so had the Khalifa.

"We must leave you now, but I entreat you to remain here on this islet until after sunset tomorrow. In doing so you trade the exhilaration of one brief and deadly charge, for the glory of leading England through another great war. That is your great duty. That is your finest hour, not here. I beg you—live to see it happen. Live to save England!"

"But they'll think I deserted, shirked my duty," said Churchill again. "I'll be ruined!'

"Not at all. You can say you were taken by Dervish scouts, and brought here to this river islet as a captive. Then simply weave a story of your heroic escape, and swim the bloody Nile if you must. It is either that, or you, and England with you, die here today. Do not worry what any man thinks of you here. Your greatest days lie ahead, and it will be just such an escape from enemy hands that lofts you to achieve your first political victory back home. I will tell you one thing more. If you believe us, and do what we now entreat you to do, then one day, you will be England's greatest Prime Minister. Yes, and one day, in another war, in yet another desert, you and I will meet again."

Garin finished translating that for Churchill, and then Fedorov extended his hand. "Give me your signet ring," he asked. "But remember it well. On that day, I will return it to you so that you remember this day and hour—the moment your life was saved for all the world."

Spellbound, Churchill removed the ring and handed it to Fedorov, and then Fedorov reached into his pocket, and handed Churchill a thick rolled cigar and a box of matches.

"Stay *here* this afternoon, and England lives. Enjoy the glee of a fierce cavalry charge, and both you and England die. Instead, I beg you to enjoy this fine cigar, a Habano Julieta #2. Then cross the Nile tomorrow night with your tale of capture and escape. We have done what we could. A satchel of food and water is there for you, and I trust you can swim the Nile. Now we must go." And they did.

The last of the men boarded the two X3 helos and they rose up in a whirl of metal and dust, racing away over another slim arm of the Nile to the east, then climbing and vanishing into the clouds. For Churchill, it was as if this small legion of guardian angels had swooped down to find him and save his life. He lay upon the tall grass, then struck a match and savored that fine cigar. It would be one of tens of thousands he would enjoy in the years to come.

As for Paul Dorland, his retraction scheme kicked in an hour after he went into that lifeboat, and he was pulled safely back to his own time at the Meridian complex in Berkeley, California. Fedorov and company returned to their ships, and the next day their 48 hour visa expired and they found themselves back in 1941.

21st Lancers made its brave charge, but one man short. In Churchill's place, Mother Time took Lieutenant Grenfell, who failed to safely cross that *khor*. When Sir Roger leapt off the *Nasr* to see if Churchill survived that charge, he would learn he had been sent back to report to Kitchener, but was not seen again. Walking back to the gunboat, he felt something lumpy in his pocket, and reached in to pull out a perfect diamond. Its yellow amber hue told him this was the Churchill Diamond, and now he knew for certain that the history replay here had saved him.

Back on the *Nasr*, the gunboat would be on the river the night of 2 September, and they would see a soldier on the bank of a river island shouting and waving his arms. The *Nasr* then spared Churchill a long wet swim across the Nile, and forestalled the possibility of any harm coming to him there. When Sir Roger saw him, and heard his tale of capture and escape, he was elated, for he knew this had never happened on the Old Meridian. Someone else was out there, he realized, possibly Walkers from his own future, operating to save Churchill's life. They had been very clever.

Once back aboard *Kirov*, Fedorov went to his quarters to look for the one book that would tell him whether or not their mission was successful— *The River War*, by Winston S. Churchill. It was right there on his shelf where he expected it.

"Good" he said aloud, greatly relieved. "Oh England: Arm yourselves, and be ye Men of Valour."[14]

That night he found a recording of that speech and listened to it, a sublime smile on his face as Churchill concluded his oratory:

"...Side by side the British and French peoples have advanced to rescue not only Europe but mankind from the foulest and most soul-destroying tyranny which has ever darkened and stained the pages *of history. Behind them, behind us, behind the Armies and Fleets of Britain and France, gather a group of shattered States and bludgeoned races: the Czechs, the Poles, the Norwegians, the Danes, the Dutch, the Belgians—upon all of whom the long night of barbarism will descend, unbroken even by a star of hope, unless we conquer, as conquer we must, as conquer we shall.*

Today is Trinity Sunday. Centuries ago words were written to be a call and a spur to the faithful servants of truth and justice:

Arm yourselves, and be ye men of valour, *and be in readiness for the conflict.... As the will of God is in Heaven, even so let it be."*

Thank you for reading *The Sands of Honor*. If you have enjoyed this book, I hope you will post and on-line review to help others discover and enjoy it too. Many thanks!

If Sir Roger Ames and his elaborate and dangerous meddling with the history intrigues you, there are three more books in this series, which can be read in any order, all alternate histories like this one:

I – *Field of Glory* – The Battle of Waterloo

II – *Zulu Hour* – Isandlwana and beyond

III – *The Devil Ship* – The Opium Wars

IV – *The Sands of Honor* – Khartum and Omdurman

—John Schettler

TIME GLOSSARY - Terminology
From Dorland's Time Theory

ABSOLUTE CERTAINTY - A condition brought about by willful determination that serves to limit variation in the continuum, creating a kind of tunnel in the Time Meridian that restricts outcomes to an absolute certainty.

ATTENUATION - A property of an incomplete Time shift, where the traveler manifests across a range of several milliseconds, slightly out of synch or phase with his correct manifestation point.

CLARITY – Clear or good understanding of a temporal locus, pattern, event, *Outcome* or *Consequence*.

CO-LOCATION - The presence of an object transported back through time to any point or Meridian on the continuum where that object already existed. This is expressly forbidden by Time, and therefore impossible. In like manner, no person can ever shift in Time to a point where they co-locate with themselves.

EXCEPTION: See Vanishing Point.

CONSEQUENCE – An undesired result achieved by a temporal *Transformation* – Usually referring to the negative. (i.e.) Sometimes certain *Consequences* must be accepted in order to achieve a desired *Outcome*.

CONVOLUTION – The relative difficulty or complexity of a given temporal event or condition.

DEEP NEXUS – Sometimes called a "Void" – A crucial, significant *Nexus Point* where radical alteration of the time line is possible. A Deep Nexus has a universal effect on all moments in Time until resolved, and can therefore be a portal into any potential Meridian passing through the Nexus.

DENSITY – A relative term describing factor counts in temporal events.

ELASTICITY – The tendency of Time to resist alteration and reassume its original shape. Also known as "Quantum Memory Foam."

FACTOR – An element contributing to convolution in temporal events.

FINALITY – A catastrophic *Grand Imperative* (like the Cuthulu asteroid strike that led to the eradication of the dinosaurs and other life.)

FREE RADICAL – A dangerous, erratic variable in the course of temporal events – usually only existing within a *Deep Nexus*.

GOLEM - A special search program written by Kelly Ramer and distributed to hundreds of thousands of computer users via the Internet. Golems are able to search and report on information on the net and can perceive data on every Meridian during a time of Deep Nexus through the phenomenon known as "Resonance."

GORDIAN KNOT: A knotting of a time Meridian that had doubled back on itself or started to loop. A Gordian knot can prevent the normal progression of time and prevent the creation of the future. Such events often arise from Paradox.

GREAT VOID – An interminable shadow or *Penumbra* cast by a *Grand Imperative*.

HAZE – Obscurity in the understanding of a temporal situation or event.

HEISENBERG WAVE – A kind of temporal shock wave, like a seismic wave, that propagates away from the locus of a major variation in causality. These waves are transformative, and can cause sudden, chaotic and disruptive changes, or Time-Quakes.

IMPERATIVE – An event in Time which <u>must</u> happen – Usually a natural event. A *Grand Imperative* is a natural event of special significance. Some Grand Imperatives can become a *Finality*.

INEVITABILITY – A progression of events that is inexorable and unalterable.

INHERENT VARIATION – The tendency for a time progression to mutate slightly every time it is replayed do to deliberate intervention.

INITIATOR – A person directly responsible for a new *Time Meridian* (Like Mohammed, or Christ). A *Prime Mover* of great significance.

LEVER – A secondary contributor to movement in a series of events.

MERIDIAN – An established line of temporal events on the continuum.

MILIEU – A particular point on the continuum, and all physical things in the immediate surrounding area. A location that on the MERIDIAN that is both Temporal and physical. See also: NODE. A MILIEU might encompass many NODES linked to one another on the continuum.

NEXUS POINT – A point of connection, intersection or branching of one or more *Meridians* in the Time continuum.

NODE – An exact Temporal location on a MERIDIAN, as distinct from its physical surroundings. See MILIEU. There may be many temporal NODES clustered or lined up in a typical MILIEU on a MERIDIAN, and these nodes will share the same physical space, while differing only in time from one another.

OUTCOME – A desired result achieved by a temporal *Transformation* – Usually referring to the positive.

PARADOX – Time's way of correcting errors in the Time continuum. Paradox is a real force, and quite dangerous. It kills or erases people and objects from the *Time Meridian* when unaccountable complications arise from their actions. A Paradox is NOT simply a thorny problem; it is a real effect and force of annihilation—a kind of "Anti-Time."

PENUMBRA – The shadow of influence on future events cast by an *Imperative*, or a very serious variation in Causality on a Meridian.

POINT OF ORIGIN – The temporal locus where a person or object becomes a *Prime Mover*.

PRECEDENT – Any given outcome from a replayed segment of the continuum can create a Precedent that influences the outcome of subsequent replays.

PRIME MOVER – A primary causative lever or agent for an event – usually a person but sometimes an object.

PUSH POINT – A moment of insignificance that gives rise to a key event on a *Time Meridian*. Often associated with a *Prime Mover*.

QUANTUM KARMA – The influence of causality on a *Time Meridian*. Each moment on the Meridian affects the next, and certain Prime Movers accumulate an aura of Quantum Karma around them that also has profound effects on the configuration of future moments in Time.

RADICAL TRANSFORMATION – A catastrophic alteration of the *Temporal Condition*.

RESONANCE - Information available in the intersection of a Nexus Point, where many alternate Meridians "resonate" data concerning the outcome of events.

TEMPORAL CONDITION – The matrix, pattern or state of affairs in a given time period.

TIME-QUAKE – A sudden disruption at the end of a Heisenberg Wave that can cause unforeseen and sudden changes.

TRANSFORMATION – Any change in a *Time Meridian* that alters a future *Temporal Condition*.

TRANSFORMER – A person who causes a *Transformation*.

VANISHING POINT - The exact moment in Time when an object is removed and transported elsewhere in the continuum, possibly to avoid entanglement from the prohibition against co-location. Either one object must fail to arrive, or the other must be removed from that milieu.

VARIATION – A subtle change in a *Time Meridian* that does not significantly alter *Temporal Conditions*.

WEIGHT OF OPINION - The culmination and likely outcome of future events as a result of a potential *transformation*, as perceived and reported by the Golem search cloud.

WILLFUL EVENT - Events resulting from decisions or actions taken by human beings

ZOMBIE - The walking dead. A person, fated to die, but whose life has been spared due to a willful intervention in a Time Meridian. Paradox will allow the elimination of a Zombie by restoring the moment of his natural death to the continuum.

---

[1] This letter will be presented verbatim, as the *Mahdi* wrote it—here you are witness to the history few have read. Peace be upon you!

[2] Too Late for Gordon and Khartum – Alex MacDonald

[3] The movie depicting this battle placed a large fortress at Abu Kru, with Dervish disguised in British uniforms. No fort existed there historically.

[4] The Maxim Gun was the first practical rapid firing Machine Gun.

[5] This scene was a documented event, presented in: *With Kitchener in the Soudan, by G.A.* Henty, 1902. I recount it in my own words here.

[6] Winston Churchill – *The River War, Vol I.*

[7] Churchill, The River War, Vol I

[8] As reported by Churchill, *The River War*

[9] Osman was an honorific title, a name derived from the 3rd 'Rightly Guided Khalif,' one of the ten companions of Muhammed

[10] The River War, Volume II, Winston S. Churchill

[11] Churchill, The River War, Volume II

[12] As presented in my book *Golem 7*, Meridian Series Volume V

[13] The British nickname for the twin battlecruisers, *Scharnhorst* and *Gneisenau*.

[14] This was the title of Churchill's first BBC radio broadcast speech to the nation after becoming Prime Minister.

Ingram Content Group UK Ltd.
Milton Keynes UK
UKHW042001200623
423745UK00001B/35